A Call to Service

Holly Green writes historical sagas about love and war, and her books are inspired by the stories she heard from her parents when she was a child. Holly is from Liverpool and is a trained actress and teacher. She is married and enjoys spending time with her two delightful grandchildren.

Also by Holly Green

Women of the Resistance

A Call to Courage
A Call to Service

A Call to Service

HOLLY GREEN

hera

First published in the United Kingdom in 2024 by

Hera Books
Unit 9 (Canelo), 5th Floor
Cargo Works, 1–2 Hatfields
London SE1 9PG
United Kingdom

A CIP catalogue record for this book is available from the British Library.

Print ISBN 978 1 80436 390 4
Ebook ISBN 978 1 80436 389 8

This book is a work of fiction. Names, characters, businesses, organizations, places and events are either the product of the author's imagination or are used fictitiously. Any resemblance to actual persons, living or dead, events or locales is entirely coincidental.

Look for more great books at www.herabooks.com

Printed and bound in Great Britain by Clays Ltd, Elcograf S.p.A.

I

An extract from Alix's notebook

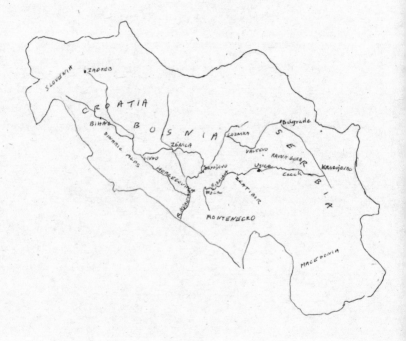

Chapter One

The explosion jolted Leonora Malkovic out of a deep sleep. She sat up and gazed around the room, unsure of what she had heard. The early light of the spring morning was showing round the edges of the curtains and illuminating the tousled dark hair of her husband Sasha as he, too, shook himself awake. Before she could speak there was a second explosion, closer this time, and then a third.

'Dear God! It's started!' he groaned. 'The Germans are bombing the city.'

'But there hasn't even been a declaration of war!' Leo exclaimed. 'It's Easter Sunday! The swine! Bombing civilians without warning – and on this day of all days.'

'What did we expect?' her husband asked, scrambling out of bed. 'Hitler can't forgive us for spoiling his plan to bring Yugoslavia into the German camp.'

His words were drowned in a new explosion that rattled the windows and shook the house to its foundations.

'Quick! We must get everyone into the cellar!' He grabbed his trousers from the hanger and thrust his legs into them.

Leo was already pulling on a pair of slacks and a sweater. The door of the room burst open to admit Gregor, Sasha's manservant, and Jana, Leo's maid.

'Sir! Let me help you…'

Sasha cut him short. 'Never mind that. Get all the servants into the cellar, as quickly as you can.'

Jana had hurried to Leo's side. 'What's happening? I don't understand…'

'We are being bombed, Jana. Come with me. We must get everyone downstairs.'

The explosions were coming so fast now that they were fusing into a single wall of sound. Jana screamed as the glass in the windows smashed and a blast of air swept through the room. Sasha was already heading for the stairs and Leo followed, pulling Jana after her. In the hallway other members of the household staff were milling about in their nightclothes. There was a hubbub of exclamations and oaths and screams.

'Ivo!' Sasha addressed the butler, who was at the foot of the stairs. 'Open the door to the cellar. Get everyone down there.'

As the butler began to shepherd the others towards the cellar, Sasha moved to the front door and wrenched it open. Leo followed and they peered out onto a street that had become almost unrecognisable. Knez Mihailova Street was one of the main thoroughfares of Belgrade, lined with elegant houses interspersed with a few upmarket shops. Several of the houses had been reduced to rubble where fires were smouldering and the street was littered with broken bricks and smashed glass.

Leo turned away. 'I'll fetch my first aid box.'

He grabbed her arm. 'No! It would be suicide to go out there now. Wait till the raid is over, then we'll see what has to be done.'

She pulled free. 'I've worked under fire before. So have you. There are people who need help out there.'

She ran back upstairs, and by the time she came back Sasha was waiting by the door with two tin hats in his hand, relics of another war, distant in time but not in memory.

'Where the hell did you find those?' she asked with a half laugh, but she did not wait for an answer.

As they stepped outside they were almost knocked off their feet by another blast, followed by the sound of yet another building collapsing. As they recovered their balance Sasha gripped her arm again.

'The king! Leo, I have to make sure Peter is safe.'

'Yes,' she agreed immediately. 'Of course. Go! I'll do what I can here.'

It was only ten days since they had both been involved in the bloodless coup that had placed seventeen-year-old Prince Peter on his father's throne and displaced his uncle, the regent, who had been prepared to sign a pact with Hitler. But Sasha had been the young man's guide and counsellor for years and Leo knew that Peter was almost like a son to him – the son she had been unable to give him. She watched him disappear, threading his way through the fallen debris, then picked up her first aid box and turned to where a few survivors were crawling from the wreckage.

–

Some miles outside the city, in Kuca Magnolija, the family's country mansion, Alexandra Malkovic was also woken by the sound of explosions. For a moment she thought she was back in Paris and wondered why the Germans were dropping bombs on the city they had occupied for months. Then she opened her eyes and saw the outlines of her old bedroom, where she had slept since she was a child and which she had not seen for almost three years. The sound of further explosions, distant but still enough to make the windows rattle, brought her to her feet. Opening the curtains, she gazed across the orchards and vineyards surrounding the house to where a pall of smoke, underlit by the glow of flames, was rising into the morning sky.

'No!' The word came out as a sob. 'Oh no! Not now!'

Grabbing a robe, she ran downstairs to where Bogdan, her father's steward, was trying to calm the men and women of the household staff.

'Bogdan! It's the city, isn't it?'

'I fear so, Miss Lexie.' The childhood pet name would have annoyed her in different circumstances but not today.

'I must go! My mother and father will need me.'

'No, Miss Lexie! It's not safe. You must wait here till they come back.'

'And if they don't come back?' Her voice trembled. 'Bogdan, I haven't seen them for three years and now... I can't just wait here. I have to find them.'

The front door opened to admit a tall man in his thirties with broad shoulders and straw-coloured hair. Alix ran to him. 'Drago! I have to get to the city. Will you drive me?'

Dragomir looked from her to the steward. 'I'll do anything you ask me, miss, but are you sure that's wise?'

'It's not a question of what's wise!' She almost stamped her foot with frustration. 'I came home to see my parents for the first time in three years and they're not here. I have to find them.'

'They did not know you were coming home,' Bogdan said placatingly. 'Otherwise they would have been here to greet you.'

'I know that! But there was no way I could let them know and now… Drago, please!'

He hesitated a moment longer, then he nodded. 'We can get to the city and find out what is happening. But they may already be on their way here.'

'Thank you!' She turned to the stairs. 'I'll get dressed. Bring the car round.'

When she came down Bogdan tried again to persuade her to wait. 'I have tried to telephone but I can't get through. Perhaps the count and countess have left already.'

'Or perhaps the whole telephone system has gone down,' she said. 'Let's go, Drago.'

When they were on the road together Drago said, 'I only heard this morning that you had come home, Miss Lexie. Why didn't you let anyone know?'

'For God's sake, don't call me Miss Lexie,' she exclaimed. 'My name is Alix.'

'Miss Alix, then,' he said.

She looked at him, suddenly in need of the comforting familiarity of childhood. 'Drago, how long have we known each other?'

Drago glanced sideways at her. He had been born to a simple peasant couple on her father's estate, educated in the school her father had set up for his tenants. He had done well and progressed through the ranks of men who worked on the estate until he had achieved his current position as second in command to the estate manager. It was a big step up for someone from his background but he never forgot his lowly origins. 'I remember the time they brought you home for the first time after everyone thought you were lost for good. You were – what? – two years old.'

'And you were?'

7

'Nearly ten, I reckon.'

'You used to give me piggybacks. You showed me where the birds' nests were and when I was bigger you taught me to climb trees. And when I got stuck high up in the old chestnut tree you climbed up and helped me down. You were like a big brother to me.'

She saw him flush slightly.

'We were children then. It was different.'

'So different that you can't just call me Alix?'

He hesitated. 'If… if that is what you want. But not in front of the count. He wouldn't approve.'

'Oh, I don't know…' she began, then thought again. 'No, perhaps you're right. Well, just between ourselves then.'

'All right – Alix. You were going to tell me why you couldn't let us know you were on your way home.'

'Well, for a start, getting out of occupied France is not easy.'

'Why not? Yugoslavia is still neutral – at least, it was yesterday. What stopped you from just presenting your passport at the border?'

'Because I should probably have been arrested by the Vichy police and handed over to the German intelligence service.'

'Why on earth would they do that?'

'Because my name was on a "wanted" list – or it probably was.'

'Wanted? Why?'

'Because I was working for the Resistance.'

He slowed the car and stared at her. 'You were with the Resistance? Doing what?'

'Escorting escaped POWs and downed airmen south over the line of demarcation between the occupied north

8

and the Vichy south and then on to Marseilles. But the circuit was infiltrated and betrayed and most of the leaders were arrested. I was out of Paris at the time, which is why I wasn't picked up, but I couldn't be sure that the Gestapo didn't have my name. The man who led the group...' Her throat constricted and she had to swallow. '...he was brave, but no one holds out for ever.'

'When did this happen?'

'On the twenty-sixth of last month. The day before the coup here. I heard about it on the radio the next morning. That's when I decided to come home.'

'So how did you get out of the country?'

'In the boot of a car belonging to the American vice-consul in Lyons. She has a chalet just over the border in Switzerland. She got me to Geneva, but even then it was days before I could get a flight back to Belgrade. I tried to telephone, but international calls seemed to be blocked. So as soon as I could I got on a plane. We landed yesterday evening and I managed to find a taxi to bring me home, thinking my parents would be there. But of course, when I arrived Bogdan told me they were at the town house, so I thought, OK, I'll go to the city tomorrow and give them a surprise, but now...' A sob rose into her throat like a bubble of gas and choked her.

Drago reached down and found her hand and she gripped his tightly.

'You know, I wasn't even sure that my mother was here until last night. The last time I heard from her she was in England, but that was months ago, before Paris was occupied. I've been listening to the reports of the blitz in London and worrying that she might be caught up in it. So when Bogdan told me she was with my father in the city I was so relieved...' The tears were coming freely now. 'Drago, can't you drive faster! We must get there. They may need help.'

There had been a lull in the bombing but at that moment they both heard the drone of low-flying aircraft and then the car was shaken by a heavy concussion. Drago pulled off the road into the shelter of a copse of trees and they both stared out as fresh plumes of dust and smoke rose from the city ahead of them. They could see the dark formations of bombers as they swept over the city, released their deadly loads and veered away, heading for home. Wave upon wave of them came out of the clouds in a seemingly unending succession. Below them, white puffballs appeared and vanished.

'What's that?' Drago asked.

'Anti-aircraft fire,' Alix told him. 'I saw it once when the Nazis bombed Paris. That was just a warning, a few bombs in the suburbs, to show us what would happen if we didn't surrender. But this... Was there ever a warning here?'

'Not as far as I know.'

'The bastards! Dropping bombs on civilians. They did it to London, but Britain was already at war with them. Are we at war?'

'It seems we are now,' Drago said grimly.

He started the engine and drove back onto the road. For the moment, at least, the raid seemed to be over. When they set out, the road had been more or less empty, but now they began to see traffic coming towards them; cars at first, crammed with people, cases strapped on the roofs; then every other sort of vehicle, tradesmen's vans, farm trucks, horse-drawn traps, bullock carts, all loaded to the brim with people and luggage. After them came men and women on bicycles and on foot, pushing prams and hand carts, carrying children, bundles of possessions tied to the end of sticks carried over their shoulders.

'Where are they all going?' Drago asked.

'Anywhere away from here,' Alix replied, scanning the faces in case she might see her father and mother among them. 'I saw this once before, when Paris was declared an open city. Every train, every bus, was packed, and the roads were clogged with refugees – and they weren't even in danger of being bombed.'

'Do you think the raids are over now?' he asked.

Alix shrugged. 'Who knows? Hitler wants his revenge because we pulled out of the pact Prince Paul signed before he was deposed. I don't think he's going to stop at bombing Belgrade.'

'You think he will invade?'

'I'm sure it's what this is leading up to. The question is, can our army stop him?'

'Our troops won't fall apart like the French did,' he asserted firmly.

'No one expected the French army to collapse like it did, either,' she replied.

–

Leo finished tying a makeshift sling round the neck of a young girl. Under a veil of grey dust the girl's face was chalk-white with pain and shock.

'That's all I can do for now,' Leo told her. 'Your arm is broken and you need to go to the hospital.' She scanned the street. Men and women were scrabbling among the piles of rubble, heaving bricks and pieces of broken timber aside in a desperate effort to reach the wounded and the dead. There was no sign of any organised medical help. 'I'm sure a doctor or an ambulance will come along soon.'

She turned aside to attend to an old man whose face was covered in blood from a wound in his scalp, but as she reached into her first aid box she realised that she had neither lint nor bandages left. A hand grasped her arm and a woman's voice pleaded, 'Help me, please! My son! My son is trapped. I can hear him but I can't lift the stones off him.'

She tugged Leo across the street to where half a house had been sheared away. A heavy beam had kept back some of the rubble, leaving a small cavity beneath it, and from there a hand and part of an arm protruded and a child's voice called, 'Mamma, help me! Help! Please help!'

'Help me lift it!' the woman begged, heaving at the beam.

Leo stooped and grasped the other end. The rough wood drove splinters into her hands but she hauled at it with all her strength. The beam shifted a fraction, sending a shower of small fragments into the cavity, but in spite of their efforts it remained in place.

Leo raised her head and shouted, 'Some help here! Someone! There's a child here.'

There was no response and she bent again to struggle with the beam.

A hand gripped her shoulder. 'Leo! Come away!'

She shook the hand off. 'Help me lift this beam.'

'Leo, it's me, Sandy – Sandy Glen. Sasha sent me to find you. You need to come with me, now!'

She twisted round and peered up at him, pushing her hair out of her eyes. A russet-haired man in naval uniform was standing behind her. Alexander Glen was a naval attaché at the British legation and a close friend of her husband's. 'Sandy? What are you doing here?' she asked.

'Looking for you. Listen to me. We're evacuating the city. Sasha has gone with the king. He asked me to find you and take you to join him,' Glen answered.

She shook her head. 'I can't. Look at all this. I'm needed here.' A wail from the rubble beneath their feet recalled her attention. 'There's a child trapped down here. Help me to lift this beam.'

For a moment he hesitated, then he stepped round her to the far end of the beam and threw off some bricks. Gripping the end of the beam, he said, 'Right. On three… One, two three…'

Sweating and straining, they managed to raise the beam a few inches and push it to one side, revealing the figure of a small boy curled in a ball below it. Glen leaned in and lifted him out.

'Oh, thank God! Thank God!' The mother sobbed and reached out her arms.

'Wait! Let me check him.' Leo ran her hands over the small head and the thin arms and legs. There was no sign of blood and the limbs seemed to be intact. 'Praise heaven! I don't think he's badly hurt. Here!'

She handed the child to his mother who hugged him to her, weeping. 'Oh, thank you! May the Lord reward you!'

Alexander Glen took hold of Leo's arm again. 'Now, we must go. There may be another raid and we could find the roads are blocked.'

She stood up. 'We can't just leave these people. Where are the doctors? Where are the ambulances?'

'God knows! Leo, there's no more you can do here. Look around you. It's a job for the authorities, not for one person with her bare hands. Sasha needs you! He'll be waiting for you to join him. We have to go!'

Leo looked around as Alexander ordered. She ran her hands over her face and realised for the first time that they were bleeding. She had no idea how long she had been here. It seemed like hours. Her face and hair were covered in dust, her eyes were smarting with it, her trousers and shirt were filthy and torn, and she was shaking with fatigue. When she tried to swallow, her throat burned as if she was swallowing ashes. Wearily, she nodded.

'Listen,' he said. 'Your house is still standing. I checked there first. You need your passport and Sasha's…'

'Passport? Why?'

'In case… in case you have to leave the country. Don't think about that now. Just get any documents you need and a change of clothing.' He was walking her along the street as he spoke and they had arrived at her front door. Miraculously, the house had survived, though there was no glass in the windows.

She pulled free of his hand. 'I need to wash and change.'

'No! There's no time for that. The bombers could be back at any moment. Just grab the essentials and come.'

The hall was empty and she guessed that the servants were still sheltering in the cellar. Upstairs she threw a change of underclothes and a clean shirt for herself and Sasha into a bag, then went to Sasha's study and found the passports. At the last moment it occurred to her to open the safe and cram some banknotes into her purse. There was no time for more. Alexander was urging her to hurry. She allowed him to lead her out of the front door and pulled it shut behind her. As she did so the thought struck her that it might be a very long time before she walked back through it again; but Glen was holding her arm and tugging her forward and there was no chance to dwell on the thought.

The legation building was more or less untouched and several cars were parked outside while men and women hurried backwards and forwards with arms full of files and boxes of documents. A small group were huddled together, obviously waiting for something. Leo recognised Baroness Zorica Collaerts, Glen's beautiful wife, a diplomat she knew slightly called Hugh Seton Watson, and Alexi Gavrilovic, the son of the Yugoslav minister in Moscow – all of whom had been implicated in one way or another in the coup that had unseated the regent, Prince Paul, and replaced him with the seventeen-year-old King Peter.

Glen said, 'I've been tasked with getting these people out of the country. They would all be in great danger if the Nazis caught them. We still have to collect Tupanjanin. We can pick him up on the way. Right, everyone. All aboard.'

'Where are we going?' Leo queried.

'West, towards Sarajevo. The king and the heads of government have set out that way and we expect to catch up with them somewhere in that area.'

'Why Sarajevo?'

'Because it's about as far from the border as it's possible to get – and if the worse comes to the worst the Adriatic coast is reasonably close for an evacuation by sea.'

Leo said no more. The warning signs of an impending invasion had been clear for the last few days. The German embassy staff had been recalled and other foreign diplomats had been advised to leave as well. Yet somehow they had clung to the hope that it might be a false alarm, or that if the invasion did occur the Royal Yugoslav army would be able to resist it. The preparations Glen was making made it obvious that the British, at any rate, did not have much faith in that possibility. Suddenly the prospect of being exiled from the country she had come to regard as home was very real.

There were two cars, Glen's Packard and an old brown Cadillac driven by another colleague, John Bennet. Leo found herself packed into the back seat of the Packard between Zorica and Hugh Seton Watson, who immediately opened a volume of *War and Peace* in the original Russian and became totally absorbed in it. The others followed in the Cadillac. There was a short delay while they waited for Milos Tupanjanin and his son. He was the leader of the Serbian Peasants Party, which had supported and encouraged the coup. He had been entertained many times by Leo and Sasha at the dinner parties where the plot had been discussed and finalised. Like the rest, he was almost certainly on Hitler's wanted list.

With all the passengers onboard they set off for Sarajevo.

–

As Alix and Drago drove into Belgrade, another raid began. In the previous one the planes had come from the north, laying down a pattern of bombs from north to south. This time, they came in from the west so that the city was cross hatched with a grid of destruction. They were close to a bridge over the Sava when they heard the drone of the bombers. Drago stopped the car and they both ran for shelter under one of the arches, crouching there with their heads buried in their arms until the sound of the explosions ceased. It was clearly impossible to drive any further, so they abandoned the car and began to pick their way across the city. In her worst nightmares Alix could never have imagined the horrors that awaited them. Dead bodies lay among the rubble of fallen buildings; sometimes there were only fragments – an arm with part of the torso, severed legs, headless bodies. In one small park shattered limbs hung from the trees like terrible fruit. Small groups of survivors huddled together or attempted to staunch each other's wounds. In some places groups were attempting to clear the debris and voices called out for missing friends and relatives buried underneath. There was no sign of anyone in authority or any real organisation.

In one street they spotted a man in a doctor's white coat tending the wounded. Alix made her way over to him.

'Why isn't there any proper help for these people? Where are the other doctors, the nurses, the ambulances?'

He raised a soot-smeared face towards her and answered in a voice cracking with shock and exhaustion. 'There was a direct hit on the hospital. I got out. I don't know what happened to the others.' He waved a hand towards the rubble-strewn streets. 'You couldn't get an ambulance here even if there was one. If you want to help, see if you can find some clean linen – or some clean water.'

Alix looked around her and was overwhelmed by a feeling of helplessness. The need was so great and the task seemed impossible. She stepped back, shaking her head. 'I have to find someone. I'm sorry!'

It was three years since she had last been in the city and so many of the familiar landmarks had been destroyed that she would have had difficulty finding her way, but Drago had driven there more recently and with his guidance they succeeded in reaching Knez Mihailova Street. For a moment it seemed that the destruction had been as complete here as elsewhere. But as they came closer, they saw that some buildings were still standing.

Alix gave a cry of joy. 'Drago! Our house! It's still there.'

She ran forward, jumping over piles of brick and timber, and up the steps to the front door. The house was more damaged than she had realised at first sight. There was no glass in any of the windows and the front door hung open, half off its hinges. Alix stepped into the hall, feeling broken glass crunch under her feet. The chandelier that used to hang there had shattered into a thousand pieces. There was no sign of life.

'Matti!' she called. 'Papa!' There was no reply. 'It's me! Alix,' she called again. 'I've come home.'

Still there was silence, until the cellar door opened with grinding and scraping over broken tiles and a face peered out.

'Ivo!' Alix cried. 'It's me. Are you all right?'

The butler shoved the door fully open and advanced towards her. His clothes were covered in dust and his hair and face were grey with it, but his expression lit up with joy at the sight of her.

'Miss Lexie! Is it really you? Welcome home! But what am I saying? What sort of welcome is this?'

'Ivo,' she said, 'where is everyone?'

'We are all down in the cellar, miss. The count ordered me to get everyone down there when the bombing started.'

'And my mother and father? Are they down there too?'

'Oh no, miss. They went out to see what they could do to help. Haven't you seen them?'

'No. When did they go out?'

'First thing, miss, as soon as the first raid started. I haven't seen them since.'

Alix suddenly found her legs giving way. She groped her way to the stairs and sank down with her head in her hands. 'Oh no! No! I've come all this way and they're not here. Where are they? Where can they be?'

'Quite likely they have gone to the country house, don't you think, miss?' the butler suggested.

'No! I've just come from there. And we didn't see them on the road. If they were out there while the bombs were falling they could be anywhere. They could be under the rubble like... like thousands of others.' It was too much to bear. She began to sob helplessly.

It was Drago who put an arm round her shoulders. 'Don't cry. They are probably out there somewhere helping. You know they would never just walk away and leave people to suffer. They will probably be back before nightfall.'

Alix huddled under his sheltering arm and struggled for control. Her sobs subsided into sniffs and she found a clean napkin being held out to her by Ivo. She wiped her eyes and sat up.

Drago was saying, 'Could you find something for Miss Alix to drink? And is there any food? We didn't stop for breakfast.'

At his words the routine of the household swung into action. The rest of the staff were called up from the cellar, the kitchen was found to be more or less intact and the dining room was swept and cleaned. A glass of brandy and water was put into Alix's hand and she was led to sit at the table. Coffee appeared, and bread – a day old but perfectly edible. There was butter and cheese and honey.

Alix looked round. 'Where's Drago?'

'He's gone down to the servants' quarters, miss,' Ivo said, 'to get something to eat himself.'

'Oh for heaven's sake!' she exclaimed. 'Go and fetch him. I want him here with me.'

When Drago reappeared he started to apologise. 'I didn't think you'd mind if I grabbed some breakfast.'

'Oh, don't be such an idiot!' she replied. 'I don't mind you getting something to eat. You just don't have to go to the servants' quarters to have it. This whole business of servants and masters is completely outdated. Sit down here and eat with me.'

He hesitated a moment. 'Ivo will be shocked.'

'I don't give a damn about that. I want you with me.'

'Very well.' He fetched a cup and plate from the sideboard and helped himself to coffee and bread.

'Oh, what am I doing?' Alix wailed suddenly. 'We should be out there, looking for my parents, not sitting here eating.'

'We can't go on indefinitely without food,' he said reasonably. 'Finish your breakfast. Then we'll go and look.'

Alix looked at him. For the last year, or more, she had seen herself as a leader; a strong person who was capable of taking charge in a dangerous situation. She had had her own little group of young men and women all working together for the Resistance, who looked to her for their orders. Now, suddenly, she was the one who needed a shoulder to lean on. For the time being she was content for that shoulder to belong to Drago.

Leo had experienced some hair-raising journeys in her time, most recently driving an ambulance across Finland in that country's 'winter war' with Russia. But this one, she decided, topped the list for sheer discomfort and moments of unadulterated terror. The route took them across the Dinaric Alps, which separated the central plain from the Adriatic coast. It might be spring in Belgrade, but here in the mountains winter had not lost its grip. Yugoslavian roads were poor at the best of times and the surface of this one consisted of ruts frozen solid and coated with ice. To add to the hazard, the delays in starting out meant that by the time they reached the mountains it was dark. The road climbed up the side of a valley, twisting round a series of hairpin bends, with a sheer drop on one side and a rock wall on the other. The car suddenly skidded sideways and came to a jarring stop that sent Leo flying forward to strike her head against the seat in front. When her eyes could focus again she saw that the front wheels were suspended among the upper branches of a tree growing lower down on the steep slope and beneath that was a bottomless void. The tree was the only thing that had stopped them from careering off the road and ending up thousands of feet below in the river.

Glen opened his door and climbed cautiously out, easing his way back along the running board until he could stand on solid ground. Dazed and shaken, the rest of the passengers followed his example – except for Hugh, who opened his book and seemed ready to stay where he was and continue reading. The Cadillac had stopped a few yards away. The passengers climbed out and joined the rest in a dejected huddle on the road.

At that moment something occurred that intensified the sense of unreality which had been growing in Leo's mind as the events of the day unfolded. Incredibly, from somewhere down the road behind them came the creaking of wheels and the sound of plodding hooves, and from round the bend there appeared an ox cart led by an elderly peasant. What he was doing or where he was going at that hour Leo had no idea. Glen accosted him in English and to everyone's amazement received a reply in the same language. It seemed the old man had been living in Manchester and had only recently returned home. The ox was unhitched from the cart and attached instead to a tow rope at the rear of the Packard. There was a moment's tense wait while the old peasant growled words of encouragement and the beast threw his weight against the harness and then, with a crash of breaking branches, the car slid back onto the road. The ox was unhitched and reattached to the cart and the old man went on his way, shrugging off their words of gratitude.

It was obvious from a cursory glance that the car was a write-off. The axle had simply fractured in the middle so that the central section of the vehicle was resting on the ground.

'Right! There's nothing for it,' Glen declared. 'We shall all have to pack into the Cadillac.'

It sounded like an impossibility but somehow they all crammed themselves in and Leo found herself perched uncomfortably on Tupanjanin's lap. In gloomy silence they set off again.

For Leo the rest of the journey passed in a haze. She had not eaten for over twenty-four hours and the shock at what had happened combined with her efforts to help the injured had brought her to the edge of exhaustion. In spite of the discomfort of her position she dozed in snatches until voices raised in relief awakened her. It was light and they were driving into Sarajevo. Bennet parked outside the principal hotel and they climbed stiffly out. Inside, the lobby was a seething mass of people and there was an air of panic. Fighting his way through the crowd, Glen managed to get hold of the manager and commandeer the use of a telephone. It was some time before he got through but at length he returned to where the rest of them were waiting, slumped on whatever surface they could find.

'It's not good,' he reported. 'The Germans have attacked through Bulgaria and taken Scopje, and there are rumours that Croat units in the army north of here have mutinied. But the good news, Leo, is that the king and his entourage passed through here yesterday and they have gone on to Pale. The prime minister is with them and most of the rest of the government. Pale's only a few miles south and I've managed to find a man who is willing to drive you there.'

'Oh, Sandy, thank you so much,' Leo responded. 'But what about you and the others?'

'My job is to get these people out of the country before it's too late,' he said. 'We shall head for the coast and hope I can get a signal out to HQ asking the navy to pick us up. Now, we need to move on. Will you be all right?'

'Yes, of course I shall, if I can just get to Pale.'

'I'll introduce you to the chap who's offered to drive you.' Glen shouldered his way through the crowd again and came back with a large, red-faced man who introduced himself as Milos, the local taxi driver.

'I am almost out of petrol,' he said with a shrug, 'and there's none to be had for love nor money. But God willing I shall get you to Pale.'

Leo got to her feet. 'I'll make sure you are not out of pocket, Milos. I'm very grateful to you for making the offer.' She turned to Zorica. 'My dear, I pray you and Sandy will get away safely.'

'Never fear for us,' the baroness replied, hugging her. 'Sandy will find a way. Give my love to Sasha when you see him. Perhaps we shall all meet again in England.'

Glen was already shepherding his passengers out to the car. Leo kissed him on both cheeks and wished the others good luck, and very soon the Cadillac, now slightly less loaded, disappeared out of sight.

She turned to Milos. 'Shall we go?'

–

Pale was a resort town in the wooded hills south of Sarajevo, a pleasant place where many wealthy businessmen had summer homes. In spite of Milos's misgivings, his fuel held out and he deposited Leo at the front of the main hotel. She did not forget her promise and paid him generously. Her legs were shaking as she got out of the car and it took an effort just to climb the steps to the main entrance. Inside, she went to the reception desk.

'I believe the king and his entourage are in Pale. Are they staying here?'

The man behind the desk stared at her with a look of supercilious horror. 'And what business might you have with His Majesty?'

Leo suddenly understood what he was seeing – a filthy, ragged woman with wild hair and bloodshot eyes. 'You don't understand…' she began.

Behind her a voice cried, 'Leo! Oh thank God!' and she turned to see her husband running down the stairs towards her. He swept her into his arms and held her tightly. 'I've been so worried. Thank heavens you're safe.' Then he took her by the shoulders and held her away from him. 'My God! You're filthy! Whatever have you been doing?'

She blinked at him from eyes blurred with a mixture of tears and dust. 'Digging, mostly – in the ruins.' Her voice was hoarse and suddenly her lips trembled. 'Please can I have something to eat and drink? I can't remember when I last ate.'

Chapter Two

Sarajevo, 6 April 1941

Stefan Popovic, known to his friends as Steve, was encoding a message for his handlers in the Special Operations Executive in London from his post as an attaché to the Royal Yugoslav 2nd Army.

The invasion has started and, as we expected, the army has been caught unprepared. Mobilisation is still incomplete, with around 90 per cent of the men reporting for duty. There is still a lack of motorised units with many relying on draught animals, of which only 40–50 per cent have been obtained, many of them of poor quality. There is also a lack of basic equipment and weapons. In some cases there are not enough boots for the men who have reported for duty.

The plan, as I understand it, is for us to be deployed along the Hungarian border between Slatina and the Danube. There has been some attempt to construct fortifications along that line but they are incomplete and so far only one unit, the 1st Battalion of the 30th Infantry, has reached its designated position. Other units are moving forward, but it is a slow process. Our HQ is supposed to move to Dakovo, but so far we are still in Sarajevo.

One other cause for concern is the morale of the Croat troops. There is a long history of mistrust between Croatia and Serbia and there is some doubt as to whether the Croats will fight for an army officered almost exclusively by Serbs. There is a fascist-leaning organisation in Croatia, the 'Ustashe', which is spreading pro-German propaganda and there are some Croats who feel that they are at greater risk from the Italians, who have territorial ambitions on the Adriatic coast, from which a German occupation would protect them.

All in all, the prospects are not good. In my judgement, if the Hungarians decide to attack immediately they could walk across the border virtually unopposed.

Stefan Popovic, Flt Lt.

Stefan let out a sigh as he finished encoding the disheartening message. Contrary to what his name might suggest, he was not Yugoslavian but American, the son of Serbian immigrants. The outbreak of war the previous September had found him in Paris pursuing his hopes of becoming a writer, and rather than return to the safety of neutral America he had opted to volunteer for the RAF. Since then he had been shot down, taken prisoner and escaped over the Pyrenees. All of which had brought him to the attention of Colin Gubbins, the head of SOE, who had seen in him an ideal recruit for his team of agents.

Up to this point he had fulfilled his brief, making regular reports on the military capability of the Yugoslavian forces and the morale of the troops; but as he considered the import of what he had just written he found himself wondering how much longer he would survive to continue.

Belgrade, 7–9 April

For two days Alix and Drago combed the ruins of the city for Alix's parents. As they searched, the full impact of the blitz came home to them. On the evening of the first day the Germans dropped incendiary bombs, turning the ruins into a blazing inferno. They found the National Library, the home of a great collection of rare books, collapsed and gutted by fire. The power station and the main post office had been hit, so there was no electricity and no telephone service, and the building housing the Supreme Command of the Forces was also destroyed. Trucks negotiated the rubble-strewn streets, loaded with the bodies of the dead.

Nobody seemed to know what the situation was in the rest of the country. There were no newspapers and the radio station had been destroyed. But in the evening, when they gave up their search for the day, Alix combed the wavelengths to find a station that was still broadcasting. Eventually she succeeded in tuning in to the BBC and heard, through a barrage of static, that a German thrust over the border with Bulgaria had captured the city of Nis, to the south of Belgrade, and that other Axis forces had crossed the River Drava on the Hungarian border to the north. It seemed that there was no concerted opposition to these incursions.

'How long can it be before they take Belgrade?' she asked Drago.

'Our troops will make a stand before they get anywhere near here,' he assured her, but she found it hard to share his optimism.

'That's what people kept saying last summer when they were advancing on Paris,' she told him.

Initially, Alix found a glimmer of hope in talking to local people who had survived the bombing. Several told her how her mother had been among them, ministering to the wounded, but no one seemed to know where she had gone after that. There were no sightings of her father. The plight of these people, sheltering in the wreckage of their homes, banished for a few minutes her own worries and she sent for Ivo.

'This place is relatively undamaged,' she pointed out, 'and we have empty rooms that could accommodate a dozen people easily. What is our position as regards food?'

'There is no fresh produce to be had but the cellars are still well stocked,' he told her. 'The countess advised me to lay down provisions, things that would keep, in case of shortages.'

'She guessed what was coming then,' Alix commented.

'So it would seem.'

'Good. I'm going to invite some of the women and children from the houses that have been worst hit to come and stay here. Please ask the staff to prepare as many beds as possible – mattresses on the floor if necessary. And tell Cook to start preparing some nourishing food for them.' She saw the butler hesitating, unsure whether to accept her authority. 'It's what my mother would have done if she was here. You know that.'

He nodded, an expression of relief on his face. 'Yes, Miss Alix, I'm sure you are right.'

Drago was watching her with a smile. 'You are right. Your mother would approve. Would it be presumptuous of me to say that you take after her?'

Alix returned his smile in a rare moment of happiness. 'I can't think of a greater compliment. Thank you.'

The next couple of days were occupied with the business of choosing which of the displaced families were in most need of help and getting them settled in the house. Several of them had wounds that needed to be dressed, or re-dressed after her mother's attentions, and Alix had to call upon her limited knowledge of first aid.

'I wish I'd paid more attention to what my mother was doing when she went out to the villages to look after people who needed medical care,' she said with a sigh. 'I just thought it was a bit of a chore when she asked me to help out. I did take a course with the Red Cross in Paris when war was declared but it was pretty rudimentary.'

Then, on the third day of their search, a woman came to the house carrying a small boy.

'I'm afraid we are getting a bit overcrowded,' Alix said, 'but we'll find you a corner somewhere.'

'Where is the lady? Your mother?' the woman asked.

'I wish I knew,' Alix replied with a catch in her throat.

'She was here, after the first bombing. She helped me to rescue my son. He was trapped under a big beam of timber and I couldn't lift it. She tried, but it was too heavy. Then a man came and helped us, but after we got my boy out he took the lady away.'

'Took her away?' Alix repeated. 'Where to?'

'I do not know. I only heard him say "you must come with me".'

'What sort of man was he? A policeman? An officer of some kind?'

'I don't know… He was in uniform, but I didn't recognise it.'

'What did he look like? Did he have dark hair?'

'No, not dark. His hair was your colour.'

'My colour? Are you sure?'

'Oh yes. Quite sure. He helped rescue my son. I shall not forget him.'

Alix looked at Drago. 'So it wasn't my father. I don't know who it could be.'

'I think I do,' he replied. 'Your mother and father were working with some English men. They seemed to be diplomats of some sort but I think that was just a cover for some other organisation. They were preparing some kind of resistance in case the Germans occupied the country. One of them was a naval officer, a Commander Glen. He had red hair, like you. I think it must have been him who took your mother away.'

'And he will have taken her somewhere for safety! Thank God! Where do you think they might have gone?'

'He was based at the legation.'

'Let's try there… If it's still standing in the middle of all this.'

–

When they reached the legation building, they saw that it had been damaged but not as severely as some others. Nevertheless, it quickly became apparent that all the British diplomats had left. Some of the locally recruited staff were still camping out in the shell of the building. At first, no one seemed to be able to tell them where the diplomats had gone until one said, 'They went to join the king.'

'Is the king still in Belgrade?' Alix asked.

The response was a shrug. 'Who knows?'

Abruptly Alix clapped a hand to her head. 'What an idiot! Of course that is where my father will be. Why didn't I think of that? He will have felt that his first duty was to make sure that Peter was safe. Come on, let's go to the palace.'

It was only a short walk from the legation to the palace compound on its hill, but it took them some time to negotiate their way through the rubble. As they approached, they saw that one end of the Old Palace – which had been the royal residence until the 1920s – had collapsed, but the New Palace seemed to be undamaged. The gates to the compound were usually guarded but there was no sign of any soldiers, so they walked up the slope to the front of the New Palace. The white stucco frontage was blackened with soot, but the main doors were still intact and two men in the sky-blue tunics of the Royal Guard were on duty.

Alix walked up the steps to face one of them. 'Vasily! Do you remember me? Alexandra Malkovic. I used to come here with my father.'

He peered at her. 'Miss Alexandra! Of course I remember. But what are you doing here? Why aren't you with your father?'

'I don't know where he is. I've been away in France, studying, and I only got back just before the bombing started. I haven't seen my parents. Please, is my father here?'

'No, miss. He went with the king.'

'Went where? When?'

'As soon as the first wave of bombing finished. It was thought essential to get the king to safety.'

'Was my mother with them?'

'I couldn't say, miss. It was all bit of a rush. But I don't recall seeing her.'

'Where did they go?'

'I heard they were heading for Sarajevo.'

'Why there?'

'Further away from the bombing, I suppose, miss.'

'Then that's where we must go.' She paused. 'There's no one on guard at the gates. Where is the rest of the regiment?'

'Most of them went with the king, miss. Just a few of us were left here to look after the palace.'

'I see. And are you all right? You weren't hurt?'

'Oh no, miss. I'll be fine. Someone has to keep the place safe for when His Majesty comes back.'

'Yes, of course. Thank you, Vasily. I must go and find my father, but I expect we'll all be back before long.'

The guard saluted and Alix returned to where Drago was waiting at the bottom of the steps.

'You heard? They've gone to Sarajevo. We must follow them.'

Drago looked doubtful. 'How are we going to get there? The chances of the car being where we left it and undamaged are very small, and anyway, there wasn't enough fuel in the tank to get us that far.'

'Good point.' Alix frowned, then her face cleared. 'If my father went with the king he probably wouldn't have taken his own car. I wonder if it's still in the garage.'

Her guess proved to be correct. Her father's Daimler, brought over from England before the war, was in the garage and by some miracle was undamaged. What was more, it had a full tank of petrol.

Alix turned to Drago triumphantly. 'There you are! Let's go.'

He looked at the clock above the garage door. 'It's getting late and it's not an easy drive over the mountains. We should wait until tomorrow morning.'

For a moment she was disposed to argue but she saw the sense of what he had said.

'Yes, I suppose you're right. One more day can't make any difference.'

Dakovo, 10 April

Steve was encrypting another message.

> *This may be the last chance I have to send for some time. The situation here is very bad. We reached Dakovo on the 7th and most of the units were deployed as planned along the Hungarian border. We could see Hungarian troops massing on the other side of the river and there were some exchanges of fire but no attack in strength. On the 9th we received a signal informing the commanding officers that the 6th Army, on our right flank, had been ordered to withdraw south of the Danube and form a line to defend against attack from Bulgaria. Today we learned that a German motor-ised column had crossed the Romanian border and attacked them, preventing their planned redeploy-ment. Also, another column has crossed the Drava with strong air support. As things stand, we expect them to reach our left flank at Slatina by tonight. It seems that resistance is crumbling all over the country.*

We have just received a signal from Prime Minister Simovic. It reads 'All troops must engage the enemy wherever encountered and with every means at their disposal. Don't wait for direct orders from above, but act on your own and be guided by your judgement, initiative and conscience.'

I am afraid that this will have very little effect. The situation is dire and as I feared might happen our Croat units are defecting en masse. We have also suffered sabotage of essential machinery and communications by fifth columnists urged on by the Ustashe.

In short, we expect to be overrun at any moment and we shall be faced with the alternatives of surrender or taking to the mountains to adopt guerilla tactics.

I will do my best to keep you informed of developments, but it may be some time before I am able to make contact.

Stefan Popovic, Flt Lt.

Steve dispatched his report and stood up, stretching his arms. He went to the opening of his tent and stood looking out. They were encamped in the middle of an orchard and the cherry trees were thick with blossom. It was hard to believe that within a few hours they could be ripped up by the tracks of German tanks.

He thought back to what he had just written about the desertion of the Croats and with the thought came a sudden memory; a chestnut-haired girl telling him that there was no such thing as Yugoslavia, only Serbs and Croats and Bosnians and Slovenes and Montenegrins, who were divided by religion, by culture and by ancient

history. The memory brought a pang of regret. For a few
heady days, when he was living in Paris before the war,
he had thought he was in love with that girl. But she
already had a lover and he had left to volunteer for the
RAF and they had lost touch. He wondered where she
was now. Still in Paris, presumably, caught there when
France collapsed and the Germans walked in unopposed.
Well, she was probably safer there than she would have
been if she had decided to come back to Serbia. What
were the chances of finding her again after the war?

He shrugged the idea off. Any thought of 'after the
war' presupposed he survived that long and right now the
prospects did not look good.

En route, 10 April

Alix and Drago set off early towards Sarajevo but as they
approached Zvornik, Drago had to brake to avoid a head-
on collision with a car coming in the opposite direction.
Behind that one there were others, filling the road, all
travelling at full speed. The road was narrow and the
Daimler was blocking the way, so the other car was also
forced to skid to a stop. The driver wound down the
window and began shouting and gesturing wildly. Alix
scrambled out of the car and ran over to him.

'What is the problem?' she began, but she had hardly
got the words out before he shouted at her, 'Clear the
road! You bloody fools, you're going the wrong way. The
Germans are coming.'

'Germans? Where? I can't hear any fighting.'

'There isn't any fighting. Their tanks are coming. No
one is trying to stop them. They'll be in Zvornik in ten
minutes. Now, get your bloody car off the road and let us
pass!'

'How can German tanks be this close?' she asked. 'Where are our troops?'

'God knows! But if you don't believe me get up to the top of that hill. You'll be able to see them from there.'

His words were almost drowned by a cacophony of horns from further back. Alix turned to Drago, who had followed her. 'We'd better let them get by. Then we can have a proper look.'

He pulled the car off onto the edge of a field and the other car surged forward. Half a dozen others followed, all going at a reckless speed.

Alix shook her head. 'Where do they think they're going?'

'Belgrade, I suppose,' Drago said.

'God knows what they expect to find there,' she said wearily. 'Come on. Let's get up the hill and see what's made them panic.'

Even before they reached the top of the hill they could hear the rumble of heavy engines and from the summit the source of the noise was plain. A column of tanks was grinding along the road from the north, with no sign of any opposition; and in the fields and lanes ahead of them men and women were scattering in all directions, some on tractors or mounted on donkeys, most on foot, carrying whatever they had been able to snatch up in their panic. On the road behind them there was now a steady flow of cars and bicycles and oxcarts.

'Oh no! Look!' Alix exclaimed suddenly.

One little group of men was heading in the opposite direction, towards the oncoming tanks, carrying rifles.

'Oh, no, you fools! What are you doing. Get back!' she yelled, but they were too far away to hear.

In impotent horror she and Drago watched as the men lined up across the road and raised their rifles. They heard the shots, but the tanks rolled on impervious. Most of the men threw themselves aside at the last moment but one remained standing in the path of the leading tank, his arms outstretched as if to prevent its passage. The advancing leviathan neither slowed nor deviated from its course. He was mown down and the column moved on.

'The bastards! The bastards!' Alix sobbed. 'How can they do that?'

Drago had gone very white. 'Now I understand,' he muttered. 'This is not a war between men. It is a war against monsters.'

They watched the tanks grind on in silence for a few moments. Then Drago pointed. 'That's Zvornik over there. He was right. The Germans will be there in ten minutes.'

'And there's no way we can get through before them,' Alix said. 'They've cut us off from the route to Sarajevo.' She clenched her fists and forced back another sob. 'If only we'd started sooner! Just a few hours and we'd have been ahead of them.'

He dropped his head. 'My fault. We should have left last night, as you wanted to.'

She saw his dejected expression and laid a hand on his arm. 'Don't blame yourself. What you said was sensible. Neither of us could have guessed this would happen.'

'I don't understand it,' he said. 'Where is our army? Does this mean we've been defeated, so soon? Almost without a fight?'

Alix sighed. 'I don't know. Maybe this is just an isolated column that has broken through the defences. The question is, what do we do now?'

'Perhaps,' Drago suggested, 'when they have passed, we could slip through behind them.'

Alix shook her head. 'They won't have left their rear unguarded. There are probably sentries posted at cross-roads, and detachments occupying the villages they've passed through. And there will be others bringing up the rear, reserves, logistical support... We got some idea of how they operate in France. Is there any other route we could take?'

He frowned. 'There are other passes through the mountains but how are we to know whether or not they are guarded? If this wasn't just an isolated column, other towns and villages will have been overrun. Perhaps even Sarajevo.'

'No! Surely they can't have got that far. Sarajevo must be defended.'

'I hope so,' he said. 'But we need to know what the position is before we try to go further.'

'I don't know how we are going to do that – unless there is something on the radio. If it's as bad as we think there might be a report on the BBC, if we can get a signal.' She turned to look back at the road behind them. 'I suppose the only thing we can do is go back to Belgrade and hope to get some news somehow.'

'I'm not sure that's a good idea,' he said. 'Those tanks are almost in Zvornic. If nothing happens to stop them they could be in Belgrade by nightfall.'

'Dear God! I suppose you're right.' She gazed from the tanks to the road behind them. 'So now what?'

'Why don't we go back to the country house? They probably won't bother with places like that – not at once anyway. We should be safe there for a while and we may be able to get news from somewhere.'

Alix heaved a deep sigh. 'I suppose you're right.' Once more, tears threatened to overcome her. 'I'm beginning to wonder if I'll ever see my parents again.'

Drago put his arm round her shoulders. 'You mustn't think like that. Remember, they are with the king, and every effort will be made to keep him safe. Our army may be preparing a counterattack even at this moment. Who knows, in a few days he may be able to make a triumphant return to his palace. And your parents with him.'

Alix allowed herself to be comforted, but at the back of her mind was the memory of how quickly France had collapsed a year earlier. If that huge, modern army had been unable to withstand the Nazi war machine she could see little chance of the Yugoslav army surviving.

As they drew up outside Kuca Magnolija, Alix was swept by a sense of déjà vu. Was it really only five days since she had arrived here as the taxi's headlights illuminated the long, cream painted frontage of the house? Her joy at returning home had been tempered by a twinge of anxiety about her father's reception. The last time they met had been three years ago, a fraught occasion in which she had finally and adamantly refused to accept his plan for her to marry the man he had chosen for her. He was the son of another old family, one with which in the past there had been a long and deadly feud. The marriage had been intended to heal that once and for all, but Alix had seen no reason why her own life should be circumscribed by ancient hatreds. The day after that interview her mother had taken her away on what was termed a 'cultural tour', ostensibly to give her a chance to experience the wider world before she had to settle down, but in practice to give time for tempers on both sides to cool. That tour had culminated in her enrolment at the Sorbonne, where she had been trapped by the German occupation. She had written to her father once or twice before the Germans moved in but had received no reply, so she had no reason to believe he had forgiven her, but her overwhelming relief at having escaped from France and evading the clutches of the Abwehr overrode any doubts about her welcome. Now the longed-for reconciliation had been postponed for an indefinite future.

Inside Kuca Magnolija, she found the household in a state of panic, convinced that she and Drago as well as her parents had perished in the bombing of the city. She called them together and told them that the count and countess were with the king and would doubtless return as soon as it was safe to do so. She omitted to mention the column of tanks they had encountered, telling herself there was no point in creating a new panic until the situation became clearer. Then, having given instructions for a meal to be prepared, she headed for her father's study and switched on the radio. It proved impossible to tune in to any of the frequencies on which the BBC normally broadcast but turning the dial she found a new, stronger voice.

'This is Radio Zagreb, the voice of the Independent State of Croatia.'

'What!' Her exclamation was echoed by Drago, who was still at her side.

'Earlier today our German friends were welcomed into the city by cheering crowds, and with their agreement the creation of the new state was announced by Slavko Kvaternik, commander-in-chief of the Croatian Armed Forces. The new state has been recognised by Vladko Macek, head of the Croatian Peasant Party and deputy prime minister of the now defunct Yugoslavia, and Ante

Pavlic has been pronounced leader. He is expected to return from exile in Italy within the next day or two.'

Alix switched off the radio and gazed at Drago in consternation. 'Welcomed by cheering crowds! How can that happen? Who is Pavlic?'

Drago shook his head sadly. 'He's the leader of the Ustashe. They are a nasty lot, extreme nationalists and fascists, but they have the support of the Roman Catholic clergy because they are against the Orthodox Church. They hate all Serbs. My mother was regarded as an outcast because she married one.'

'Of course! I'd almost forgotten that your mother was Croatian. That's where you get your fair hair from. This must feel very personal to you.'

'It does, but mainly because I pity any Serbs still living there – also any Jews or Roma people. The Ustashe are merciless.'

'But to welcome the Germans! Why would they do that?'

'I suppose they see them as liberating them from the government in Belgrade.'

Alix put her head in her hands. 'If the whole of Croatia is in German hands, how long can it be before they take Sarajevo? How long before my parents, and the king, are prisoners of war?'

Chapter Three

Pale, 10–14 April 1941

Dusan Simovic's face was grave as he rose to address the royal council. 'I have just received very grave news. Croatia has surrendered to the Germans and declared itself an independent state.'

'Treason! That is treason!' The exclamation came from the king but was echoed around the improvised council chamber.

'There is more,' Simovic went on. 'There are reports of four armoured columns advancing across our borders, one from Romania towards Belgrade, one across the Drava from Hungary, one from Austria towards Celje and another towards Zagreb.'

'But our men are counterattacking, of course. What is the situation?' Peter demanded.

'We are being forced back on all fronts. The 4th Army has all but disintegrated, the 2nd and the 6th are retreating. Skopje has fallen and the enemy is closing in on Belgrade.'

Peter's face was deadly white and his lips trembled. Leo looked at her husband and saw that he, too, was badly shaken by the news.

'How can this have happened?' Peter asked.

'The prime cause has been the disloyalty of Croatian units. Many of them have deserted. I have received

43

reports that in some cases men have simply laid down their arms and gone home. Others have actively welcomed the invaders. Some have been responsible for sabotaging our own equipment.'

'So what can be done?' Peter asked hoarsely.

Simovic shook his head wearily. 'I have issued a message ordering all our troops to resist by any means in their power, but I have to admit that I do not expect it to have much effect. The German panzer columns are better equipped and move much faster than we could have foreseen. Our own forces have simply been overwhelmed and overrun.'

'Then we must make urgent arrangements for the safety of His Majesty,' Sasha said.

'I am looking into the possibility of an evacuation by air,' the prime minister told him.

'I refuse to go!' Peter declared. 'I will not leave my people to face the Nazi threat alone.'

'Sir,' Sasha said gently, 'think how demoralising it would be if your people were to learn that you were a prisoner of the Germans. You can do much more to help as a free man, rallying our allies to our defence.'

Peter looked as if he was going to argue, but then he bent his head. 'What you say makes sense. But is there a real danger that we may be taken prisoner?'

'All is not yet lost,' Simovic told him. 'Loyal elements in our army are making a last stand. We may yet prevail, but we must also be ready to move at a moment's notice if it becomes necessary.'

The tension grew over the days that followed until it was almost palpable, as if the air itself was charged with electricity which might precipitate at any moment in a bolt of lightning. The news was progressively worse with every hour that passed. On the eleventh they learned that Italy and Hungary had joined in the attack. The Italians advanced on Ljubljana and took the Dalmatian coast, meeting virtually no resistance. The Hungarians, likewise, advanced on Novi Sad unopposed. On the twelfth they heard that Belgrade had fallen. The Council met for the last time on the thirteenth.

'I am afraid defeat is inevitable,' Simovic declared sombrely. 'So we must face the prospect of going into exile. There is an airfield at Niksic which is still in our hands. I have arranged for an aircraft to fly us out from there tomorrow.'

'Where to?' Sasha asked.

'To Athens, initially. The British Expeditionary Force is holding out there, though how much longer they can do so is doubtful. The Germans turned south after taking Belgrade and they have already taken Thessalonika. The Greek army is in retreat. We must hope Athens remains in Allied hands until we get there. After that, it will be up to the British government.'

There was little conversation as the car carrying the king, with Leo and Sasha in attendance, wound its way down the twisting roads through the mountains. Each of the passengers was struggling to come to terms with the shock of sudden defeat and the bitter prospect of exile, and there was the constant fear of an enemy at their backs who might catch up with them before they reached their destination. Leo was aware that for her, perhaps, the situation was marginally less traumatic. Yugoslavia was her adopted country but she had a country and a home else-where; a home that had been defended with much greater determination by its inhabitants and which still clung, in the face of all the odds, to the prospect of ultimate victory.

Nevertheless, it was Serbia she had fought for through the perilous years of another war and this flight brought back terrible memories of another retreat through these same mountains twenty-five years earlier. She knew that the same thoughts must be going through her husband's mind, and she reached across to clasp his hand.

'We'll be back. Just like last time.'

He squeezed her hand in return but said nothing.

—

They came down at last onto the wide plain around Niksic and drove straight to the airfield where the plane awaiting them was, ironically, a Junkers 88 purchased a few years ago from Germany. They were followed by a small convoy of cars carrying Simovic and the members of his government and administration who had escaped with him from Belgrade. The plane was designed as a bomber, not as a passenger plane, so as they all climbed aboard they had to settle themselves uncomfortably on benches along the edge of the fuselage, but there were no complaints. The pilot and co-pilot were waiting for them and within minutes the propellers on the twin engines were turning. There were a few anxious seconds as the plane roared down the runway and it seemed as if with its heavy load it would never take off, then came the stomach-churning lurch as the wheels left the ground and a sound between a sigh of relief and a cheer echoed round the cabin.

Time passed. There were no windows so it was impossible to see how far they had travelled. There was some desultory conversation but most of the time a gloomy silence prevailed. Then the co-pilot came through from the cockpit.

'Gentlemen, I'm sorry to tell you but we have a problem. We don't have enough fuel to reach Athens. But we have identified a temporary airfield set up by the RAF, so we are going to make an emergency landing there.'

The passengers looked at each other in consternation and there was a babble of comment, some angry, some fearful. Leo reached for Sasha's hand and gripped it.

They felt the plane bank sideways and then Leo's ears popped as they lost height. They levelled up and there was a jolt as the wheels touched the ground. They taxied for a short distance and then came to a stop, and the co-pilot came back and opened the door in the fuselage and lowered a ladder. Immediately they heard running feet and shouting, and a sergeant in RAF uniform appeared in the doorway holding a pistol.

'What the bleeding hell do you think you're doing? Who are you and who gave you permission to land here?'

Peter was nearest to the door and before Sasha could intervene he rose to his feet.

'How dare you address me like that? I am King Peter the Second of Yugoslavia.'

'Oh yeah? And I'm Father Christmas,' came the reply. 'Now get out, all of you – and don't try any funny business.'

Sasha laid a hand on Peter's arm. 'Better do as he says. We'll sort this out when we're on the ground.'

They all descended, finding a posse of airmen, all armed, awaiting them. Sasha turned to the sergeant. 'Please take us to your superior officer. This young man is truly the king of Yugoslavia and these gentlemen are members of his government. We are fleeing the German occupation of our country and need your help.'

The sergeant looked from him to Peter and then at the rest of them, clearly struggling with disbelief, but Sasha's manner and his perfect English carried conviction. 'All right, follow me – just you and the young man and the lady. The rest stay here.' He looked at the airmen. 'Keep them under guard until we can get this sorted out.'

In a temporary hut they found a squadron leader standing behind a table covered in maps.

'Well, Sergeant?'

'Young chap here says he's the king of Yugoslavia.'

'What?'

Sasha stepped forward. 'Squadron Leader, it's quite true. My name is Count Alexander Malkovic. Let me present Peter Karadjordjevic, King of Yugoslavia.'

The officer stared from one of them to the other. 'I don't understand.'

'You will probably not be aware of this, but Yugoslavia is about to be overrun by the Nazis. The army cannot hold out much longer so it was imperative that we get the king to safety.'

'Do you have any proof of any of this?'

'I have,' Leo said, delving in her shoulder bag, thankful that Glen had told her to collect their passports from the Belgrade house. She handed them to the squadron leader who leafed through them.

'You're British?'

'Yes, but I am married to Count Alexander.'

'All right. What about you?' he asked, looking at Peter.

'Squadron Leader,' Sasha said gently, 'royalty do not carry passports. Now, out there on your airfield is the prime minister and several senior members of government. I suggest you bring them in and then you can contact whoever you like to confirm the situation in

Yugoslavia. I understand that arrangements have been made for our onward passage from Athens.'

The squadron leader looked like a man awaking from a dream. 'Very well! Sergeant, take the other gentlemen to the canteen and organise some refreshments.' He turned his gaze back to Sasha. 'If you'll just give me a moment...?'

He disappeared into an inner compartment and they heard low voices and the crackle of static from a WT radio. A few minutes later he reappeared looking at once relieved and mildly embarrassed. 'I've been on to our chaps in Athens and it seems you are expected, as you said.' He turned to Peter. 'Sir... Your Majesty... Forgive this rough reception. But you arrived without warning in a German aircraft. You will understand that we had to be sure you were not enemy agents.'

'I quite understand,' Peter said. 'And I'm sorry if we gave you a bit of a shock.'

After that, the atmosphere changed completely. They were conducted to the canteen, which was housed in a large Nissen hut, and offered sandwiches and mugs of strong tea with condensed milk. The sandwiches were accepted with gratitude, the tea met with a rather different reception. In its place there was the offer of apparently unlimited quantities of gin – so much so that when the announcement came that their plane had been refuelled and was ready for take-off Dusan Simovic was incapable of walking and had to be carried out to it.

Half an hour later they were in Athens.

Kuca Magnolija, 12 April

'Belgrade has fallen!' Gregor, Sasha Malkovic's manservant, burst into the study where Alix was sitting with Drago trying to tune in to the BBC.

'Fallen?' Alix got to her feet. 'When? How? Was there no attempt to defend it? We haven't heard any gunfire, any sound of any fighting.'

'There wasn't any,' he replied breathlessly. 'Some men of the Waffen SS managed to cross the Danube last night in inflatable boats. There was only a small guard on the riverbank and they were taken by surprise and surrendered. When some of our armoured vehicles arrived the SS men fired on them and took them over. They drove to the German legation – that was untouched by the bombing, of course. The bombers avoided that whole area. They ran up the swastika and proclaimed that the city was under their control and in the morning the mayor formally surrendered. The tanks moved in an hour later. I thought I should let you know as soon as possible.'

Alix felt tears stinging her eyes, tears as much of anger and humiliation as of distress. 'It's shameful! How could they let that happen? Without any attempt at resistance!' She drew a breath and forced herself to be practical. 'How did you get here, Gregor?'

'By bicycle. I didn't want to draw attention to myself by trying to drive out in one of the Count's cars. Anyway, the streets are impassable now.'

Alix took in his dishevelled clothes and his sweating face. He was usually so immaculate. It was bizarre and unnerving to see him like that.

'Thank you for coming so quickly. Tell me, are the rest of the staff all right? What about the refugees we took in?'

'All is much as you left it two days ago,' he told her. 'The city is calm and so far no one has bothered us. But I don't know how much longer that will last.'

'Well, it's good to know no one is hurt, for now at least. Go to the kitchen, Gregor, and ask cook to find you something to eat and drink. After that, you might want to go to your room and change. You have clothes here, I presume?'

'Oh, yes, miss. I've always kept a separate wardrobe here for when the count was in residence.'

'Good. Come back when you've had a chance to rest and change. We'll talk more then.'

As the door closed behind Gregor, Alix turned to Drago. 'We must go to the city. The people at the town house will need me.'

'It's too dangerous,' he said. 'Stay here until we have a clearer idea of what is happening.'

'No. I can't leave them to fend for themselves. If my father was here, or my mother, one of them would take charge. They aren't, so it's up to me.'

She spoke the words without fully understanding their import but once spoken they crystallised a thought that had been at the back of her mind for the last couple of days. In the absence of her parents, the estate and its people, and the staff of the town house, were her responsibility. She had left two years ago as a young girl, thinking only of her own future. She had returned a woman, with experience of responsibility in the face of danger. She needed to now demonstrate that she was capable of stepping into her mother's shoes.

'I need to speak to our people here first. They will be frightened and confused.' She rang the bell and Bogdan appeared with a rapidity that suggested he had been waiting outside the door for the summons.

'Bogdan, I want you to assemble the staff, all of them, the house servants and the grooms and the gardeners and the rest. Drago, please go and find Rodovan and ask him to collect as many of the farm workers as possible. Tell them to meet in the courtyard.'

It took almost half an hour for everyone to assemble. Alix watched from a window as they arrived and saw the same fear and consternation on every face. Many had brought their families with them, children clinging to their mothers' hands, men trying to put on a brave face in front of their wives. When Bogdan informed her that everyone was ready she stepped out onto the front steps where they could all see her.

'My friends.' She pitched her voice so that those at the back of the crowd could hear her. 'I know we are all shaken and confused by what is happening. It is hard to get reliable news but it seems that German columns have penetrated our defences and I have just heard that Belgrade is now in enemy hands.' A sound somewhere between a sob and a gasp swept through the assembly like a gust of wind through the forest. 'The good news is that there seems to have been no fighting, so it is unlikely that our friends and colleagues – those who survived the bombing – have been hurt. What has happened to our troops in other parts of the country we have no way of knowing. There may still be fighting going on in other areas but it seems that the city is calm, and since the Germans are meeting no resistance I see no reason why there should be any fighting round here. So I do not think we are in any immediate danger. I am going now to visit our house in the city to make sure that our people there are all right. I shall be back in a day or two. Until then, Bogdan and Rodovan are in charge and I want you all to carry on with your normal tasks as calmly as possible. Do not be too downhearted. We may have been defeated but we shall survive, and one day, if God wills, we shall drive these interlopers out of our land and live as free people again. Until then, we can only commend ourselves into His hands and care for and support each other to the best of our ability.'

As she stepped back inside the house Alix was aware of Drago looking at her as if seeing her for the first time. Caught between amusement and irritation, she said, 'Why are you looking at me like that? I haven't suddenly sprouted two heads, have I?'

He dropped his eyes. 'Forgive me. I didn't mean to be impertinent.'

'Oh, for heaven's sake!' she exclaimed. 'I thought we'd got past all that. You can say what you like to me. I just wondered why you were giving me that odd look.'

He hesitated. 'It's the way you spoke. Suddenly you weren't little Miss Lexie any more. You sounded... Well, you sounded like your mother.'

She reached out and squeezed his hand. 'Oh, Drago. If only that were true.' After a pause, she went on. 'But I did sort of surprise myself. I hadn't thought what I was going to say. That bit about God's will and commending ourselves into his care – it's not something I would normally say. I'm not sure if... Well, if I believe in God any more.'

'But they do,' he said. 'And it's what they needed to hear. It was the right thing to say.'

Chapter Four

Colonel Draza Mihailovic and a small band of officers huddled together in a half-ruined barn in the shadow of the ancient castle of Doboj. In the fields around it the exhausted remnants of their forces tended their wounded, scavenged for food or simply lay on the ground waiting for the advancing enemy to kill or imprison them. Steve stood in a corner, listening. Of all the officers he had met during his time with the 2nd Army he had most respect for Mihailovic. He had had a somewhat chequered career in the army, often speaking out against accepted dogma in a way that had not endeared him to the High Command, but he had a charisma that bound men to him. Tall and unusually fair for a Serb, his good looks undoubtedly helped to enhance his image. Two days earlier he had been given command of a small 'rapid unit' with orders to assess the situation along the front line. It had not taken long to realise that there was no longer a 'front line'. The defences had disintegrated under the pressure of attacks across the Hungarian border. As they retreated they were almost overrun by a German armoured column, but they had managed to skirt round it by taking to minor roads and tracks in the hills, and had regrouped here to consider their next move.

As they were talking, a dispatch rider on a motorcycle drew up outside the barn and announced he had a message for the colonel. Coming inside, he handed Draza a letter.

'My God! It's unbelievable!' The colonel crushed the paper in his fist.

'What is it?' one of the officers asked.

'Miljkovic is ordering us to surrender.'

'Surrender!'

'The High Command has decided that the only solution is to capitulate.'

There was a brief silence. It seemed no one was keen to be the first to speak.

'It seems to me, sir,' one of his aides said at length, 'that there is no alternative. We are surrounded and cut off from all contact with the general staff in Sarajevo. The men are exhausted – those that are left. The rest have deserted already. We have to surrender.'

'And then?' Draza cut in sharply. 'Then what? Do we expect them to allow us to go back to our homes? Or do we go meekly into a prison camp? And what of the rest of the country? Do we accept the prospect of being occupied? They will split the country between them – the Germans, the Italians, the Bulgarians and the Hungarians will all want their bit. Already Croatia has declared independence. Yugoslavia will cease to exist.'

'It already has,' someone muttered.

'And what of Serbia? Do we let them dismember our homeland and make it part of Greater Germany?'

'What option do we have?'

'Resistance! Let us take our arms and go to the mountains. I refuse to bow to the enemy.'

The aide shook his head wearily. 'That must be a futile gesture. We should either starve to death or be hunted down. Better to make what terms we can and at least preserve our lives.'

'If life means more to you than honour, then that is your choice. I will choose death before I break my oath to my king and betray my country. Any of you who feel the same can come with me.'

With that, Mihailovic marched out of the barn. There was a pause and then most of the other officers followed him. Steve caught him up.

'Excuse me, Colonel. What do you intend to do?'

'Do? Exactly what I said. I shall collect those men who are prepared to follow me and head for the mountains.'

'Then I will come with you, if you will allow me.'

'You? Why would you want to do that?'

'Because I prefer that prospect rather than spending the rest of the war in a German prison camp.'

'But you are an American, yes? Your own people would repatriate you, would they not? After all, America is still not involved in this war.'

'Perhaps that is another good reason why I should be involved,' Steve replied grimly.

'I see. Well, if you are determined to fight on, I am happy to welcome you to join the Chetniks.'

'Chetniks. It means "a band of men", yes?'

'But it has a noble history. In the Balkan Wars of 1912 and '13 we fought the Ottoman Turks. Chetniks were used as the advance guard to soften up the opposition before the main army attacked, and for operations behind enemy lines. We shall do the same.'

'And will men follow us?'

'We are about to find out. There is still some honour among the Serbs. It is to them that we shall appeal.'

In the course of the next hours Draza Mihailovic moved among the men sprawled on the ground around them, and in ones and twos they dragged themselves to their feet and assembled around his tent, bringing with them their rifles and what ammunition they had left. Steve counted upwards of fifty.

While they waited for the last few to join them, Draza said to Steve, 'You are coming dressed like that?'

'Why not?'

'The men may wonder why a man in British uniform is among them. They may wonder if you are a spy of some sort. And apart from that you will not survive the winter in the mountains in those clothes. Make no mistake. This is not an enterprise that will last only for the summer.'

'I have my greatcoat.'

'Not enough. Wait.' He dived into his tent and brought out a well-worn sheepskin coat. 'Put this on. You will be glad of it later. What is in that case?'

'A radio. We may want to contact London.'

'We may indeed! But it is too heavy to carry around if we need to move quickly and secretly. Let me think.' He looked around and called one of the men over.

'Find me a donkey or a mule. Pay for it if needs be. Here.' He gave the man some coins. 'Be quick.'

Minutes later the man returned leading a mule, and the case containing Steve's radio was loaded into a pannier slung across its back, balanced on the other side by a sub-machine gun. Steve had already packed his other posses-sions into a rucksack and he tied the sheepskin to it and slung it over his shoulders. Around him the other men also hefted their packs and their rifles. Mihailovic looked around the camp. He raised his rifle.

'Forwards! Follow me.'

Someone raised a cheer and the little band moved off.

Instead of taking the Daimler, Alix and Drago decided to drive to the city in the American Dodge truck her mother had bought for taking medical supplies to the local villages. It was still difficult to negotiate the rubble-strewn streets but with the vehicle's more robust construction it proved possible and no one attempted to question their right to pass. There were armoured cars parked at most of the main intersections and sentries in German uniform outside most of the public buildings – or in many cases the burned-out shells of them; but there were no disturbances. As they came to the centre of the city they saw gangs clearing the rubble under the guard of more soldiers. They were a strange sight: men and women, young and old, some in working clothes but others quite smartly dressed.

They found matters in the house, as Gregor had said, much as they had left them. Every room now accommodated as many refugees as it was possible to fit in, whole families in some, groups of strangers in others. The main salon had been turned into a hospital ward to care for the wounded who were lying on mattresses on the floor. The billiard room was now an improvised operating theatre. By lucky chance, one of the neighbours displaced by the bombing was a doctor and he had taken charge in this area, helped by several of the female servants. Alix conducted a rapid tour of inspection and then dispatched Drago to the kitchens to check on supplies, while she rolled up her sleeves and set to work changing dressings and replacing soiled sheets. Several of the patients had suffered horrific burns and many had broken bones, and the limbs of others had been so badly crushed by falling debris that the only real treatment would be amputation, but without access to anaesthesia the doctor was unwilling to go to those lengths. Two of the male servants were even now combing the city to find a hospital that was still operational, or failing that, one that could supply chloroform or some other anaesthetic. There were moments when Alix found herself having to choke down nausea and resist the urge to drop what she was doing and run out into the fresh air.

To distract herself she remarked on the work she had seen going on outside. 'It's noble of them to volunteer for that job. But some of them don't really look up to it.'

'Volunteer?' the doctor said. 'Those people did not volunteer. They are all Jews. The Nazis rounded them up as soon as they took over and set them to work.'

Alix stopped what she was doing and rested her brow on the back of her hand. 'Oh God! It's started already!'

'What do you mean?'

'I was in Paris when the Germans occupied the city. It didn't happen so quickly there, but soon they brought in laws preventing Jews from owning businesses. They banned Jewish children from using playgrounds. Then the arrests started. I had a friend, a Polish girl. She was a Jew. She was terrified. She had heard that awful things were happening there. We had to get her out of the country.'

He glanced up, one hand holding the wrist of a small child. 'Get her out? How?'

Alix pulled herself together. 'Oh, that's a long story. But we were able to put her in touch with someone who could probably get her on a ship to America.' She sighed. 'I just hope she got there.'

Drago joined them. 'They are running short of things in the kitchen, especially fresh food. There's nothing to be bought here.'

Alix stood up. 'Take the Dodge and go back to the country house. See what they can spare. You should be able to get some potatoes and some milk and eggs. Bring whatever you can.'

This set the pattern for the next day or two. Alix helped the doctor, or carried round bowls of soup and wedges of bread and tried to amuse some of the children who were recovering from the shock of the bombing and becoming a nuisance. Drago went backwards and forwards between the two houses, collecting whatever supplies he could find.

On the seventeenth, armoured cars with loudspeakers toured the city announcing the unconditional surrender of the country. 'Your king and his ministers have fled. Your army has been defeated. Any further resistance is futile. Submit and you will be well treated.'

That evening Alix made another effort to tune in to the BBC. The batteries in the wireless set were getting low but she suddenly picked up a new, strong signal. It announced itself as Radio Belgrade, but it was obvious that it was being run by the Germans. There was no news. The programme was devoted to music of various kinds. It was not what she was looking for, but simply to hear music lifted her spirits. She asked Drago to carry the set down to the salon so the patients would have the benefit of it, at least until the batteries ran out.

Next day there was an announcement. The surrender had been formally signed by the ex-foreign minister Aleksander Cincar-Markovic and General Jankovic. Serbia was now to be known as the Territory of the Military Commander. Large parts of what had been southern Serbia had been annexed by Bulgaria; Montenegro was now an Italian protectorate and areas to the north had been divided between Hungary, Germany and Italy. Independent Croatia now included the whole of Bosnia.

The whole concept of Yugoslavia as a united state had collapsed.

Chapter Five

In the mountains of Bosnia, 15–29 April 1941

All day Mihailovic and his men marched south-east, keeping to the high ground and following the mule tracks that wound round the contours of the hills. Here and there they came upon small groups of Serb soldiers who had not waited for the order to surrender but had taken their weapons and headed for the hills. Their numbers grew until there were eighty of them. At evening they came to a small village and Mihailovic called halt.

'We may be able to shelter here for the night, and perhaps buy some milk or some eggs. You three men, come with me. The rest wait here.'

The four men walked forward until they came within fifty yards or so of the first buildings. The first shot seemed to come from nowhere and one of the men fell to the ground. Three more shots followed but by that time Draza and the other two had thrown themselves down and the bullets passed harmlessly over their heads.

'With me!' shouted Draza's second in command. 'Keep down.'

Crawling on their bellies, the rest of the men moved forward to join Draza and the others.

'Come out and show yourselves!' Mihailovic shouted. 'Are you cowards sheltering under your mothers' skirts?'

The answer was a volley of shots and Steve heard another man somewhere behind him cry out in pain.

'It's coming from that barn,' one of the officers said.

'Right, let's teach them a lesson,' Draza responded. He got to his knees and sent a burst of fire in the direction of the barn. Others followed his example and Steve saw the timber walls pock-marked with bullet holes. There was a rattle of return fire and then, in the lull that followed, Mihailovic shouted again.

'We are soldiers of the Royal Yugoslav Army. Firing on us is an act of treachery to the crown. Surrender your arms.'

There was a pause, then a voice shouted back, 'Fuck off, Serbs! We are the Ustase and this is a Croat village. You have no rights here.'

Draza did not respond for a moment, then he turned to the men behind him. 'Withdraw and regroup.'

When they were out of range, he and his officers clustered together. 'How many injured?' he asked.

'Three and one dead.'

The colonel's expression was grim. 'We can't afford to lose men and use up our ammunition on one insignificant village. We'll move on and find somewhere else to camp for the night.'

That night they slept under the stars and with empty stomachs. Before he settled down, Steve unloaded his radio set and tried to make contact with London, but it was impossible to get a signal here in the mountains.

In the days that followed they met with similar hostile receptions, sometimes from villages occupied by the Ustase, twice from Bosnian Muslims determined to protect their communities from the depredations of either side. They were reduced to hunting rabbits and stealing chickens and eggs from outlying farms. Once one of the men came in with a lamb he had taken from a flock when the shepherd boy's attention was elsewhere. One day they encountered a peasant returning with his donkey from market in the nearest town and from him they learned that the final unconditional surrender had been agreed on the seventeenth and formally signed in Belgrade the following day. What the terms were he had no idea. It was enough that the whole country was now in the hands of the enemy.

Looking down from the heights, they frequently saw traffic moving on the roads below. Dispatch riders on motorcycles sped backwards and forwards and convoys of heavy lorries carried supplies for the occupying army.

'If only we could disrupt their communications…' Draza Mihailovic mused.

'It wouldn't be hard to shoot one of the dispatch riders,' someone suggested. 'Or shoot out the tyres on some of the lorries.'

'We can't afford to waste ammunition,' the colonel said. 'And we don't want to draw attention to ourselves by starting a fire fight. We don't have the men or the resources.'

Steve was remembering techniques he had learned at the SOE 'finishing school' at Beaulieu. When practised in the leafy lanes of Sussex they had seemed so bizarre that he could not envisage himself employing them. Now he said, 'There are other ways.'

The next day, several dispatch riders were brought crashing to the ground when a rope, stretched across the road and hidden by fallen leaves, was suddenly raised to the level of their throats by men concealed in the bushes. Breaking cover, the Chetniks made short work of them.

A day or two later the group came upon a small village which was obviously occupied by a German detachment. What had happened to the original inhabitants it was impossible to tell. Watching through field glasses, Steve had the impression that the commanders were overconfident and that the sentries were not as alert as they should have been. He outlined his plan to Draza and was given permission to ask for volunteers. He chose six men from those who put themselves forward, all of whom had some knowledge of internal combustion engines. As night fell, they smeared their faces with mud from a nearby stream and crawled on their stomachs to within a few yards of the village. A single road led through it and one man stood sentry at either end. In the centre, two trucks and two armoured cars were parked, and there was a tent which they had observed being used as a field kitchen. The village houses where the rest of the detachment were presumably sleeping were dark and silent. Lying in the ditch close to where the sentry was standing, Steve had to call upon everything he had been taught by the SOE instructor in unarmed combat. 'You only get one chance,' he had said. 'Make it count.' But could he do it? Was he, when it came to it, capable of killing a man in cold blood? He reminded himself of a scene he had witnessed a few days earlier. As a German tank column rolled into a village, some men had rushed out armed only with sickles and axes and blocked the road. While he and the remnants of the 2nd Army had watched helplessly, the tanks had simply rolled over them and on through the village, leaving distraught women and terrified children in their wake. *You can do this!* he told himself. Gesturing to the other men to stay back, he wriggled forward. The sentry was facing away from him, looking along the road.

Silently, knife in hand, Steve rose to his feet. He felt hot blood pulse over his hand and the man fell without a sound.

He beckoned the others forward and they crept down the street to where the vehicles were parked. Each man had been given a target and it was the work of seconds to remove the rotor arms. Steve himself headed for the field kitchen. He had a sack stuffed inside his battle dress tunic and his first thought was to fill it with tinned goods. But that presented a problem. Tins would make a noise. There were loaves of black bread in a bin and strings of sausages hanging from hooks. He filled his sack and slipped out of the tent. The other men were already heading out of the village. Incredibly, not one person had stirred in the darkened houses. Scarcely able to believe his luck, Steve crept back along the village street, averting his eyes from the motionless body of the sentry. Minutes later he was back with the rest of the Chetniks, being pounded on the back in congratulation. They did not wait to find out what the reaction was when the watch was changed in the village, but melted away into the forest like ghosts, distributing the rotor arms in the leaf litter as they went.

Steve was glad to have proved himself, but the success of the mission left a bitter taste. In his former life with the RAF he had dropped bombs and felt a surge of triumph when they hit their target, knowing quite well that this involved the death of an unknown number of men on the ground below. But that was very different from feeling the warm blood of another human being on his hands. Telling himself that it was what he had been trained to do did not make it any easier to come to terms with.

Day by day they came closer to the border of Serbia and on 29 April they crossed the Drina river.

'Where are we heading now?' Steve asked.

'Ravna Gora, in the foothills of Mount Suvabor,' Draza told him. 'I have friends there and it is too remote for the Germans to bother about.'

They were to be made to pay for the success at their small attempts at sabotage. To reach their goal at Ravna Gora they had to cross the River Detinja somewhere in the region of the town of Uzice. The river here ran through a deep gorge and the only way across it was by a narrow bridge that carried the Belgrade to Bar railway. Both sides of the gorge were heavily wooded and an advance party reported no sign of enemy activity. They could not hear any sound of an approaching train, so they set out across. The leaders were almost at the far side when a fusillade of fire broke out and several men dropped to the railbed or toppled over the parapet into the river.

'Back!' shouted Draza, but even as he spoke, more fire broke out from the bank they had just left. They were caught in a well-designed trap.

Men were falling all round him and Steve saw that there was only one way to escape. He threw off his pack, scrambled over the parapet and let himself fall into the fast-flowing water below. He surfaced, gasping, to hear the patter of bullets striking the surface all round him. He dived and let the water carry him downstream. When he could hold his breath no longer he surfaced again and saw that the current had carried him round a bend and out of sight of the bridge. Looking around him, he could see no sign of any of his comrades. Panting, he searched for a point on the riverbank where he could haul himself out. The weight of his boots was threatening to pull him under and he had to struggle to stay afloat. He was tempted to kick them off but he had done that once before, when his plane ditched in the English Channel, and he had not forgotten the pain of trying to cover any distance in bare feet. The riverbank rose steeply and he could see nothing he could grab onto, and the current was sweeping him downstream at an alarming rate. Then, by luck, even as it seemed he would have to sacrifice the boots, an eddy carried him close to the bank and he was able to grab hold of the root of a willow growing by the water. The struggle to pull himself out almost took the last of his strength, but he managed it at last and lay panting on the bank.

As his mind cleared it struck him that he had seen no sign of any other survivors. The fear gripped him that he might be alone in a hostile country.

A voice from the river made him twist round. Draza Mihailovic was clinging to the same root and trying to pull himself out. The relief gave Steve a new burst of energy and he reached down and grabbed his arm. In his sodden clothes he was a dead weight and obviously almost exhausted, but with the strength born of desperation Steve succeeded in hauling him up onto the bank. They lay side by side, gasping, and it was a while before either of them could speak.

'Did any of the others survive?' Steve asked at length.

'I saw several jump into the river,' Draza replied wearily. 'God knows where they may have ended up. I doubt if I could have got out without your help.'

Steve reckoned he was probably right. For a man of his age, Draza was undoubtedly fit, but the fact was that he was no longer in the prime of life.

'How did they know we would try to cross that bridge?'

'You can't move eighty men around the country without someone noticing – and we haven't exactly kept a low profile. They must have guessed where we were heading and this was the only way to cross the river without going into the centre of the town.'

'So now what?' Steve asked.

Draza pulled himself into a sitting position and emptied the water out of his boots. 'Keep going and hope some of the others join us.'

Steve looked at him in admiration. Many men would have been crushed by what had happened but Draza seemed to have a reserve of courage that put his own fears to shame.

They got to their feet and managed to haul themselves up the slope by holding onto the trunks of the trees. At the top they found themselves on a narrow lane and followed it away from the town. But a noise in the bushes beside the road brought them both to a standstill. Steve's rifle had gone the same way as his pack. He still had his pistol but the likelihood of that firing after its soaking was remote. His knife was in its sheath at his belt. He drew it and saw that Draza was similarly armed.

'Come out and show yourself,' Draza commanded.

There was a crash of breaking branches and three men in the uniform of the 2nd Army appeared on the road.

'Colonel! Thank God!' one of them said. 'We thought you'd had it.'

Draza embraced them all in turn and Steve shook their hands with renewed optimism.

'Are there more of you?' Draza asked.

'I saw a couple in the river near me,' one replied, 'but I don't know if they got out.'

As they walked on, more men joined them, including three of the officers. Looking around at them, Steve was struck by a sudden thought.

'What happened to the mule?'

He had entrusted the animal to one of the men who seemed to have the knack of keeping it moving, but now there was no sign of either man or beast.

'I presume the Germans have got it,' Draza said.

'Which means they've got the radio set, too.'

'Maybe not,' someone else suggested. 'I was at the rear of the line and I saw Spiro struggling with the brute. It didn't like the look of the bridge and was refusing to go across. It probably bolted when the firing started up.'

'So it may be wandering about somewhere,' Steve said.

'On the wrong side of the river,' Draza pointed out. 'The chances are someone has caught it and taken it in.'

'But the radio would be no use to them,' Steve said.

'No, but the mule would. To a small peasant farmer, a mule is a very valuable item. The radio set is probably dumped in a corner of a barn.'

'So no chance of getting it back?'

'You never know. I'll put the word out that there might be a reward for handing it in. It may find its way back to us one day.'

Grudgingly, Steve had to accept his conclusion but he had little hope that the set would ever reappear. Its loss left him feeling strangely bereft. He had willingly thrown in his lot with Draza and his Chetniks, but he only realised now that at the back of his mind there had always been the thought that some rescue plan was being hatched by his masters in Baker Street to get him out of the country. He wondered what had happened to the other SOE agents who had been caught by the invasion and the sudden collapse of the Yugoslav army. Had they been rescued? Were some of them also embedded with other groups planning guerilla warfare? Or perhaps there was no one else. Was Draza Mihailovic alone in refusing to give in?

There was no point in pursuing that train of thought. For better or worse he was stuck with his decision, and since the alternative was a German prison camp, he could not regret it.

The little party moved on and they were joined by others who had also escaped from the ambush, but there were very few of them. When they finally reached their refuge on the high plateau of Ravna Gora, they numbered seven officers and twenty-one men.

Chapter Six

Belgrade, May 1941

The citizens of Belgrade were slowly coming to terms with what had happened and trying to recreate something approaching normality. The occupying forces had a part to play here. As Alix admitted to herself, the Germans, hate them as you might, were extremely efficient. The gangs of Jewish men and women were stood down and bulldozers were brought in to clear the rubble and retrieve the hundreds of bodies lying trapped beneath it, the stench of which was beginning to permeate the city. The dead were loaded onto lorries and carted away to be buried in a common grave. Estimates of their number varied. The official figure given by the Germans was 2,271 but most people put the figure much higher, at least five thousand and maybe more.

Electricity and water supplies were restored, though both were somewhat intermittent, and the main hospital reopened. This allowed the most serious casualties who were being sheltered in the Malkovic house to be moved. Others had recovered sufficiently to take care of themselves and many of the refugees Alix had taken in decided to move out, some going to families or friends in the countryside, others to camp out in the ruins of their homes while they worked to make them habitable again.

Relieved of the pressure to look after them, Alix found her mind turning to memories of her time in Paris and the friends she had left behind there. What had happened to Boris Vildé and Agnes and Yvonne, whose arrest by the Abwehr had triggered her own flight from occupied France? Were they still in prison, suffering God knows what tortures at the hands of the Gestapo? Or had they been executed? And what of Paul Rivet, the director of the Musée de l'Homme, whose contempt, as an anthropologist, for the racial doctrines of the Nazis had led him to start the very first resistance organisation in Paris? An organisation to which they had all belonged. Was he still at liberty? And then there was Marie Louise and her parents who had risked so much in the cause of returning escaped POWs and downed airmen to Britain to continue the fight. Were they still safe in the secret hiding place they had established deep in the hills of the Auvergne? And would she ever see any of them again?

These reflections brought other, more personal ones, to mind. Thinking of those she knew she wouldn't encounter again – those who met darker endings. Raoul, for one, her one-time lover – if their relationship could ever be called love. It was Raoul who had introduced her to communism and to his circle of ardent, dogmatic friends. Her memories of him were clouded by his jealousy, his often violent love-making, and contrasted sharply with those of another man – a dark-haired, dark-eyed man who spoke French with an American accent but whose Serbian was perfect. His name was Stefan but he called himself Steve, and his gentle kisses had fired her blood in a way that Raoul's never had. Raoul was dead now. She retracted Raoul's history. Killed in battle while the French army was still resisting the German invasion, but it was her misguided loyalty to him that had sent Steve to England to volunteer for the RAF. She still wondered guiltily if Raoul had chanced to die sooner whether she and Steve would still be together. And where was Steve now? He had written to say he was being posted to a bomber squadron and rumour had it that losses had been very heavy among them. There was a good chance he had not survived, and despite the lapse of time and the many experiences she had been through she found that thought painful.

Although some semblance of normality had been restored to the city, Alix realised that there were still families sheltering in the ruins and eking out a precarious existence, so she set out with Drago at her side to see what help she could provide. They were walking through the Karadordev Park, where some of those who had lost their homes were camping out, when a voice hailed her.

'Miss Malkovic! Alexandra!'

Looking for the source of the voice, she saw a young man waving at her. There was something familiar about him, but she could not at first work out why. He was of medium height, solidly built, dark-haired like most Serbs and with a closely trimmed beard and moustache. What made him stand out from the crowd were his clothes. His grey flannels and tweed jacket would not have looked out of place in a London park, and unlike most of the men and women in the area he was not covered in the grey dust that rose from the debris. He strode across the grass towards her, his expression eager.

'Alexandra! You're home! When did you arrive?'

It was the voice that finally jogged her memory.

'Nikola!'

'Yes! For a moment I thought you didn't recognise me.'

How could she not have known him at once? This was the man her father had wanted her to marry; the man she had rejected with such determination.

'It was the beard,' she said, trying to recover herself. 'You didn't have a beard when… when we last met.'

'Ah ha! No, of course not.' He tilted his head, turning it from side to side. 'What do you think?'

'It suits you.' It was true. Alix knew he was six years older than she was, but her memory of him was of an over-grown schoolboy, round-faced and a little on the plump side. He had certainly slimmed down and his features were more defined. In fact, he was quite good looking.

Nikola was looking past her at Drago, standing a few feet behind her.

'Who's this?' The question was abrupt, suspicious.

Alix turned and drew Drago forward. 'This is Dragomir Pesic, my father's estate manager. Drago, this is Nikola Dordevic. He…'

'I know.' Drago's tone told her that he remembered the history of their relationship. He bent his head. 'Sir.'

Nikola ignored him and turned back to Alix. 'What are you doing here? You should be at Kuca Magnolija. You would be safe there.'

Alix felt a tremor go through her nerves. If she had been an animal, her hackles would have gone up. 'We've been helping out here where we can. Until yesterday, I had people who'd been bombed out staying in the house.'

Nikola frowned. 'In your house? What did your father have to say about that?'

'He doesn't know. But I'm sure he would approve. It's what he and my mother would have done.'

'Your mother? Ah, Lady Leonora.' He had clearly not forgotten her mother's part in preventing their marriage. 'How is she?'

'I don't know.' To her intense annoyance Alix felt the tears that were all too easily provoked stinging her eyes. 'She isn't here.'

Suddenly Nikola's manner changed. The slightly supercilious tone was replaced by one of genuine concern. 'Not here? And your father? Don't tell me they were caught in the bombing.'

'No, no. At least, yes, they were here when it happened but they weren't hurt. Or I don't think so. I haven't seen them.'

'Why not?'

'I'm not sure where they are. My father went with the king and I think my mother followed them. That's all I know.'

'And you are here all on your own? You poor girl! That must have been terrible for you.'

'I haven't been all on my own.' Alix forced back the tears. 'I've had Drago with me. He's been a tower of strength. I couldn't have coped without him.'

'Oh, well. That's good, of course.' He dismissed Drago's presence as insignificant. 'But you should be back at the country house, not wandering around here without a chaperone. My car is not far away. Let me drive you back.'

Alix looked at him and suddenly burst out laughing. 'Wandering about without a chaperone? Where do you think I've been for the last couple of years?'

He looked taken aback. 'I was told your mother had taken you abroad. I assumed you were with her in England.'

'In England? No, I was in Paris. Paris! This is not the first time I've lived under German occupation. And believe me, for the things I've been doing I certainly did not need a chaperone!'

He looked at her as if he was seeing her for the first time. 'You were in Paris? Until when?'

'Until a few weeks ago. I got back the night before the bombing started.'

'What did you mean, the things you were doing?'

She wanted him to know that she was not the sheltered young girl in need of protection that he imagined. She cast a swift glance around them. No one was close enough to hear. 'I was working with the Resistance.'

'You? You were with the Resistance?'

'Yes. Don't you believe me?'

'It's not that. No, of course I believe you. It's just…' It was his turn to look over his shoulder. 'Look, can we go somewhere we can talk privately?'

She studied him for a moment. His manner had changed since they first met. But was this request for a private talk just an excuse to get her on her own? It occurred to her that her declaration that she did not need a chaperone might have given him the wrong impression. Well, if that was the case she would soon correct that misapprehension.

'We can go back to the house, if you like. It's more or less empty now, apart from the staff.'

'That would be good.'

'All right,' she said. 'Let's go.'

As they walked back she asked, 'Where have you been, since the war started?'

'I was visiting my family at our country house when the bombing started. I came back a few days ago. I've been staying in my rooms at the university. Thank God the building was hardly touched by the bombs.'

'The university? You have rooms there?'

'I teach there – modern languages.'

Alix looked at him. This was a surprise. She had assumed that he would still be pursuing the life of a country gentleman, as heir to his father's estate.

'I thought the university had closed down,' she said.

'Yes, sadly. The Nazis ordered it to close as soon as they took control. But some of us are still hanging on, waiting.'

'Waiting for what?'

He shrugged. 'Who knows?'

'I didn't expect...' She struggled to formulate the words. 'I never imagined you having a job. You don't need to work, surely?'

'Need? Not financially, no. But after... after you went away I wanted to do something. Anything was better than being stuck at home with my increasingly cantankerous father. Besides, I wanted to be useful in some way.'

'Modern languages,' she pondered. 'How? I mean, were you qualified?'

He laughed, but there was a hint of bitterness in the sound. 'We never really got to know each other, did we? You are not the only one who has spent time in Paris. I have a degree from the Sorbonne.'

'The Sorbonne? That's where I was studying, too. When was this?'

'I qualified in '37. It was after I got home that... that negotiations started between our fathers.'

'Negotiations,' she repeated. 'You make it sound like a business deal.'

'That's the way I saw it, to start with, until... until I met you, properly.'

She glanced sideways at him. It was her turn to see him in a different light.

They had reached the house. The front door had been repaired and the glass window boarded up. Alix produced a key and let them into the hall and the noise brought Ivo, the butler, up from the kitchen regions.

'Ivo, you remember Gospodin Dordevic? He's dropped in for a chat. Do we have any coffee left?'

Ivo took Nikola's hat. 'Good morning, sir.' Then, to Alix, 'I'll enquire with Cook, Miss Alix. I am sure she will be able to find something acceptable.'

Alix led Nikola into the drawing room. Normally she and Drago had used the smaller morning room and until recently the drawing room had served as a ward for those wounded in the bombing. On this occasion, however, the more formal surroundings seemed suitable. Much of the best furniture was protected by dust sheets but she uncovered a couple of chairs.

'Please sit down.' It was the first time she had acted as hostess in her father's house and she felt slightly awkward. Unusually, she could not think of anything to say.

It suddenly struck her that something was missing. She looked around.

'Drago?'

He was nowhere to be seen. She went to the door and called, but he did not appear. She realised with a pang of conscience that since her meeting with Nikola she had not addressed a word to her faithful companion.

'I'm sorry the place is a bit shabby,' she said. 'We only got rid of the last patient the day before yesterday.'

He looked around. 'You actually had wounded people in here?'

'What else could we do? The hospitals were either demolished or overwhelmed. We couldn't leave people lying in the street.'

He dropped his eyes. 'You make me feel ashamed. I just stayed comfortably at home until I heard things were getting back to normal.'

Ivo came in with a tray. There was a pot of coffee and the best china cups, which had been stored away, and, miraculously, two portions of *lenja pita*, a light sponge split and filled with honey and walnuts.

'Ivo,' Alix asked, 'where is Drago?'

'He is downstairs, in his own quarters,' Ivo replied, his tone implying that that was precisely where he thought he should be. He had never approved of the informality with which Alix had treated him. Alix's first impulse was to tell the butler to send Drago up to her immediately, but then she remembered that Nikola had asked if they could speak in private. She was half afraid that he was going to propose marriage again, and if that was the case Drago's presence would be embarrassing for all of them. So she just nodded.

'Thank you, Ivo. That will be all.'

He bowed and withdrew and Alix busied herself with pouring the coffee.

'I'm afraid there's no fresh milk. I hope you don't mind. I got used to drinking it black in France.'

'That's fine,' he responded.

He accepted one of the cakes and declared them delicious and then Alix decided it was time they got to the point.

'You wanted to talk in private, but before you say anything I should tell you that my decision about marrying you was final. I don't want to reopen that subject.'

She saw him flush. 'No, no. I wouldn't dream of doing that. It would be… inappropriate, as your parents are not here, and I have no reason to think you might have changed your mind. No, what I wanted to ask you was, have you heard any suggestion of any resistance to the occupation here?'

'Resistance?' The word sent a chill through her bloodstream. 'No,' she said. 'I have to admit I hadn't even thought about it. Why do you ask?'

'There have been rumours, whispers, among some of my colleagues at the university – those that haven't left the city. I thought, perhaps, if you had some experience… I don't know. Would you want to be involved? This is our own country, after all, not France.'

Alix was silent for a moment. Then she said, 'You are right, of course. We should resist, by any means in our power. But it's not something two or three people can do on their own. There has to be some kind of organisation.'

'Yes, of course,' he agreed. 'There needs to be a leader. I think I know exactly the right man, if he can be persuaded. I'd like you to meet him.'

'Who is he? One of your colleagues?'

'No. His name is Josip Broz, but everyone calls him Tito. I first met him in Paris when I was there as a student. He's a remarkable man, a born leader. But there's one thing you should know. He is a communist. In fact, he is the general secretary of the Yugoslav Communist Party. Does that matter to you?'

'A communist?' Alix lifted her eyebrows. 'No. I had…' She stopped. She had no intention of discussing her relationship with Raoul with him. 'I had a lot of friends who were communists when I was at the college.'

'And did you agree with their ideas?' he asked.

'Some of them. But we fell out when they refused to join the Resistance because of the friendship pact between Russia and Germany. They changed their minds when they found out what swine the Nazis are, but by then I'd made other friends.' She paused and looked at him. 'But you? Surely you don't agree with communism.'

'What makes you say that?'

'Well, I just assumed… I mean, you are a member of the aristocracy. Your father is a great landowner.'

'That doesn't mean I can't see the wrong things that are happening in this country, the terrible conditions some of the poor people live in.'

She met his eyes. 'You know, you were right when you said we never really got to know each other.'

He smiled. 'Well, better late than never, as they say.'

'So, this man you want me to meet?'

'I'll have to make the arrangements. He's here incognito, passing himself off as an engineer on a business trip. If the authorities knew his true identity he'd be arrested. Can I call in tomorrow to let you know?'

She nodded, with a quickening of her pulse. Something was happening, something new and unexpected, and she was not sure whether the prospect frightened or excited her.

When Nikola had gone she went in search of Drago and found him in his room on the top floor, gazing out of the window. He looked round as she knocked and entered.

'My lady! You should have sent for me instead of coming up here.'

His tone was flat, his face expressionless, but she recognised that she had reset their relationship to that of mistress and servant, something she had thought they had gone beyond weeks ago.

'I need to talk to you,' she said. 'Something important has happened.'

His expression did not change. 'I think I should go back to the estate. There will be work to do, organising the planting of new crops for one thing. I have been away too long.'

'No! You can't do that. I need you here.' She looked at him, shaken by guilt and distress. 'Drago, I've behaved very badly. I was rude to exclude you from my conversation with Nikola. I was taken by surprise when he suddenly appeared out of the blue. I didn't know how to react. And then he said he wanted to speak privately...'

'So you have accepted? You have said yes?' His tone was neutral but there was no concealing the pain in his eyes.

'Said yes? To what?'

'To his proposal.'

'How do you...? Oh! No, you've misunderstood. He didn't propose marriage. We talked about something quite different.'

'Different?'

'Yes. That's what I need to tell you about.'

'You don't need me any longer. You have someone else to protect you. I should go back.'

'Protect me? Is that all you have been doing? Drago, I don't need protecting. I need a friend, a companion... A brother. Isn't that how we have been these last weeks? I hurt your feelings and I'm sorry. It was thoughtless of me. But please, can't you forgive me? Can't we be friends again?'

She saw the first sign of softening in his face. 'Brother and sister?'

'Yes!'

There was something in the way he looked at her that she could not interpret, but he nodded. 'Very well. What is it you want to tell me?'

She repeated the conversation she had had with Nikola.

'If he's right and this man he wants me to meet is planning to start some kind of resistance, I think I should support him. We can't just sit back and let the Nazis do whatever they like. I've seen what that leads to.'

'So what do you want me to do?'

'If Nikola arranges a meeting I want you to come too. I want your support, and your advice.'

'Of course,' he agreed. 'You will always have that.'

She reached up impulsively and kissed his cheek. 'That's what I needed to hear.' Then she drew back, struck by a sudden thought. 'Oh God! What am I thinking of? If this plan goes ahead, everyone involved is going to be in danger. I've seen what can happen. I've had friends arrested and I don't know if they are still alive. I've no right to drag you into this.'

He frowned. 'Do you imagine I would let you do this alone? If there is danger, I want to be there to share it, to protect you if I can.'

She took his hand. 'Then we stick together, whatever happens. And forget any idea of me being romantically involved with Nikola. He's changed a lot since I first knew him, but I turned him down once and I'd do it again. Understood?'

He nodded gravely. 'Understood.'

Nikola reappeared the next morning. Alix was sitting with Drago in the morning room when Ivo announced him. Drago got up and bent his head politely but Nikola did not acknowledge him.

'I've made the arrangements. Tito will see us straight away. Are you ready?'

Alix rose to her feet. 'I'll get my hat.'

In the hall, Ivo was waiting. 'We're going out, Ivo. I'm not sure if we shall be back for lunch.'

'Very good, miss.'

She took her hat from the hallstand and put it on. 'I'm ready. Let's go.'

Nikola moved towards the door, which Ivo held open, and then turned back. Drago was at Alix's side.

'Where do you think you're going?' he demanded.

Alix said, 'Where I go, Drago goes. He is the nearest thing to a male relative I have while my parents are away and I rely on his protection.'

They had agreed on this as a way of explaining their relationship. It fitted with prevailing Serbian attitudes to unmarried girls and was less likely to provoke questions. Nikola frowned, obviously unhappy with the situation but unable to find any way out of it.

'Can he be trusted? I've explained our friend's situation.'

'I trust Dragomir with my life,' she responded. 'Now, shall we go?'

—

Nikola had his car outside and he drove them to the affluent suburb of Dedinje. He rang the bell at a pleasant house in a tree-lined street and they were admitted by a good-looking young man with thick curly hair.

'Alix, this is Ivo Lola Ribar,' Nikola said. 'We met at the university. Lola, this is Alexandra Malkovic. I told you about her yesterday.'

Ribar offered his hand. 'Delighted to meet you. And this is…?' he asked, looking at Drago.

'Dragomir Pesic,' Drago said.

To Alix's pleasure Ribar shook Drago's hand as well.

'Come this way,' he said. 'Tito is waiting for you.'

In the drawing room Alix found herself facing a man in his middle years, compactly built and good-looking, with a high forehead and eyes that commanded attention; deep set and bright with a piercing gaze that held her own and was hard to look away from as they were introduced.

'So,' he said. 'Nikola tells me you were with the Resistance in France. Tell me about it.'

For the next half hour Alix recounted her activities in Paris, beginning with distributing anti-Nazi propaganda and her attempts to gain useful intelligence by flirting with German soldiers on leave and then moving on to her exploits, chaperoning escaping Allied airmen across the line of demarcation between the occupied and unoccupied zones and on down to Marseilles. Tito listened closely, occasionally interrupting to ask a question, usually to pinpoint an exact location or date in order to establish, she presumed, the reliability of her story.

He then questioned her about her family and her upbringing. 'Your father is an aristocrat and the owner of serfs,' he said. 'What sympathy can you have for the principles of communism?'

'My father did everything in his power to improve the lot of the people who lived on the estate,' she said. 'He established schools and a hospital, and my mother is English. She has some training as a nurse and before the war she used to go out to the villages with medical supplies and help to vaccinate children and care for expectant mothers.'

Drago spoke for the first time. 'I can bear witness to that. I was educated in the school on the count's estate and later I drove Lady Leonora on her visits to the villages.'

'And where are your parents now?' Tito asked Alix.

'As far as I know they are with the king. My father was – is – one of his closest advisers.'

'A royalist, then. How would he feel about his daughter consorting with communists?'

Alix hesitated for a moment. This was a question she had been asking herself. 'My father is above all a patriot. He would approve anything that helped to drive out the enemy and make Serbia a free country.'

Tito was silent for a moment. Then he leaned forward in his chair and fixed Alix with those remarkable eyes. 'You have shown great courage in defying the Nazis in France. Are you prepared to take the same risks to defy them here, in your own country?'

For a moment Alix hesitated. She had spent a year living on her nerves, under constant threat of discovery. She had no regrets, but the thought of starting again in another country made her stomach turn over. Then she nodded. 'I will do whatever you need me to do.'

Tito looked at Dragomir. 'And you?'

'I, too, will do whatever is needful.'

For a moment Tito continued to look from him to Alix. Finally he said, 'Very well. Lola, give me some of the leaflets.'

The younger man passed him a handful of leaflets from a table nearby and Tito handed one to Alix. It was a call to all citizens of Yugoslavia to resist the occupying forces in any way possible.

'You have had experience of this kind of activity before. I don't need to tell you how to go about distributing them. But be warned, if you are caught with them the punishment will be draconian.'

Alix looked down at the papers and a picture of the Paris streets and of Paul Rivet's face rose in her mind's eye. She had worked in conjunction with one inspiring leader and now, she realised, she had found another.

'Very well,' she agreed. 'When do you want us to report back?'

'There is a meeting in two days. Nikola can bring you,' Tito replied.

Over the next days Alix and Drago quartered the city. She used the same techniques that had served her well in Paris and passed them on to him. Some of the hotels had opened up again, so they left leaflets in the toilets and slipped them under bedroom doors. They interleaved them with menus in bars and restaurants and they rode the trams and left leaflets on the seats. By the time Nikola picked them up to take them to the meeting they had disposed of all that they had been given.

The room was already crowded by the time they arrived and a cloud of tobacco smoke hung over the gathering. Nikola pointed out two men.

'That's Alexander Rankovic and that's Milovan Djilas. They are Tito's closest friends, them and Lola Ribar.'

'Who's the woman sitting beside him?' Alix asked.

'Ah.' Nikola's tone changed. 'That's Zdenka, his mistress. She's a foul-tempered bitch, if you will excuse the word, but for some reason he's devoted to her.'

The first part of the meeting reminded Alix of the interminable discussions about ideology she had sat through round the café table in Paris with her communist fellow students. Then someone cut through the chatter with a question.

'This is all very well, but when are we actually going to take action? We know there are groups of peasants outside the city who are already arming themselves. We should be joining them and starting an armed uprising.'

A silence fell and everyone looked at Tito. His expression was stony. 'You know perfectly well that we are under orders from the Comintern not to take any aggressive action against the Germans. So long as the friendship pact between Russia and Germany remains in force we are not permitted to take up arms.'

Alix sighed deeply. She had heard all this before but it was disappointing to find herself mired in the same old controversy. There was a mutter of discontent in the room that told her many of those present felt as she did, but no one was prepared to argue.

Tito looked around at them. 'Take heart. If the rumours are true, Hitler has no intention of honouring the pact. If he attacks the Soviet Union, we shall be free to act. Until then we must content ourselves with sabotage and propaganda.' He stood up. 'Patience, my friends. Our time will come.'

Chapter Seven

Ravna Gora, May 1941

The high plateau of Ravna Gora had been virtually unaffected by the German invasion. It was a region of small villages whose pastoral lifestyle had continued unchanged for generations. Here and there were rough shepherds' huts built as shelters from the elements. Mihailovic and his small band of followers found one that seemed abandoned and the colonel claimed it for his headquarters. Men were dispatched to collect firewood while Draza and some of his officers prepared to go to a nearby village in search of food; but before they could leave they heard the sound of voices approaching and a group of men in peasant dress, some of them armed with sickles and axes, appeared.

Draza Mihailovic stepped forward to meet them.

'We mean you no harm, friends. We are soldiers of the Yugoslav Royal Army, seeking refuge from the German invaders.'

One of the peasants spoke up, glancing at his fellows for confirmation. 'We apologise for seeming inhospitable. We are plagued with bandits who steal our sheep and terrorise our women and children. We thought you were more of them.'

'Bandits?' Draza echoed. 'If we stay here I guarantee you we will find these fellows and arrest them. In return, we wish to buy food, if you have any to spare for starving men.'

'If you can free us from these men who prey on us, we will happily supply whatever you need,' was the response.

Draza and three of his officers went with the peasants and returned shortly with the carcass of a lamb, some wine and several loaves of bread, generously donated by the villagers. The fire was built up and the lamb was impaled on an improvised spit above it and before long the whole group sat down to the best meal they had had for many days. When they had eaten, however, Draza called the officers, including Steve, into the hut. The only furniture was a rough table and a stool, which Draza took, so the rest of them sat round on the beaten earth floor.

'My friends,' Draza began, 'we have been received with great generosity but we cannot expect these poor people to go on feeding us for nothing. We must pay our way. Our first priority, if we are to become the nucleus of a fighting force to combat the German occupiers, is to obtain funds. But until they arrive we must depend on our own resources. How much money can we muster between us?'

Nobody could argue against that, so they all turned out their pockets and put whatever money they had on the table. The sum total was enough to keep the company fed for a few days, if they could buy from the local villagers, but that was all.

'Very well,' Draza said. 'I thank you all for your generosity. Tomorrow I shall send out couriers to anyone we can think of who might help us with funds. I have a cousin, a widow who inherited a considerable sum from her husband. I am confident she will wish to support us. Meanwhile, we need to keep our promise to the villagers regarding these so-called bandits who are preying on them. Tomorrow I shall send out small groups under the command of some of you to search the local woods or anywhere else these men may be hiding. If you find them, arrest them and we will hand them over to the local gendarmes. We need to have them on our side if we are going to be free to operate in the area. Any questions?'

There were none and the group dispersed to bivouac around the fire. Steve lay looking up at the stars, wondering how long it would be before he slept in a real bed again. He was worn out after the long trek through the mountains and it seemed that there was to be little comfort in the foreseeable future. He thought of his lost radio set. If he still had it, he would have been tempted to ask his masters in London to arrange for him to be exfiltrated. At that point he checked his wandering thoughts. He had made the decision to join Draza and his Chetniks and now he must stick with them, come what may.

By mid-afternoon next day the search parties had rounded up two small groups of brigands and brought them back to camp. They were a sorry-looking lot, filthy and unkempt, men who had been driven out of their villages for one reason or another or who had lost their jobs. Draza took half a dozen men as guards and marched them off to the largest village in the area where there was a police station. He returned looking satisfied.

'We got a warm welcome. These men have been plaguing the neighbourhood for months and the gendarmes don't have the resources to deal with them. They are all loyal to king and country and willing to support us in any way they can.'

Over the next weeks the outlook for the Chetniks brightened considerably. Draza's cousin took up a collection among her friends and a courier arrived at the camp with a satchel containing 50,000 dinars. Couriers sent to Belgrade brought back the news that there were many uncaptured soldiers in the city and the Germans were apparently making no effort to round them up. As news spread of Mihailovic's escape from the debacle at the front, others were emboldened to follow his example and set up their own Chetnik companies. Day by day more men arrived and the camp grew until it accommodated several hundred soldiers. This strained their resources to a point where Draza called a meeting with some of their leaders.

'We need to be clear about our objectives. We are too few and too poorly armed to fight the German occupiers, and any attacks will inevitably result in reprisals that will bring suffering and death to innocent Serbs. I firmly believe that Hitler will not win this war. The time will come when he will be forced to withdraw his troops. The great danger is that when that happens the country will descend into chaos and areas will fall into the hands of the communists. That is the moment when we shall come into our own. Our plan must be to establish Chetnik units all over the country who will rise up as the enemy retreats and take control in the name of the king and the legitimate government. To this end I am proposing to send many of you back to your own towns and villages, where you will recruit and train men ready to perform that vital task.'

'You mean we are to sit back and take no action against the Germans?' someone asked incredulously.

'Until such time as we have the men and means to be effective,' Draza replied. 'I confidently expect the British to land troops on the Adriatic coast when the moment is ripe. That will be our cue to rise in support.'

The meeting broke up but Steve sensed that not all the officers were in agreement with the policy. He wondered what the reaction of the men who had sent him out here would be, if he could communicate with them. He regretted ever more bitterly the loss of his radio set. He certainly did not relish the prospect of remaining passive and waiting for someone else to win the war.

He was even more disturbed by Draza's next move. He called together some of the men closest to him and said, 'We need more money. It's impossible to sustain any kind of force with the funds at our disposal. I'm going to send you, Lenac, to Belgrade, to Dmitri Ljotic. Ask him to prepare a list of wealthy civilians who might be prepared to contribute.'

'Ljotic?' Lenac objected. 'I thought we heard that he is collaborating with the Nazis.'

'That is why he will be free to circulate among the people we need to contact. But there is another important point. We must at all costs avoid the Germans getting the impression that we pose a threat. We need to encourage in them an attitude of salutary neglect. Let it be known that we are concerned with countering the communist threat, not with killing Germans.'

Rumours reached Ravna Gora that another Chetnik band was now in action under the leadership of Kosta Pecanic, a veteran who had led Chetnik bands in World War One. In the interwar period he had set up an organisation for ex-Chetnik fighters who now regarded themselves as the 'official' Chetniks. A few days later another group arrived at the camp, led by a General

Novakovic. When informed of Draza's policy of organising and waiting for an Allied invasion, he was furious.

'I outrank you, Mihailovic! From now on I give the orders round here and I want nothing to do with your namby-pamby attitude! I propose that we set up three units, one commanded by me, one by you and the third by Kosta Pecanic. And then we go on the offensive. We resist these Nazis in every corner of the country.'

'And we shall be decimated in a matter of weeks,' Draza replied. 'To say nothing of the reprisals exacted by the enemy. I refuse to accept your authority.'

Novakovic turned to the other officers present. 'Well, men. Are you with me or with Mihailovic?'

There was a brief moment of hesitation then Lieutenant Jovanovic, one of Draza's most loyal companions, said, 'I've given my loyalty to Colonel Mihailovic, sir. I'm sticking with him.'

All the others who had escaped from the battle with Draza expressed the same loyalty. Novakovic glared round at them but he was clearly outnumbered. Next morning it was discovered that he had left the camp overnight. Later they learned that he had joined Pecanic and been put in charge of a Chetnik group in the Sumadija region.

Alone with Steve, Draza admitted to a rare moment of doubt. 'I don't have the rank to impose my ideas on men like that. If only we could contact the members of the government who escaped with the king. They must have set up a government in exile somewhere. I feel sure I am doing what is best for the country but I need their support.'

Steve sighed. 'If only that damned mule hadn't taken off with my radio set, we wouldn't have a problem.'

Chapter Eight

London, June 1941

Leo looked down as the plane made its approach to Northolt aerodrome, taking in the green fields and the wooded hills, with the silver line of the River Thames threading through them, and then, as they flew lower, the encroaching buildings of the London suburbs. They were low enough for her to make out the gardens of the houses and to see that, though large parts of each one were now given over to crops – potatoes as far as she could tell – there was still room for brilliant splashes of colour, a rose bed here, a narrow border of marigolds and petunias there. She drew a long breath. Although so much of her time over the last twenty years had been spent in Serbia, the sight of the English countryside still gave her the feeling of coming home.

The feeling was enhanced now by a sense of relief that her wanderings were over. Since their precipitate flight from Belgrade, she and Sasha and the young king and his entourage had been almost constantly on the move. First there had been a few days in Athens, then a short stay in Jerusalem. After that they had been moved on to Cairo while harassed government officials tried to work out what to do with them. Finally, a day or two ago had come the message that they were all to come to London.

After the dust and heat of the desert, the sight of the green fields of England was a balm to her heart as well as her eyes.

She touched Sasha's arm. 'Home at last!'

He grunted. 'Not really.'

'No.' She reproved herself inwardly for being insensitive. 'Not really home, but somewhere we can feel comfortable, on familiar ground at least.'

He stretched himself in the cramped seat and nodded. 'At least it looks as though they have stopped shunting us around, though why we couldn't come straight here I shall never understand.'

It had been a long, roundabout journey from Cairo, avoiding the dangerous skies over the Mediterranean and flying instead across North Africa to the Atlantic. Here they had been picked up by a Sunderland flying boat that had taken them to Southampton, where they had changed again onto an ordinary plane. They had made several overnight stops to refuel on the way but there had been little comfort and they were all tired and travel worn.

The plane touched down and a small convoy of cars drove out to meet them on the tarmac. Peter was the first to disembark. The last weeks had taken their toll on him and he had lost the glow of healthy boyhood he had enjoyed when he succeeded to the throne, but Leo was impressed to notice that Peter nevertheless made a point of shaking hands with the pilot and co-pilot and the stewards and thanking them before he left the plane. He was followed by Prime Minister Simovic and several other members of what they were now beginning to recognise as the government in exile. Some of them had chosen to go elsewhere, to the USA or South Africa, and one, Bogoljub Ilic, had chosen to stay in Cairo where he was attempting to assemble any troops who had succeeded in escaping from the German advance to create a new army.

There were handshakes with officials on the tarmac and then they were all loaded into cars and the cavalcade set off for Central London. Watching the suburbs pass the window, Leo's delight in the sight of her home country yielded to horror at what had happened to it. From the air she had seen the occasional bomb crater but as they got nearer to the centre of the city the damage became more and more obvious.

'Dear God!' she murmured to Sasha. 'I knew the blitz was bad but I had no idea it was as bad as this.'

'Wasn't it like this when you were here last summer?' he asked.

'It had started, but the destruction was nothing like so widespread.'

'Well, they should see Belgrade,' he said bitterly.

'That was terrible, certainly,' Leo agreed. 'But it was all over in twenty-four hours. This has been going on for months. How have people lived through it?'

'Do we know if the raids are still happening?'

'The consul in Cairo said it seems to have stopped, but who knows for how long?'

As they drove through the centre Leo was more and more horrified by the extent of the damage. Blocks of flats had been sheared in half, leaving the walls of rooms still clinging to the remaining structure. Wallpaper hung in shreds, and here and there she saw a picture or a mirror still hanging on, or a wardrobe with clothes spilling out of it; the pathetic remnants of someone's life. The roads were so potholed and blocked with rubble and burned-out vehicles that the cars had difficulty finding a way through. Even in Mayfair the destruction was widespread, and Hyde Park was lined with anti-aircraft gun emplacements.

'I wonder where they are taking us,' Sasha said.

The question was soon answered as the cars drew up outside an imposing red brick frontage.

'Claridge's,' Leo pronounced. 'At least that is still standing.'

One of the grandest hotels in London, Claridge's was clearly suffering from the lack of staff due to conscription but was determined to keep up appearances. The major-domo conducted them up to the top floor where a suite had been prepared for King Peter. On the floor below, rooms had been allocated to the various members of the government. When they were all accommodated the major-domo looked doubtfully at Sasha and Leo.

'Forgive me, sir. We were not told to expect anyone else. May I ask what your connection is to King Peter?'

Sasha drew himself up. 'I am Count Alexander Malkovic. I have a hereditary position at the royal court, and I am here in the capacity of friend and adviser to the king.'

The major-domo looked worried. 'I am not sure if we have any vacant rooms that would be suitable.'

Sasha looked at Leo. 'Never mind. We have a place in London. We can go home.'

Leo shook her head. 'I'm sorry. I should have thought of it earlier. We don't have anywhere. I gave up the lease on the little flat I was renting before I came back to Belgrade last year.'

He frowned. 'But the town house in Kensington...'

'It's rented out. Remember, we decided there was no point in it standing empty when we are here so infrequently.'

He ran his hand through his hair and Leo saw that the recent weeks had taken their toll on him, too. 'Of course. Stupid of me.'

Leo turned to the major-domo with a look of appeal. 'You see? We have nowhere else to go. Surely you can find a corner for us.'

At that moment, Yuri, the king's valet and the only one of the household staff who had been able to accompany him, came running down the stairs.

'Oh, Count. His Majesty is asking for you. Please can you come?'

'Of course.' Sasha turned to go. 'I shall have to leave you to find us some form of accommodation, my dear.'

The major-domo's expression had changed.

'Please don't worry about that, sir. I am sure something can be arranged.'

Leo gave him a triumphant smile. 'I knew you wouldn't let us sleep in the street. Can you have our bags taken to our room, please, while we are with the king?'

They found Peter sitting disconsolately in the drawing room of his suite and Leo felt a sudden pang of sympathy. He looked so young and so lost. He looked up and said, 'Oh, Sasha! I'm sorry to send for you. I know you must both be longing to put your feet up.'

Sasha bowed. 'Not at all, Your Majesty. I am always at your service.'

Leo said, 'Has anyone offered you something to eat or drink, sir? Shall I ask them to send up some tea?'

Peter's face brightened. 'Of course! The universal English cure for anything – a nice cup of tea.'

'In my experience,' she told him, 'life always looks less daunting after that.'

'I'm sure you are right,' he agreed. 'Please do send for some.'

While Leo used the house phone to order, Sasha said, 'Was there something in particular you wanted to discuss?'

Peter sighed, the momentary lightening in his expression vanishing. 'The future, I suppose. How soon can we assemble a sufficient force to retake our country?'

Sasha indicated a chair and Peter nodded. 'Yes, yes. Sit. Now, how soon?'

Sasha weighed his words carefully. 'I'm afraid it may be some time. You know that British resources are already stretched to breaking point. There is no chance that they can spare enough troops to make up a sufficient force at the present. I think you will have to be patient. Once victory is in sight, things will be different.'

'Well, if I can't lead an army to take back my kingdom, I want to do something to hasten that victory.' Peter leaned forward in his chair. 'I want to fight.'

'Fight?' Sasha queried.

'I'll join the British army. Or better still, the Air Force. I want to fly a plane to drop bombs on the people who bombed Belgrade.'

The tea arrived, with sandwiches and slices of rather bright yellow Victoria sponge, and there was a pause in the conversation while Leo poured. Peter took a gulp of tea and smiled suddenly.

'This makes me feel as if I'm back at Eton.'

'You enjoyed your schooldays here, didn't you?' Leo asked.

'Oh yes! I had a great time. I've always enjoyed being in England.' He turned his attention to Sasha. 'That's another reason why I want to join up. I'd like to be part of the fight to preserve the English way of life.'

'It's very creditable of you,' Sasha agreed. 'But there is one slight stumbling block. You won't be accepted into the RAF until you are eighteen. Not to train as a pilot, anyway.'

Peter looked suddenly bereft. 'Then what can I do? I can't just sit here doing nothing.'

'Of course not.' Sasha paused. 'I'm just thinking aloud now and I don't know what your prime minister will say, or indeed what our government will say, but it seems to me that this would be an ideal time to complete your education.'

'My education? You mean go back to school?'

'No, no. Not that, of course. I was thinking of university. A few terms at Cambridge would broaden your outlook and make you better fitted to take your place in governing the country when we finally get back. What do you think?'

Peter chewed his lip. 'I don't know. It doesn't do anything to hasten victory, or to revenge myself on those monsters who bombed Belgrade.'

'Not directly, I agree,' Sasha said. 'But if it makes you a better ruler when the time comes… And I suspect the war will still be going on when you are old enough to join up, if that is what you want. It's better than sitting around doing nothing, isn't it?'

'Of course,' Peter agreed. 'And I think I might enjoy it. Some of the chaps I was at Eton with were going on there. I might catch up with them.'

'Very possibly,' Sasha said.

Peter looked at Leo. 'What do you think?'

'It sounds an excellent idea to me. You remember our daughter, Alix?'

'Yes, of course.'

'Well, she was thoroughly enjoying life at the Sorbonne until…' A sob caught her unexpectedly in the throat and she had to stop. 'I mean, I think university is something that most young people enjoy.'

'As I said,' Sasha put in, 'it's just an idea. Mr Simovic may not agree, and it would depend on the authorities at Cambridge being willing. But you did well at school. I can't see there would be any problem there.' He sat back in his chair. 'It's too soon to make any decisions yet. We've only just got here and we all need a long rest. But it's something to think about.'

'Yes.' The young king's whole manner had changed. 'Thank you, Sasha. I will definitely think about it.' He got up. 'Now I think I shall have a bath and get changed. And I might have dinner sent up. I'm very tired. I'll see you tomorrow?'

'Of course, Your Majesty.' Sasha and Leo had risen too. He bowed and she curtsied. 'Good night, sir.'

'Good night.'

Going down in the lift, Leo pressed her husband's hand. 'Well done, darling. That was just what he needed.'

'Poor boy,' Sasha said. 'I wonder, will we ever be able to give him his throne back?'

The following morning they had to turn their attention to more immediate matters. They had left Belgrade with nothing more than the clothes they stood up in. Leo had been given some underwear and a dress by a secretary at the British consulate in Athens, and the wife of the British ambassador in Jerusalem had taken her shopping for some other essentials, but after weeks in Cairo and the long journey she was painfully aware how shabby and unkempt she must look to the other guests at the hotel. There was also the question of money. Fortunately she had always retained her account at Coutts bank. Her grandmother had been a wealthy woman and, although her father had squandered much of his inheritance on his passion for archaeology, there was still the income from dividends, plus the farm at Broomhill and the rent from the hall there and from the house that had once belonged to her grandmother. So a visit to the bank manager was her first priority. With cash in her purse her first impulse was to go shopping, but to buy clothes in this time of rationing she had to have clothing coupons. She and Sasha both needed ration books, so the next hours were spent in negotiating the bureaucracy involved in establishing their identities and obtaining the necessary documents. It was late afternoon before she was able to head for Harrods department store to buy herself a new wardrobe. It was a dispiriting experience. The choice was limited and the number of garments she could buy with the coupons she had been given meant that she had to stick to the basic essentials. Nevertheless, by dinner time she was able to appear, if not glamorously, at least respectably dressed.

There was one useful new development. Peter was invited to meet the British King and Queen at Buckingham Palace. Sasha and Leo accompanied him and Leo found herself, somewhat belatedly, fulfilling her grandmother's ambition for her to be presented at court. Queen Elizabeth was obviously sorry for the young man whose reign had started with such promise and ended so abruptly. She took him under her wing and introduced him to other young people, some of whom shared his current predicament. One of them was Princess Alexandra of Greece and Denmark, who had fled to London with her mother after the Germans invaded Greece.

Simovic and the other members of the Yugoslav government, with Sasha in attendance, were closeted with British officials discussing future plans, but the main conclusion was simply a confirmation of what he had told Peter. There was no prospect of military support to regain the country.

With Sasha busy and Peter spending time at the palace, Leo had the chance to think about her own position. It occurred to her that she should report to the man who had sent her back to Yugoslavia to be his eyes and ears on the preparation of the coup. She had sent her last message back just days before the invasion, reporting on the success of the coup and the general rejoicing it had generated. Since then she had had no means of getting in touch. Her radio set and code books were still, as far as she knew, hidden in a storeroom at Kuca Magnolija. Thinking back to her escape from Belgrade reminded her that there was an important question she wanted answered.

Accordingly she set off for the Inter-Services Research Bureau in Baker Street, the building that housed under its bland pseudonym the headquarters of the Special Operations Executive. The WAAF at the reception desk looked at her askance when she requested an interview with Brigadier Gubbins but a phone call announcing the presence of Countess Malkovic produced an immediate invitation to go up to the third floor.

Colin Gubbins advanced across his office with his hand outstretched.

'My dear Leonora! It's such a relief to see you. I didn't know if you had been killed in the bombing or were still trapped in Belgrade. How long have you been in London?'

'Just a few days,' Leo told him. 'We came back with King Peter and the prime minister and others.'

'Ah! Of course, I was aware of the king's arrival. I didn't realise you were with him. And your husband?'

'He's with the king.'

Gubbins gestured to a chair. 'Please, sit down. I'm eager to hear how you escaped.'

'There's one question I want to ask first,' Leo said as she seated herself. 'Do you know what has happened to Alexander Glen and the other SOE agents who were out there?'

'Currently interned in Italy,' he told her. 'I'm informed they are being well treated. We are negotiating their release.'

'Will you succeed, do you think?' Leo asked.

'I'm hopeful. I get the impression that the Italians are not at all convinced that they are fighting on the winning side and are keen to bank some good will in case they are defeated.'

Leo breathed a sigh. 'That's a relief. They got me out of Belgrade and I've been wondering what happened to them after we parted.'

'They got you out? Can you tell me how that happened?'

Leo recounted the events of the day the city was bombed and the hair-raising drive through the mountains to reach Sarajevo. 'We found out that the king was at Pale and I knew Sasha was with him. Sandy Glen managed to find a taxi to take me up there so that's when we separated. They were hoping to get taken off by sea from Dubrovnik or somewhere like that. What went wrong?'

'Several attempts were made, but the Italian navy managed to pre-empt all of them. In the end we were able to send in a Sunderland flying boat to bring out all the Serbian contingent, because they were at greatest risk if the Germans caught them. But there just wasn't enough room for Glen and the others. So their only option was to give themselves up to the Italians in Montenegro.'

'That's such a shame!' Leo sighed regretfully. 'But they are all right?'

'I understand they are being accommodated in a hotel in Foggia until such time as we can come to an agreement with the Italians. But you were able to join your husband and the king?'

'Yes, and we were flown to Athens, then Jerusalem, then Cairo and finally back here three days ago.' She hesitated. 'I suppose I should have reported in sooner.'

'Never mind that,' Gubbins said. 'I'm greatly relieved to find you safe and well. So, what are your plans now?'

Leo spread her hands. 'I honestly don't know. I haven't really had time to think.'

'A holiday, perhaps?'

'Maybe. But it feels wrong to be idle. There must be something useful I can do.'

He looked at her in silence for a moment. Then he said, 'When you were in Cairo, you didn't happen to bump into any familiar faces, did you?'

'No. Why?'

'You remember Tom Masterson, of course.'

'Of course. He was in charge while we were preparing the coup. Was he able to get out? He wasn't with us.'

'No, he found a different route and ended up in Cairo. He is now heading our Balkans desk there.'

'Oh, so you are still... well, taking an interest in the area?'

'Of course. In due course I hope we shall be able to infiltrate agents back into Yugoslavia. Which is why I was thinking…' He paused. 'Do you really want to make yourself useful?'

Leo looked at him with a thrill of nervous anticipation. 'Yes.'

'Your ability with languages, particularly Serbo-Croat, would be invaluable there.' He leaned towards her. 'I'm not suggesting anything clandestine. You would be in uniform, accredited to the bureau. Your job would be to analyse information coming out of Yugoslavia and possibly, in due course, to help prepare agents to be dropped to any resistance organisations we are able to contact. What do you say?'

Leo hesitated. It meant being separated from Sasha, but he had his own job to do looking after Peter and advising Simovic and the rest. She needed some new purpose.

She nodded. 'Yes. I think that would suit me very well.'

Chapter Nine

Belgrade, June–July 1941

An uneasy peace had established itself in Belgrade. The Germans had set upa collaborationist government under Milan Acimovic, the one-time minister of the interior. Alix longed for some way to hit back at the oppressors but she had to resign herself to the fact that as long as the pact between Germany and Russia held, Tito would refuse to undertake any direct action, and she contented herself with distributing propaganda leaflets urging non-co-operation with the regime.

There were more refugees in the city now, not local people who had been bombed out but groups of men and women, ragged and hollow-eyed, clutching bags or sacks containing a few personal belongings.

'Where have you come from?' Alix asked.

'From Otosac, in Croatia,' one of the men said wearily. 'We have come to seek refuge. Terrible things are happening in our country.'

'You are Serbs, yes?' Drago asked.

'Yes. If we were not we should not be here, begging for your protection.'

A woman burst into tears. 'They are killing us! They are brutes, without mercy.'

The man beside her put his arms around her. 'Hush! We are safe here. We are with fellow Serbs. They will protect us.'

Alix asked, 'What is happening? What are these terrible things?'

The refugees looked at each other, as if unsure where to begin. Then one of them drew a deep breath and began to speak, hesitantly at first but then with greater fluency.

'Since Croatia became independent, life for all us Serbs has become unbearable. President Pavlic has launched a policy of cleansing the country of all who are not Croats. The Catholic Church is backing him. There is a war against all those who follow the Orthodox church. To start with all Serbs were forced to wear blue armbands with the letter P on it – Pravoslav, Orthodox. We were forbidden even to use the Cyrillic script. Then, a few days ago, there was an article in the newspaper. Deputy Prime Minister Budak says his policy towards us is "convert a third, expel a third, kill a third".'

'Dear God!' Drago exclaimed. 'That is unbelievable! They cannot mean that.'

'Oh, they do,' another man said. 'And it has begun. Some Serbs have already been sent to concentration camps. Others have fled to Belgrade.'

'You say the Catholic Church is party to this?' Alix asked.

'They have a policy of forced conversions. The ordinary peasants are rounded up and made to undergo baptism.'

'How can that be, unless they have been instructed in the Catholic faith?'

'Oh, no one worries about that,' the first man said sarcastically. 'As long as the bishops can say they have converted hundreds to the "true" faith.'

'Who is doing this?' Drago asked.

'It is the Ustashe. They carry out the orders of the prime minster, Ante Pavlic.'

The woman who had wept earlier began to sob again. 'They haven't heard the worst. Tell them what happened in our village.'

There was a brief silence. The men who had spoken so far had been restrained, as if struggling to hold back emotions that threatened to overwhelm them. Now, one spoke with a voice that cracked with horror.

'The Ustashe came to Otosac. We were out in the fields cutting hay, and when we heard them we hid in a barn, but we saw what happened.' He choked and stopped, then gathered himself and went on. 'They made all the villagers line up in the village square and they grabbed our priest and held him. His son ran forward, calling out to him. They... they cut the boy to pieces in front of his father. Then they turned on the rest. They had knives and swords. They...'

He choked again and fell silent. His friend took up the tale. 'They butchered them like animals, killed everyone. Then, then they took the priest. They cut off his beard, and his ears and his nose, gouged out his eyes and then they killed him.'

There was a long silence while the listeners took in his words. Then Drago said, 'How many did they kill?'

'Three hundred – more than that. It must be three hundred and fifty.'

Alix reported the conversation to Tito. 'What can we do?'

He shook his head. 'Nothing yet.'

One morning she and Drago were returning from distributing leaflets when they both stopped abruptly.

'Listen!' Alix said.

'What can it be?' Drago asked. 'It sounds like people in trouble. Has there been some kind of disaster?'

'It's coming from the river,' Alix said. 'Let's go and see what's going on.'

They hurried towards the source of the noise and came to a bridge across the River Sava. Men and women were leaning over the parapet, others pressing behind them to see, and from them arose a cacophony of groans and screams and profanities. Alix and Drago forced their way through the crowd until they could look down. Floating down the river there was a barge, with no one at the helm. For a moment Alix could not comprehend what she was seeing. When she did she swung around and fought her way out of the crowd, her hand clamped over her mouth to stop herself from vomiting. The barge was loaded with the decapitated heads of hundreds of children. Displayed on the bow was a notice: *Meat for St John's Market.*

Drago struggled out of the crowd to join her. She was leaning over the opposite parapet, retching. He put his arm round her shoulders but said nothing, and she could feel him trembling. Eventually she recovered enough to look up at him.

'Who? Drago, who could have done such a thing?'

He bit his lip and shook his head. Then he muttered, 'You know what is upstream on the Sava.'

She stared at him for a moment, uncomprehending. 'Croatia. It has come from Croatia? But who can have done such a terrible thing there?'

'The Ustashe,' he said. 'They are a brutal fascist organ-isation. Even when I was a child my mother used to speak of them with horror.'

'Of course!' She felt for his hand and squeezed it. 'I'd forgotten for a moment. Your mother was a Croat.'

There were tears in his eyes. 'Yes, and when she fell in love with my father the Ustashe threatened to kill her. They hate all Serbs. But I never imagined they were capable of something like this.'

Back at the house in Dedinje the macabre arrival was the main subject of discussion. Tito himself had a Croat father and had been living in Zagreb until a few weeks earlier.

'When the government welcomed in the Nazis and proclaimed Croatia an independent state I knew some-thing like this was going to happen, but I never imagined such brutality,' he said sadly.

'So what can we do about it?' asked Lola Ribar.

Tito shook his head. 'Nothing at the moment. The time is not ripe. But there is some good news. Germany is withdrawing some of its troops. They are leaving Acimovic to run the country, with just a skeleton force in support.'

'Why are they doing that?' Lola asked. 'Are they so convinced that we have all accepted the status quo and there will be no resistance?'

'There may be other reasons,' Tito said. 'The rumour is that they need the troops elsewhere, for a new front.'

'A new front? Where?'

'We shall find out in due course,' Tito said, but Alix had a feeling that he knew more than he was admitting.

The answer came a few days later, on 22 June. The radio announced the launch of Operation Barbarossa.

Hitler had launched a massive attack on the Soviet Union along a 2,900-kilometre front.

Next day Tito announced that the Comintern had sent out a general order for all communists to do whatever they could to disrupt the German forces wherever they might be, in an effort to force them to withdraw troops from the eastern front. He called a meeting at the villa of Vladislav Ribnikar, the owner of the newspaper *Politika*, a long-standing supporter of the Communist Party. For the first time Alix discovered that the men she had met at Tito's house were only a small proportion of a much larger organisation, the Central Committee of the Yugoslav Communist Party. It was agreed that now that the pact between Germany and Russia had been broken the time had come for action. The meeting established the Supreme Headquarters of the People's Liberation Partisan Detachments and elected Tito as commander in chief.

As the meeting broke up, Nikola pushed his way through the crowd and took Alix by the arm.

'At last! Now we shall be able to get down to some real fighting – well, we men, I mean. But I'm sure there are going to be plenty of jobs for you girls. Did you say you had learned a bit of First Aid when you were in Paris?'

Alix looked at him askance. 'I'm not going to be pushed into some kind of backroom job, if that's what you're thinking. I'm not a nurse. I can be useful in other ways.'

'I'm sure you can,' he agreed, smiling. 'But not on the front line. I'm not having you put yourself in harm's way.'

She pulled her arm away. 'What do you mean, you're not having? I shall do as I like. You don't have any authority over me.'

He looked momentarily taken aback but recovered himself with a laugh. 'Still the same little spitfire! I should have remembered. Don't be angry. It's just that it's up to us chaps to do the fighting. We don't want you getting hurt. Do we, Pesic?'

Drago, whose presence Nikola now acknowledged for the first time, said quietly, 'Alix will do as she wants. We are in no position to give her orders.'

Nikola glared at him. 'You are not, certainly. Don't presume to speak for me. And how dare you use her name so casually? To you she is Lady Alexandra.'

Alix intervened. 'Ignore him, Drago. We haven't seen you for the last week or two, Nikola. Where have you been?'

He shrugged. 'I had business to attend to, back at the estate. I've got better things to do with my time than push leaflets under people's doors.'

Alix started to say, 'You mean you didn't want to risk being picked up by the police...' but Nikola saw someone across the room and hailed him.

As he pushed away through the crowd, Drago said, 'I wonder if he will be so brave when there is real fighting to be done.'

One of the first tasks Alix was given was an extension of her propaganda work, or rather a reversal of it. Since the German attack on Russia, the local media, which was under the control of the occupiers, had been churning out a stream of announcements of Nazi victories. Posters stuck on walls showed maps of German advances and newspapers carried gloating accounts of battles won and Russian losses. Alix and Drago and a small team were given the job of removing the posters and preventing the papers being distributed. She developed a scheme for removing the papers from newsagents' shops which worked well for some time. She would go into a shop on the pretext of trying to buy sweets for an imaginary child. There were very few to be had but she would start a conversation with the owner, flirting if it was a man, gossiping about the shortages of goods and the difficulties of bringing up children under the current circumstances if it was a woman. Meanwhile Drago would browse the newspapers and magazines on the shelves. When he saw that the owner's attention was fully occupied he would grab a sheaf of papers and pass them out to another member of the group waiting outside. If the owner was still distracted he would repeat the operation. After they had carried out the same routine in three or four shops the resulting pile of newsprint was taken to one of the many vacant bombsites and burned. Wall posters were simply ripped down while other members of the group kept watch for police.

Harsh penalties were advertised for anyone performing such acts of 'vandalism' but with fewer German troops on the streets the Acimovic regime's control was beginning to slip.

Now that Tito had the full backing of the Central Committee he swung into action. Some of his closest lieutenants were dispatched to distant areas of the country to recruit and train men with a view to a general uprising. One of those was Milovan Djilas, who was sent to Montenegro. Others were ordered to set about the same task in the local area. Nikola had done his military service, so he was put in charge of a company of his own based in one of the suburbs.

The communists had a good following in Belgrade among students and factory workers but they had little success in recruiting among the peasant farmers in the surrounding area. Hearing Tito complaining about this gave Alix a sharp reminder. For several weeks she had almost forgotten about the country estate, except to send Drago there to pick up supplies.

'We should go back to Kuca Magnolija and see how many we can recruit from among the estate workers,' she told him.

He frowned. 'I'm not sure if that would be the right thing to do.'

'Why not? We need every man we can get.'

'Ask yourself what your father would think. He is a supporter of the king. How would he feel about his people serving with the communists?'

Alix frowned. The question of what her royalist father's attitude would be was something she had been avoiding.

'I told you before,' she said, 'that he would believe we should do anything we can to get rid of the enemy, and the traitors who have taken over the government in support of them.'

'I'm sure he would agree with that,' Drago said, 'but he would also want to be sure that when it was accomplished the king and the legitimate government could come back and take their rightful place.'

'But why wouldn't that happen?' she asked. 'Once the Germans have been defeated there will be nothing to stop the king returning.'

He rubbed a hand through his hair. 'I suppose not. But if the communists are mainly responsible for getting rid of the Germans, won't that give them a lot of power? Will they be prepared to let the old regime take over again?'

'I see what you're saying,' Alix conceded. 'But we've agreed that things do need to change. I think my father would agree with that and I believe that he would encourage the king and his advisers to co-operate with Tito to bring those changes about. Wouldn't that be the ideal solution?'

'Maybe,' Drago agreed doubtfully. Then his face cleared. 'Perhaps you are right. I think your mother would agree. I remember on one of our expeditions, when I was driving her to some remote village, I was horrified by the conditions people were having to live in. She told me that she and your father were trying to get the government to put in place some improvements, but it was terribly difficult to get past the bureaucracy. Maybe the kind of compromise you are suggesting would achieve that.'

'I'm sure it would,' Alix agreed. 'So on that basis isn't it right for me to encourage everyone to join the struggle? After all, nothing could be worse than finding ourselves stuck under the Nazi's thumb for the foreseeable future.'

He smiled at her. 'Yes, of course. You are right, as usual.'

–

The next day they drove out to the country estate and, as before, the household staff and the workers were assembled in the courtyard in front of the house. Alix stood on the top step leading up to the front door and spoke.

'My friends, as you know, in the absence of my father and mother, the responsibility for ordering the affairs of this estate, this community in which we all live, has fallen to me. I am sorry that I have not been here very much in the last few weeks but I have been involved in some important developments that will affect all our lives. I know that, like me, you hate the idea that our country is no longer free. I'm sure you all want to see the back of these invaders who think they can ride roughshod over our customs and our beliefs. I am here to tell you that there are moves afoot now to drive these invaders out, but we need men and women who are prepared to work and fight with us. I must warn you that it will be hard and it will be dangerous. It will require courage. But those who are prepared to risk everything for their country will be heroes. I am asking for volunteers to join me in the fight.' She paused and looked around at the assembled company. She could see that some of the younger men were already excited by the challenge, but their elders were doubtful. 'Does anyone want to ask a question?' she concluded.

Zoran, the estate manager, raised his hand. 'Who is to lead this effort? With the king in exile and most of the government with him, who has the authority to command us?'

'The leader is a man who is known by the name of Tito,' she told him. 'He is not a member of the government or of the aristocracy. He is a man of the people, but he already has many followers.'

'He's a communist,' a voice from the crowd called out.

A murmur of disapproval went through the assembly. 'We don't like the communists,' someone said. 'They are not like us. We're not commies!' Similar objections went from mouth to mouth. 'They don't believe in God. They are godless men.'

Zoran spoke up. 'Mistress, we hear what you are saying and we support you in wanting to rid us of the invaders. But we are simple people and we are loyal to our king, our country and our religion. We will not fight for men who do not share our beliefs.'

Alix's heart sank. She had hoped her words would bring supporters to her chosen cause but now she was afraid she had lost them. She sought for some argument that would convince them.

'I know your loyalty to God and the king, and I share it. We may not approve of everything the communists teach. I certainly do not. But we have to consider the greater good. Think what will happen if we do not rise up and throw these men out of our country. They are Nazis. They believe that they belong to a superior race, a master race. They look down on us as lesser beings. They have driven their tanks across our land and mown down all those who oppose them. And now they have put into power a group of toadies who will carry out their orders. They are not God-fearing people. If they were they would not behave as they do.' She took a step down, bringing herself closer to the people she was addressing. 'I have seen what these men do to conquered peoples. I have lived in France. I know that they arrest and torture and kill anyone who dares to oppose them. Do you want to live under such a regime?'

She knew from the change in the tone of the comments that she was winning.

'In France brave men and women are mounting a resistance, refusing to lie down under the boots of the aggressors, risking their lives for the sake of their unborn children. Are we going to be less heroic? What will history say about us if we meekly succumb?' She pressed her advantage home. 'Maybe we don't approve of the ideas of the communists. But they are the only people who have the courage and the organisation and the will to stand up against the invaders. When we have achieved our aims, when the country is free again and our king is allowed to return, then will be the moment to discuss what sort of a government we want. Then we shall be able to say, we fought for our king and our country and our religion.' She looked around. 'Who will join me?'

There was a breathless pause, then one young man broke away from the restraining hand of his father and stepped forward. 'I will!'

The dam was broken then and within minutes Alix had a dozen recruits.

'You have an hour to collect your belongings and say goodbye to your family and your friends,' she told them. 'Then we leave for the city.'

There were too many to cram into two cars, so they hitched up a farm trailer to the Dodge and four of the young men climbed into that. With Drago at the wheel of the Dodge and Alix driving her father's Bentley, they headed for the city. There she installed her recruits into the rooms in the town house which had previously accommodated refugees and went to report to Tito.

'A dozen recruits from your own estate?' He smiled at her. 'You will soon have your own platoon. Perhaps I should make you a lieutenant.' Alix's heart jumped but it was said lightly and Tito moved on. 'They can join Nikola's company. I will make arrangements for them to be transferred.' His expression darkened. 'Unfortunately I cannot give them weapons at the moment. We are attracting more and more recruits but we are desperately short of arms and ammunition.'

Drago stepped forward. 'I think I may be able to help,' he said diffidently.

'You?' Tito asked. 'How?'

He glanced at Alix. 'You remember I told you that your mother and father were working with some British men who belonged to some kind of secret organisation? I used to drive your mother out to some of the villages so she could hold clinics and provide some medical help. When she and your father were involved in the preparations for the coup, that became a cover for something else. The British agents arranged for shipments of rifles and grenades and ammunition to come here in the diplomatic bag and the idea was to distribute them around the country so they would be available to the Resistance if the country was overrun. Your mother volunteered to do that. We would drive to a village and while she was vaccinating children in the front room of whichever house we were invited to, I would be round the back with the village headman and the others unloading the weapons.'

Tito was leaning forward eagerly. 'Can you remember which villages?'

Drago nodded. 'Oh yes. But there might be a problem.'

'A problem?'

Drago shifted uncomfortably. 'The head men may not be willing to hand them over. Most of the peasants do not like the communists.'

Alix said, 'I'm afraid Drago is right. They are all very traditional and they cling on to the way of life they have always known. I had difficulty convincing the men on my own estate that this was for the greater good.'

Tito leaned his head to one side. 'Maybe you could use the same arguments to persuade these villagers to give up their weapons.'

'I could try, I suppose,' Alix said doubtfully.

'Then try!' Tito urged. 'We need every rifle and every grenade we can get hold of.'

Over the next days, Alix and Drago traversed the countryside with mixed success. Some village heads maintained immovably that the weapons could only be handed over to a representative of the exiled king. Others insisted that they needed them to defend their own village in the increasingly lawless times. But in around half of them Alix's eloquence bore fruit and they were able to return with the truck laden with armaments, hidden under boxes of produce from the estate.

When they handed over the last consignment Tito slapped Drago on the back.

'Well done, comrade! I shall not forget the part you have played when victory comes.' He turned to Alix. 'And you, clever lady, you have proved your usefulness. I need men and women such as you around me.'

Alix paid a visit to the suburb where Nikola's company was training to see how her men were getting on. Nikola declared himself well satisfied.

'I have brought in men from my own estate to join them and I have told them they are fighting for your honour and mine. I have promised them that when all this is over we shall be in a position to reward them.'

Alix frowned. This use of 'we' was rather unsettling, but she decided it was just a form of words and chose to let it pass.

Next day Drago came to where Alix was sitting.

'I think I should join them.'

'Join? Join who?'

'Dordevic's company.'

'Nikola's company?'

'Yes. I cannot sit back and let them do all the fighting. We have agreed that Tito needs men. I am going to volunteer.'

'But you already do useful work, helping me,' Alix protested. 'I need you.'

'I think you can manage without me,' he said quietly. 'You inspired those lads with the desire to become heroes in the defence of their country. Can you deny me the same chance?'

She gazed at him, contrary emotions warring within her. 'I don't want to lose you, but you are right. I can't hold you back. But I can't bear the thought that you might be killed.'

He shrugged slightly. 'At the moment there's no fighting. Who knows what Tito's plans are? I shall have to take my chance.'

She thought hard. 'Nikola's company is not far away. I can come and watch you training. And when we move out of the city, as I suppose we must soon, I shall come with you.'

'Will Tito allow that?'

'I don't see how he can stop me. I'm a free agent.'

'Dordevic will object.'

'Let him. He'll just have to get used to it.'

'I should be urging you to stay in the city, where you will be safe, or safer at least.'

'And you know I won't listen to you either, if that's what you are saying. Forget I'm a woman, Drago. We're comrades in arms now.'

He looked at her in silence for a moment. Then he said heavily, 'If that is what you want, so be it.'

Chapter Ten

Cairo, July 1941

Leo walked down the gangplank from the houseboat and strolled along the palm-tree-lined avenue to the point where it met the main road at the beginning of the bridge that connected Gezira Island to central Cairo. It was not yet seven thirty and under the shade it was still blessedly cool. She had only been in Egypt for a few days but she relished this early morning walk. The island was an oasis of green with its well-watered gardens and golf course, and it offered a welcome interval of calm before she was plunged into the noise and heat and dust of the city.

Her first few nights had been spent in a boarding house where the floors were alive with cockroaches and she had been reacquainted with bedbugs, something she had not encountered since her days working at the front line in the First World War. Her outspoken protests had resulted in the offer of alternative accommodation on a houseboat moored to the island. It had recently been requisitioned by SOE and she had a small cabin and access to a bathroom that she shared with an ATS sergeant called Glenda. The contrast made her new assignment bearable.

She had only a few minutes to wait before the 'bus' arrived that would take her to work. The bus was a three-ton truck fitted with benches along the sides. A fleet of them had been commandeered by General Headquarters and SOE to collect operatives from around the city and take them to work, either at GHQ in a large building known as Grey Pillars or at Rustum Buildings where SOE was based. The bus carried her across the bridge and into the heat and bustle of the city, navigating a path through donkeys and camels laden with a multitude of goods of various sorts, driven by men in grubby white robes, avoiding statuesque women in black with their heads and faces veiled. In contrast, it had to give way to sleek chauffeur-driven limousines carrying wealthy businessmen in smart suits and red fezzes. Mixed in among all these were soldiers from different regiments in baggy shorts with knee-length socks and heavy boots, and officers in smarter uniforms and polished shoes. The bus would collect her at 1:15 p.m. and then the afternoon was hers, to sleep out the heat or perhaps take tea on the terrace of the Gezira sporting club. Work began again at five p.m. and went on until eight o'clock.

She found Tom Masterson already at his desk in Rustum Buildings and with him was a stranger, a tall, broad-shouldered, extremely good-looking young man in the uniform of an army captain. His close-clipped dark hair grew to a widow's peak above a wide brow and eyes with a direct, almost challenging gaze. His nose was straight and the firm set of his lips suggested a man not easily diverted from his chosen purpose; but she soon discovered that those eyes could gleam with amusement and the lips could part in an appealing smile.

Masterson stood up. 'Leonora, this is Duane Hudson. Hudson, this is Leonora, Countess Malkovic.'

The young man held out his hand. 'Call me Bill, everyone does. I'm delighted to meet you, Countess. I've been aware of the work you and your husband the count have done in Yugoslavia, though we've never met.'

Leo shook his hand. 'I'm afraid I can't say the same about you. Have you lived in Yugoslavia?'

'Bill's a mining engineer,' Tom told her. 'He was managing an antimony mine in Zajaca when war broke out. But he was also working for us.'

'I didn't know.'

'Well, we don't actually publicise such things,' Masterson pointed out.

'And now you are coming to work here?' Leo asked.

'Yes. I hope I can make myself useful.'

'There's no doubt about that,' Masterson said.

'How did you get out?' Leo asked. 'So many of the others didn't make it.'

'I was lucky. I managed to get the last train out to Istanbul. I got stuck there for a while but I finally made it here.'

'Now, to business,' Masterson said. 'Sit down, both of you.' When they were seated he went on. 'As you are well aware, we know very little, in fact nothing, about what has happened in Yugoslavia since the German invasion. The Yugoslav government in exile in London understandably wants to know as much as possible. Of course, they have their own people here. General Ilic has established himself as supreme commander of what's left of the Yugoslav Army and Jovan Djonovic has been given the job of collecting whatever information he can find about the situation over there. Now he is beginning to get scraps of information coming out via couriers to Istanbul, some of which he is prepared to share with us. The most important item to date is this. It seems a man arrived recently in Istanbul with a message from someone called Mihailovic saying that he was forming a resistance organisation and asking for financial support. What I want you two to do, with your shared understanding of the country, is to analyse these scraps. In particular, we want to know if there is any organised resistance and if there is who is leading it.' He sat back. 'I know it's asking you to make bricks without straw but until we can establish direct communication with someone out there it's all we have.'

'What about dropping someone back in there to see what he can find out?' Bill said.

'All in due course,' was the reply. 'Dropping a mission blind, without any idea of who to trust or where to go, would be a recipe for disaster. Once we have a clearer picture of the situation we can consider sending someone in, but not yet. Now, can I leave you to get to work? You can use the office next door and this' – he held out a thin buff folder – 'this is all we have at the moment. Top secret, of course, and not to leave this building, but I'm sure you are well aware of that.'

Leo found that the hours that followed were at once some of the most interesting and some of the most frustrating in her experience. The paucity of the information in the folder meant that they could do little more than speculate. On the other hand, they found that by pooling their combined knowledge of the country and how things worked there they were able to make some informed guesses. At the basic level, she enjoyed talking to someone who shared many of her own feelings about the state of the country before the invasion. Bill, for his own part, was eager to quiz her about the coup and the preparations that had led up to it, and about the part she and Sasha had played in helping to develop new ideas and ways of thinking in the period before the war.

He was good company, well-informed and intelligent with a mischievous sense of humour. When the bus came to take her back she found she was looking forward to their next session.

At eight o'clock, when the working day ended, he said, 'Do you fancy going somewhere for a drink?' and she accepted.

He took her to Shepheard's Hotel, the famous watering hole for expats and wealthy Egyptians. She had been there once with Sasha while they were waiting to be transferred to London, but she had been so uncomfortably aware of her shabby dress in the midst of the elegant crowd that they had not gone back again. Now as they got out of the taxi she asked, 'Do you think I'm dressed for Shepheard's?'

'Why not?' Bill asked. 'There will be plenty of people in uniform.'

'Men, yes…'

'And women too. Don't worry. You look great.'

Before leaving London, Leo had paid a visit to FANY headquarters to talk to the commanding officer, her old friend 'Dick' Baxter Ellis. She had been granted indefinite leave when she made the decision a year ago to return to Serbia, but she was still technically a FANY officer. She had been given an allowance and had managed to get herself fitted for a new uniform. She did feel quite smart in it, so she allowed herself to be persuaded.

The decor in the hotel was both ornate and exotic. Huge granite columns based on ancient Egyptian models lined the façade and the interior was replete with stained glass and Persian carpets. The famous 'long bar' was packed, and the dance floor in the ballroom was crowded with men in uniform and women in evening dress. Leo made a mental note to go shopping and get herself something suitable.

They found a table on the terrace and as they sipped whisky sours Bill said, 'Do you mind if I ask how you met Count Alexander?'

Leo sat back in her chair with a smile. 'Oh, that's a long story. You have to go back to 1912, the First Balkan War. You won't remember that.'

'1912? You must have been just a child.'

'I was eighteen. A friend and I had run away from home to join the Women's Sick and Wounded Convoy, which was run by a remarkable woman called Mabel Stobart. They were nursing the wounded right up close to the front line. We'd got as far as Thessalonika but we didn't know how to get from there to the front line, which was almost at the Turkish frontier by then. I made the mistake of asking Sasha for help.'

'The mistake?'

'He was horrified at the very thought of women anywhere on the field of battle, so we got very short shrift. Fortunately, we found another officer who was more sympathetic and smuggled us onto a train heading in that direction.'

'But obviously that wasn't the end of the story. You met again, in more propitious circumstances.'

Leo sighed as memories crowded in. 'Oh, we kept meeting, off and on, in all sorts of circumstances. When the Great War started I volunteered to join Stobart in Serbia and got caught up in the retreat through Albania. That's where...' She hesitated. 'That's where we really got together.'

He sat back and looked at her admiringly. 'What an amazing story. What happened to the friend you went out there with in the first place?'

'Victoria? She lives in Australia now. We keep in touch, as far as possible.'

'And do you and the count have children?'

'One, a daughter.'

'Where is she now?'

Leo shook her head, frowning. 'I wish I knew for certain. She was studying in Paris when war broke out and got trapped when the Germans marched in. As far as I know she's still there but... Well, there's no way of communicating. I haven't heard from her for over a year now.' She blinked back tears and took a mouthful of her drink. 'That's enough about me. Tell me your story.'

'It's nothing like as exciting as yours,' he said. 'But here goes...'

He told her that he had been educated in South Africa and then at the Royal School of Mines attached to Imperial College, London. He had worked as a mining engineer in South Africa and then moved to Yugoslavia to act as a mining consultant and later as a mine manager. It was there that someone from SOE had recruited him.

'I was based in Croatia, in Zagreb,' he said, 'and as you know there were some strongly pro-German elements among the Croats. They murdered one of the chaps I was working with and put a bomb under my office. Luckily for me it wasn't as lethal as they hoped, but it was a near thing. When war broke out, I decided to do my bit by planting limpet mines on Italian ships in the Adriatic and sank one of them. Then the Nazis moved into Yugoslavia and the Croats, the bastards – sorry, pardon my language

– they welcomed them in. So I decided it was time to get out. The rest you know.'

'Well, that sounds like a pretty exciting story to me,' Leo said with a smile. She finished her drink. 'I think it's time we called it a day, don't you? We have to be up early in the morning.'

He offered to see her back to her accommodation but she told him she would be perfectly safe in a taxi and they said good night on the hotel steps. Leo went to bed feeling that life in Cairo had suddenly become a whole lot more interesting.

Next day she felt it was her turn to offer him some form of hospitality and invited him to have tea with her on the terrace of the sporting club. There were two bakers who had shops on the island and in the absence of rationing the club provided a selection of mouth-watering cakes.

'I've never been here before,' he said. 'What sort of facilities do they offer?'

'Oh, there are tennis courts and a swimming pool,' she said. 'And then there's the golf course and the polo field.'

'Tennis? Do you fancy a game one day?'

'I've never learned how to play,' Leo had to confess.

'Never played tennis? Not at school?'

'I never went to school. I'm afraid my education was, well, somewhat haphazard.'

That led her to explain her childhood growing up with her archaeologist father, following him from one dig to another. 'He decided to educate me himself and I learned more from him than I would have ever learned in a girls' school in England – history, geography, some basic physics and chemistry, and languages of course. Though most of those I picked up from the children I played with around the various digs. By the time I was twelve I was fluent in Greek, Turkish and Arabic – though perhaps my vocabulary was not what you might require in polite company – and I had a smattering of German and French from the other archaeologists my father worked with.' She laughed. 'It was a very useful education, as I realised later, but not one that fitted me for London society. So when I was sent back to live with my grandmother at the age of sixteen she found herself saddled with a hoyden who had no idea how to behave. I heard her once pronounce to some friends that there was no chance I would ever find a husband because I was "too tall, too clever, and too arrogant".'

He laughed out loud. 'And how wrong she was!'

'Oh, I don't know,' Leo responded. 'I could never have settled down to the sort of conventional marriage my brother wanted for me.'

'You have a brother?'

'Had. He was killed in the trenches in France.'

'I'm sorry. You must miss him.'

'I didn't see much of him when we were growing up. And later... Well, we didn't have much in common. He was sent back to school in England, so he had a "proper" education, and then he went into the Guards. So we had very different points of view.' She shook off the memory. 'More tea?'

As they prepared to catch the bus back to work he said, 'Tomorrow's Saturday so we can look forward to a day off on Sunday. Do you fancy going dancing tomorrow night?'

She looked at him with a quickening of her pulse. 'Why not? That would be very nice.'

Leo spent her time off the following afternoon shopping and as soon as the bus dropped her back to the island in the evening she hurried to get ready. She had bought an evening dress in green silk, shot through with kingfisher blue. The privations of recent months and the limitations of rationing had burned away any extra flesh she had developed in the years of peace so she was as slim as a girl and the dress suited her perfectly. She did her makeup with extra care and when she looked at herself she felt a frisson of pleasure at the result. Then she stopped and addressed her reflection.

What the hell do you think you're playing at? You're forty-seven years old and you're acting like a giddy girl because a man more than ten years younger is taking you dancing. For goodness' sake, pull yourself together!

Nevertheless, she experienced the same thrill at the expression on his face when he came to pick her up.

He raised his hands. 'What a vision! Lady, you take my breath away!'

She gave a small self-deprecating shrug. 'I suppose I scrub up quite well, considering.'

'Never mind "considering",' he responded energetically. 'You, madam, are a sight for sore eyes. Come on. I can't wait to get you on the dance floor and see the envy in the other fellows' eyes.'

Shepheard's was even more crowded than it had been on their first visit and Leo was glad that she was properly dressed for the occasion. As Bill led her onto the dance-floor she was aware of appreciative glances from some of the officers sitting at tables round the edge. Then he took her in his arms and she forgot about anything else.

On the way back in the taxi he said, 'What do you usually do on a Sunday?'

'I have a long lie in and do some washing. Then I sometimes go over to the sporting club for lunch.'

'Excellent!' he said. 'While you are engaged in domestic duties, you won't mind if I go to the club and see if I can get myself into a game of tennis? Then we could meet for lunch.'

She accepted, but her mind was on other things. When it was time to say good night, would he try to kiss her? And if he did, how should she respond? No, that was not the right question. She knew what she should do. But could she avoid it without offending him? And did she want to?

He walked her to the gangplank and thanked her for a wonderful evening. As she returned her own thanks he took her hand and looked into her eyes. Her heart thumped faster. For a moment they teetered on the brink. Then the mood was abruptly broken by two of the other young women who were billeted on the boat tumbling out of a taxi in a flurry of giggles. He glanced round, raised an eyebrow ironically and wished her good night.

Next morning, she could not prevent herself from hurrying through her washing in order to get to the sporting club. He was on the tennis court with two girls and another young man and it was clear that he was a superb athlete, streets ahead of the other players.

When he joined her on the terrace after showering she said, 'You are obviously a keen sportsman.'

'You could say that,' he agreed. 'I box a bit, and ski when the opportunity offers, and I swim and ride. I'll have a go at most sports given the chance.'

'Well,' she said, 'there is one thing we have in common. I love to be on horseback.'

'Then we must see if we can borrow a couple of horses,' he responded.

They spent the afternoon lazing by the pool – well, Leo lazed, while Bill powered backwards and forwards doing lengths.

After tea he said, 'What shall we do this evening?'

Leo was prepared for this. She shook her head. 'I really need to get an early night or I shall be useless in the office tomorrow.'

If he was disappointed he did not show it. Shortly afterwards he took his leave and Leo retreated to her cabin.

Next morning, she received a much-delayed letter from Sasha.

> *My darling,*
>
> *I pray to God you are safe and have not succumbed to any of the horrible bugs that seem to plague Egypt. Are you making friends and enjoying yourself? I think of you stuck out there in that heat and find I am grateful for this English climate where it rains three days out of four.*
>
> *Matters here go on much as they did before you left. Peter is becoming reconciled to the idea that he will be here for some time. I am still pushing the possibility of him going to Cambridge, even if only for one year. Simovic and his crew are driving me mad. They seem to spend more energy on fighting with each other than in planning for the future.*
>
> *I have been trying to find some way of getting back into the country. There must be people prepared to resist if they had someone to lead them. I've had several meetings with your friend Brigadier Gubbins but he says he can't help. It seems there is no thought of infiltrating anyone until they know more about the situation, and*

even if it was a possibility, he suggested, very tactfully, that perhaps I am too old to learn to parachute! I suppose he's right but I am desperate to do something. To think of those Nazi swine tramping their jack boots across our lovely country makes me feel sick with rage. I pray they have not invaded Kuca Magnolija. I worry about Bogdan and the rest of the staff.

On a lighter note, I find I have developed quite an active social life. With so many men away fighting, the male of the species is thin on the ground here, so I am constantly bombarded with invitations to play bridge, or make up the numbers at dinner parties. I also have to navigate my way around a number of ladies 'of a certain age' and some younger ones too, to avoid giving offence.

I have no doubt that the opposite situation applies where you are and attractive women are at a premium. You will be much in demand, I am sure. Please don't hold back on my account. I know you are just as adept at dealing with these situations as I am – probably more so. I have absolute faith in your good sense.

Oh, how I miss you, my daring. I find all the women I meet here vapid and lacking in spirit compared to you, my brave love.

Take care of yourself. God willing we shall be together again soon.

All my love,
Sasha

Leo read the letter through twice. Then she spent several minutes sitting in silence. When she stood up she knew what she must do.

That afternoon, as they were packing away documents and preparing to leave the office, Leo said, 'Bill, before we go, there's something I want to say.'

His easy-going expression changed. 'Looks like it's something serious.'

'Yes, well it's something I need to get straight.'

She sat down and he drew a chair closer and sat facing her. 'Go on.'

She took a breath and then stopped. 'Oh, this is difficult. I'm afraid I may have made assumptions, jumped to the wrong conclusion…'

'Just tell me,' he said.

'OK. This is it. I really like you, Bill, and I enjoy your company. I find you very attractive, perhaps too much so. But I want you to know… This is where I may have got the wrong end of the stick… Whatever your intentions, your expectations may be, I will not, cannot, be unfaithful to my husband.' She felt herself blush scarlet. 'There, now I've made a complete fool of myself.'

He reached across and touched her hand. 'No, you haven't. I suppose I should pretend to be outraged at the mere suggestion that I might try to seduce you, but that wouldn't be honest. You've been straight with me, so I owe it to both of us to be the same with you. Yes, I did have hopes that our relationship might develop along the lines you suggested. I cannot think of anything I would rather do than entice you into bed with me. But I knew all along that it would be a dishonourable thing to do. I won't pretend innocence. I've had affairs, several of them. But I've always had the feeling that if I succeeded with you I should regret it, because I would have spoiled something, something fine. So thank you for putting me straight.'

She breathed a sigh of relief. 'I'm glad you understand. And if that means that in future you would rather we confined our time together to office hours I shall understand. I shall be sorry because I love being with you, but…'

He interrupted. 'I love it, too. But it's up to you. If you feel you'd rather…'

'No! It's not that. I just don't want to cramp your style. There must be dozens of girls around who would jump at the chance. You'd have much more fun with them.'

'Fun?' he queried. 'You are the most interesting woman I've met for a very long time, and one of the most beautiful. Why would I want to swap your company for some silly WAAF who giggles all the time?'

She looked at him. He seemed sincere. 'Well, then, on that basis…'

He got up and reached out a hand to draw her to her feet. 'On that basis, let's go back to Gezira and have tea. I really fancy a cream cake.'

Chapter Eleven

Belgrade, August 1941

Alix was in Tito's house drafting an article for *Borba*, the newspaper of the Communist Party. Officially it had been banned, but Tito had decided to resurrect it as a counter to the German propaganda machine. Finding that Alix had had some experience of a similar publication in occupied Paris, he had co-opted her onto the staff. She was pleased that her function had been upgraded from merely distributing propaganda to helping to compose it, but she still felt that she was not being allowed to join the real action. Over recent weeks Tito's men had carried out a number of attacks on the transport and communication apparatus so important to the quisling regime imposed by the Germans. Because direct attacks on the occupying soldiers would be met with reprisals, they had concentrated on those who chose to collaborate, or on the machinery of the state. She was at that moment composing an article describing the destruction of a train carrying coal from Serbian mines to boost the German war effort. It had been blown up and in the process the railway line from Nis to Leskovac had been cut.

Lola Ribar came into the room. 'Where is Comrade Tito?' he asked urgently.

'In the next room,' she answered. 'Why?'

'I must speak to him. Something bad has happened.'

Hearing his voice, Tito came out of his room. 'What is it?'

'We think Marco has been arrested.'

Alix knew that Marco was the *nom de guerre* of Alexander Rankovic, one of Tito's most trusted lieutenants.

Tito swore softly. 'He was planning to blow up the radio station. Somebody must have talked. How do we know he's been taken?'

'It's bad,' Lola said. 'I got a message from Mihailo Svabic. He had heard that someone was arrested in the street yesterday and taken to the hospital in Vidal Street. From the way it was handled he got the impression it was someone important. Marco's been out of contact since then so we are pretty sure it must be him.'

'We need better information,' Tito said. 'If it is him, we need to get him out before the Gestapo get their hands on him again. Do we have any contacts within the hospital?'

'Svabic says he is already having discussions with a medical student called Guja Lasovic. There are several women who have been arrested and mistreated by the Gestapo in the hospital. His sister Vera is one of them and he's desperate to get her out. Also, Mitra Mitrovic has just been transferred there from a concentration camp. Their idea is to rescue both of them.'

'Is there any chance of getting in touch with one of them?' Tito asked. 'They may know if it is Rankovic. Can this medical student do it?'

'Apparently he's not permitted in the women's ward. It needs to be a woman.'

Alix's stomach churned, but she knew this was her chance to prove she could do more than write articles. 'I could do it.'

'You? How?' Tito asked.

'If you can get me a nurse's uniform I could go in and try to speak to one of the women.'

'Too risky!' Lola exclaimed.

'Maybe not,' Tito responded. 'There must be a lot of nurses coming and going in a busy hospital. It should be possible to pass a note to either Vera or Mitra and collect a reply.' He looked at Alix. 'Are you prepared to try it?'

Alix found she was trembling but she nodded. 'If someone can get me a uniform...'

'I'll get back to Svabic,' Lola said. 'The medical student may be able to help there.'

That evening he came back carrying a bag containing a dress, an apron and a cap. The dress was too large but one of the women in Tito's circle had a sewing machine and offered to alter it. Next morning, suitably dressed, Alix was sitting in the car with Lola at the entrance to the hospital. Men and women, some in military uniform, others in the white coats of doctors and many in nurses' uniforms, were coming and going.

'It doesn't look as if they are having to show identity cards or anything like that,' Lola said.

'No, it doesn't,' Alix agreed.

'Well then...' he said.

'Wish me luck.'

She got out of the car quickly, feeling that if she waited any longer her nerve would fail her. She followed a small group of nurses up the steps and in through the main door. The vestibule was busy with people moving in all directions and for a moment she hesitated, not sure where to go.

'Looking for something?' a voice said from behind her.

She swung round to face a man in a brown overall pushing a trolley.

'Oh, yes,' she said, managing to keep her voice steady. 'I'm new here. I'm looking for the women's ward.'

'Third floor,' the man said. 'Turn left out of the lift.'

Alix followed his instructions and found the ward, but she came to a sudden stop at the sight of two armed gendarmes standing guard at the door. She knew that she had a choice. To turn back, her mission unaccomplished, or to somehow brazen it out. On a trolley nearby was a stack of bedpans and clean towels. She grabbed one, slipped into it an envelope containing a note, a pencil and a sheet of paper, covered it with a towel and marched as confidently as she could manage towards the door. The guards let her pass without a glance.

Inside, she scanned the row of beds. Slotted into a holder at the head of each one was a card bearing the name of the patient. She moved along the row until she came to the one with the name *Mitrovic, M* above it. Her heart thumping, she approached the bed. The woman lying in it was emaciated, her lips dry and cracked, and there was a livid bruise on her left temple. It was not hard to believe that she had been held in a concentration camp until a day or two earlier.

As Alix came closer with the bedpan, the dry lips parted. 'I don't need that.'

Alix looked around. Nobody seemed to be taking any notice of her. She lifted the towel and tucked the envelope under the pillow. 'Sorry, I thought you called for one.'

As she moved away she saw a thin hand grope under the pillow for the envelope. The ward was busy and it was clear that the staff were all fully occupied; too busy, she had to hope, to pay attention to what a patient might be reading. Her problem now was to seem to be as busy as they were until there was an opportunity to collect a reply.

'Nurse! Nurse!' a voice appealed from a bed further along.

Alix responded hesitantly, praying that her lack of expertise was not about to be revealed.

'Oh, thank goodness!' the woman exclaimed. 'I've been asking for one of those for the last half hour. Pull the curtain round for me, will you?'

Alix realised with a mixture of relief and reluctance that she had found herself a job.

As she moved to leave the ward, with the full bedpan, she saw Mitra haul herself out of bed and limp towards a door at the far end. Guessing that she was heading for the sanitary facilities, Alix followed. She emptied the bedpan into one of the toilets, wrinkling her nose at the state of it. As she was hesitating, wondering what to do next, another nurse came along.

'What are you doing with that?' she asked briskly.

'I… I'm not sure…'

'You're new, aren't you?'

'Yes.'

'Right. Sluice room is at the far end. Come on, I'll show you.'

Alix spent the next twenty minutes cleaning bedpans. Then, judging that Mitra should have had time enough, she went back to the ward.

'Nurse?' Mitra called her over. 'I need a drink of water. Can you help me, please?'

Alix bent and helped her into a sitting position and passed her the glass of water that was on the bedside table. As she did so a piece of paper was pressed into her hand. She laid Mitra back on the pillows and hesitated a moment, wishing she could find some words of encouragement or comfort. Unable to think of anything, she simply whispered, 'Thank you.' She pushed the paper down the front of her apron, straightened up and headed for the door. As she walked, the hairs on the back of her neck prickled with the anticipation of a voice calling her back, but none came. She passed the guards, forcing herself to move purposefully but not to run. In the lift, pressed in with doctors in white coats and officers in uniform, she shrank into a corner and tried to make herself invisible. She crossed the vestibule, expecting a German voice shouting '*Halte!*', and then she was out in the street.

Lola was waiting in the car, half hidden by the rubble of a bomb-damaged building.

'Well?' he asked tensely.

Alix produced the crumpled piece of paper.

'Wonderful!' he said. 'Let's get this back to Tito.'

Back at the villa in Dedinje, Tito unfolded the note and read out:

'One of the guards is a sympathiser. Told me prisoner is held in private room off men's ward on first floor, guarded. Unconscious. No name.'

He folded the paper and put it in his pocket. 'Well done, Alix. Once again, you have proved your worth to the cause. It will not be forgotten.'

'No name?' Lola said. 'Is it possible they don't know who they've got?'

'Possible, I suppose,' Tito said. 'He must have stood up to a lot to have kept his identity from them. The bastards must have gone too far, which is why he's in the hospital. We need to get him out before he regains consciousness.'

Over the next hours a plan was drawn up and word went out to loyal supporters. The following day sixty of them succeeded in blocking all roads leading to the hospital. At the same time eight partisans entered the hospital, led by an intrepid woman called Cana Babovic. One of them was bandaged and in handcuffs, and they pretended to be special police bringing in a prisoner.

Cana reported later, 'One of the guards outside the room got suspicious, so we had to shoot him and the noise brought one of the soldiers down to investigate. He raised the alarm and we had to shoot our way out, but we got Marco away and got him to Jenekov's apartment. He provided some fresh clothes and then we put Marco into a horse carriage and told everyone he was a construction worker who'd been injured. He's in the clinic now.'

The clinic was a private facility set up at Tito's insistence to treat partisans injured in the course of operations. He regarded it as an obligation on anyone leading a resistance movement to make sure that the wounded were properly cared for.

Alix found that her standing in the group had risen considerably and she was seen as part of Tito's inner circle. Nevertheless, she could not help comparing herself with Cana Babovic. Would she have the courage to lead an armed group like that? She had tested herself in a number of risky situations but she had never carried a weapon. Could she, if the need arose, shoot another human being?

Momentum behind the movement was building. As well as further acts of sabotage, reports were coming in from the representatives Tito had sent out around the country with instructions to raise recruits. These units had grown into well-trained companies, ready for action.

Several raids had been carried out on local gendarme headquarters, where arms and ammunition had been captured. The question was being asked, more and more urgently, 'When are we going to rise up and drive the enemy out?'

Nikola's company was ordered south into the Podrinje region. This area of forests and mountains, along the valley of the River Drina, was judged to be the most promising area for an armed insurrection to begin.

Nikola came to say goodbye.

'At last!' he crowed. 'Some real action.'

'Yes,' Alix agreed. 'I almost wish I was coming with you. Or at least…'

He overrode her. 'The battlefield is no place for a woman. You've got a job to do here. Just be grateful you can stay where it's comparatively safe. Anyway, it wouldn't be suitable. A single girl, out there mixing with men from all sorts of different backgrounds. It wouldn't be acceptable.'

'I can look after myself,' she said.

He smiled. 'You don't have to. That's my job now.'

'No, it isn't!'

She began to protest but he spread his arms. 'Come along. Don't let's quarrel. Won't you give the departing soldier a kiss? Who knows when we shall meet again.'

She hesitated but it seemed unfeeling to refuse so she moved closer and reached up to kiss his cheek. Immediately his arms went round her and he pulled her to him, pressing his lips hard against her own. In a vivid flashback, she felt herself fighting off Raoul's attempt to take her in a dark alley in Paris a year ago. She struggled free and pushed Nikola away.

'Don't do that! We agreed, you promised that all that was behind us.'

'But that was before we knew each other properly,' he said. 'It's different now.'

'No, it's not,' she said.

For a moment he looked angry, then he smiled. 'It will be, given time. I shall just have to be patient. So, just a little kiss, to wish me good luck?'

Unwillingly she stepped forward and pecked him briefly on the lips. 'Good luck.'

'That's my girl!' He saluted and turned to the door.

She said quickly, 'I must say goodbye to Dragomir. Will you tell him to come and see me, please?'

He spoke over his shoulder. 'Don't worry about him. I'll give him your good wishes.'

'No!' she said. 'I want to see him. Tell him to come – or I shall come and find him.'

Drago arrived later that afternoon. She told herself that women all over the country were having to part with husbands and brothers and she had no right to expect to be the exception, but she found herself on the verge of tears.

'I just wanted to say goodbye, and good luck.'

He nodded gravely. 'Thank you.'

'We shall meet again soon,' she promised.

'I hope so,' he responded, but she could see in his eyes that he was as fearful as she was.

'Take care of yourself,' she begged him. 'Remember, I need you.'

He took her hand and kissed it. 'I shall do my best.'

Impulsively she pulled him closer and kissed his cheek and this time it was his arms that went round her. They held each other for a moment then he stepped back and made a little bow.

'I pray God to keep you safe, my lady.'

He turned away and went to rejoin his comrades.

Chapter Twelve

Ravna Gora, September 1941

The camp at Ravna Gora had grown from a cluster of improvised shelters housing a small band of men to an organised settlement occupied by several hundred. Huts had been built from the wood of trees felled in the surrounding forests, and men, most of them army officers who had escaped being rounded up by the Nazis, had continued to flock in. Draza had held to his policy of dispersing his forces, and the officers he had put in charge in the different areas reported that the number of recruits continued to grow. Rumours suggested, however, that there were other groups calling themselves Chetniks who did not answer to his authority.

By the middle of August he was presiding over an increasingly restless company. Reports were coming in of partisan attacks on local gendarme stations and on German trucks and garages and trains. His officers were asking why he expected them to remain inactive. Some of them sought Steve's opinion.

'We joined Draza to redeem ourselves after our defeat by the Germans,' one said. 'We are ashamed of the way our army crumbled in the face of the enemy. Now he asks us to sit by and watch students and teachers and other civilians taking the fight to them while we soldiers stay here safe and out of sight.'

Steve was inclined to agree with that attitude but he was careful not to appear to take sides, reminding himself that his role was to observe and report. He had his own source of frustration in his inability to carry out his orders.

Draza countered by reminding everyone that Prime Minister Simovic had broadcast from London, exhorting his people not to provoke German reprisals but to await the arrival of an Allied army.

'We are the Royal Yugoslav Army of the Homeland. We represent the king and the legal government,' he reminded them. 'This war is not going to be over quickly. There is no point in wasting ourselves and our armament against forces we cannot hope to overcome.'

His position was made more difficult by reports from the village of Bela Crkva. At the midsummer fair a group of partisans had gathered the people together and encouraged them to join the fight against the invaders. Such a public gathering was forbidden by the authorities and two gendarmes attempted to break it up. In retaliation, they were shot by the partisans. Mihailovic responded by issuing a directive ordering all army reservists between the ages of thirty and forty to report to Chetnik detachments in their area, for the purpose of maintaining order.

On the first of September a courier galloped into camp and pulled his horse to a standstill in a shower of gravel.

'Colonel Mihailovic!' he shouted. 'I have great news!'

Draza came out of his hut. 'What news?'

'Loznica has been liberated!'

'Liberated? What do you mean? By whom?'

'By some of our men, with support from the local partisans.'

'Partisans? Who gave orders for that?'

'There was a meeting at the monastery of Tronosa. Lieutenant Colonel Misita was there and Captain Racic of the Jadar Battalion. It was decided to attack the next day.'

Draza was frowning. 'Go on. What happened?'

'The town was only lightly defended but the Germans were dug in. We surrounded it and invited the Germans to surrender but they refused. So at nine o'clock Colonel Misita personally led the attack.' The messenger's face lost its triumphant expression. 'Sadly, I have to report he was killed. But the Germans saw that resistance was useless and they surrendered.'

'Misita killed? What did the fool think he was doing?'

'Sir!' the messenger objected. 'He is a hero. It is our first victory. We took ninety-three Germans prisoner.'

Many of the other officers had gathered round to hear the news and there was a collective cheer.

Draza looked at the messenger in silence for a moment. Then he said, 'You are right. He is a hero. But I should have been consulted before anything like this was attempted.' He turned to one of the officers. 'See this man is given food and somewhere to rest.' Then he went back into his hut.

Steve followed him in. 'It's good news, isn't it?'

'Is it? How am I supposed to hold the rest of these fool-hardy idiots back now? And it was done in co-operation with the communists! How can we work with them when everything they stand for is contrary to what we believe in?' He shook his head. 'We may have to change the whole way we operate.'

In the following days further reports came in of successes achieved by joint forces of Chetniks and

Partisans, including the liberation of the towns of Krapanj and Gornji Milanovac. Draza ground his teeth and exclaimed, 'There is only one thing to do. I shall have to meet the leaders of these partisan brigades and bring them under my command. They must accept that I am the leader accredited by the king and the government in exile.'

One evening a peasant appeared in the camp leading a mule with something heavy in the panniers slung across its back.

'I have something for the colonel,' he announced.

Steve was just about to sit down to his evening meal when a boy rushed into the mess hut. 'The colonel wants you, now!' he exclaimed breathlessly.

In Draza's hut, Steve found him standing at a table on which was an object covered by a hessian bag. Draza indicated the peasant standing by.

'See what this man has brought us!'

He whipped away the bag and Steve gasped. 'It can't be! My wireless set, after all these months!'

'According to him, the mule wandered into his farm soon after that disastrous river crossing. He regarded it as a gift from God as his previous mule had recently died. He had no idea what it was the beast was carrying, so he stored it away in a barn and forgot about it, until his son found it. The boy thought it might be of some use to us and persuaded his father to bring it.'

Steve turned to the man. 'Thank you! Thank you. Your son was right. This is very useful.' He looked at Draza. 'He should be rewarded.'

'He will be,' Draza promised. 'I shall see to it. The point is, will it work?'

'We'll have to see. Is my code book here?' Steve turned back to the peasant. 'There should have been a book, some papers. Did you find them?'

The peasant shrugged. 'No use. I threw them away.'

'Does that mean you can't use the set?' Draza asked anxiously.

'No. It just means any messages I send will have be in clear, not in code.'

'That won't matter,' Draza said. 'As long as you can make contact with London.'

Steve opened the case and took out the equipment. 'It's all here. The question is, what state is the battery in?' He switched it on and shook his head sadly. 'It's very low. The signal will be very weak. There's no way it will reach London.'

Draza's shoulders slumped. 'Then it's useless?'

'Not completely. I can send out a message on an open frequency and hope it might be picked up by a local station. Perhaps on a ship out in the Adriatic. I can ask for it to be passed on. It might work.'

'Then try it!' Draza said. 'We need them to know what is happening here.'

Steve deployed the aerial and seated himself in front of the set. 'What do you want me to say?'

'Just tell them that I, Mihailovic, have established a force to resist the enemy and I await their instructions. Say I need supplies of money and of arms and equipment. Ask whoever receives the message to pass it on to the Serbian government in exile in London.'

Steve put on the headset and started to tap away at the Morse key. After a few minutes he sat back and looked at Mihailovic.

'I've sent it but so far there has been no acknowledge-ment. I can keep sending at intervals, as long as the battery holds out. That's the best I can do, I'm afraid.'

Draza put a hand on his shoulder. 'You chose to throw in your lot with me, and for that I am thankful. If this message gets through, all Yugoslavia will have reason to be grateful.'

Chapter Thirteen

Belgrade, September 1941

News came in daily of the progress of the uprising in the Podrinje area. A combined force of partisans and Chetniks liberated the towns of Koviljava and Sabac and Baja Koviljaca. In other parts of the country railway lines were blown up and gendarme stations attacked. It was obvious that the weak quisling government of Acimovic was unable to quell the unrest.

On the last day of August Tito met with his close colleagues. Alix was with them.

'Dankelmann has sacked Acimovic and put Milan Nedic in his place,' Tito said.

Heinrich Dankelmann was the military commander left in charge when most of the German troops were withdrawn.

'That's not good,' commented Lola Ribar.

'No. Nedic is a fanatical fascist. He's going to broadcast tomorrow and I'm afraid we shall not like what we hear.'

Next day they all gathered round the radio set. Nedic proclaimed that he was going to head a 'Government of National Salvation'. His aim, he stated, was to preserve the core of the Serbian people by accepting the German occupation in the key areas of Serbia, including the Podrinje.

He ordered people not to join in any form of resistance, particularly that organised by the 'communist Jewish rabble'.

Tito switched off the radio. 'It's time we joined our comrades in Podrinje. The Nazis have pulled out of Uzice and the surrounding area. This shows that we now have forces capable of taking the fight to them. Now we need to organise a coherent army with a proper approach to strategic objectives.'

'What about these Chetnik detachments who seem to be co-operating with our men?' Lola asked.

'They need to be brought under our overall command. I shall write to Mihailovic and suggest a meeting to discuss co-operation. Meanwhile, I intend to leave tomorrow for Valjevo to link up with Milos Minic and establish a central command position.'

'We will come with you,' Lola exclaimed.

'No. It will attract less attention if I travel alone. You and Rankovic and Milutinov can follow the next day.' He glanced across the room. 'Bring Alix with you.'

Alix caught her breath. At last she was going to be part of a great enterprise. For a moment, until she heard Tito's last instruction, she had been afraid that she would be left behind in Belgrade, charged with some propaganda function, or forgotten completely. Now the prospect ahead of her filled her with trepidation, but also with excitement. She went back to the family house and made her preparations. It still housed two refugee families from Croatia but in recent weeks she had left the running of the place to Ivo, the butler.

She called him into the morning room and explained that she had to go away.

'I'm leaving you in charge, Ivo. I want the refugees to stay as long as they need to. Apart from that, I trust you to look after the place until I get back, or' – the breath caught in her throat – 'until the count and my mother return.'

He looked grave. 'Miss Alexandra, I don't know where you plan to go, or who with. I know you believe you are doing the right thing but I seriously question whether your father the count would approve. Should you not think again?'

'No, Ivo,' she said. 'My father is a patriot. I know he would wish us to resist the enemy occupation in any way we can.'

'If only he were here…' the butler lamented.

His words struck a chord in Alix's mind. She understood that her father's first duty was to the young king, but she could not help wondering why he did not return to join the struggle against the invader.

'He's doing his duty looking after King Peter,' she said. 'So for the time being I have to decide for myself what I should do. And that means leaving the city for a while…' She held out her hand. 'You have been a tower of strength, Ivo. I know you will take care of everything till I get back.'

Next day she drove out to Kuca Magnolija and explained the situation to Bogdan, the butler there, and to Zoran, her father's steward. Their reaction was much the same as Ivo's and she used the same arguments to convince them. Then she went up to her bedroom and rifled through her wardrobe for suitable clothes to take with her. She knew she could not carry much, so she had to guess what conditions would be like. She had had to leave all her French clothes behind when she fled the country, so now she had to fall back on what she had worn as a teenager. Fortunately the restrictions of rationing meant that she had not put on any weight so they still fitted her. She pulled out and cast aside pretty summer dresses, cashmere sweaters and fur-trimmed jackets. For a moment she lingered over her first grownup evening dress, running her hand over the blue silk, but she knew it might be many months before she could contemplate wearing something like that again. She had already packed the practical skirts and blouses she had been wearing over the summer but now winter was coming. Searching the wardrobe, she came across a pair of sturdy corduroy trousers. She teamed them with boots and a couple of warm sweaters and a lined waterproof jacket she had kept for riding out in bad weather. There were riding breeches too, but it seemed they would have a limited use so she left them behind. That gave her a twinge of nostalgia. She had been a keen horsewoman but there had been no opportunity since her return to revive the habit. She pushed everything into a case and headed back to the city.

According to plan, on the following morning she met Lola and the others at the railway station and they took the train to Valjevo. From there the only available transport was by horse and cart, so it was evening when they were challenged by the sentries guarding the town of Uzice.

'Comrade Tito is in the bank,' they were told. 'He has made his headquarters there.'

They found Tito in what was once the bank manager's office with Milan Mijalkovic, the man he had sent out in July to recruit and train partisans. It was plain he had succeeded brilliantly. Spread on the desk were lists of names and maps showing positions.

Tito welcomed them warmly and added, 'You need to eat and sleep. Milan will show you where the canteen is and there is a house set aside for you to live in. Tomorrow we will get to work. We have a whole city administration to set up.'

The town was thronged with troops. They wore a mixture of uniforms, some army, some police or even fire brigade, while others were in civilian clothes where the variety and quality gave a clue as to their position in society before the war. All wore sturdy boots and knitted hats and many had scarves in various colours round their necks. To Alix's amazement, mixed in with the men were many women. They were dressed like the men in trousers and boots and many of them carried rifles.

'Who are those women?' she asked Milan.

'Those? We call them *partizanke*. They are all women who have volunteered and fought alongside their comrades in the recent battles.'

In bed that night, in the unfamiliar room, Alix thought about those women with a mixture of envy and reluctance. Could she ever be like one of them? Did she want to be? In all the work she had done for the Resistance in France her femininity had been one of her strengths. The Germans were less likely to suspect a woman. She had always dressed as well as she could and taken care of her hair and used what makeup she had been able to obtain. Recently, in Belgrade, she had been more concerned with practicality than style but she had still taken care of her appearance. As a girl she had been regarded as something of a tomboy, but her whole education and background had been directed to making her a 'lady'. Now she began to see that that was no longer an option. If she wanted to participate in the struggle she would have to leave all that behind her.

The following morning, she reported with Lola and the others to the bank where Tito was already at work.

He looked up with a broad grin. 'Welcome to the Soviet Republic of Uzice! Our men, with the help of the Chetniks, have liberated a large area of western Serbia. It is up to us now to see that it is properly run.'

In rapid sentences he outlined the work ahead of them. There were to be 'people's councils' to deal with local matters but the final authority would be in the hands of the Central Committee as set up in Belgrade. Uzice was a busy town with a number of thriving enterprises, the most important of which, and the jewel in the crown as far as the partisans were concerned, was a factory that produced guns. They needed now to take on the administration of all the various departments; transport, communications, hygiene, law and order, and so on. By the end of the morning Tito had allocated the responsibility for all these to his lieutenants.

'I want this to be a model of how a socialist state should operate,' Tito said. 'There will be kitchens to feed the disabled and proper health care for all. And, of course, a hospital. It has always been a point of honour among freedom fighters to care for those injured in the cause. I have found the ideal man to run it. His name is Gosko Nikolis. He is a graduate of the Belgrade Medical School and served with the International Brigade in Spain. We need nurses to assist him. That will be a job for the *partizanke*. I don't want women fighting at the front line. We shall establish a medical brigade and they will serve in that.'

No one raised any objection but Alix felt a simultaneous sense of relief coupled with one of disappointment. She wondered how some of those women she had seen the day before, in their easy comradeship with the men, would feel about the new regime.

'And we shall continue to publish the newspaper,' Tito went on. 'Milutinov will take over as editor. Alix, you will assist him.'

The confusion in Alix's emotions deepened. This was the same job, just in a different place. But what had she expected?

'How is all this to be paid for?' Rankovic asked.

Tito slapped the desk he was sitting at. 'This is a bank. The money is under our feet, in the vaults.'

'What are we doing about the Chetniks?' Rankovic asked.

'I have had a reply to my letter. I am going to meet Colonel Mihailovic tomorrow in Struganik. We shall have to see what transpires.' He looked across at Milutinov. 'We should have a full report in the newspaper. You should be there.'

'I've got more than enough to do here,' Milutinov said. 'Alix can go.'

Chapter Fourteen

Ravna Gora, September 1941

'I am meeting this man who calls himself Tito tomorrow,' Draza Mihailovic said. 'It seems he has quite a lot of men under his command. He could be dangerous.'

'In what way?' Steve enquired.

'These attacks on towns and villages are not going to go unnoticed by the enemy. If they go on the Germans will be forced to react. I've said many times that we should not provoke them until we have a real chance of victory. I do not want to see innocent men and women killed in reprisals. I do not know what we can expect from this meeting, but it is important that our government in exile is kept informed. You had better come with me and take notes, so if we are able to establish radio contact you can give a clear account.'

'Very well,' Steve agreed. He had grave doubts about whether any of his radio messages would be picked up but he was already keeping a written record of everything that happened for future reference. This was a golden opportunity to be right at the heart of what might be an important development.

Soon after dawn they mounted up and rode to the village of Struganik, accompanied by a small escort. They had acquired several horses when a group of cavalry officers who had avoided capture opted to join them. Steve had never ridden before, but he had been given a couple of lessons by one of the officers and was reasonably confident in staying in the saddle as long as they didn't go too fast and nothing happened to spook his horse.

They reached the village in good time and Draza expressed his satisfaction.

'Always better to be in possession of the scene before any encounter.'

The headman of the village had offered his house for the meeting, and on Draza's instructions the escort dismounted in the village square and he and Steve went into the house. They were followed by Draza's batman, Goran, who was carrying a chest containing a field telephone and various other bits and pieces which Draza insisted on taking with him wherever he went. It was a simple place with just one room on the ground floor but it was clean and a fire burned in the grate.

'Good!' said Draza. 'Goran, we will have some tea ready for our guest when he arrives.'

Steve smiled inwardly. Draza's idea of tea might come as something of a surprise to the uninitiated. Goran put down the chest and got out a bottle, a pan and two tin cups. He filled the pan and put it to heat over the fire.

A few moments later they heard horses outside. The door opened and a tall man in a neat grey uniform stepped inside. In the doorway stood two other men, both carrying rifles. Behind them Steve glimpsed a shorter figure in boots and trousers, wearing a felt cap. A boy, perhaps?

Draza got up quickly. 'Who are these men?'

'My escort,' was the reply.

'This was supposed to be a private meeting, man to man,' Draza said.

'So who is that?' the new arrival asked, pointing to Steve.

'My radio operator.'

'You have radio contact? With London?'

'Yes.' The lie seemed to come easily.

Tito turned to leave. 'I won't have anything we discuss here passed on to your government in exile. The meeting is off.'

'No,' Draza said hastily. 'If you dismiss those men behind you, I will send my operator away. Anything we say will remain confidential. You have my word.'

'Very well.' Tito looked round at the figures behind him. 'Wait for me at the entrance to the village.'

They turned to leave. The boy followed but looked back, and for a moment Steve had a disconcerting feeling that he should recognise him. Before he could pursue the thought, Draza said, 'You too. Wait for me with the rest.'

i —

Walking back to where they had left the horses, Alix was troubled by a nagging sensation that she had missed something. She had been unable to see into the room because the two men had blocked her view until the last minute. She had looked back, wanting to catch a glimpse of the Chetnik leader she had heard so much about, but who was the other man with him? She was certain she had seen him before somewhere.

Rejoining the rest of the escort, she forgot about him. Vlodimir, the man in charge, was grumbling about being denied a chance to listen to the discussion between the leaders. Alix concentrated on her horse. He was a big bay gelding and when they were preparing to leave Uzice, Vlodimir had led him over to her.

'Don't be afraid. He's very docile,' he said reassuringly. 'But I'll put him on a leading rein if you prefer.'

Alix burst out laughing, then apologised. 'I'm sorry. It's kind of you but you really don't need to worry.'

Ignoring his offer to give her a leg up, she swung herself into the saddle and took up the reins.

'You've ridden before,' he said.

She grinned down at him. 'I more or less grew up on horseback. But thanks for offering to help.'

They had to wait nearly an hour before Tito rejoined them. On the ride back he refused to be drawn about what had passed between him and the Chetnik leader but when they reached Uzice he called a meeting of his inner council. Alix slipped into the room, clutching her notebook, so she could use the excuse that she still had to write a report for the paper.

'Well?' Rankovic asked. 'How did it go?'

Tito ran his hand through his hair. 'I don't know what to make of the man. Do you know the first thing that happened? He offered me tea. But it wasn't tea. It was warm slivovitz!'

Rankovic laughed. 'Sumadije tea! It's a well-known local drink. They make it from a very weak form of plum brandy.'

'Well, it was not what I was expecting,' Tito said. 'Anyway, we eventually got down to outlining our aims. Mihailovic wants, as we do, to liberate all Slav territories from the German and Italian occupiers. Then he is hoping to establish a "greater Serbia" within the bounds of Serbia itself together with Montenegro and Bosnia Herzegovina.

I get the impression he would like to remove all non-Serbs, all Muslims, all Croats. I told him I didn't see the future like that. That my aim is to unite all the different nationalities into a socialist republic of Yugoslavia.'

'Quite right!' exclaimed Lola Ribar.

Tito acknowledged the comment with a lift of his eyebrows and went on. 'It was when we got down to tactics that the real difference in our approaches became obvious. Mihailovic is obsessed with the need to avoid German reprisals. I told him you can't make an omelette without breaking eggs. Anyway, the final conclusion was that we will continue to co-operate, for the time being at least, and meet again at some point to discuss matters further.'

An animated discussion followed, with some members of the group objecting to the idea of working with a man whose aims were so contradictory to their own, while others pointed out that the joint forces of partisans and Chetniks had produced some important gains. Alix slipped away, intending to go and write up her report. As she reached the street someone called her name.

'Alexandra! Alix!'

She looked round and saw Nikola hurrying towards her. Like the majority of partisans he was in civilian clothes, but whereas when they had said goodbye he was immaculate, now his breeches were dusty and his boots caked with mud and he was growing a beard.

She suppressed a sigh and forced herself to smile. 'How are you? It looks as though you've been busy.'

There was no answering smile. 'Never mind how I look. What are you doing dressed like that?'

Alix glanced down at her trousers. 'I've been riding. I went with Comrade Tito to an important meeting.'

'For goodness' sake, go and change! Think what sort of impression you are making.'

'I don't know what you mean. All the *partizanke* wear trousers.'

He stared at her. 'You aren't trying to bring yourself down to their level, surely! Most of them are just ignorant peasants. You have a position to keep up.'

'What do you mean, position?'

'You are the daughter of a count. What do you imagine your father would say if he saw you now?'

That thought made Alix pause. In the end she said, 'I don't think who your father is matters much these days.'

He glared at her. 'Well, if you are not worried about your family's reputation, what about mine?'

'Yours? What has it got to do with you?'

'Everyone knows we are betrothed.'

'Then everyone is wrong. I turned you down, remember?' She saw pain replacing the anger in his eyes and thought for the first time that her refusal must have caused a severe blow to his self-esteem. She spoke more gently. 'I'm sorry, Nikola, but that's the truth. I thought we'd agreed to put that behind us.'

'And I thought we had agreed to think again, now we know each other better.'

'No, we agreed to be friends. Nothing more than that.'

He changed his tack and his voice was almost pleading now. 'But can't you see the danger you are putting yourself in? A single woman, among all these men. They are not the sort you are used to mixing with. Yes, we have doctors and lawyers and university professors in our ranks but most of them are either peasants or working men from the factories. I know the men in my own company and I know the way they talk about women. You don't understand. You are too innocent.'

Alix was silent for a moment. It was true that even in the short time she had been in Uzice she had noticed men passing her in the street and seen the way they looked at her and nudged each other and muttered some presumably ribald comment.

She shrugged. 'So, do you really think I would be safer in a dress?'

'It's not a question of that. It's the matter of letting them see that you are not like them, that you have a position in society.'

'Oh, really!' She sighed. 'Nikola, I do think all that is irrelevant now.'

'It's not. People still think the same way. These are men who would have touched their forelocks or doffed their caps to you before the war. You need to maintain their respect. A single woman, without any male protector, is fair game to some of them.' He reached out to touch her arm and then drew back. 'Listen, all I want to do is keep you safe. If we gave out that we are betrothed, everyone would know that if they laid a hand on you they would have me to answer to. If… When all this is over… If you still want to think again, that will be up to you. What do you say?'

Alix hesitated. She could see the force of Nikola's argument. Her sense of independence rebelled against the idea that she needed a male protector but she had grown up in the rigid traditions of Serbian society and she knew that what he was saying was true.

She nodded reluctantly. 'As long as you understand that this is simply for public consumption. It doesn't actually change anything between us.'

He smiled warmly. 'I understand. Thank you. But please, as my fiancée, think of my feelings and take care of how you appear to people.'

Alix sighed. She had a feeling that she had been talked into a situation she was going to regret. But, she reflected, she might as well use it to her advantage where she could.

'I'd like to see Dragomir to make sure he's all right. Could you tell him to come and find me? I shall be in the newspaper offices.'

He smiled again. 'Of course. Now that we know where we stand I can't object to that.'

Before going back to work, Alix went to her room and looked at herself in the mirror. It was true that her first encounter with the *partizanke* had made her think that dressing to make herself look attractive was inappropriate but she had had to revise her first impressions. She had noticed that most of the members of the committee had pretty secretaries whose principal function, she suspected, was of a more intimate nature. Tito himself, of course, made no attempt to disguise his relationship with Zdenka and she certainly would never have appeared in trousers and boots. Alix changed into a skirt and combed her hair.

Drago arrived half an hour later, while she was writing up her report. She jumped up and held out her hand.

'How are you? You haven't been wounded in the fighting?'

He took her hand and bent his head but he kept his eyes lowered. 'I'm well, thank you, madam.'

She almost shook him with exasperation. 'What's the matter with you? You don't speak like that to me. I thought we had got over all that.'

He looked up. 'Count Nikola tells me you are now officially betrothed.'

'Drago, that's just for show. Nikola thought I would be safer if people believed that. But nothing's changed, really.'

'He thinks it has,' he said.

'Well, it hasn't. Certainly not as far as you and I are concerned. You are still my big brother.'

He met her eyes and in a moment of revelation she saw in his gaze something that had nothing to do with brotherly love. A lump rose in her throat and she felt she had lost something very precious.

'Oh, Drago!' she murmured.

He took a step back. 'Count Nikola does not see things that way. He will not permit us to spend time together as we did.'

'Never mind what Nikola says. It is not for him to permit or withhold permission.' She was furious that she had allowed herself to be manoeuvred into this position.

He said simply, 'He is my commanding officer. I must do as he tells me.' He looked round as if seeking a way of escape. 'If you will allow me, I should go back.'

She had to swallow back tears but there was nothing she could do but nod. 'Take care of yourself, Drago.'

For a moment he hesitated, but all he said was, 'You, too.' Then he turned and left the room.

Ravna Gora

When the Chetniks arrived back at camp, Draza called a meeting of his senior officers. He gave them a summary of his discussion with Tito, and ended gloomily with, 'I don't trust the man. He is not a Serb, of course. He's a Croat. He seems to me to be completely reckless and doesn't care how many innocent lives are lost in pursuit of his aims.'

His pessimism was reinforced the next day by a broadcast on the German-controlled Belgrade radio. Hitler had announced that from now on 100 civilians would be shot in reprisal for every German killed and fifty for every German wounded.

The atmosphere in the camp was uneasy. Most of the older officers supported Draza's stance but some of the younger ones were eager to take the fight to the enemy, whatever the cost. One or two even declared their intention of defecting to the partisans. In a number of areas, individual Chetnik leaders were taking matters into their own hands and continuing to mount joint operations with Tito's men.

One evening Steve burst into Draza's cabin without waiting to knock.

'I've done it! We've made contact.'

Draza jumped to his feet. 'With London?'

'No, not yet. But my signal has been picked up by a British warship somewhere out there in the Adriatic. They have promised to forward the message to a radio station in Malta, who will send it on to London.'

'At last!' Draza exclaimed. 'If I can tell the men that I have the complete backing of the government in exile that will put an end to the arguments. So what will happen next?'

'I'm not sure,' Steve said. 'I suppose they can relay an answer via the same route. We shall have to wait and see.'

Chapter Fifteen

Cairo, 13 September 1941

Tom Masterson came into the office where Leo and Bill were working.

'I've had a signal from London. It seems they have made contact with someone working for a Colonel Mihailovic, who is raising an army to resist the Germans. The message was sent in clear and the signal was very weak, so there's no way of knowing who is sending it but the Simovic government is extremely keen to have first-hand information. They want us to send a mission to seek out Mihailovic and confirm the situation.'

'Mihailovic?' Leo said. 'I seem to have heard that name before.'

'Yes, we were interested in him when I was based in Belgrade,' Masterson said. 'A bit of a rebel, not popular with the High Command, but a good soldier. If it's true, then he is probably just the man for the job.'

'Will we be sending someone in?' Bill asked eagerly.

'Yes, but the plan is to send in a couple of local men for a start. Ilic seems to want to keep it a strictly Yugoslav affair. He's suggested a couple of chaps who are here in Cairo already. They are both majors, Zaharije Ostojic and Mirko Lalatovic. I know Ostojic. He was involved in the coup last April. He was put in charge of getting

King Peter out after the invasion and ended up here in Cairo. Lalatovic was in the Air Force. He flew his plane out of Montenegro to Greece to escape the Germans. He's been here for a while, too. They both work for Djonovic. I'm going to suggest that they join you to prepare for the mission. We'll have to work out the best way of infiltrating them.'

Leo could see that Bill was disappointed. She knew that, pleasant as their life was, he was getting restless and eager to be doing something more active. Since they had arrived at their agreement to keep their relationship purely platonic, they had settled into a comfortable routine of tea at the sporting club, dancing at Shepheard's Hotel or one of the other popular night spots in the city and riding out on borrowed horses on their days off. She still found him very attractive but in a strange way their mutual restraint seemed to bring them closer together and she had developed a deep affection for him. The thought that he might be sent away on some dangerous mission frightened her.

Over the next weeks they both worked with the two Serbian officers on the details of the mission. The Yugoslavs were both punctilious in their courtesy to her and she had no doubt about their courage and dedication to the cause of restoring the king to his rightful position, but she found it hard to warm to them. She had the impression that they were co-operating with SOE because it was the only way they could get back into their country, and that they were working to a private agenda that they were unwilling to share. They received their instructions direct from Djonovic, who was in communication with his government in London, rather than from SOE.

It was decided that the best way to get them into the occupied territory was by submarine. This would entail a train journey to Alexandria, then a flight to Malta where they would join the sub which would drop them somewhere on the coast of Montenegro. There had been rumours of an uprising in Montenegro which suggested there must be some active resistance going on. It was hoped that the two officers would be able to link up with the men involved who would then be able to tell them where the colonel was. They would be accompanied by a radio operator, a non-commissioned officer called Veljko Dragicevic, with two radio sets.

They were to leave Cairo on 12 September and Bill was going with them as far as Alexandria, just in case there were any last-minute problems. On the evening before he was due to leave he took Leo dancing as he so often did, and escorted her back to the houseboat afterwards.

'I've got an early start tomorrow,' he said, 'so I'll be gone before you get to the office. I'll see you when I get back the day after tomorrow.'

'Be careful,' she said, and he laughed.

'Not a lot can happen to me between here and Alex.' He kissed her lightly on the lips and wished her good night.

Just before midday next day Masterson came hurriedly into the office where Leo was listlessly scanning through a file.

'Change of plan. I've just had a signal from London. Hudson is to go with the others. I need you to go to Alex and tell him.'

'Go?' Leo exclaimed. 'But he's not prepared. He hasn't got any of the right kit with him.'

'You know where he is lodging?' Masterson said. 'You've just got time to go there and pick up a few essentials for him. There's a train at two thirty. All being well that will get you there by six. Take-off is scheduled for six a.m. tomorrow, so that gives him just twelve hours to get himself organised.'

'Organised!' Leo snorted. 'What can he possibly do? You're sending him out completely unprepared.'

'He's a resourceful chap and he knows the country,' Masterson said. 'And the captain of the sub may be able to help with extra supplies.' He changed his tone. 'I know it's not the right way of doing things, but I'm only following orders. It seems the top brass at HQ have suddenly realised that the Serbs are only going to report to their own superiors, who may not choose to share information with us. So we need our own man on the ground. And Bill is ideally suited.'

'Have you got written orders for him?' she asked.

'No time,' he answered. 'But you need to give him these.' He handed over a sealed envelope. 'The two Yugoslavs have already been given the necessary ciphers and other information for Mihailovic to use. These are personal ciphers for Bill. All radio traffic will go initially to Malta for onward transmission and they will send copies to us. The beauty of this arrangement is that, because Mihailovic is using our codes, we shall be able to read all the traffic between him and the government in London, while Bill's messages can only be read by us.'

'So what do I tell him his mission is?'

'Pretty vague, to be honest with you. It's to contact, investigate and report on all groups offering resistance to the enemy, regardless of race, creed or political persuasion.'

'That sounds pretty comprehensive,' Leo said.

'I think he'll like that. It gives him a free hand. Now, you'd better get going. It's vital you make that two thirty train.'

Leo took a cab to the house where Bill had a room. The housekeeper recognised her and let her in and she spent several minutes rifling through drawers and cupboards, trying to work out what items might be most useful. In the end she selected a pair of stout boots, a sweater, some clean underwear and a razor. She looked for an oilskin but could not find one. She found a rucksack in the bottom of a cupboard and shoved everything into it, then she set off for the station.

She reached Alexandria on schedule and took a cab out to the airfield, where she found Bill having dinner in the officers' mess. The Serbs were sitting together at a different table. He jumped to his feet at the sight of her.

'What's happened? Don't tell me there's a hiccup and the whole thing's been called off.'

'Quite the opposite,' she said. 'You are to go too.'

'Go? Are you sure? Whose orders?'

'From on high, I gather. They've decided we need our own man out there.'

'Absolutely right!' he said. 'To be honest, I don't trust Ostojic to give us an honest assessment of the situation. But it's a bit late in the day to decide. All I've got with me is a toothbrush.'

She showed him the rucksack and he examined the contents and declared himself well pleased. He introduced her to the RAF officers he had been sitting with and she was made welcome and offered dinner while he contacted the necessary authorities about the change in the arrangements. Later, they found a few moments to sit with their backs to the mess hut and look up at the desert sky.

'The stars look so close I almost feel I could reach up and touch one,' Leo murmured.

He put his arm round her shoulders. 'We need one to fall, so we can make a wish.'

'I shall make one anyway,' she said. 'I wish for you to come back safely.'

He murmured, 'I want you to know, whatever happens I shall always look back on these last few weeks as a very special time.'

When he turned towards her and pressed his lips to hers, she yielded, and for a few moments she was almost lost. It was he who drew back and whispered, 'No. Much as I long to, I don't want to spoil things. I don't want you to look back on this with regret.'

'Thank you,' she responded. 'I don't want that either.'

After that they didn't speak again until the next morning. It seemed there was nothing left to say. Leo fell into a doze with her head pillowed on his shoulder until he shook her gently and said, 'It's almost dawn. I need to get myself ready for take-off.'

Half an hour later, she watched his plane soar away into the infinite blue of the sky over the Mediterranean.

–

A week followed during which Leo found it almost impossible to concentrate on her work. Then Masterson called her into his office.

'The first part of the plan seems to have gone OK,' he said. 'I've just had a message from HQ. The captain of the sub radioed to say he put them ashore on the twenty-first.'

What followed was a flurry of sometimes contradictory messages. On the twenty-sixth the SOE radio station in

Malta reported that they had received a message from Bill. They had met up with a group of guerilla fighters who had taken them to a nearby village. There were, he told them, 'about a hundred, led by a man called Djilas'. Later messages reported that there were a number of bands of freedom fighters in Montenegro, possibly totalling around five thousand men. On 9 October Leo was instructed to encode a message ordering him to proceed as rapidly as possible to Serbia, to find Mihailovic. More signals had been received from Mihailovic's radio but they were still being sent *en clair* and it was imperative that he should be given new wavelengths and the necessary ciphers.

On 16 October, Bill sent a message saying that the communist groups in the area seemed to him to be better organised than the Chetniks and that they wanted everyone to join together to fight the occupiers. The Nationalists, however, were standing aside and waiting for something. He recommended that support in the way of weapons and supplies should be given to the communists. At the same time, separate signals were being received from the Serbian officers stating that no help should be given to any groups who did not support the Yugoslav government, and that Mihailovic had been told to refrain from any aggressive activities other than sabotage of railway lines and trains, so that the population was not exposed to reprisals.

On 19 October Bill sent a message saying he was setting out to find Mihailovic with an escort of communist partisans.

After that there was silence.

Chapter Sixteen

As the days passed, Alix was regretting more and more bitterly that she had agreed to Nikola's suggestion. He strutted around, puffed up with pride, and made a point of informing everyone that they were engaged. He became increasingly possessive and objected if he saw her talking to another man. When she complained, he insisted that he was only concerned for her good name but she knew it was actually his own standing he was concerned about. She thought back to her row with her father when he wanted her to marry Nikola. Did he have any idea of the character of the man he was trying to tie her to? Surely he could not have wanted her to be treated like this. The memory brought back to the forefront of her mind her anxiety over the whereabouts of her parents. She had heard that King Peter was in London, but that was no guarantee that her mother and father had escaped with him.

The Republic of Uzice was thriving, in partisan terms at least. They were now in control of a large swathe of territory from Montenegro through a considerable portion of the area known as the Sanjak. It was home to more than three hundred thousand people. The local population, while not entirely behind the partisans' cause, seemed prepared to tolerate them. Much of the production of the various industries in the town itself had been turned over to providing essential equipment. The output of the armament factory had been increased and diversified. There was a weaving factory which was set to producing towels and sheets and bandages, and a tailor's shop which was making uniforms, another workshop was producing shoes and boots and there was a bakery to provide bread for everyone. Hydroelectric plants on the river provided power and even the railway continued to function, though over a limited distance. As a final gesture of triumph Tito had installed an illuminated red star on top of the bank.

On 26 September Tito called a conference of leaders from all over the country at the village of Stolice. In her role as reporter for the newspaper, Alix was allowed to attend. On her return she he wrote an account of proceedings.

> *At the request of Comrade Tito, representatives from Macedonia, Bosnia Herzegovina, Croatia and Slovenia gathered in the house of the manager of the Zajaca mine. The principal topic under discussion was the organisation of the Army of Liberation. The General Committee under the leadership of Comrade Tito will henceforth be known as the Supreme Headquarters. Each province will have its General Staff. The main military units will be detachments, and each detachment will be divided into battalions which will be composed of companies. Each detachment will be led by a commander and a political commissar. It was agreed that close attention must*

*be paid to discipline, to the gathering of intelli-
gence and to the provision of medical facilities. It
was also agreed that there should be a universally
agreed symbol by which members of the army could
be recognised. This will take the form of a green
titovka cap carrying a badge in the form of a red
star. The meeting concluded with an oath-taking
ceremony in which all present swore to be loyal to
the cause of liberation.*

There was one additional rule. Sexual relations between
partisans were forbidden as it was not considered condu-
cive to corporate morale and a misuse of energies that
should be directed at the struggle. 'If you love someone,'
Tito dictated, 'show it by offering to carry her rifle, or
by sharing your food with him. That is the correct way
between comrades.'

Alix returned to Uzice with a renewed feeling of
optimism. She was part of a much greater movement than
she had at first realised and she had no doubt that the result
must be the liberation of her country from the Nazi thrall.
How it was to be governed when that had been achieved
was not clear, but many of the old ways were going to be
swept away and that must be a good thing.

The next news that reached her, however, put a damper
on her cheerful mood. There had been a partisan attack
on a garrison in the town of Gornji Milanovac in which
ten Germans had been killed and twenty-six wounded.
Following Hitler's decree that for every German soldier
killed a hundred men should be executed and fifty for each
one injured, the local commanders had instituted terrible
reprisals. Local villages had been burned to the ground and
400 men had been shot. Then the killing had moved to the

city of Kragujevac. Altogether over 2,300 men had been executed. The numbers included many Jews, communists, Romany people and at least 144 boys of high school age.

While the massacre roused a burning desire for revenge among the partisans, the local people reacted differently. Alix found herself being spat at in the street.

'It is you people who have caused this,' a woman selling vegetables told her. 'Before you came we lived at peace with the Germans. We didn't bother them and they didn't bother us as long as we obeyed their rules. Now you communists have stirred everything up and you see the consequences. And most of you are not even Serbs. You are Croats and Montenegrins and God alone knows what. You don't belong here.'

Worse news was to follow. Tito called a conference of senior officers.

'The Boche are sending in reinforcements. Several divisions have been recalled from Bulgaria and there has been fighting between some of them and our men on the road between Sabac and Loznica. We have incurred heavy losses.'

Some four or five days later a group of men coming from the direction of Montenegro was stopped by sentries on the road into town. The leader was Milovan Djilas, the man Tito had sent to organise resistance in that area. Alix remembered him from the early days in Belgrade where he had been one of Tito's inner circle, but he had been in Tito's bad books lately because he had backed an uprising that had broken out in August against the Italian occupation force. Tito was angry because he knew the partisans were not yet strong enough to drive them out, and so it had proved. The Italians had counter-attacked in force and the rebels had been broken up and had to take refuge in the mountains. Alix wondered how Djilas would be received.

But it was not Djilas who was the focus of attention as the group made their way towards the centre of the town. To Alix's enormous excitement he was accompanied by a man in the uniform of a captain in the British army. With him was another man in Serbian army uniform.

The visitors were taken to Tito's office in the bank and the rest of the council were summoned. Alix lurked in a corner with her notebook as usual. Though she appeared to be taking notes, her attention was focussed on the new arrival. He was taller by several inches than the Montenegrins who accompanied him, with broad, muscular shoulders and an athletic bearing. He was good-looking, with a strong face and sharp, observant eyes.

Tito welcomed his old friend with an embrace, then looked beyond him at the stranger. 'Who is this?'

Djilas drew the big man forward. 'Comrade, I present to you Captain Bill Hudson. He is English and his government has sent him to see what we are doing to free ourselves from the Nazi occupiers. And this is Major Ostojic of the Royal Yugoslav Army.'

Tito offered his hand and welcomed them both and the Englishman replied in fluent Serbo-Croat. More chairs were brought in, everyone was seated and the slivovitz circulated. At that point Tito noticed Alix, who had made herself as small and inconspicuous as possible.

'Ha!' he exclaimed. 'Captain Hudson, you have a fellow countrywoman here.'

Hudson turned and took her in for the first time. 'You're English?'

'Half English.' Alix felt herself flushing as the attention of the whole gathering focussed on her. 'My father is a Serb but my mother is English.'

Hudson's gaze took on a sudden intensity, but Tito's attention had moved elsewhere. 'So, tell us how you got here. What have you been doing in Montenegro?'

'We were landed by submarine,' Hudson told him. 'Some of your men were watching the coast. They took us to a local village and from there we were able to make our way inland until we met up with these gentlemen here,' he said, indicating Djilas and his colleagues.

'And why has your government sent you?' Tito asked.

'We had heard rumours that there were insurgents who were rising up against the Italians and the Germans. My people want to know the strength of these movements, with a view to possibly offering support.' He took a sip of slivovitz. 'To be honest, we had no information about your group. But I must tell you I have been extremely impressed by the discipline and organisation of the communist detachments I have encountered.'

Ostojic spoke for the first time. 'We do, however, know about the Chetnik forces raised by Colonel Mihailovic of the Royal Yugoslav Army. He is the official representative of the government in exile and it is to find him we have been sent.'

Alix noticed that Hudson cast a glance at his companion and she read a hint of exasperation in it. She could understand why. To make it so obvious that Tito and his men were regarded as less important struck her as tactless if nothing worse.

Tito, however, accepted the interjection with equanimity. 'I have already met with Colonel Mihailovic. In fact we have another meeting planned for the twenty-sixth.'

'Do you see any possibility of co-operation between your two forces?' Hudson asked.

Tito lifted his shoulders. 'It's possible. We are conducting joint operations now. But ultimately our aims are so different I do not see how that can be sustained.'

'Surely your ultimate aim must be to free your country from enemy occupation,' Hudson said.

Tito smiled. 'That is the immediate aim. The ultimate goal is something rather different.' He rose to his feet. 'But come. You are all tired after your journey. We must find you somewhere to sleep and then you must eat. We will talk again when you are rested.'

Major Ostojic left for Ravna Gora the next morning with a guide and a small escort, but Hudson remained for further talks with Tito. He left two days later and to Alix's frustration there had been no opportunity for a private meeting.

Nikola came to find her looking more pleased with himself than ever.

'My battalion has been appointed as personal escorts to Tito. That means we shall be going with him to Brajici, for the meeting with Mihailovic.'

'Congratulations,' Alix responded less than enthusiastically.

'You'll be going too, won't you? So I'll be there to look after you.'

'You mean to keep an eye on me,' she said. 'I don't need you to look after me. I can take care of myself.'

'Now, now,' he chided her, as if speaking to a recalcitrant child. 'You know we agreed that you will be safer under a man's protection.'

She shook her head wearily. They had had this conversation too many times. 'Yes, all right. You'll be there. Satisfied?'

He looked wounded. 'You know I'm only thinking of you. Don't be angry with me. Come on, give me a kiss.' He moved towards her, reaching to put his arms round her.

'No, not here!' she said. 'I'm working. Anyone could come in.'

'So what? In the eyes of the world we are engaged. What's wrong with an engaged couple kissing?'

To Alix's relief Milovan Djilas came into the office. 'Comrade Tito has asked me to take over as editor of *Borba*,' he said. 'I thought we should go through what we're putting in the next edition.'

Alix was not sure how to react to this. She had never had a chance to get to know him well while they were in Belgrade. He was extremely handsome and she knew he had a reputation for bravery, but he had always struck her as a rather gloomy character.

Two days later she left with Tito and his entourage for Brajici, a small town in the foothills below Ravna Gora. This time the meeting was to be held in the local school rather than the peasant cottage of the previous occasion, and each leader was permitted to bring two advisers. As before, Mihailovic and his company had arrived early and were already inside, but Alix saw Bill Hudson looking out of one of the windows. She wondered if there might be a chance to speak to him, to find out what his reception by the Chetnik leader had been like. Tito went in with Rankovic and Milovan Djilas, and the rest of them were told to wait outside. It was a perfect autumn day, one on which to treasure the last warmth of the sun before the onset of winter. On the hills above the town, the trees were gold and bronze, and nearer at hand in the orchard belonging to the schoolhouse, a few apples too high to pick glowed scarlet against the blue of the sky. The grass below them was strewn with windfalls and Alix picked up two. One she ate, the other she fed to her horse. The men of the escort tethered their mounts and found places to sit on a fallen log or the grassy bank above the road. Even Nikola seemed relaxed. He came over to talk to her and for once they chatted without acrimony.

An hour passed. Then the door opened and Tito and his two companions came out. Nikola moved away to call his troops to attention. The door opened again and two more men came out. One of them was the one Alix had glimpsed at the last meeting and thought she recognised. He was wearing a sheepskin jacket but underneath that she saw the unmistakable blue trousers of the British Air Force. Impulsively she moved forward and at that moment he turned towards her. He had a full, dark beard but it was the eyes she recognised.

'Steve? It is you, isn't it?'

'Alix! You! How? What...'

The exclamations were simultaneous. 'Steve! I thought I recognised you. But how did you get here?'

'I can't believe it! What on earth are you doing here?'

'Are you all right? You weren't wounded? It's so wonderful to see you again!'

'I never imagined...'

The words still tumbled over each other and instinctively they moved together. Then a hand grabbed Alix's arm and jerked her violently backwards.

'What do you think you are doing!' Nikola yelled. 'How dare you talk to this stranger? Come here!'

She swung round, fighting to get out of his grip. 'Let me go! You brute, let go of me!' Over her head he shouted, 'This woman is spoken for! Get away from her. Bugger off!'

She beat her hands against his chest, still yelling, 'Let go! Let go!'

Steve started forward, his fists bunching, but at the same instant the door of the house slammed open and Mihailovic came out.

'No more! I've had enough! Get your horses. We're leaving.'

Nikola was still shouting. 'Get back, damn you. This is my affianced bride, not some slut you can pick up for your amusement.'

Steve stopped, as if frozen in place, an expression of incredulity on his face. Then he shook his head and turned away.

There was a general rush as his companions mounted up. Alix twisted out of Nikola's grip in time to see Steve swing himself into the saddle.

'Steve!' she shouted after him, but he was already following the others as they rode at a smart canter out of the village.

'Who was that?' Nikola demanded. 'Come on, you little whore, who is he?'

Alix stood quite still and looked at him. She had been called a whore once before, by Raoul all those months ago. It was not true then and it was not true now, but the memory struck a chill into her heart.

Men from Nikola's company had gathered round, watching with fascination. Alix drew herself up.

'You have no right to call me by that name. You have no rights over me at all. We are not engaged. We never have been. I rejected you once and I do so again now.' She looked around the circle. 'Hear this, all of you. This man is not betrothed to me. I want nothing to do with him.'

She turned away and mounted her horse and as she rode away, she heard him trying to laugh it off. 'Women, eh? What can you do with them?'

—

Drago found her an hour later in a small back room at the newspaper offices leaning over the desk with her head pillowed on her folded arms. He knelt beside her and touched her hand.

'I saw what happened. That man is a swine. I am going to kill him.'

She jerked her head up and gazed at him with tear-reddened eyes. 'No, Drago! You mustn't even talk like that.'

'Why not? He deserves it.'

'That isn't the point. You would be putting yourself in danger, and even if you thought you could get away with it I won't have you committing murder on my account. Anyway, he's not worth it. I've made it clear that I want nothing more to do with him. That's the end of the matter.'

'You know he is going round telling everyone that you are just playing hard to get? He says the betrothal stands and you will marry at the end of the war, because both your fathers have agreed to it.'

'Well, he's wrong. Nothing would induce me to marry him. I don't care what he says.'

'But you are upset. You have been crying.'

'Not about Nikola.'

'About the young man you were speaking to?'

'Yes.' She sniffed and found a pocket handkerchief to wipe her eyes. 'He is someone I used to know when I lived in Paris. He went away to volunteer for the RAF and we lost touch. It was a shock to meet him again so unexpectedly.'

'What is his name?'

'Steve. Stefan, really, but I always knew him as Steve.'

He looked into her eyes. 'You were in love with him?'

'No. Well, perhaps I was. I could have been if we had had more time together.' She forced a smile. 'It was a long time ago.'

'So why were you crying?'

'Oh, I'm upset because of what Nikola did. I should have liked to talk to Steve, find out what he's been doing, how he comes to be here, working with Mihailovic. Now he's gone away thinking I am engaged to another man and I may never see him again.'

'There may be another meeting. He might be there.'

She shook her head. 'I don't think so. The meeting went badly. Tito thinks it would be a waste of time.'

Drago sat back on his heels, thinking. 'You could write to him. I saw the Englishman there. If he comes back here, you could give him a letter to pass on.'

Alix's face brightened. 'That's an idea. I presume Captain Hudson is here as some kind of go-between and I'm sure he would pass on a letter.' She laid a hand on Drago's shoulder. Now that she had guessed his real feelings for her she was deeply touched by his undemanding loyalty. 'You are a true friend, Drago. I'm lucky to have you.'

He took her hand and kissed it. 'You know I will do anything for you. You have only to ask.'

Looking at his honest, open face and the devotion in his eyes, it occurred to her that it would be very easy to lean down and kiss him, to give him the kind of love he longed for. But instinct told her that that would only end in heartbreak for both of them. She stood up and pushed the hair out of her eyes.

'I'd better go and tidy myself up. Djilas will want a report of some kind for the paper.'

'How will you know what to write? You weren't there.'

She shrugged. 'I'll be told. Tito will decide what the official line is.'

Chapter Seventeen

Ravna Gora, October 1941

A hundred yards outside Brajici, Steve pulled his horse to a standstill and looked back. He had a strong urge to return and challenge the man who had so brutally ended his conversation with Alix, but after a moment he thought better of it. The man had said Alix was 'spoken for'. He had called her his fiancée. If he went back it would only start an argument, maybe even lead to a fight. He had no right to interfere in Alix's private life. He was amazed to see her here, but after all this was her country. Obviously she had decided to go home rather than stick out the war in Paris; but why was she working for the communists? Then he reminded himself that she had had a communist lover when they first met, and when it had come to a choice between them she had chosen to stay loyal to him. Thinking of it like that, he wondered why he had cherished such fond memories of her for so long. He kicked his horse forward and rode away.

Mihailovic, when he caught up with him, was involved in an angry argument with Hudson.

'The meeting was a waste of time! I have had messages from our government in London appointing me as commander in chief but Tito refuses to accept that. He offers co-operation but will not desist from his attacks on German garrisons. He must accept my authority.'

'Perhaps,' Hudson suggested, 'the meeting might have been more productive if I had been allowed to take part. Tito was prepared to accept that. It was you who banished me to another room.'

'Why should I trust you, after you have been spending time with that communist rabble?'

'Colonel Mihailovic,' Hudson protested, 'my only concern is to see you and the communists working together for the common end.'

'And what, in your terms, is that?'

'To carry the fight to the Germans. To make life as difficult as possible for them, so that they have to withdraw troops from the eastern front in order to keep control over what happens here.'

'And at what cost?' Mihailovic demanded. 'More massacres, like the one at Kragujevac? That is what will happen if Tito is allowed to go on killing Germans. I am beginning to think that he and his communists are a greater danger than the Nazis.'

Hudson said, 'Maybe when I go back to Uzice I can persuade Tito to take a more conciliatory approach.'

Mihailovic turned in his saddle, his eyes flashing with fury. 'I tell you now, if you go back to Tito, or attempt to communicate with him in any way, that will be the end of any relationship between us. I shall regard you as a traitor.'

At that he spurred his horse forward and cantered ahead, putting an end to the discussion.

Back at camp, Mihailovic held a meeting with his closest advisers.

'As you know, my instructions are to make life difficult for the occupying forces by sabotaging rail lines and trains but not to undertake any actions that would bring down reprisals on the civilian population. Most importantly, we are to build forces that will be ready to take over when the liberation comes and to maintain law and order until the legitimate government can be reinstalled. I have come to the conclusion that if we are to fulfil those instructions we must first defeat the communists.'

'You are suggesting that we attack them?' one of the officers asked. 'We do not have the arms or ammunition to do that.'

'I am aware of that,' Mihailovic said. 'I have taken steps to remedy the situation. Some days ago I sent Branislav Pantic and Nenad Mitrovic to speak to Prime Minister Nedic in Belgrade. My message was that in return for weapons we would undertake to rid the country of the communist rabble.'

'You are suggesting we co-operate with the quisling government?' another man asked in disbelief. 'That is tantamount to collaborating with the enemy.'

'There is an old saying that "my enemy's enemy is my friend",' Mihailovic reminded him. 'As I see it, the communists are a greater threat, in the long term, to the restoration of the king and the legitimate government of the country.'

'And what was the result of the meeting with Nedic, sir?' Lieutenant Misic, Mihailovic's ADC, asked.

'They were put in touch with a Captain Matl of German Intelligence and he has agreed to arrange a meeting to discuss the proposition. We are asking for at least five thousand rifles, thirty or more sub-machine guns and twenty heavy machine guns. With those we shall be able to wipe out Tito and his partisans and then we can turn our attention to the Germans.'

Steve had listened to all this with mounting horror. The prospect of collaborating, even temporarily, with the forces of occupation was in opposition to everything he felt he had been sent to Yugoslavia to do. But he did not have the standing among these senior officers to speak up. He left the meeting feeling completely disillusioned.

Later he saw Hudson pacing moodily around the perimeter. There had been no opportunity to talk privately since he arrived so he took the chance to join him.

'Captain Hudson? We haven't been formally introduced. My name is Stefan Popovic.'

He spoke in English and Hudson stopped abruptly and looked at him. 'Popovic? That's a Serbian name, but you speak very good English.'

Steve grinned. 'That's probably because it's the language I grew up with.'

'How come?'

'I'm not actually a Serb. My family come from Macedonia but I'm American.'

'American? What the hell are you doing here – and in RAF uniform?'

'It's a long story, but to give you the broad outline, I was in Paris when war broke out. I volunteered for the RAF and got shot down and picked up by the Boche. I managed to escape and made my way back to the UK where I came to the attention of a chap who runs a pretty secretive organisation devoted to sending agents to work behind enemy lines. Knowing I speak the language, he sent me here.'

'You're a secret agent?'

'Actually, no. I was sent here officially as a British liaison officer. When the balloon went up last April I chose to throw in my lot with Draza Mihailovic rather than risk being caught by the Nazis again. Now I work as his radio operator.'

'Well, that's quite a story. And you're just the man I need to talk to. I've brought new ciphers and wavelength information so you can communicate with Cairo. You've been sending your messages *en claire*. Why is that?'

Steve explained about the loss and recovery of his radio set. 'So I got the set back, but the farmer who had it had fed the cipher information to his pigs.'

'Your first message was very weak. It's lucky it was picked up at all.'

'That's because the battery was virtually flat. But we've managed to improvise a way of boosting it.'

'How?'

'Come and see.'

He took Hudson to his cabin and stood back with a wave of his hand.

'Good God!' was Hudson's reaction.

Ranged across one wall was an array of torch batteries which were all connected up and finally connected to the radio set.

'And it works?'

'After a fashion. They can read the signal in Malta now. But you must have your own set, surely?'

Hudson shook his head. 'Sadly, no. When we left Montenegro my set was left behind with the other Yugoslav officer I arrived with. He promised to bring it when he came to join us but he hasn't arrived yet. Tito wasn't keen to let me use his set, so I'm relying on yours to keep in touch.'

'OK,' Steve said. 'We'll just have to do the best we can.' He hesitated, wondering if he should take the Englishman into his confidence about his meeting with Alix, but he was fairly sure that he had not witnessed the encounter. He had still been inside the schoolroom with Mihailovic when it happened. Steve decided that to embark on such a personal story would just be to embarrass them both.

Hudson reached into an inside pocket and withdrew two envelopes. 'Right. In this envelope are the ciphers to be used when you are transmitting messages for Mihailovic. In this one are different ciphers for use on my messages.' He met Steve's eyes. 'I don't want the colonel to know there are two. There may be information I don't want to share. Can I trust you on that?'

Steve hesitated for a moment. The idea seemed disloyal to the man he had accepted as his commander but at the same time his faith in Mihailovic's judgement had been shaken and it was a reasonable guess that ultimately he and Hudson were working for the same organisation. He nodded. 'I understand. You can rely on me.'

Hudson patted his arm. 'Good man.'

Chapter Eighteen

Cairo, October–November 1941

Leo passed the month of October in an agony of suspense. The lack of any radio contact from Bill filled her with foreboding. The only likely explanation was that he had either been captured or killed. Then, on the last day of the month, Masterson came into her office carrying a slip of paper.

'I've just received this decrypt of a message from Mihailovic to Simovic.'

'What does it say?'

'"In the name of God send help while the weather is good. In a short time we could form an Army corps. Ostojic and friends are here."'

'And friends?' Leo caught her breath. 'That must mean Bill, surely?'

'Well, he's using the cipher we gave Ostojic to pass on to him, so he has obviously made it there. I think we can presume that the phrase "and friends" includes Bill.'

'Oh!' Leo felt suddenly weak with relief. 'Thank God!'

'It looks as if Mihailovic is getting ready to go on the offensive,' Masterson said. 'So that's good news.'

'What about those partisan units Bill mentioned in his earlier message?' Leo asked. 'He seemed to think they were better organised and more likely to cause the Germans a problem.'

'Well the obvious answer is for them to be put under Mihailovic's command and create a joint force. Compose a cable to Bill telling him to do everything in his power to bring the two groups together.'

Two days later Leo received a response in Bill's personal code.

> *It is now impossible to establish communication with the partisans. Mihailovic insists that communicating your message will end relations between us. Fighting between Chetniks and partisans broke out yesterday.*

On 9 November they learned that the first air drop of supplies and arms to Mihailovic's troops had been successfully completed.

Bill sent another message suggesting that Mihailovic should be told that there would be no more supply drops unless he came to some agreement with the partisans. He informed them that he intended to go to Uzice to intervene personally with Tito. He also suggested that Moscow should be asked to bring pressure to bear on Tito to agree to place his forces under Mihailovic's command.

Leo was collecting her things ready to leave for the lunchtime break when the door opened and Sasha walked in. She dropped the bag she was carrying and threw her arms round him, almost sobbing with joy.

'How did you manage to get here? Why didn't you let me know you were coming? Oh, it's wonderful to see you!'

He pressed her close and nuzzled his face into her hair. 'It's marvellous to see you too, my darling.' Then he held her at arm's length and looked at her. 'How are you? You look well.'

'I'm fine,' she assured him. 'How about you?' It seemed to her the lines round his eyes were deeper than before, and his face was paler.

'I'm well, thank you. Much better for getting away from London.'

'What's wrong with London?'

'Well, the weather for one thing. I forgot how dreary November can be in England.'

'Well, you'll have the opposite here,' she assured him. 'At the end of the week you'll be longing to feel rain on your face.'

'I shan't care about the heat, or anything else, as long as I'm with you,' he said.

'I can't get over you just walking in like this. Why didn't you let me know you were coming?'

'I got a call saying there was a spare seat on a plane going to Malta if I could get to Northolt within the hour. Then when I got there someone managed to squeeze me onto a flight to Alexandria. I tried to get a call put through to you from Malta but all the lines were busy.'

She kissed him. 'Well, you're here now. That's all that matters. But you must be exhausted. Come along, I'll show you where I'm living and then if you're not too tired we can have lunch at the sporting club.'

'Sounds wonderful,' he said.

The chef at the sporting club had trained in France and the menu reflected the tastes of the club's clientele of British officers rather than showing any influence from Middle Eastern cuisine. So Leo and Sasha lunched on fillet steak followed by strawberry gateau and washed down with a bottle of Pomerol. Keeping the mood light, Leo entertained her husband with anecdotes about some of the wilder escapades of the officers stationed in Cairo and some of the odd quirks of the personnel manning the SOE office.

After they had eaten, Sasha sat back with a contented sigh. 'That's the best meal I've had in months. Even the best hotels in London are struggling to produce anything edible under rationing.'

Leo nodded. 'I feel guilty sometimes, eating so well, when I know how hard it must be for everyone back home.'

He raised an eyebrow quizzically. 'You still think of England as home?'

'Don't Australians and Canadians still refer to England as "home"? But when I think about our real home, about Kuca Magnolija, my heart fails me. I can't imagine what's going on there.'

He became serious. 'Do you have any up-to-date information about things in Serbia?'

'Only scraps. It seems the Nazi occupation is not quite as onerous as it is in France, by all accounts. They seem to leave most things in the hands of the quisling government under Nedic.'

'I've got one bit of good news,' Sasha said. 'Simovic has had a radio message from Colonel Mihailovic saying he's on the verge of raising an army corps to start fighting back.'

'I know,' Leo said.

'How do you know that?'

Leo shrugged. 'We have our sources.' She knew she could trust Sasha completely, but she had signed the official secrets act and she knew it was forbidden to reveal secret information even to him. It was vital that Simovic and his government did not know that their messages were being read.

'I remember Mihailovic,' Sasha said. 'He's a strong character. If anyone can organise some meaningful resistance it's him.'

'Hmm. Maybe,' Leo murmured.

'You don't agree?'

'It's just that we have a man on the ground out there now and he had met up with another resistance group. They are communists and they are led by a man who is known as Tito. He says that from what he has seen they are far better organised than Mihailovic and his Chetniks and much more active in attacking the Germans.'

'Communists!' Sasha exclaimed. 'We don't want to put our trust in them, for God's sake. They've been banned in Serbia for years.'

'I know,' she said. 'But surely what matters now is promoting active resistance and making life as hard as possible for the occupying forces.'

'That's all well and good, but if we let them get too strong there's no knowing where it will end. Mihailovic is our man. He's a regular army officer and loyal to the king. If this Tito fellow wants our support he will have to put himself under Mihailovic's command.'

'That's the official line from here,' Leo told him, 'but I doubt if it will work. Our man says his men and Mihailovic's have actually come to blows.'

'That fits with what I've heard. Mihailovic's last message said that they were being attacked by the communists and were having to fight them and the Germans. He's begging for more arms and says that if they are forthcoming a lot of the partisans will come over to the Chetniks.'

'Bill says he's trying to arrange a meeting between Mihailovic and Tito to iron things out.'

'Bill?' he queried.

'Bill Hudson. He's our man on the ground. We sent him in a couple of months ago.'

'What's he like?'

Leo fidgeted in her chair. The thought of describing the man she had so nearly fallen for to her husband was very uncomfortable. 'He's a good chap. He's always been a bit of an adventurer, from what I can gather. He has travelled a lot. He's a mining engineer and was working in Croatia when the war started, so he's fluent in the language. I think, we think, he will do a good job.'

Sasha grunted. 'As long as he isn't letting those communists pull the wool over his eyes.'

'I don't think he's likely to do that,' Leo said, and she changed the subject. 'Tell me what's been happening in London.'

'With the government in exile, you mean?' He ran his hand through his hair. 'To be honest, they are driving me insane. Constant bickering and in-fighting. Just at the time when we all need to pull together and support the king. Why do we Serbs always have to fight each other?'

'How is Peter?' she asked.

Sasha's face relaxed a little. 'He's fine. He's gone up to Cambridge as I suggested and I think he is really enjoying it. A chance to behave like an ordinary young man.'

'Sow a few wild oats?' Leo suggested.

He chuckled. 'I shouldn't be surprised.'

Leo stood up. 'Do you fancy a swim, or would you rather go back to the boat for a nap? I've only got a single bed but it's quite comfortable.'

He raised an eyebrow. 'Back to bed sounds a good idea. I don't know about the nap.'

Chapter Nineteen

'We're under attack!'

A courier jumped off his sweating horse and rushed into the bank where Tito had his headquarters.

In the newspaper office, Alix heard the sound of boots running over the cobbles.

'What's going on?'

Djilas left his desk. 'I'll find out.'

He returned a few minutes later.

'It seems the Chetniks have attacked our men outside Loznica. Tito has ordered full mobilisation.'

'The Chetniks?' Alix queried. 'But only a few days ago we were having talks with Mihailovic. I know they didn't go well, but I can't believe they would turn against us without warning.'

Djilas's expression was grim. 'I have the impression that Mihailovic is hardly in control of some of his officers. I've never trusted him, but it's possible some of his men have carried out this attack without his knowledge.'

'How serious is this?' Alix asked. 'Is there any danger they may break through and attack us here?'

Djilas shook his head. 'From what I can learn about them, they don't have the men or the armament to pose a real threat. Tito will see them off.'

He was proved right. By nightfall the battle was over and the troops returned to their barracks. Tito summoned his council.

'We need to teach these Chets a lesson they won't forget. Tomorrow we attack their HQ in Posega.'

Two tense days followed.

Posega was captured and when Tito refused to withdraw, the Chetniks attacked nearby Cacak.

Tito returned triumphant. The Chetniks had been defeated, with heavy losses in men and equipment.

Ravna Gora

Steve was becoming increasingly concerned about Draza Mihailovic's state of mind. He was becoming very secretive, confiding in only one or two of his closest associates, a circle which did not any longer include Steve. Meanwhile, clashes between the Chetniks and the partisans were becoming more frequent and usually the partisans came out on top. One day Draza disappeared on some mysterious errand accompanied only by Branislav Pantic and Nenad Mitrovic. He came back in a filthy temper and Steve overheard him saying, 'Is there no one you can trust? I offered in good faith to destroy the communists if only they would give me the means. I thought I was entering into meaningful negotiations and what did I get? A demand for total surrender! So now we find ourselves fighting the Germans as well as the partisans.'

The next day Draza walked into the hut where Steve had set up his radio.

'You have been transmitting messages from Hudson. Secret messages in a different code.'

'He has asked me to send messages, yes,' Steve hedged. 'It's not surprising that he has his own ciphers.'

'I want to know what he is saying. Come on, you know. You have to encode them.'

Steve hesitated. Hudson had gone away on a tour of inspection of the areas where the fighting between the Chetniks and the partisans was occurring. Steve was reluctant to betray his confidence but against that he had a loyalty to Draza. It struck him that it would be salutary for him to know what Hudson was telling his superiors in London.

'He's very concerned about the conflict between us and the partisans. He feels strongly that we should be combining with them against the Germans. He has suggested that there should be no more drops of arms until that is resolved, otherwise they might just fuel a civil war.'

'I knew I could never trust that man!' Mihailovic exploded. 'And you! I thought better of you. You are no more than a traitor!'

Steve winced. The accusation was too close to what he was feeling himself. 'I am only doing my job to the best of my ability in difficult circumstances. You must remember that I was sent out here as a liaison officer with orders to keep my superiors in London informed about what is happening out here. Captain Hudson works for the same department, so he is my superior officer. It would have been very awkward for me to refuse his request.'

'But there is nothing to stop you alerting me to the content of his messages,' Draza responded.

'I admit I have felt divided loyalties,' Steve said, 'but I am, when all is said and done, a British officer. I know that my bosses in London would be very disturbed if they knew of the negotiations you have entered into with the men who are our real enemy.'

'Are you trying to blackmail me?' Draza asked, his face dark with fury.

'No, I am not. I have not sent any messages on my own account and I will not. I am just trying to point out what an invidious position I find myself in. But if Captain Hudson were to suspect what is going on and tell them in London, that would be the end of any possibility of support.'

Draza began to pace around the hut and Steve saw that his warning had hit home.

He persisted. 'Also I cannot help thinking there is a lot of sense in what Hudson is saying. We should be fighting alongside the partisans against the common enemy. If Hudson could assure his superiors that this is what is happening I think arms drops would be resumed quite quickly.'

Draza grunted. 'I've told you. I don't trust that man. He's too thick with that communist rabble.' He glowered at Steve for a moment. 'Any further messages he sends I want to know about them. Understand?'

Steve shook his head. 'I can't promise that. I've told you why.'

Mihailovic glared at him a moment longer, then he turned and stamped out of the hut.

-

Hudson returned later that same day in time for Steve to hand him a message that had just come in.

'I think this looks hopeful,' he commented.

The message began, *His Majesty's government now consider fight should be Yugoslavs for Yugoslavia, not revolt-led by communists for Russia.* It went on to say that the Soviets were being asked to urge the communists to co-operate with Mihailovic and to 'put themselves unreservedly at his disposal as national leader'. The message concluded by saying that Simovic was to be asked to urge Mihailovic to refrain from any retaliatory action.

'That should resolve a lot of problems, don't you think?' Steve asked.

Hudson grunted. 'Warm words, but will Tito listen? I'm trying to arrange another meeting between the two of them. We shall have to see what that produces.'

Mihailovic's reaction was a great deal more positive.

'At last! Now we can put that upstart Tito in his place. I shall go to the meeting and tell him to his face that this is how it has got to be.'

Chapter Twenty

Uzice, November 1941

It was increasingly clear that the German reinforcements were all in place and they were determined to destroy Tito's Republic. Bombing raids were becoming more frequent and the armaments factory had to be relocated more than once to preserve it. Tito's illuminated red star on the roof of the bank provided an excellent target for the bombers. Messages from the troops guarding the borders told of a large buildup of enemy tanks and artillery.

Alix had been given a room in a house belonging to a widow who was happy to earn some extra cash by renting rooms to Tito's followers. Another room was occupied by Irina, Rankovic's secretary, and soon after their arrival Milovan Djilas had moved in with his wife Mitra. It was during a lull in the bombing that there was a knock at the door. The three women had just finished their evening meal and Mitra went to answer the door.

'It's Nikola,' she announced. 'He wants to speak to you. Shall I ask him in?'

Neither of Alix's companions had witnessed her argument with Nikola at Brandiji and she had simply told them that they were no longer engaged, but she guessed that rumours had filtered back from others who were present.

She got up hastily. 'No. I don't want to talk to him.'

Mitra lifted her shoulders. 'Well, you'd better tell him so yourself.'

Alix grabbed a coat and went out to where Nikola was standing on the doorstep.

'What do you think you are doing here? I told you it's all over between us.'

He drooped his head and gazed up at her from under his eyebrows. Alix was reminded of a dog that had been punished and come slinking back looking for forgiveness.

'Please, Alix. I've come to apologise. I know I behaved badly. It's just that I can't bear the idea of another man coming between us.'

'That's rubbish!' she told him. 'I was simply talking to an old friend who I haven't seen for years. Anyway, what do you mean by "come between us"? You know perfectly well that our engagement was just a matter of convenience. You persuaded me into it to protect my reputation, that's all.'

'You don't understand,' he whimpered. 'It may be a matter of convenience to you, but it is much, much more to me.'

'What do you mean?'

'Don't you realise I'm in love with you? I always have been, ever since our fathers introduced us. I was devastated when you turned me down. Then you disappeared off to Paris and I told myself I had got over it, but when I saw you again I knew at once that you are the only woman I could ever love.'

'That's not what you told me,' Alix said, shaken. 'You said we could just be friends and I accepted that. Otherwise I would have told you from the start that I don't love you and I never could.'

'But why?' he asked. 'Am I so repulsive?'

'No, of course not! Lots of women would find you very attractive. You must know that.'

'But I'm not in love with any of them,' he said. 'Please, Alix, I've said I'm sorry. Can't we pick up where we were a day or two ago?'

She shook her head. 'No, Nikola. That's just not possible. I can't cope with your jealousy. If you are going to behave as you did every time I speak to another man my life would be insupportable.'

'Then if I promise that will never happen again…?'

Alix sighed. It distressed her to see this arrogant young man reduced to this hangdog condition and she felt obscurely guilty. 'Look, if we can just go back to the way things were when we first met again back in the summer. If you can accept the fact that I am a free agent and I can go where I like and speak to whomever I like. That's the only basis for any future relationship I can agree to.'

His face brightened. 'Yes! Yes, anything you say. Just so I can see you sometimes and talk to you.'

'All right, then,' she said. 'We'll see how it goes. But I want you to leave now. I'm not standing out here in the cold any longer.'

'Yes, of course. I understand. Thank you, darling Alix.'

Before she could prevent him he grabbed her hand and kissed it. She stepped back.

'Good night, Nikola.'

'Good night. Sleep well, my dearest.'

She went back into the house and closed the door. She had a feeling that she had been manipulated again into a relationship not of her choosing but she could not see an alternative.

Mitra had tuned the wireless to a Moscow station. The signal was faint and intermittent but it was their only way of finding out what was happening in the rest of the world. As Alix came in, Mitra exclaimed, 'Listen! Just listen to this! They are saying that Draza Mihailovic is leading all the forces of resistance.'

'How can they believe that?' Alix asked.

'It must be propaganda from the Yugoslav government in exile.'

'It's so unfair!'

Mitra shrugged her shoulders. 'What do you expect?'

Djilas arrived from talking to Tito at the bank.

'Mihailovic has agreed to another meeting,' he told them.

'Where? When?' Alix asked.

'At Cacak, on the twentieth.'

'Can I go?' Alix's heart was beating fast.

Djilas shrugged. 'I don't see much point. Last time he refused to let any witnesses in to the discussions.'

'Things might be different this time. He must be ready to compromise, surely, if he's agreed to more talks.'

'Well, you can go along with the others if you like, but I doubt if you will learn anything,' Djilas said.

Alix spent the intervening days in a state of suppressed excitement. This time there would be nobody to stop her talking to Steve. She longed to know what he had been doing since they parted two years earlier. She found herself remembering fondly their meetings at Chez Michel and their walks back to the college where she was living afterwards. She remembered his kisses and the way he never pressed her to go any further than she felt comfortable with. What misguided loyalty had made her stay with Raoul when she could have been with Steve?

Now they seemed to be on opposite sides of a conflict that was nothing to do with either of them. Was it too late to pick up where they left off?

Chapter Twenty-One

Steve was looking forward to the meeting with mixed feelings. There was a good chance that Alix might be there but he was not sure if it would be wise to try to speak to her. How she had managed to get herself engaged to that brute he failed to understand, but he had no wish to make life difficult for her. He reminded himself of his earlier recollection that she had chosen Raoul rather than himself, but then he remembered the affectionate letters they had exchanged while he was training with the RAF. In all the months since, and through all the many crises and adventures he had experienced, he had always kept a fond memory of them. Even during his affair with Yvette in Brussels, the thought of Alix had never been far from his mind. It would be good to catch up, even if there was no chance of resuming their former relationship.

Mihailovic and his aides, together with Captain Hudson, were preparing to set off for Cacak. Steve shouldered his rucksack and picked up his rifle and went to join them.

Mihailovic turned to him. 'No point in you coming. If there is anything to report I'll tell you when we get back.'

Steve understood that he was being punished for his collaboration with Hudson. There was nothing he could do but return despondently to his radio hut.

They came back a few hours later and Mihailovic's face was grim. It was Hudson who came to the hut to explain the situation.

'It's a truce of sorts but I can't see it lasting. The partisans refuse to accept Mihailovic as commander and insist on keeping their own structure and organisation. They say they have no faith in the Yugoslav military after the way they collapsed during the invasion and I can't say I blame them. I think Draza has all the qualifications to be a leader. He's intelligent, principled, disciplined, but he hasn't got the strength of numbers to overcome the partisans and if we send him arms to do that there will be a continuing civil war. Right now, the partisans are the stronger group and they will only combine with the Chetniks on their terms.' He sighed. 'OK. Let's get down to composing a signal.'

Over the next few days, messages went backwards and forwards between Simovic and Mihailovic and Hudson and his superiors in an attempt to produce some kind of united front. Simovic seemed convinced that the partisans had agreed to put themselves under Mihailovic's command, while the latter insisted that he had done everything in his power to halt the 'fratricidal conflict' and if he only had enough ammunition he was ready to begin operations against the Germans.

Hudson came into Steve's hut one morning. 'I'm going to make a last attempt to talk sense to Tito. I know Draza won't like it but I think it's worth a try. I don't think the majority of the men supporting Tito are actually communists. Most of them are just peasants who see him as the only person who can protect them and their families.'

Soon after he left, a message came through telling him to pass on the congratulations of His Majesty's government on reaching an understanding with the partisans and promising to send arms and money 'within a week'. But Hudson was not there to receive it and there was no word of when he might return.

Uzice

Alix had watched and waited in vain for any sign of Steve at the meeting and returned with an empty feeling of disappointment. Had he deliberately stayed away to avoid meeting her? It seemed the most likely explanation.

Djilas came into the office. 'Here's the report to go into the paper.'

Alix read: *On the occasion of yet another agreement, the signing of this act is a reflection of the sincere readiness of the leadership of the military Chetnik units to abandon fratricidal war.*

She looked at Djilas. 'Is this what really happened?'

'It's what people need to hear,' was the response.

When Hudson rode into Uzice a day or two later and asked for a meeting with Tito, Alix remembered Drago's advice and wrote a letter to Steve. In it she explained that she was not engaged to Nikola and never had been. She reminded him of the happy times they had spent in Paris and expressed a hope that they might be able to meet again. She sealed the envelope and waylaid Hudson as he came out of the bank.

'Excuse me, sir. Can I ask you a favour?'

'Certainly. I'm happy to help if I can.'

'There's a man working for Mihailovic. I saw him briefly at Brajici but we didn't have a chance to talk. His name is Stefan Popovic and I knew him when we were both in Paris.'

'You mean Steve, the radio operator? He told me he was in Paris when war broke out. Does he know you are here?'

'Like I said, we saw each other but... Well, there wasn't a chance to talk properly. And he wasn't at the last meeting. So could you give him a letter from me when you go back?'

'Of course I will. Who shall I say it's from?'

'Alix.'

He looked at her with that sudden sharpness of focus she had noticed when they first met.

'Short for Alexandra?'

'Yes.'

He came a little closer, studying her face as if he thought he ought to recognise her. 'Would I be right in thinking that your surname is Malkovic?'

An electric shock ran through her nerves. 'How could you possibly know that?'

'Because I know your mother. You are amazingly like her.'

'You've met my mother? Where? In England?'

'No, in Cairo.'

Alix felt her knees might give way. 'My mother is in Cairo? Why?'

'She is working for the same organisation that sent me. Collecting intelligence about what is happening here.'

Alix swallowed. Her heart was pounding. 'And my father? Is he with her?'

'No. He's in London with King Peter.'

219

'So they are both safe?' She reached out to rest her hand on the wall for support. 'I've been so worried. Thank you! Thank you for telling me that.'

He looked around. 'Let's find somewhere we can sit down, shall we? Over there, perhaps?' There was a wooden bench outside a baker's shop on the far side of the road. Hudson led the way to it and Alix sat down gratefully. He took a seat beside her. 'The thing is, your mother has no idea where you are. She thinks you're still in Paris.'

'Yes, I suppose she must. I didn't have a chance to tell her I was coming home. Anyway, I thought she was still in England.'

'She told me she came back to Belgrade a year ago, but of course there was no way she could let you know. But how come you missed each other when you arrived back from France?'

As briefly as possible, Alix related the story of her resistance work in France and the reason for her hasty departure. 'I got back the night the Germans started bombing Belgrade. I went to the country house but my parents were in the city. By the time I got there they'd disappeared. It took me a long time to discover they had left with the king.'

He sat back. 'What an extraordinary story! But you and your ma are two of a kind, aren't you? She told me how she ran away to nurse at the front line when she was no older than you.'

'Younger,' Alix said. 'I've always looked up to her and I suppose tried to follow her example.' She leaned forward. 'She must be wondering what's happened to me. Will you be able to contact her?'

'When I get back to Ravna Gora. Comrade Tito doesn't seem to want to let me have the use of his radio. I've offered to give him the necessary ciphers and wavelengths so he can communicate directly with London and ask for weapons and supplies to be dropped to him, but he seems to prefer to rely on the Russians.'

Alix nodded. 'I'm not surprised. He doesn't trust what he calls "the West". He is very committed to the cause of communism.'

Hudson looked at her with a frown. 'How does that sit with you? Are you a communist?'

Alix shook her head. 'I'm not committed to any party. I just want to see the Boche driven out of my country. I've seen how they behave to conquered people. I hate the thought of it happening here.'

Hudson stood up. 'I'd better get on. As soon as I get a chance I will let your mother know you are here.'

'On second thoughts,' Alix said, 'perhaps it's better she doesn't know. She'll only worry. At the moment I suppose she thinks I'm quietly getting on with my studies in Paris.'

He grinned. 'I'm pretty sure she doesn't see you "quietly getting on" anywhere. She knows you too well for that. I think she will be happy to know you are "doing your bit" here. Let's have that letter, then.'

Alix handed over the envelope and Hudson stowed it away in an inside pocket. She noticed he was wearing simple peasant clothes.

'What happened to your uniform?' she asked.

'Makes me too much of a target. I think I'm better off just merging into the background,' he said.

-

Late in the night they were all shaken out of their beds by a huge explosion.

Alix rushed out of her room and found Mitra standing at the window looking out onto the street.

'It's the powder store and the factory!' she exclaimed. 'Dear God! Now what are we going to do?'

Tito called a meeting.

'There was no bombing last night, so I suspect sabotage. We are no longer welcome here. But the cause is immaterial. The fact is that the German tanks are on our doorstep and we do not have the means to repel them.'

'What are we going to do?' Rankovic asked.

'We shall have to evacuate the city. We shall head for Bosnia. Our first rallying point will be on Mount Zlatibor. The walking wounded will leave today. The rest will follow as soon as practicable.'

He proceeded to allot specific commands to his lieutenants and give instructions about the order of evacuation. No one argued. It had been obvious for some time that they could not stand up against the sort of onslaught the Germans had mounted.

A period of frantic activity followed. Supplies and equipment were loaded onto trucks, including the printing press and several boxes of silver from the bank's vaults. Alix was busy packing up paper and ink and burning files containing compromising or secret material. As she worked she could hear the drone of enemy aircraft overhead and the sound of shells exploding. At intervals she was aware of the tramp of feet as another detachment left for the mountains.

Towards evening Djilas came into the office.

'Alix!' he exclaimed. 'What are you doing here?'

'Packing up,' she said.

'You should have gone hours ago. There won't be any chance of producing a newspaper under these circumstances.'

'Gone where?'

He looked for a moment at a loss. 'You should go home, back to Belgrade. You will be safe there.'

'How can I?' she asked. 'And anyway, I don't want to. I want to go with you and Comrade Tito.'

After a brief hesitation he came to a decision. 'Very well. You had better attach yourself to Tito's personal guard. Nikola will take care of you.'

Alix opened her mouth to say that she had no wish for Nikola to take care of her, but the realisation came to her that she needed to join an organised detachment of some kind, and there was the compensation that she would also have the company of Drago.

'Very well,' she agreed.

'Go now and collect whatever you need,' Djilas said. 'Only what you can carry. We have a long march ahead of us.'

Alix crammed a rucksack with thick socks and extra clothing, and added a toothbrush and some basic sanitary items and a packet of biscuits that had been left on a shelf in the kitchen. She pulled a blanket off one of the beds, rolled it up and strapped it to her pack. At the last moment she remembered to add a bottle of water. She had just finished when she heard a hammering on the door.

Drago stood outside. 'They told me you were still here. You should have been evacuated hours ago. Come along. I've been sent to fetch you.'

She pulled on her warm coat, shouldered the rucksack and thrust her gloved hand into his.

'Right, big brother, we're off on another adventure!'

Chapter Twenty-Two

Ravna Gora, 4 December 1941

The German offensive was drawing in on Ravna Gora, too. It would not be long before the plateau was surrounded. Steve gathered with the other officers in Draza Mihailovic's hut.

'What are we going to do?' Pantic asked. 'We have lost too many men. If we hold out here we shall be wiped out.'

'My efforts to come to some agreement with the enemy have come to nothing,' Draza said heavily, 'and the perfidious British have failed to send us more arms.'

'So I have a suggestion,' Pantic said. 'We should go underground. We should attach ourselves to Nedic's gendarmerie. That way we would legalise ourselves and we could continue to fight the partisans with weapons supplied by Germany.'

'That is collaboration,' another officer objected.

'The purpose of the gendarmerie is to maintain law and order and to look after the well-being of the population,' Pantic said. 'They are loyal to the king and hate the communists. In that respect our aims are the same.'

'But they take their orders from the German military commander,' someone else interjected. 'How can we ally ourselves with them?'

'What's the alternative?' Pantic persisted. 'Stay here and die?'

The argument continued for some time, growing increasingly heated. Steve noticed that Draza said very little. He looked defeated and at a loss. At length, he stirred himself.

'It is for each of you to make his own decision. I am not prepared to collaborate to that extent but those of you who wish to join Nedic's force have my permission to do so.' He stood up. 'The meeting is over. We will talk again in the morning.'

When Steve woke next day he was aware that the sounds he was used to hearing as the company roused itself for a new day were absent. Going to the door of his hut, he saw that the camp was almost deserted. A short walk around the area confirmed the impression. Before dawn almost all the officers who had spoken in favour of Pantic's proposal the night before had departed, presumably for Belgrade.

'What now?' he asked Draza.

'We withdraw into Bosnia,' was the answer. 'We must go underground until circumstances are more favourable.'

Mount Zlatibor, 3 December

Alix lowered her pack to the ground and stood, drawing deep breaths of the icy mountain air. She had never been so tired. Nikola's battalion, with Tito at its head, had left Uzice as the winter darkness closed in and the sound of German tanks echoed through the streets. They had almost been cut off by them as they marched out along the road to Zlatibor and they had come under rifle fire from an infantry battalion not more than one hundred and fifty yards away. For the first time in her life Alix heard the whistle of bullets and cries as some of them found a target. Drago, still at her side, pulled her towards him, sheltering her with his own body. Luckily for them, the firing was haphazard and they were soon out of range. After that it was a matter of plodding onwards and upwards as the air grew colder and thinner and the first snowflakes fell. More than once Drago had offered to carry her pack but she had refused. Nevertheless, she was reminded of Tito's dictum about love between partisans.

At last, when she felt her legs would carry her no further, they had arrived at a small cluster of huts in a fold of the hillside where some of those who had left earlier were waiting for them, under the command of Djilas and Rankovic. She had seen the two men embrace Tito with tears of relief and understood how close she and the others with her had come to being captured.

'How far have we come, do you think?' she asked Drago.

'Must be twenty miles,' he responded.

All around them men were sinking down on their packs and gulping from their water bottles. Alix did likewise and Drago hunkered down beside her. She looked round for Nikola, but he was engaged in a tense conversation with the other commanders.

After a few minutes he came back and called out, 'On your feet, men. Comrade Tito says the enemy are still close behind us. We cannot rest yet.'

'He expects us to walk further?' Alix exclaimed incredulously. 'I don't think I can.'

Drago pulled her to her feet. 'You must. You can't let yourself be left here. If the Germans don't get you the wolves will.'

How she endured the next hours Alix was never sure. After the first mile or so she lapsed into a dream-like state where she was conscious of nothing but the need to place one foot after another. Her toes and fingers were numb and every muscle ached. This time, when Drago offered to carry her pack she accepted, and towards the end it was only his arm around her shoulders that kept her upright.

Eventually they reached the village of Drenova, sheltered from the worst of the weather in a valley, and Tito called a halt. Drago guided her to a little wooden house where she found several female *partizanke*. There was one room which smelled strongly of goat droppings and a loft area reached by a ladder. Three other women were already up there, rolled in blankets and fast asleep. An old lady gave her a bowl of turnip soup and as soon as she had drunk it she hauled herself stiffly up the ladder. The others were lying close together for warmth. In other circumstances it would have been unimaginable to lie so close to strangers, but she was past caring for such niceties. She wrapped herself in her blanket, snuggled close to one of the others and fell asleep.

Next day word went round that Tito had decided it was safe to remain here for the time being. They were now in the Italian sector so the German pursuit would have been called off and the general feeling was that the Italians were unlikely to bestir themselves to attack.

Alix spent most of the morning sitting on a stool close to the fire huddled in her blanket. The old woman who owned the house seemed quite happy to let her be, and the others had gone to rejoin their comrades. Drago called in to make sure she was all right but he had his duties to perform and could not stay. At noon Nikola came to find her.

'Ah, here you are. Thank God! What's wrong? Are you ill?'

Alix shed her blanket and got stiffly to her feet. 'No, just tired.'

He shook his head reprovingly. 'You should have gone back to Belgrade. This is no place for a gently brought up girl. I would have been there to help, but, you understand, I have my duties as a commander. I sent Drago to look after you. I hope he carried out my orders.'

'He was magnificent,' she said. 'I wouldn't have got here without him.'

Her whole-hearted endorsement did not please him but all he could say was, 'Well, good. Now, is there anything you need?'

'No, thank you. I'm fine.'

'Well, then…' He dithered. 'I'd better get on. Have a good rest. We may have to move on again soon.'

When he had left, Alix found herself comparing his abject appeal during their last conversation with his condescending manner now. It was a case of role reversal. Now she was the one in need of help and support and he was enjoying his position as a commanding officer. It was not comfortable and she was determined not to show any further weakness.

He had not been gone long when Mitra Djilas came in. There was nothing in her manner to suggest that she had just undergone a gruelling overnight trek and Alix recognised that she was truly a seasoned campaigner.

'Alix, are you all right? I only just heard you were here. I thought you had been sent back to Belgrade.'

'I couldn't bear the thought of leaving you all,' Alix said.

'Well, good for you! Now, what are you doing here? Milovan and I are with Tito in the headman's house. You'll be more comfortable there.'

'Are you sure?' Alix queried. 'I don't want to be in the way.'

'Nonsense. We'll find a corner for you. I don't think Tito knows you are still with us. Come along.'

The headman's house was still little more than a cottage but it had more than one room and in the living area a table was spread with dishes of stew and loaves of flat bread. Tito and Djilas and Rankovic were sitting round it, together with Irina, Rankovic's secretary, and Zdenka, Tito's mistress.

'Who's this?' Zdenka demanded.

Tito rose to his feet, exclaiming, 'Alix! My flame-haired good luck talisman! I thought we had lost you. Come and join us.'

With a good meal inside her, Alix felt better and made herself useful clearing the table and helping to wash up. The three men were discussing their next move.

'We should make for Foca,' Tito said. 'Our detachments in eastern Bosnia have established themselves in that area and cleared out most of the opposition.'

'Will the Italians let us pass?' Rankovic asked.

'In my experience the Italians want as little trouble as possible,' Tito said. 'They haven't given our people in Montenegro much to worry about.'

'There's no proper road from here on,' Djilas said. 'Only mule tracks. We shan't be able to take the trucks.'

'That's true,' Tito acknowledged. 'Can we buy mules?'

'We can try but I think the local people won't be keen to part with them.'

'Then we must carry what we need.'

'What about the wounded?' Mitra asked. 'Do we leave them here?'

'We never leave our wounded,' Tito said. 'You know that. Those unable to walk will have to be carried. Tomorrow we must think about constructing stretchers.'

'And the silver?' Rankovic asked.

'Divide it up between the strongest men. They will have to carry it. We need that money.'

The headman's wife, Sara, was heavily pregnant, so big that any movement was an effort.

'If you ask me, it's twins,' Mitra said. 'And any day now, I should think.'

Two days passed, during which Alix's stiffened muscles began to ease and she began to feel more herself. She had washed her underclothes and some of Mitra's and was hanging them out in the cottage garden when Captain Hudson called her name.

'I've decided to make my way back to Ravna Gora so I just wanted to say goodbye.'

'Are you going on your own?' she asked. 'Won't that be dangerous?'

'I don't see why.' He made a gesture that encompassed his peasant garments. 'I'm just a harmless shepherd wandering the hills in search of a lost sheep. No threat to anyone.'

'Well, I wish you the best of luck,' she said.

'I promise I'll deliver your letter as soon as I get a chance,' he said. 'And once I'm back in radio contact I can let your mother know where you are.'

Alix felt a lump in her throat. 'Yes, please do that. And give her my love. Make sure she knows I did come home. It was just rotten luck that I was a few hours too late.'

'I'll tell her, don't worry,' he promised. 'And I'll tell her she has a daughter to be proud of. Just take care of yourself. Perhaps we'll meet again sometime.'

'I hope so.' On an impulse she reached up and kissed his cheek. 'Goodbye. Good luck.'

She had just gone to bed that night when she was awoken by the screams of a woman in pain. Coming out of her room, she ran into Mitra.

'It's the twins!' she said. 'Sara has gone into labour.'

'Can I help?'

'Get some water boiling. Baldo has gone for the midwife.'

Baldo was the headman's name.

Alix had never attended a birth before and by midnight she was convinced that she never wanted to have children of her own. The midwife was an old crone with lank hair and grubby hands and it was Mitra who insisted that she should wash them and that everything should be sterilised with boiling water. The labour seemed to go on for ever, but at last, first one baby, a girl, and then the second, a boy, were safely delivered. By the time they had been cleaned and wrapped and laid in their mother's arms and the bloodstained sheets had been changed, it was almost dawn.

Alix stumbled off to bed in the little attic room she had been given but she had only just fallen asleep when she was brought abruptly back to consciousness by a hammering on the door of the house.

'The Italians!' someone was yelling. 'They are almost upon us!'

Men's boots clattered on the stairs. Alix, coming out of her room, saw Tito with shaving foam still on his cheeks and a sub-machine gun in his hands run for the door. Her heart thumping, she grabbed the clothes she had just taken off and ran downstairs. As she did so she heard gunfire echo round the village. In the lower room, Mitra grabbed her arm.

'Don't go out there! You'll be shot.'

'But…But Tito,' Alix babbled.

'We must pray he has got away,' Mitra said.

'What can we do?' Alix asked.

'Stay here. It's him they are after. If we're lucky they won't bother with us. Give me a hand here.'

By this time Baldo and Irina had joined them and together they overturned the heavy oak table and laid it across the room facing the door. Mitra had a rifle and Irina was carrying a pistol, while Baldo produced an ancient shotgun. They crouched together behind the table, their weapons trained on the door. Alix crouched with them, feeling useless. If they survived, she promised herself, she would get hold of a gun somehow.

Outside, the shooting continued and they heard shouts in Italian and running feet. A window shattered on the floor above but little by little the noise died away into the distance. When all was quiet, Mitra got to her feet.

'It sounds as though they've gone after Tito. I think we are safe enough here.'

Irina said, 'We'd better go and check on Sara. She must be terrified, poor woman. After all she went through last night…'

'Baldo should go,' Mitra said.

The man made his way upstairs and the women set to right the table. They were stopped by a howl of distress from above.

Alix was first up to the main bedroom where Sara had given birth. In the doorway she stood paralysed with horror. It was the window of this room that had shattered, and the bed below it was bathed in blood. Bruno was kneeling by it, dragging away the blood-soaked sheet that covered his wife's body, sobbing and calling her name.

Mitra shouldered Alix out of the way and bent over the bed. Alix saw her put a hand to Sara's throat, feeling for a pulse. Then she touched Baldo's arm.

'I'm sorry, Baldo. It's no use. She's gone.'

A wail from the corner of the room made them all jump. 'Oh my God!' Irina said. 'The babies!'

She picked one of them up and thrust it into Alix's arms, then turned to pick up the other one. Alix looked down at the small, wriggling, surprisingly heavy bundle and was reminded of the first puppy she had been given as a child.

'What are we going to do with them?'

'We shall have to find a wet nurse. Another woman who's recently given birth and has enough milk to feed two.'

'Three in this case,' Mitra said. 'That's a tall order – unless her own child didn't survive.' She turned to the distraught Baldo. 'Listen to me. We can't save Sara but we have to save your children. Where can I find the midwife who was here last night?'

He mumbled incoherently for a moment but then managed to give directions. 'I'll go,' Mitra said. 'Can I leave you two to clean up here?'

Alix looked out of the broken window. The village street was empty, the residents cowering behind their closed doors. There seemed to be no sign of the Italians.

'I think it's clear,' she said. 'But take care. They may have left someone to watch the house.'

'I'll have to take a chance,' Mitra said, and she went quietly down the stairs.

Irina held out the twin she was carrying. 'Can you manage them both?'

Alix took the other bundle and found it came quite naturally to rock them gently. Both of them had stopped crying and two pairs of amazingly blue eyes gazed up at her trustingly. Suddenly she felt that perhaps motherhood might be worth the suffering she had witnessed.

Irina removed the bloodied sheet and found a clean one to lay over Sara's body. Baldo was kneeling by the bed with his hands folded in prayer.

'What shall we call them?' Alix asked.

'We should call them Slobodan and Slobodanka,' Irina said. 'Freedom.'

Mitra came back sooner than they expected, bringing a woman with her.

'I hesitate to call it luck,' she said, 'but it just so happens that this woman gave birth to a stillborn child two days ago. Her name is Agata. She has agreed to take these two.'

Agata was a stocky woman with muscular arms and legs, the build of a peasant used to hard manual labour, but her shapeless dress could not conceal her flabby, empty belly and her swollen breasts. She looked around at the three strange women in the room, her expression inscrutable, and then focussed on Baldo, who had risen to his feet.

'My condolences. Sara was a good woman.'

He moved towards her. 'And mine for your loss.'

She lifted her shoulders. 'God decided to take my baby to him. I am blessed. I still have my two boys.'

'And you are willing, willing to feed my two?' Baldo asked tremulously.

'It is the will of God. Perhaps that is why he took my little one.'

'And he will bless you,' Baldo replied.

Agata looked at Alix. 'Let me see the little ones.'

Alix held out the two small bundles and Agata took them in her arms, crooning softly. Then she seated herself in the only chair and put the two of them to her breasts. Alix watched, feeling a constriction in her throat, moved and humbled by these simple people's acceptance of the will of God.

Mitra touched Alix on the arm.

'Let's leave them to it. I've arranged with the midwife to see to the laying out of the body. It seems she's responsible for that as well.'

Downstairs they had time to take stock of their own situation.

'Do you think Tito and the rest got away?' Alix asked.

'I'd lay odds on it,' Mitra said. 'He would never surrender and I can't hear any sound of fighting. I think the Italians may have given up.'

'So, what do we do?' Alix asked.

'Wait. If he's still free he will get word to us somehow.'

Irina found some oatmeal and some goat's milk in the kitchen and made porridge for all of them. Two women had arrived and went upstairs to attend to Sara, and Baldo was persuaded to come down and eat something. They had just finished when they heard marching feet and voices raised in a patriotic song.

'They're safe! Thank God!' Mitra said.

Moments later Tito and his two lieutenants came through the door.

'What happened? Where are the Italians? How did you get away?' Several voices overlapped.

'We regrouped up on the hill and fought back,' Tito said. 'It was only a small contingent of Italian cavalry. Once they saw they were outnumbered they wheeled round and galloped off. One of the buggers has stolen my horse, though. And my camera was in the saddlebag.'

Alix looked at him and saw that he was genuinely distressed. She had learned over the weeks that he was a good horseman and cared deeply for his horse.

From upstairs came the wail of a baby.

'What the hell…?' Rankovic asked.

'We've had our own battles while you were gone,' Irina told him.

When Tito heard about Sara's death he embraced Baldo with tears in his eyes. Then he asked to see the babies. The wet nurse brought them down and Tito cradled them in his arms with a tenderness that surprised and moved Alix.

'Slobodan and Slobodanka,' he murmured. 'Well named. May you live free, little ones.'

For the next eight days the forest around Drenova rang with the sound of axes as the partisans cut down trees to provide wood for the construction of stretchers while negotiations went on for the purchase of mules. Alix and the other women were busy sewing bags to carry the silver, and when it proved impossible to distribute all the treasure among the men, a large hole was dug at Tito's command and the heavier items were buried, to be retrieved later. Finally, on 13 December, they said goodbye to Baldo and the twins and a long column of men and women, headed by Tito and his staff with stretcher bearers bringing up the rear, set off along the mountain track heading for the town of Rudo.

Chapter Twenty-Three

Cairo, 1 December 1941

The steady flow of messages from Bill Hudson during November had reassured Leo. Towards the end of the month he signalled that Mihailovic had agreed to recognise the partisans, so it seemed his efforts were bearing fruit.

On the last day of November they intercepted a signal from Mihailovic to Simovic informing him that the partisans had evacuated Uzice and were retreating to Mount Zlatibor. *They are few in numbers and poorly led.*

Masterson flourished the transcript. 'Looks like things are turning out the way we hoped. If the communists are finished, the way will be clear for Mihailovic to turn his attentions to the Germans.'

'But Bill thought the partisans were better organised and a greater threat to the Boche,' Leo pointed out.

'But the last thing we want is for them to take over,' Masterson said. 'Mihailovic is our man, a loyalist fighting for the restoration of the king.'

'Bill says not all the partisans are communists. Most of them are just patriots who have attached themselves to what they see as the most likely people to get rid of the Germans.'

'Never mind that,' Masterson responded dismissively. 'Mihailovic has the backing of the government in exile. He's the man we should be supporting.'

On 1 December, they intercepted another message from Mihailovic. *The morale of my troops remains excellent. Captain Hudson has not returned. He is cut off from us.*

'What do you think that means?' she asked Masterson. 'What has happened to Bill?'

'Hard to be sure,' he replied, 'but it could be that he is with Tito.'

'On Mount Zlatibor?' Leo felt a stab of anxiety. 'From Mihailovic's signal it sounds as if the partisans are being defeated.'

'Bill's no fool. He won't stick around if there's any danger of being captured. My bet is he'll make his way back to Mihailovic as soon as he can.' He gave her a smile. 'Don't worry. I expect we'll hear from him soon.'

Mihailovic's next signal proclaimed that he was now 'at war with the Germans'.

Three days later his message had a very different tone. He was retreating and unable to maintain radio contact or receive further supplies. *I am continuing guerilla warfare as it suits the reality of the situation.*

There was no further message from Bill.

Chapter Twenty-Four

Ravna Gora, 3 December 1941

Mihailovic called his senior officers together.

'All our intelligence points to the fact that the Germans are now mounting a major operation against us. My spies report that there are four columns of tanks and infantry approaching from different directions. We cannot hope to withstand a concerted attack so we must take evasive action. We will break up into small groups, not more than a dozen men, and disperse into the mountains. Meanwhile, Major Jovanovic in Valjevo has been organising a disinformation campaign to convince the enemy that we plan to confront them in strength. Hopefully, this will cause them to proceed more cautiously and give us time to disperse. The Germans will not be able to sustain a prolonged campaign in the remote mountains and if we break up into small units there is a good chance they will sweep through the area without making contact. Once that has happened we can regroup.'

No one disputed his analysis and the Chetniks still in Ravna Gora began to leave a few at a time as he suggested. There were still active units in other areas, particularly the Cer Brigade under the command of Captain Racic south of Valjevo and a smaller unit commanded by Aleksander

Misic near Struganik. Racic was ordered to create a diversion but the rest were given the same order to disperse.

On the fourth a courier brought the news that Misic had decided to confront the advancing Germans.

'The imbecile! Why can't he obey orders?' Mihailovic stormed. 'I shall have to go to Struganik personally to enforce obedience.'

Most of the men at Ravna Gora had already left but Major Ostojic, the agent who had arrived by submarine with Bill Hudson, was still there. He had become one of Draza's closest confidants. Mihailovic summoned three of the remaining men to him.

'Mount up! We are going to Struganik.' He turned to Steve who was hovering nearby, wondering what his orders were to be. 'Get the radio packed up and come with us. We can't have it falling into German hands.'

With the help of one of the other men, Steve dismantled his equipment and packed the radio into its case, shoving the rest into a canvas kitbag. Carrying it out of the hut, he found Mihailovic already mounted. Someone had found a mule and the radio was loaded into its panniers, then Steve scrambled into the saddle of the remaining horse. They were already moving out when one of the sentries who had been left on guard until the last moment shouted to Mihailovic.

'Sir! Captain Hudson is here.'

Steve looked round and saw Hudson waiting at the sentry post. He was in peasant dress and he looked unkempt and worn out.

Mihailovic answered. 'Don't let him pass. I want nothing to do with that traitor.'

'But sir,' came the reply, 'what is he to do?'

'Tell him to go back to his communist friends. We're leaving. If he tries to follow I shall have him shot.'

He spurred his horse forward and the other men went with him. Steve had no option but to follow. His last sight of Hudson was standing gazing after them, an expression of hopeless amazement on his face.

When they arrived in Struganik they were greeted by Misic.

'What are you doing here?' Draza demanded. 'I told you to disperse your men.'

'It's too late,' Misic told him. 'The Germans are upon us. They are driving a large group of civilians ahead of them as human shields.'

'Then we must retreat into the forest and hide until they have passed through,' Draza said.

Already Steve could hear the rumble of tanks on the road to the south. Misic relayed Draza's order and in small groups his men ran for the cover of the trees. Draza and his escort did likewise and Steve dragged the unwilling mule after them. They were only just in time. The roar of the tanks subsided as they came to a halt and a voice on a megaphone shouted an order for the Chetniks to give themselves up. When no one responded the guns on the tanks opened fire.

'The swine!' Misic exclaimed. 'They are firing on innocent civilians.'

'They don't care about that that,' Draza responded grimly. 'They think you and your men are still there.'

'We can't let them devastate the village,' Misic said. 'Those people have been good to us. They have given us shelter and food.'

'Do you see any way to stop them?' Draza enquired ironically.

Misic conferred in undertones with a colleague, Major Ivan Fregl. He then spoke to some of his men. He came back to Draza.

'We will give ourselves up. I shall tell them I am Mihailovic. That will stop the shelling and give you time to get away.'

Draza looked at him for a long moment. Then he embraced him. 'You are a hero. When all this is over your name will be known throughout Serbia.'

Misic freed himself and called Fregl and a small group of others to him. Steve watched in awe as they walked out of the forest with their hands in the air. They were quickly surrounded and hustled away through the ranks of tanks. A command rang out and the shelling stopped.

Mihailovic turned to his companions. 'We must not allow their heroic sacrifice to go for nothing. We must get away from here and find refuge in the mountains.'

It was already late and the winter dusk was falling as they pushed their horses through the undergrowth until they came to a forest track leading uphill.

'This will do,' Draza proclaimed. 'The deeper we are in the hills the better.'

Darkness had fallen and the horses picked their way along the rough track by moonlight. It was bitterly cold and the ice on the puddles along the way gleamed in the fitful light. The bushes beside the track were stiff and rimed with frost, and the horses' breath hung in the air in clouds. Steve huddled into his sheepskin but before long his hands and feet were numb with cold. He was still far from being at ease on horseback and they had ridden hard that day to reach Struganik. His RAF trousers were not designed for riding, and before the dawn spread its chilly light over the mountains his thighs were rubbed raw and every muscle in his body ached unbearably. When they finally rode into the village of Kadina Luka, he had to be helped down from his mount.

The villagers welcomed them and to Steve's great relief Draza declared that they would rest there until the next day. Down below in the valleys they could hear the distant rumble of the German tanks converging on Ravna Gora. Three of the young men of the village agreed to act as scouts and set off through the woods. That evening they returned to say that the tank columns had passed on and the area between the village and Ravna Gora appeared to be clear of them, but they had seen smoke rising from villages in the area.

'I foresaw what would happen,' Draza said. 'They have encircled our camp at Ravna Gora and found it empty. The trap they thought they had set has netted them nothing. Tomorrow we move on to Teocin. From there we can make a reconnaissance and assess the situation.'

They were not welcomed in Teocin. The village headman's greeting, while not actively hostile, was grim in tone and content.

'The Boche came. They drove through here and took some of our people as hostages. When they reached Ravna Gora and found no one there they searched all the surrounding villages. When they found no trace of you or your men there they burned the villages to the ground. There was no reason to do that. It was pure revenge because you had outwitted them.'

Draza sighed deeply. 'I cannot tell you how profoundly I regret that. But what was I to do? If we had remained there we would have been massacred, and the last force to stand up for God and the king would have vanished.'

The headman bowed his head. 'We are simple people. Our loyalty is to God and King. We respect what you are doing but the price is too great.'

'But the Boche have left the area now?' Draza asked.

'Yes. They reformed their columns and moved off to search elsewhere.'

Draza gathered his small group together. 'We shall return to our headquarters at Ravna Gora. The Boche will get tired of searching and finding nothing. The men who have dispersed into the mountains will soon learn that the enemy have gone and they will come back to join us. It is time to regroup and reconsider our tactics.'

Chapter Twenty-Five

Cairo, 7 December 1941

The Cairo office was thrown into uproar by the news of the attack by the Japanese on the American naval base at Pearl Harbour.

'Surely the Yanks can't go on sitting on the fence any longer,' Masterson exclaimed. 'They will have to declare war now.'

The next day he was proved right and there was a general cheer at the news.

'Hitler's bitten off more than he can chew on the eastern front,' Masterson said. 'Now with the Yanks on our side we shall be able to take the fight to him in Europe.'

On the same day they had also intercepted a signal from King Peter to Mihailovic proclaiming him supreme commander of Royal Yugoslav Forces in the Homeland and promoting him to brigadier general.

A few days later Masterton thrust a copy of a magazine onto Leo's desk.

'Look at this! *Times Magazine* has named Mihailovic as the most popular general after MacArthur.'

'That's amazing,' Leo said. 'I'm surprised they've even heard of him.'

'Well, I guess now that they are in the war with us they are keen to look for heroes to keep the general public onside,' Masterson suggested. 'Anyway, he's anti-communist. That's bound to make him popular.'

'I wonder if they would be quite so admiring if they had seen his last signal to us,' Leo mused.

'It's probably just a temporary setback,' Masterson said.

'I wonder,' Leo responded. 'I wish Bill would get in touch. If Mihailovic is under attack he is in danger too.'

'Give him time,' Masterson said. 'It's only a couple of weeks since we last heard.'

Sasha was still with her, in spite of messages from Simovic requesting his return to London. Shepheard's Hotel was decorated with coloured lights and paper chains to celebrate Christmas but Leo found it hard to summon up any sense of occasion in the dust and heat of Egypt. There were carol concerts in the messes of the various army and air force detachments stationed in the city and an ENSA group put on a pantomime at the Opera House. Leo and Sasha were invited to so many parties, they had to turn some of them down. She tried to enter into the spirit of jollity but she found herself frequently remembering the last Christmas they had celebrated at Kuca Magnolija. Then although most of Europe was enveloped in the turmoil of war, Serbia still existed as a peaceful island in the midst of chaos. But even then their celebrations were not complete. Without Alix there was a terrible gap in the family. Repeatedly she found herself wondering what her daughter was doing. What sort of Christmas could they have in occupied Paris? There seemed to be no shortages in Cairo and as she tucked into roast beef and the local chef's version of Christmas pudding she wondered if Alix was getting enough to eat.

Adding to her unease was the nagging worry about what had happened to Bill Hudson. With every day that passed without any contact the suspicion that he must have been captured or killed grew.

Tom Masterson was finally obliged to agree that something must have gone wrong.

'What can we do?' Leo asked.

'We shall have to send someone else in to try and find him,' he said reluctantly.

'Send me!' Sasha demanded. 'I know the country and I have good contacts there. If anyone can track him down I must have the best chance.'

Masterson shook his head. 'It's not on, Sasha. For one thing, you're too old to learn to parachute, and even if we sent you in by submarine, like Bill Hudson, there would be no one to receive you. We've lost radio contact so there's no way we can organise a reception committee.'

'As I understand it, there was no reception committee for Hudson either,' Sasha said.

'That's true. He was lucky to be picked up by a company of partisans who arranged for him to travel to where Tito was based. At the time there seemed to be good contacts between Tito and Mihailovic. But now it seems that Tito's forces have been dispersed and nothing has been heard from Mihailovic for nearly a month, so I am coming to the conclusion that the Boche have mounted a pretty successful campaign against both of them. For all we know, there may be no organised resistance force left.'

'Isn't that exactly why you need someone on the ground to report back?' Sasha asked, pressing his case. 'You could send someone with me as a radio operator...'

'I could go!' Leo said. 'I can work a radio set.'

'No!' Sasha exclaimed. 'I'm not having that.'

'Neither of you is going,' Masterson said. 'Apart from any other consideration, you are too well known, Sasha. Everyone knows that you are a royalist and you were instrumental in the coup that brought Peter to the throne. That might make you acceptable to the Chetniks, but certainly not to the partisans. The last intelligence we had suggests that the partisans and the Chetniks are now fighting each other. If they haven't been wiped out altogether they have probably been broken up into small groups. You might well fall into the hands of one side or the other. If it was the partisans, if they didn't dispose of you outright they could hold you as a hostage. But the chances are you would be picked up by the Boche, and think what a propaganda coup that would be for them. I'm sorry, Sasha. You are just too high profile.'

Sasha sat back with a sigh. 'So what do you propose to do?'

'We can't just abandon Bill,' Leo said.

'We are not going to abandon him,' Masterson said, 'but it's no good sending someone else in without due preparation, and we have to liaise with the Yugoslav government in exile. I'm working on the idea of sending in two, or possibly three, teams to different areas, but there is nothing definite yet. Meanwhile, don't give up hope. We may get another message from Bill any day now.'

Chapter Twenty-Six

The ragged column of partisans trudged wearily along a track following the bed of a stream that had carved itself a deep ravine. On either side the ground rose steeply to a snow-covered ridge. Here in the valley there was less snow but anyone stepping aside from the rocky path felt ice crackling underfoot. Little sunlight penetrated so deep and the air was bitter. At the head of the column was Tito with the other members of the Supreme Council, followed by the men of the Escort Battalion and then the rest of the army, and bringing up the rear the long line of stretcher bearers carrying the wounded. At intervals the line was broken up by men leading mules loaded with the supplies that kept the army moving. Nikola marched at the head of his troops, with Drago close behind.

Alix was a little further back, with Mitra and Irina. She plodded along with her head down, her face muffled in her scarf so only her eyes were visible. The time since they left the village where the twins had been born had resolved itself into an endless succession of days like this, where conscious thought was reduced to two things: keep warm and keep walking. Over time her muscles had strengthened and she was no longer afraid that she would not be able to keep up with the rest of the column, and there were brief interludes when she raised her head enough to take in the scenery they were passing through, but soon one mountain ridge looked very much like the last, all its features obscured under a blanket of snow. Sometimes she and the other women sang, and occasionally the song was taken up by the men in front and behind, but mostly they did not have the breath to sustain it for the same reasons they did not have the breath for conversation. Where they were going and how long it would take to get there no one seemed to know.

She was jolted out of a semi-trance by several voices raised in a yell of alarm.

'The Boche! They're on us! We're under attack!'

Men were pointing up to the ridge opposite them. Whirling round, she stared in that direction. The snow covering the ground was dotted with small, rapidly moving figures and as she stared, the first bullets whistled overhead.

'They're on skis!' Mitra shouted. 'And we've no cover!'

Tito had halted the column and now he raised his voice. 'Up! Up the ridge. Fast!'

Swinging round, Alix saw what he intended. Down here in the valley they were sitting ducks. The only shelter would be on the far side of the ridge. Already men were scrambling up the cliff, clinging to whatever handholds they could find.

'Come on!' Mitra shouted, and Alix forced herself into action. The rocks were glazed with ice and between them the surface was obscured by snow. Her feet scrabbled to find purchase and her fingers slipped as she grabbed for a handhold, but somehow she pushed herself upwards. As she climbed she heard bullets ricocheting off the rocks on either side. A man above her cried out and fell backwards, missing her by inches. Suddenly she was aware of a shower of tinkling silver pieces falling all round her. It took her a moment to understand what they were. At Tito's orders some of the men were still carrying the bags of silver looted from the bank at Uzice. Now they were casting them aside in the struggle to reach safety.

She ducked her head and scrambled on. The top of the ridge seemed very far away.

Suddenly Drago was there, a few feet above her, reaching down to grasp her hand, and with his help she gained the summit and half fell into the shelter of a rock on the far side.

'Thank you!' she panted. 'My faithful friend.'

He was peering over the top of the rock. 'They're giving up. They know there's no way they can reach us over here.' He gripped her arm. 'Come on. Let's join the others.'

In the lee of a cliff, the column was reassembling and captains were counting numbers. Voices called the names of friends. Often there was an answer, too often there was none. To Alix's relief Mitra and Irina were both there and, miraculously, little by little, the stretcher bearers with their burdens came to join them. How they had hauled them up the cliff under fire Alix could not imagine.

When it seemed the last stragglers had joined them, the column reformed, slanting down the hillside into another valley. Towards evening they came down to a forest of golden pine, a local species from which Mount Zlatibor got its name. The trees here had protected the ground from most of the snow and they walked on a thick carpet of pine needles. As night fell they made camp in a clearing and men collected fallen branches to make fires.

That night, for the first time since they left Uzice, the men began to sing, the haunting, melancholy songs born from generations of struggle against oppressors. After a while some of them raised the energy to form a circle and dance the kolo. Arms linked, feet moving to the rhythm of a tune picked out on a flute, they swayed first one way then the other. It was a simple dance, earthbound, but to Alix, who had seen it danced many times by the men on her father's estate, it had the feeling of a sacred ritual, an affirmation of fellowship. For the first time since they left Uzice, she felt her heart lift.

Three days later they reached Rudo, a little red-roofed town perched above the gorge of the River Lim. The citizens welcomed them. They were mostly Serbs who had suffered at the hands of the Ustashe and were glad of the protection the partisans could offer.

Tito took up residence in the house of the mayor, and the officers and their women found accommodation in the homes of some of the leading citizens. The army bivouacked in the fields around the outskirts. There were 1,200 of them, mostly Serbs, who had come with them from Uzice, and the commanding officer was a veteran of the Spanish Civil War called Koca Popovic. The first time Alix heard that name it sent shock waves through her nerves; but Popovic was not an uncommon surname and she knew it was almost impossible that he could have any connection with Steve. Steve's parents, after all, were the second generation of Popovices to live in Alaska.

The day after they arrived, Tito called a meeting of all his senior officers in the town hall. Alix went along, clutching her notebook. After all, she told herself, there might not be a newspaper at the moment to report the outcome, but one day, perhaps, a record might be valuable.

'Comrades,' Tito began, 'I have decided it is time to make a change to the way our forces are organised. Until now, detachments have been based in the particular locality where they were raised. The men have joined up largely in order to protect their own villages and their own families. Some of them even returned to their homes every night to sleep. When it comes to battle, morale suffers a terrible blow if they are killed in front of their families.' There was a general murmur of agreement. 'There is another point, a more important one,' Tito resumed. 'If we are to free more territory from German or Italian control, and to hold it until peace comes, we must have a large, mobile, disciplined army. The men with us now have followed us away from their homes. I propose to form them into the First Proletarian Brigade. They will be the core of our new army, under the command of Koca Popovic. I have called this meeting to set down the statutes under which this new brigade will function.'

The rest of the meeting was devoted to drawing up those statutes, the first of which stated that 'the proletarian people's shock brigades are the military shock formations of the peoples of Yugoslavia under the leadership of the communist party.'

As the officers dispersed Alix heard Djilas murmur to a friend, 'This brigade is proletarian in name only. True, there are peasants among our ranks, but many are lawyers and doctors and university graduates who have been inspired to join us.'

Listening to the discussion had brought to the forefront of Alix's mind thoughts that had been nagging at her for days. While they were in Uzice she had thought that she did fulfil a useful function in her work on *Borba*, but since they were forced to leave she had felt increasingly useless. As soon as she left the meeting she sought out Drago. Nikola had appointed him as his batman, making him a soldier servant in what Alix recognised was a deliberate attempt to emphasise the difference in their social positions. It infuriated her to see him being ordered to perform menial tasks, but in the circumstances there was nothing she could do about it.

She found him cleaning Nikola's boots. He looked up with a warm smile.

'Drago,' she said. 'Teach me how to use a rifle.'

'A rifle?' He frowned. 'Why?'

'Because I need to be able to fight, like the others.'

'You mean like the *partizanke*? You are not like them. They are peasants, mostly.'

'Mitra is not a peasant. She carries a rifle and knows how to use it.'

'You say you want to fight, to kill people? That's what it means.'

'I know that! But we are in a war. I saw men killed when we were attacked in that valley. We have to fight back.'

'Perhaps you should ask Nikola.'

'Ask Nikola? Why? You know he doesn't have any authority over me.' She moved closer to him. 'Come on, Drago. You taught me to use a shotgun when we were just kids. My father wouldn't have approved, but you did it anyway.'

He sighed and stood up. 'I just don't want you to put yourself in danger.'

'If the Boche attack us, they won't distinguish between people holding guns and those who aren't. At least I would have a chance of defending myself.'

She saw that she had won the argument. He fetched his rifle and they found a place in some woodland on the edge of the river gorge. He had picked up some empty bottles left outside one of the houses and set one up on a convenient tree stump.

'Do you remember how I taught you to fire a shotgun?'

'More or less.'

He showed her how to load the rifle. 'Lie down and use that log to rest the rifle on. Now get the butt tight against your shoulder and look down the barrel. There will be a kick when you fire. Be ready for that. Line up the sights with that bottle and when you're ready squeeze the trigger. Don't pull it. Squeeze it.'

Alix put the gun to her shoulder. It was heavier than she expected. She remembered her original lessons with the shotgun. She was, what? Eleven or twelve. She had been scared, scared of the noise more than anything. She felt the same now, but she lined up the sights and squeezed. The recoil almost knocked her off balance and the bottle remained undisturbed.

'Want to go on?' Drago asked.

It was as if they were back to the days when he had been the big brother she admired and longed to impress.

'Yes.'

On the third attempt she hit the bottle. He made her keep going until she was hitting more than she missed and her shoulder was bruised, but when he finally said, 'Well done! You've got a good eye,' she glowed with pride.

'Now what?' he asked.

'I need a gun of my own.'

'You'll have to ask the armourer for that.'

They found the company armourer putting some new recruits through their paces. A shooting range had been improvised where the army was encamped outside the town, with targets set up against bales of hay. He looked askance at Alix's request but Drago spoke up for her.

'We've been practising. She's not a bad shot.'

'All right,' the armourer said. 'Show me.'

Alix dropped to the ground and put the gun to her shoulder. She felt suddenly confident. She could do this! She aligned the sights and squeezed the trigger.

'There you are!' Drago exclaimed triumphantly. 'I told you she was good.'

The armourer came back from examining the target. 'Very well, comrade. You can have your gun. You are now a member of the First Proletarian Brigade.' He looked at Drago. 'Which company?'

'First company, the Escort Battalion,' Drago said promptly.

'Very good. Report to Comrade Dordevic.'

He walked away and Alix and Drago exchanged glances. 'Is this what you wanted?' he asked.

'It's not what I expected,' Alix confessed. 'But yes. I suppose it is what I want.'

Nikola, when she reported to him, was outraged. He turned on Drago.

'How dare you manufacture this? Have you no respect?'

'It isn't Drago's fault,' Alix said firmly. 'I persuaded him. I need to feel I am part of what we are doing.'

'And you will take orders from me?'

'As my commanding officer, yes. Not as the man I refused to marry.'

He glared at her for a moment, then he turned his back. 'Very well. Report for duty first thing tomorrow.'

Next day the whole battalion assembled in a field outside the town. There was none of the strict military drill Alix associated with a regular army. The men collected in their different companies and formed rough ranks but that was as far as it went. Alix followed Nikola and Drago and found a place in the ranks behind them.

A voice from behind her called her name and she looked round to see Mitra.

'Alix? What are you doing here?'

'I've joined up. I didn't know you were in the battalion.'

Mitra laughed. 'I didn't think of it like that until the other day. I've always just fought beside Milovan as a matter of course. Now it seems we are going to be much more organised, which is a good thing.'

'Yes, it must be,' Alix agreed. She admired Mitra for her courage and resilience and it was comforting to feel that they were going to fight side by side.

Some boxes had been set up at one end to form a rough podium and when Tito mounted it there was instant attention in the ranks. He told them that they were now the elite of the army and had been entrusted with a great responsibility. 'You will fight now, not just for your village or your town but for the whole of Yugoslavia, and when we achieve victory, as we will, people will look on you as the men who saved their country from all those who seek to dominate it and who set it on the path to freedom.'

There was a wholehearted cheer as he stepped down. His place was taken by General Popovic, who spoke of the need for order and discipline and the responsibility of each man for the men who fought alongside them. The rest of the day, he told them, would be devoted to an exercise to promote these virtues.

He was still speaking when a rider galloped across the parade ground and jumped off his horse in front of the podium. Sentries had been posted on all the access roads to the town and Alix realised this must be one of them.

'Sir!' His voice carried clearly to where she was standing. 'There is a large company of the enemy approaching from the west.'

'Germans?'

'No, sir. It looks like a guerilla force. Chetniks perhaps.'

'To action stations!' Popovic shouted. 'Defend the approaches.'

Orders were shouted. Men began to run, and Alix ran with them. On the western side of the town there were a scattering of small holdings with vegetable gardens and pigsties and yards where chickens scratched and goats were tethered. Nikola's company had been at the front of the assembly and were some of the first to reach the area.

'Take cover!' he yelled.

Alix jumped a low fence and threw herself down behind a wall, her rifle at the ready. Mitra dropped down beside her. For a few minutes nothing seemed to be happening. Then they saw figures running down a small hill opposite them, dodging from bush to bush and tree to tree. Moments later the first bullets sang over their heads.

After that, for Alix the situation developed a dreamlike confusion. A man appeared, running towards her. She loaded and fired and he disappeared. Beside her, Mitra was firing too. Another figure emerged from the dust and smoke and she fired again. The sound of firing and the smell of cordite filled the air, and her eyes smarted but she kept firing until, quite suddenly it seemed, the noise stopped except for the occasional single shot.

'Fall back! Fall back!' came the command, and she scrambled wearily to her feet.

Nikola appeared a few yards away.

'You're safe! Thank God!'

'Is it over?' she asked.

'Yes, we've seen the bastards off. Come on, back to base.'

Alix looked round at Mitra. 'I think I shot someone.'

'Yes, you did.' Mitra put her arm through Alix's. 'You've also got pig muck on your trousers. Come on. Your baptism of fire is over.'

Chapter Twenty-Seven

'Malta has picked up a message purporting to come from Bill.'

Leo looked up from her desk, feeling her pulse quicken. Masterson was standing in the doorway holding a sheet of paper.

'Purporting?' she queried.

'Let's not get too excited,' he said, coming into the room. 'They think it's probably not from him. It doesn't use his own personal code and they say it didn't sound like his set.'

'What does it say?'

'At the moment there are no communists on the ground. On account of their inexpert handling they were dispersed by strong German forces. Their leaders have retreated to Montenegro.'

'Doesn't sound like Bill,' Leo said reluctantly. 'Inexpert handling sounds more like someone who doesn't actually speak English.'

'I agree,' Masterson said. 'I suppose it could be Mihailovic. But why would he say it was from Bill?'

'We know Bill wasn't with Mihailovic when the last message was received,' Leo said. 'Could Bill have found someone else who would allow him to use their set? If he had lost his ciphers that would explain why it is not in his code.'

'Is there any way we could check? A personal question only he would know the answer to?'

Leo thought for a moment. 'Ask him what breed his first dog was. I remember him saying once that he was given a beagle puppy when he was a kid in South Africa.'

'Good idea!' Masterson said. 'I'll get that sent off right away.'

Sasha had remained in Cairo, unwilling to abandon his hope of finding a way to get back into his own country, but one morning he came into the office looking worried.

'I'll have to go back to London. God knows what's going on there but I've just had a telegram telling me that Simovic has been ousted as prime minister and his place has been taken by Jovanovic.'

'Why?' Leo asked.

'I've no idea, but you remember I said when I came out here that I was sick of all the in-fighting.'

'Jovanovic is OK though, isn't he?' Leo asked.

'Oh, he's sound enough,' Sasha agreed. 'Intelligent, straightforward, steers a middle course between opposing ideologies. And a Serb, of course. But I'm concerned about what manoeuvring is behind this – and Peter will be worried. He trusted Simovic. I should get back and make sure he's all right.' He rubbed his chin with a wry look of self-reproof. 'I've no business to be lounging around here in the lap of luxury, anyway.'

She got up and put her arms round his neck. 'You've been doing a great job of keeping me company. But I suppose you won't be easy in your mind until you check everything out for yourself. But I shall miss you.'

'And I shall miss you,' he said, kissing her. Then he sighed. 'How long is this bloody war going to go on? I want to go home.'

'Me too,' she agreed. 'But now the Americans have decided to join us it can't be much longer, surely.'

Masterson came in. 'Ah, Sasha. Have you heard the news?'

'About the change of prime minister? Yes.'

'It's more than that. General Ilic has been given the push too. Mihailovic has been named supreme commander of the Forces of the Homeland.'

'That's a bit optimistic, isn't it?' Leo asked. 'Considering nobody knows where he is at the moment, or what forces he has under his command.'

'I agree,' Masterson said. 'But it gets Ilic off our backs, at least.'

'Can you get me on a flight back to London?' Sasha asked. 'I really should go back to find out what has happened.'

'I can get you on a flight to Malta,' Masterson promised. 'But from there on you'll have to try to sweet talk someone into giving you a lift. It won't be easy. The island is getting a real pasting from German bombs.'

'I'll have to take my chances,' Sasha said.

Leo saw him off two days later from the airfield at Alexandria. As they waited for his flight she was guiltily reminded of how she had seen Bill Hudson off from the same airfield. *Nothing happened!* she reminded herself, but she could not forget how close she had come to doing something she would now regret so bitterly.

'I wish you were going by a different route,' she said as she hugged her husband. 'From what I hear Malta is a very dangerous place right now.'

'I shan't stay there any longer than I can help,' he promised.

'Telegraph as soon as you get back to London.'

'I will if I can, but you know what international communications are like these days.'

He kissed her tenderly and went to catch his plane.

–

Next morning, the response to the message sent to whoever was purporting to be Bill arrived.

'The dog is dead,' Masterson read.

'Well, yes, it would be,' Leo agreed. 'But it doesn't answer the question.'

'I agree,' he said. 'I'm afraid we must conclude that the Boche have captured a WT set from somebody and they are playing it back to us to give us false information. It may be that they have even captured Mihailovic himself.'

'Doesn't this make it all the more urgent to send someone in to find out what has happened to Bill?' Leo asked.

'Yes, it does,' he agreed. 'We need to start planning a new expedition straight away. And I think the man to lead it has just presented himself. His name's Terence Atherton. He's a journalist who ran several newspapers in Belgrade before the war, and also worked for us.'

'Oh, I remember him!' Leo exclaimed. 'Sasha and I had dealings with him in the run-up to the coup. Is he here?'

'He arrived not long ago, after a pretty hair-raising escape when the Boche moved in. He and some American journalists managed to acquire a sardine boat on the coast of Montenegro and sailed it to Greece under the guns of the Italian navy. Then they went by train from Patras to Athens, under fire from the Boche this time. Atherton was wounded but managed to get onto the last naval evacuation ship. He arrived here only a few days ago, but he's volunteered to be sent back into Yugoslavia.'

'A civilian?' Leo said.

'We're arranging for him to receive a commission into the Intelligence Corps. He's ideally suited to the job we want him to do. He's lived in Belgrade for years, speaks the language like a native, and he's proved he has guts and initiative. I want you to brief him on what we know and what we want him to find out.'

'How's he going in?' Leo asked.

'Same way as Bill, by submarine. We'll drop him as close to the point where Bill went in as we can, and hope he can pick up the trail from there.'

Leo spent the next two days bringing Atherton up to date with all they knew, or could deduce, about the situation in Yugoslavia. She liked him and found his company stimulating, but she was never in danger of feeling for him what she had felt for Bill.

To her great relief, on the second day she received a telegram from Sasha saying that he had arrived safely in London.

In the end it was decided to send not one but three missions into Yugoslavia. A party consisting of two Slovenes was put ashore on the island of Mjlet where there were rumours of a group of Chetniks; Terence Atherton, now Major Atherton, with an Irish Sergeant Patrick O'Donovan as radio operator and a Yugoslav Air Force officer were dropped on the coast of Montenegro, and a third party under Major Cavan Eliot with two Yugoslav officers and a British radio operator were dropped 'blind' by parachute near Sarajevo.

Once they received news that all three groups had been delivered as planned, all Leo and Tom Masterson could do was sit back and wait for radio contact.

Chapter Twenty-Eight

The nucleus of Mihailovic's force had reassembled in their old headquarters but they were a pathetically small group. Only a few of the officers closest to Mihailovic were still with him. The rest were either dead or had joined Prime Minister Nedic's gendarmes. Many of the other detachments had been broken up by the German offensive, save for the Cer Battalion, which numbered around a thousand men. Following a preprepared plan, they had withdrawn across the River Drina and were now in Bosnia. On the face of it, Mihailovic was a general without an army. It seemed the Germans had decided they were no longer a threat. The invaders did not have the troops to patrol the remote areas and they had enough on their hands with rebel activity in other parts of the country.

'So what is the plan?' Lieutenant Jovanovic said. 'Do we start trying to recruit more men?'

'No,' Draza said. 'Not here. There is very little we can do here in Serbia at the moment. Our focus must be on building up forces in other areas. And our primary objective is the defeat of that communist rabble led by Tito. I have had messages from Djurisic, whom I dispatched to Montenegro last autumn. He tells me that the Chetnik bands there are strong and have established good contacts with the Italians.'

'With the Italians?' Jovanovic queried.

'The Italians do not have sufficient forces to control the whole country. They are concentrated in the main towns and they, too, see the partisans as their main enemy. By co-operating with them our men will be able to establish themselves as the main authority in the rest of the country, so when the time comes they will be in a position to take over.'

'When the time comes?' someone asked.

'Eventually Hitler and Mussolini will be defeated. Our duty is to make sure that when that happens the legitimate government is reinstated and the country is not handed over to the communists. The Italians are prepared to supply our people with arms and ammunition so that they can exterminate the partisans.'

'So what do we do?' Jovanovic asked.

'Our role is to act as co-ordinators. Chetniks are active in the Sanjak, in Bosnia and in Croatia. We need to bring them all into a co-ordinated force under my command. I shall be asking some of you to go as my emissaries to work to that end.'

Nikola Kalabic, another of Draza's closest confidants, spoke for the first time.

'I think it would be helpful, sir, if we could clarify exactly what our aims are, so we can set them out for the benefit of all Chetnik leaders in these other areas.'

Draza nodded. 'Very well. I can set them out for you quite simply. One: to create a Greater Serbia, ethnically pure within the bounds of Serbia, Montenegro and Bosnia Herzegovina. Two: to include in our nation all the unliberated Slav territories currently under the Italians and Germans. Three: to cleanse from the state territory all national minorities and non-national elements. To create a common border between Serbia and Montenegro and to cleanse the Sandjak and Bosnia from all Muslim and Croat inhabitants.' He looked around him. 'Is that all perfectly clear?'

There were nods and murmurs of agreement, but Steve, who had listened in silence, thought he saw signs of discomfort on some faces.

He himself was becoming increasingly disenchanted with his situation. Draza refused to allow him to use his radio set because this would give the Germans a chance to pinpoint his location. This was understandable, but he knew that his superiors in London would be wondering what had become of him and, more importantly, needed to know what was going on. He felt he was failing in his duty, more so now than ever with this talk of co-operation with the Italians.

As soon as he had a chance to catch Mihailovic alone he voiced his misgivings.

Draza glared at him. 'What gives you the right to question my decisions?'

'I am only thinking that if it ever got back to the British authorities it would be the end of any support we might get from that direction.'

The Serbian drew himself up, his face contorted with fury.

'Are you threatening me?'

Steve stood his ground. 'No. I'm just stating facts.'

Draza shook his head. 'I thought I could trust you,' he said bitterly.

'You can,' Steve responded. 'I'm just wondering if the king and the government in exile are aware of what is happening here.'

Draza took a step towards him, his fists clenching. 'If I ever find out that you have been in communication with London and have told them I am working with the Italians I will have you shot as a traitor. Do you understand?'

Steve met his eyes and knew that he meant what he said. 'I understand. I will do nothing without your permission.'

Chapter Twenty-Nine

Bosnia, January 1942

The First Proletarian Brigade was on the march, heading north-west across the River Drina into Bosnia. There were several partisan detachments operating in the mountainous area between Sarajevo and the river and Tito's plan was to link up with them and incorporate them into the brigade. They had reached the small town of Bogdasici and encamped for the night when a courier rode in.

Tito and his closest associates were sitting round their campfire, finishing their evening meal. Since Milovan Djilas was one of their number it was natural that Mitra, his wife, joined him and it had become a habit that where Mitra went Alix followed. She was not sure whether it was that association that allowed her access to this privileged circle, or whether it was Tito's half-joking assertion that she brought him good luck, but she took care to make herself inconspicuous. The chance to be at the heart of discussions was too good to lose.

The courier was brought to Tito's side.

'Comrade, there are reports of German troops massing around Tusla and moving towards Zvornik.'

Tito sat up, immediately alert. 'Who sent you?'

'Comrade Markovic, the commander of the Kalesinja detachment.'

'Is there any idea of their objective?'

'I'm sorry, comrade. I know no more than that.'

'Never mind. You have done well to bring us advance warning.' Tito stood up and clapped the young man on the shoulder. 'Go and get some rest.'

'Bad news,' Koca Popovics said grimly. 'It could be the beginning of another offensive, like the one that pushed us out of Uzice.'

'This makes it all the more urgent to link up with the other detachments,' Tito said. 'As a united force we stand a chance but as individual units the Germans will be able to pick each one off. When we know which direction they are heading in we must do everything we can to delay them.'

Over the next twenty-four hours, couriers came and went in a flurry of activity. The reports told of pitched battles being fought by partisan detachments, and by Chetnik companies too. It seemed the Germans had orders to clear the area of insurgents, of whichever persuasion. They were arresting anyone who was not resident in the immediate locality, or anyone caught with weapons. Houses from which a shot was fired were burned down. Prisoners were summarily shot, after a brief interrogation.

That evening Tito's expression was grave.

'The Germans are moving south from Zvornik and we have reports of others moving in from the west, from Sarajevo.'

'So what do we do?' Rankovic asked.

'Fetch me the map,' Popovic responded.

They pored over the map for some time. Popovic stubbed a blunt finger on a spot. 'The terrain is to our advantage, particularly the number of rivers. If we can blow the bridges, that will slow them down. Here, for example, at Britunak, they will have to cross the Krizevika and again further south the River Potorijka. I suggest we start by blowing the bridges over both of them.'

'Do we have sufficient explosives?' Rankovic asked.

'We carried all we could from the factory at Uzice,' Tito reminded him. 'It will be enough for those and a few more.'

'Who do we have who is capable of setting the charge?'

'Tomaz Kostic. He's an engineer and worked for the Trepca mines. He's used to dealing with explosives.'

Scouts were sent out and came back looking troubled.

'There are advance parties scouting the route south and some of them are already in Britunak.'

Tito and Popovic exchanged looks. 'We can probably infiltrate Kostic disguised as a peasant,' Tito ruminated, 'but if he's caught carrying a rucksack full of dynamite…'

Alix had been listening to all this. A memory stirred in her mind of what she had learned in the French resistance. Fear churned in her stomach but she forced herself to speak.

'A woman could probably do it. The Germans don't expect women to be involved in anything like that.'

Tito looked at her. 'My flame of the forest! Are you volunteering?'

Alix's knees were shaking. 'Yes.' Her voice deserted her for a moment and she had to repeat herself. 'Yes, if you think I can do it.'

'Wait a minute,' Popovic said. 'The explosives and the necessary detonator and wires and so on will be heavy. Too much for a woman.'

'Not too much for two women.' It was Mitra's voice. 'Two women and a donkey, collecting wood from the forest for their fire.'

So it was decided.

–

Next day a small party detached itself from the main army and set off for Britunak. It consisted of Tomaz Kostic with two assistants, Alix and Mitra leading a donkey provided by the headman of a local village, and an escort of ten men with a local guide. Travelling along forest tracks to avoid the roads, they reached a point on a hill looking down onto the little town and the river flowing through it. Tomaz scanned the area through a pair of field glasses.

'There's the bridge, just west of the town, upstream,' he said.

'Can you see any sign of enemy activity?' Alix asked.

'There are soldiers moving around in the town, not many, probably not more than a company, and I can see a couple of armoured cars.'

'Any road blocks?'

'Not as far as I can see.'

The river here, like so many in the area, had carved itself a deep gorge with rocky sides topped by thick forest. The road crossed it on a high-arched bridge supported by two central columns.

'Shouldn't be too difficult to bring that down by laying charges at the base of the columns,' Tomaz said. 'The tricky bit is getting the explosives down there.' He turned to their guide. 'Do you know any way?'

The man shook his head. 'It's not my area. I can find my way here but I've never been into the town.'

'Can I look?' Alix requested.

Tomaz handed her the field glasses and she scanned the area where the road crossed the ravine.

'Isn't that a track going along the edge of the river, on the far side? There's a little cluster of cottages close to the riverbank, just beyond the bridge.'

Tomaz took the glasses back and peered through them. 'Yes, you're right.'

'There must be a way down to them from the road,' Alix said. 'We can't see it from here, but I'm sure the people who live there must need to go up and down. If we can find that, we can get down to river level.'

'OK,' Tomaz said. 'It's the only chance I can see, so we shall have to hope it works. This is what we'll do. I'll go down now with Goran and Teo. We can scramble down and cross the river somehow and find a place to hide. There's plenty of vegetation along the riverbank. I'll have to leave you two women to make your own way down and hope that you're right about finding a track. We can't start operations until it's dark, so you should probably wait as long as you can. Agreed?'

'Agreed,' Alix and Mitra echoed.

'The rest of you,' he said, addressing the men of the escort, 'wait here. We'll rendezvous here when the job's done and head back to join the others. If we don't reappear by dawn, you'll know we've been caught, so start back without waiting any longer.'

When Tomaz and the other two had left, Alix, remembering how crucial the right cover story had been in France, drew Mitra aside.

'We should decide what we are going to say if we are stopped by any of the soldiers.'

By the time the early winter dusk was drawing in, they had agreed on a story and had collected armfuls of dry branches and twigs to cover the contents of the donkey's panniers. They changed their clothes, putting on skirts and shawls borrowed from women in the village, said goodbye to their escort and made their way down to the road. To reach the bridge it was necessary to go through the town. It was only a small place, more an overgrown village, so it was not hard to find their way. They kept to the side streets without encountering any of the German soldiers, though they heard their voices. They sounded quite relaxed and Alix guessed that they had taken control of the area without too much trouble and were now waiting for the main force to catch up with them.

It was as they were leaving the town that their luck ran out. A sentry was guarding the approach to the bridge. It was a cold afternoon, with flurries of snow in the air, and he was hunched up in his greatcoat, obviously fed up with his lot; but as they approached he shook the snowflakes off his shoulders and stepped forward to bar their way.

'Where do you think you're going?' He spoke in Serbo-Croat and Alix realised with a shock that, though his uniform was almost indistinguishable from the regular German soldiers, he wore badges that identified him as belonging to the Croat Home Guard. They all knew that the Croatian authorities were co-operating with the invaders, but it was the first time she had seen proof that they were fighting alongside them.

She pushed the thought to the back of her mind and replied, in humble tones, 'Please, friend, let us pass. We are only taking firewood to warm our children.'

'Taking it where? Where do you live?'

'Down there, in the valley.' She pointed to the little cluster of houses and prayed that the Germans had not already searched them and identified the owners.

'What is in the panniers?'

'Firewood, as you can see.'

'Why are you alone? This is not women's work. Where are your husbands?'

Mitra spoke up, a catch in her voice. 'Both dead. Mine was killed last summer by a falling tree and my sister's died of a fever last winter.'

'Please, sir,' Alix begged, 'let us pass. Our father is old and frail and the children will be hungry and cold.'

A gust of wind blew fresh snow in their faces. The soldier looked from one to another and shrugged his shoulders. 'All right. On your way.'

They hurried past him and on across the bridge. 'Just pray I'm right and there is a way down,' Alix murmured.

At the end of the bridge they turned their eyes to the forest and Alix gave a small cry of triumph. A narrow track zig-zagged down the steep embankment of the gorge. They turned into it with relief but found their trials were not yet over. The donkey took fright at the precipitous drop on one side of the track and dug in all four feet. It took them twenty minutes of tugging and cajoling and blows to its rump to get it to the bottom.

When they finally arrived Alix looked around them. The houses were a hundred yards further on and all the doors and windows were closed against the weather, so there was little chance they had been spotted, but they could still be seen from the bridge if anyone had looked down. They pulled the unwilling donkey along the track until they were sheltered underneath it.

'Now what?' Mitra said. 'Where are the men?'

It was almost dark and they did not have long to wait before Tomaz and the other two emerged from the bushes a little further along and came to join them.

'Well done!' he said. 'Any problems?'

Alix and Mitra exchanged glances. 'Nothing we couldn't deal with,' Mitra said.

Once everything was unloaded from the panniers Tomaz said, 'There's no point in you two hanging around. You might as well make your way back to the rendezvous point. We'll join you as soon as we've finished here.'

'We can't go back the way we came,' Alix pointed out. 'There's a guard on the bridge and he thinks we live down here.'

'You'll have to get back the way we came down,' he said. 'There's a place about fifty yards upstream where there are rocks sticking up out of the river. We managed to get across by stepping on those. Then it's a steep scramble up but not too difficult.'

'That's all very well in daylight,' Mitra said. 'Pretty well impossible in the dark.'

Tomaz grunted in assent. 'OK. Wait with us. Then we'll help you across.'

After that all they could do was wait, hugging their hands under their armpits for warmth, while the men set to work by the light of a carefully shielded torch. When the charge was ready Tomaz and Teo waded out into the river and strapped it to one of the supporting columns. They came back unrolling a reel of wire.

'By Christ! That water is freezing,' Teo said as they regained the bank.

'Let's move,' Tomaz ordered.

They continued to unroll the wire until they reached the place where the men had hidden earlier. There they stopped and Tomaz attached the detonator, a box with a handle which, when depressed, would set off the charge.

'Goran, you and Teo go with the girls,' he said. 'Get them across the river. I'll be along after the bridge goes up.'

'But you'll be caught on the wrong side of the river,' Alix objected. 'The place will be swarming with Germans when they hear the explosion.'

He shrugged. 'Can't be helped. The detonator wire isn't long enough to reach to the other side. With any luck I'll be covered by the general confusion and get across without being spotted. Now, go, all of you. I'll give you time to get well away before I detonate the bomb.'

For a moment longer they hesitated, but Alix saw that there was no alternative to his plan. She held out her hand.

'Good luck, comrade.'

The others added their good wishes and then the four of them slipped out of the hiding place and made their way along the riverbank.

'Here,' Goran said. 'This is where we crossed.'

At that moment, as if the forces of nature were on their side, there was a break in the clouds and the faint light of a waning moon illuminated the scene. The river was running fast and the rocks stuck up only inches above the surface. Goran produced a torch and held it cupped in his hand to shield the light.

'I'll go first. You follow and Teo will help Mitra. I'll give you a hand where I can.'

Alix's heart was pounding. The thought of trying to balance on slippery rocks and the danger of being swept away in the icy current frightened her more than the encounter with the guard. Mitra squeezed her arm.

'Courage, sister. God is with us.'

Goran was already standing on a rock a foot or two out in the water, stretching his hand towards her. She gathered up her skirt, swallowed hard and took a leap towards him. Her feet slid on the rock but he had a firm grip on her hand and held her from falling.

'Now, stay here while I step across to the next one,' he instructed. 'Then you follow.'

In this way, balancing from one rock to the next with Goran's strong arm to help her, she managed the crossing. Turning on the far bank, she was in time to see Mitra lose her footing and slide up to her waist in the river, but Teo reached down and somehow managed to haul her up again and moments later they were with them on the riverbank. Mitra's teeth were chattering.

'Thank you, Teo! I thought I'd had it then. You saved my life!'

He shrugged, embarrassed. 'You'd do the same for me.'

'Come on,' Alix said. 'If we stand around you'll catch your death of cold.'

They began to scramble up the steep side of the ravine, clinging to roots and overhanging branches for support. More than once Alix cursed the skirt she had been forced to wear. After the weeks on the march she had come to recognise how much more practical trousers were. They were almost halfway when she felt the earth shake under her and a gust of wind ripped the branch she was holding out of her hand. Then she heard the noise.

'There it goes!' Goran exclaimed.

They all twisted round to look down into the valley. For a moment Alix thought the whole attempt had ended in failure, then quite slowly the bridge crumbled and collapsed into the river.

'He's done it! He's done it!' Mitra cried ecstatically.

'*We've* done it,' Alix said.

Below them they saw lights springing up in the town and then two armoured cars raced down the road and skidded to a halt as they reached the place where the bridge had been. Angry shouts reached their ears.

'What about Tomaz?' Alix asked.

'He'll find a way,' Teo said. 'We should keep going.'

The men of the escort gave them a cheer as they appeared, but the mood of celebration faded when they saw that Tomaz was missing.

'We can wait a short while,' the captain said, 'but we need to be as far away as possible when it gets light.'

'Mitra, don't stand around in that wet skirt,' Alix said. 'You'll get frostbite or hypothermia.'

The men gallantly turned their backs while she stripped off her wet clothes and pulled on her trousers. She had just finished when they all froze at the sound of somebody, or something, crashing through the under-growth. Seconds later, Tomaz appeared.

'You made it!' Alix exclaimed. 'How did you get across?'

He grinned. 'No problem. The collapsed bridge formed a dam and I was able to walk across more or less dry shod. It won't be long before the water flows over the top of course, but it held long enough for me.' His expression darkened slightly. 'I'm afraid the donkey didn't make it.'

'The donkey!' Alix and Mitra spoke in the same breath.

'We forgot all about it,' Alix confessed. 'What happened?'

'We'd tethered the poor beast under the bridge, remember?' he answered.

'Oh, poor creature!' Mitra exclaimed. 'How could we be so thoughtless.'

'We couldn't have brought it back with us, anyway,' Alix pointed out. 'But we should have set it free.'

'Nothing to be done about it now,' Tomaz said. 'It's the fortunes of war.'

'What matters,' Goran put in, 'is we did what we set out to do. It'll take the Boche a while to repair that bridge.'

'Quite right!' Alix said. 'Let's get back to the others and tell Tito what we've done.'

Chapter Thirty

A messenger arrived in the partisan camp.

'Bad news, Comrade Tito. When Draza Mihailovic heard that four hundred of his men had been taken prisoner he sent out orders that all Chetnik forces should withdraw to the other side of the River Drina, or if that is not possible they should lay down their arms and offer no resistance. He is telling his people that the German offensive is directed against us partisans, not against them.'

Tito's face grew dark with fury. He summoned the members of the council.

'That is the end of any co-operation between us and the Chetniks. I want the following proclamation disseminated all across the region. "To Bosnians, Serbs, Muslim and Croats. Mihailovic, Todorovic and all their associates are traitors. We partisans have fought alone all across Bosnia and Herzegovina. Long live the united people's liberation struggle!"'

In the intervening days between the blowing up of the bridge at Britunak and that day, Tomaz and his team, in which Alix and Mitra plus a newly acquired donkey were an essential part, had become known as the 'bomb squad'. Having watched Tomaz lay another explosive charge, Alix had persuaded him to teach her, and she had lost count of the number of bridges they had destroyed between them. But as fast as they blew them up the German engineers built bailey bridges to take their place. Other teams had felled trees to create roadblocks; but the German tanks shoved them aside or rolled over them and the troops marched on.

The First Proletarian Brigade had fought their way onwards, aiming to join up with the Romanija detachment, which was the largest in the area, only to discover that they had been almost wiped out in a fierce battle with forces driving in from the west. The situation was becoming desperate. During a temporary lull in the fighting, Tito called his officers together.

'The Germans have taken Sokolac and Rogatica and they are pushing in from Sarajevo. We are surrounded and the noose is tightening.'

'So, what now?' Djilas asked.

Koca Popovic said, 'The Italians are supposed to be holding the southern sector but our information is that their lines are very thin. If we can reach them we may be able to infiltrate through them and reach Foca.'

'And how do we do that?' someone asked.

'There is only one way,' Tito said grimly. 'We have to cross Mount Igman.'

'Cross Igman, at this time of year?' Djilas's face expressed disbelief. 'The weather is bad enough here. At that altitude…'

'It's that or stay here and be wiped out,' Popovic told him.

As the discussion went on Alix raised her eyes to the mountain that loomed above them. It seemed impossible that human beings could survive up there.

Nevertheless, the decision was taken. Tomorrow they must make the attempt.

As she prepared, Alix remembered something she had seen in one of the abandoned cottages where they were encamped. She found her way back to it and was relieved to see that she had not been mistaken. Hanging on a hook behind the door was a sheepskin coat. It was old and dirty and from the smell of it had not been properly cured, but it was big enough to fit over her other clothes. She put it on, wondering if lice survived at these temperatures, and deciding that lice or no lice it might be the difference between survival and an icy death.

As the column formed up Djilas called Mitra to him.

'Today, we march together, yes? We can help each other along.'

Alix felt a sudden stab of jealousy but an instant later Drago was at her side.

'Doesn't Nikola want you with him?' she asked.

'Yes, he's threatened me with court martial for desertion. I told him, fine, but not till we get to Foca.' He reached for her hand. 'I think you may need your big brother today.'

She moved closer to him. 'I've never been more grateful to see you.'

'Don't worry,' he said. 'We'll get to the other side. I won't let anything happen to you.'

The order to march was given and they fell in behind Djilas and Mitra and began the long trudge up the mountain. The top, they discovered, was a wide plateau, across which the wind blew relentlessly, whipping snow into their faces. The snow was almost knee deep in places and Alix was glad that the men in front of them had trodden a path through it. At this altitude, the air was thin and she was soon panting for breath, but Drago kept a grip on her arm and urged her onwards.

'We have to keep going. If we get left behind we won't survive.'

Hour after hour they plodded forward. From time to time they passed men who had fallen out and collapsed in the snow, but Drago would not let her stop to help. Her feet and fingers were numb, but in the sheepskin coat her body remained warm. Occasionally the column was called to a halt and flasks were produced. Alix had brought her water bottle, but the contents were frozen solid. Drago shared sips of water mixed with slivovitz from his.

After what felt like an eternity she realised that the ground was sloping away under her feet.

'I believe we may have got to the far side,' Drago said. 'I think the going will be easier from now on.'

They came to the first trees, stubby firs heavy with snow. A little further on the trees grew thicker and the wind was less fierce. Finally, in a clearing, Popovic called a halt and told them to make camp. Alix sank down on a fallen log and watched the rest of the army limp in. Some walked unaided but many were hobbling, helped along by their stronger comrades, and a few were carried on the backs of friends. There was no way of knowing until a roll call was made how many were still out there on the mountain, unable to summon the strength to go on.

There was no shortage of dead wood in the surrounding forest and the stronger men soon collected enough to make campfires. Sacks of beans were opened and the cooks set to work. Alix's nostrils flared as she picked up the odour. 'Soldiers' beans!' Flavoured with onion and garlic and plenty of paprika, with a few pieces of dried bacon, it was the most basic of dishes but one that she had always enjoyed. Flasks of slivovitz made the rounds, and little by little the men and women revived.

Drago squatted down beside Alix. 'I should go and see how Nikola is.'

'Yes, go,' she told him. 'And if he is angry with you tell him I would not have survived without you. If he cares for me, as he professes to, he should be glad you disobeyed him.'

She sat on for a while, waiting for feeling to return to her numbed feet, then she limped over to join the officers round their fire. Mitra and Irina were already there and Alix was thankful to see that they, too, had survived. She noticed that Nikola was hunched as close to the fire as he could get, his hands outstretched to the blaze.

'Careful,' she admonished him. 'You'll burn yourself.'

He shuddered under his blanket. 'I lost a glove on the way and I can't get my hands warm.'

He sat back as Drago handed him a bowl of bean stew, but he seemed to have difficulty gripping it and it nearly fell out of his hands.

'Idiot!' he exclaimed. 'Couldn't you see I hadn't got hold of it properly?'

Drago bent his head and said nothing.

'It wasn't Drago's fault,' Alix said. 'What's wrong with your hand?'

'I told you. I can't get it warm.'

'Let me see.' She took his right hand in hers and saw that the fingers were dead white with blotches of purple. 'I'll rub it for you.' She began to rub gently but after a few seconds he snatched his hand back, swearing under his breath. 'No, leave it! You're making it hurt.'

He began to eat, holding his spoon in his left hand and balancing the bowl awkwardly on his knees. Alix let him get on with it.

Next morning, as they dragged themselves to their feet and prepared to face another day, she noticed that Nikola was still having difficulty using his right hand. Studying him properly for the first time since they left Rudo, she saw that he had lost weight. His cheeks were hollow, and under the superficial weathering brought about by exposure to the elements, his face was pale.

'How's your hand?' she asked.

'It's feeling better,' he said gruffly.

'Let me see.'

He let her take his hand and she gasped. His fingers were now patched with dark blisters. 'Nikola, that looks bad!'

'It'll be all right,' he insisted, and he pulled it away.

There was another long march ahead of them, but now they were going downhill and the further they descended the warmer the weather grew. Most of the men had recovered after a night's rest, but some were still hobbling and several had to be carried.

When they made camp that night she found Nikola hunched up with his hands between his knees. He was grunting softly in what she guessed was an attempt to suppress cries of pain.

'Show me again,' she insisted.

He held out his hand and she felt his fingers. They were ice cold and the flesh was as hard as iron, but the blisters were even worse.

'You need to get something done about this—' she started to say, but she was interrupted by Djilas who had been watching.

'Let me see that,' he ordered. When Nikola unwillingly stretched out his hand, Djilas's expression grew grim. 'That's frostbite, a bad case of it. You need to see the surgeon.'

'No!' Nikola snatched his hand back. 'I know what you're thinking. I'm not losing my fingers.'

'It's them or your life,' Djilas said. 'If you don't let him do what is necessary they will rot and you will get gangrene. Come along.'

He took Nikola firmly by the arm and led him across the clearing where they had camped to a rough shelter of branches and tarpaulins that had been erected to serve as a hospital. Dr Ivanovic was a qualified surgeon who had joined the partisans while they were in Uzice and was greatly respected for the efforts he made in the care of the wounded. He rose from kneeling beside a stretcher and came over.

'I'm afraid we've got a bad case of frostbite for you,' Djilas said.

'No! It's nothing. It'll be all right in a day or two,' Nikola protested.

The doctor took his hand and sucked his teeth. 'No chance of that, I'm afraid. There's only one remedy and the sooner it's done the better. This way.'

He led them to the back of the shelter and Alix gasped at the sight of a wooden block stained dark with blood. A fire burned close by and into it were thrust several metal implements. The sight undid Nikola. He collapsed to his knees, sobbing, 'No! No! Not that.'

'Come along, man. Brace up!' The doctor spoke with barely concealed disdain. 'I've amputated more fingers and toes in the last few days than I care to count – and with a lot less fuss.'

Alix stepped forward. 'But… anaesthetic? Surely…?'

The doctor shrugged. 'We ran out of chloroform many days ago.' He looked at Djilas and Drago, who had followed them. 'Perhaps the young lady would be better elsewhere?'

'No!' Alix said. She felt she was being tested, though by whom she was not sure. 'I'll stay, if I can help.'

She knelt down by Nikola. 'I'll stay with you. I'll help you through this.'

He stopped sobbing, though she could feel him shaking.

The doctor was washing his hands in a basin of water. He turned back to them. 'Right. Put your hand here.' He pulled Nikola's hand forward and laid it on the block, fingers spread. 'Hold him.'

Drago took Nikola's arm in both his hands and held it outstretched. Alix knelt behind him and wrapped her arms round his body, burying her face between his shoulder blades. There was a crunch and Nikola screamed. The sound was repeated three more times.

'Stay still,' the doctor ordered. 'The wounds must be cauterised.'

She heard him remove something from the fire and then there was the smell of burning flesh and Nikola sagged in her grip.

By the time he regained consciousness his hand was wrapped in fresh bandages. Alix had his head on her lap. He looked up at her. 'Are they… are they gone?'

'Yes. It had to be done, Nikola.'

'What am I going to do? How shall I manage?'

'I'll help you. Drago will help you. You'll be all right.'

The doctor held out a couple of pills. 'Take these. They will help you through the night.' He looked at Alix and

Drago. 'Make sure he keeps his hands well covered from now on.'

Nikola tried to rise then sagged back. Drago stooped and picked him up as if he were a child and carried him back to the campfire. Alix fetched a beaker of water and gave him the pills and then they wrapped him in his blanket and laid him down.

He looked up at Alix. 'Stay with me! Just for tonight.'

She met Drago's eyes and he looked away. With a feeling of inevitability, she fetched her blanket and wrapped herself and Nikola in it. He laid his injured arm across her body and nuzzled his face into her shoulder. She held him like that, unable to sleep herself, until his breathing told her he had dropped off.

—

Nikola insisted the next morning that Alix marched beside him. With Drago supporting him on his other side, they found their place in the column and plodded forward.

At midday Popovic called a halt. 'The Italian lines are just ahead, along the road running at the bottom of that valley. We will break up into small groups and attempt to cross at different points. Rendezvous in Foca. Follow the River Drina.'

Officers worked along the column, dividing the men into small groups. Each was given a point to aim for along the valley and they were sent off at intervals. Alix and Mitra, with Nikola, Djilas and Drago, had to wait for almost an hour before their turn came. They spent it scanning the valley below for any sign of conflict and studying the movement of the occasional armoured car along the road. If this was indeed the line the Italians were supposed to have set up to block their escape, it was thin indeed.

When their turn came they made their way down a rough track, their way obstructed briefly by a small boy with a herd of goats. He gazed at them with wide, anxious eyes and babbled his thanks when Djilas handed him a small coin. They came to the road and stood looking left and right. There was no sign of movement. Twenty minutes later they walked into Foca.

Chapter Thirty-One

Cairo, February 1942

Leo was worried about Tom Masterson. He was not a young man, over sixty at a reasonable guess, and the strain of the job was beginning to tell on him. She remembered her initial reaction when he had been sent out to Belgrade to replace Julian Amery and act as a restraining hand on the 'bomb-happy amateurs', as the SOE agents there had been characterised. It had struck her then that he was an unlikely secret agent, a businessman in civilian life with no previous experience of clandestine activities. That had not, however, prevented him from helping to promote the coup that had deposed the regent and put King Peter in his place. He had proved his worth again in the Cairo office, and she was grateful for his friendship and support. But increasingly she was aware of the lines of strain on his face and the shadows under his eyes, and she was beginning to wonder if he was not just tired but ill.

It did not help that there had been no contact from any of the three missions they had dispatched to Yugoslavia the previous month. The inevitable conclusion was that they had either been killed or had fallen into enemy hands. There was even speculation that Mihailovic himself might have been captured.

Masterson's health apart, there were changes afoot in the Cairo Balkan Desk. A new man had been appointed as intelligence and co-ordination officer. His name was James Klugmann. He was a small man with glasses perpetually clouded by the smoke of the cigarette that never seemed to be absent from his mouth and an intense manner. He had started his military career as a private in the pioneer corps but his undoubted intellectual brilliance had seen him seconded to SOE and promoted to the rank of lieutenant. He was a brilliant conversationalist with a command of a range of topics and an ability to connect with all sorts of people, but his chief interest was politics. Leo found him a stimulating companion on the rare occasions when he was in the office, but his political views disturbed her. He was a communist, something alien to the general political bias of the men and women who worked for SOE, and she wondered how he had come to be recruited. He could make a very convincing case for his convictions but they went against everything Leo had grown up to believe in, and what she had heard of life in the USSR did nothing to change her mind.

At a more personal level, talking to him reminded her of what she had learned about Alix's life in Paris. She had mentioned that some of her friends were communists and Leo found herself wondering to what extent her views agreed with Klugmann's. Thinking along those lines brought back to the surface of her mind the perpetual undercurrent of anxiety and loss that her separation from her daughter created. She longed for the end of the war, as everyone did, but for her the overriding reason was that it would mean that at last they would be reunited.

There was a reason for Klugmann's frequent absences from the office. He had been brought in to deal with a new bunch of recruits from an unusual source. They were Yugoslavs who had emigrated to Canada but who had not found a great welcome there. They were all members of the Communist Party, which was banned in that country, and that dissatisfaction made them ripe for recruitment. They were hard-bitten, tough men, miners and dock workers mainly, and their one burning desire was to return to their homeland and free it from the aggressors.

They were quartered outside Cairo in a villa near the pyramids which had once been a high-class brothel. When Leo went to meet them she was amused to discover that the decor had not been changed. It was decorated and upholstered in shades of pink and embellished with lamps whose pink silk shades were decked now with cobwebs. She was left in no doubt that these men would be a formidable force once they were parachuted into Yugoslavia, but conditions were not yet ripe for that to happen and their impatience led to a simmering discontent. It was that potentially dangerous situation that James Klugmann had been sent to manage. He was successful to such an extent that it was generally accepted that the 'Jugs' would listen to no one else.

Unsurprisingly, Klugmann's approach to the situation in Yugoslavia was at variance with the received opinion among the SOE establishment in Cairo. He was convinced that the future of anti-Nazi operations there was in the hands of Tito and his partisans and that SOE support for Mihailovic and the royalists was mistaken. Leo remembered that Bill Hudson had been inclined to the same opinion but she found it difficult to stomach. Sasha's connection to the royal family meant that she had been closely involved with young King Peter and the coup to put him on the throne, and the only future she could imagine was the restoration of the previous regime. She was prepared to acknowledge that much would have to change; indeed, she and Sasha had been pushing for reforms for many years. But the thought of the country being taken over by the communists was abhorrent to her.

Always, of course, as a continuous background to all her more immediate concerns, there was the news, good and bad, of the war in the rest of the world. Good news of the arrival of the first American troops on British shores, and the failure of Hitler's Operation Barbarossa as the Russians drove the German forces back from Moscow; bad news of the fall of Singapore to the Japanese. More immediately important was the ebb and flow of fighting in the desert west of Cairo. In January the Germans under Rommel had captured Benghazi and besieged Tobruk; but in recent weeks Benghazi had been retaken and Tobruk had been relieved. There were times when the fighting came almost to the Egyptian border but life in Cairo continued as before. The cafés and restaurants were filled with soldiers on leave, dancing and drinking; there were shows at the Opera House, and the tea room at the sporting club continued to serve the most delicious cream cakes. Sometimes Leo felt she was living in the world of *Alice in Wonderland*.

Chapter Thirty-Two

Foca, Bosnia, February–April 1942

Alix stepped out onto the balcony of the house where they had found accommodation and stretched her arms luxuriously. The sun was shining and a soft breeze was blowing from the Adriatic, a hundred miles to the west. Alix thought Foca was the most beautiful place she had ever seen. It was situated at the confluence of two rivers, the Drina and the Tara, and was surrounded by orchards which were now washed in the pale pink of almond blossom. After the icy crags and the precipitous ravines of the area they had traversed with such difficulty, Foca seemed like the garden of Eden. Its charms were enhanced even further by the fact that for the first time in weeks she had been able to take off her clothes, wash in warm water, and sleep in a proper bed.

As Alix gazed out over the peaceful scene, her thoughts drifted to Steve. In recent weeks she had been much too occupied with the business of survival to daydream, but now she had time to wonder where he was and how he was faring. As far as anyone knew Mihailovic was still somewhere in Serbia, so she presumed Steve was with him. She wished there had been a chance to talk, to find out how he had come to be with Mihailovic. He had been in uniform when she caught that brief glimpse of him, so presumably he was still in the RAF and under orders. It was some comfort to think that perhaps he had been given no option about where he should serve. That led to the thought that her father would deeply disapprove of her own choice of leader. She could only hope that, if she survived to the end of the war, she would be able to explain.

A voice from inside the house broke into her reverie. 'Alix! Stop mooning about out there and help me with these damn buttons.'

Since the amputation of his fingers, Nikola had become more and more demanding. He required help with dressing and eating but irritably rejected Drago's assistance and insisted that Alix performed all but the most intimate tasks. So she fastened his buttons and tied his shoelaces and cut up his food. The wounds had healed well but she recognised that he must still be in pain. It was understandable that he was often bad tempered. All the same, she found his refusal to help himself infuriating. When accommodation was being allocated he had insisted that she must live wherever he was. He had even tried to persuade her to sleep in the same room with him, but she had drawn the line at that.

She buttoned his trousers and helped him on with his jacket.

'There.' She stood back. 'You're ready for the day.'

'Huh!' he grunted. 'Ready to do what?'

'Your men still need you. You are their commander. You have a duty to them.'

'What good am I to them? I can't fire a rifle or use a sword.'

'You don't need to. We have a blessed interval of peace. But General Popovic is conducting training exercises. You should be there to see your men through them.'

He shrugged his shoulders and turned away. She waited a moment, then said, 'Well, it's up to you. I have to go to work.'

'Work!' he sneered. 'Writing little pieces for a newspaper.'

She bit back an angry retort. 'Milovan thinks they are worth printing. At least I'm trying to contribute.'

'Oh, go on then.' He waved her away. 'I'll find someone to talk to, I suppose, if you can't spare the time.'

She looked at him in exasperation for a moment and then turned away to the door. 'I'll be back at lunchtime.'

'I may not be here.' He shot the words after her but she ignored them.

Since the partisans had arrived in Foca, Tito had established a very similar regime to that he had created in Uzice. He and his aides had taken over the hotel, which was now Supreme Headquarters. A hospital had been established and *Borba*, the newspaper, was being published again. There was even talk of founding a music club and a dramatic society.

They had been made welcome by the citizens but Alix was only beginning to learn why. Foca was part of the new independent Croatian state, the NDH, which was controlled by the Ustashe. In the past few months the Croats and Muslims had committed atrocities, slaughtering Serbs in large numbers. They had started with the sons of the twelve most prominent citizens. In another nearby village, they had cut the throats of the Serb inhabitants over a vat normally used for grapes. Alix remembered with a shudder the barge loaded with the heads of children that had floated down the Sava river into Belgrade. Tito's army at least promised protection from further outrages.

Alix had mixed feelings about returning to work at the newspaper. After her decision to enlist in the brigade and the adventures that had followed, it seemed a tame occupation; but she consoled herself with the thought that, as there was no fighting at the moment, she was at least making herself useful. And it had the added bonus of keeping her at the heart of the decisions of the Supreme Council.

She had just settled at her desk when Milovan Djilas put his head round the door.

'Tito has called a meeting. It seems there is news of some sort. Bring your notebook.'

Alix grabbed her book and followed him through the streets to the hotel. The Council was assembled in the dining room and she took a seat at the back.

'It seems,' Tito began, 'that the British have not completely lost interest in what is going on here after all. I have had a message from Milutinov, the commander of the Lovcen detachment in Montenegro. They have picked up a new mission that was landed by submarine a few days ago. It consists of a British major and a Yugoslav captain with an Irish radio operator. They say they want to come here and meet with me. Milutinov has asked them for arms to be dropped and they have apparently agreed to facilitate this.'

There was a murmur of mixed appreciation and suspicion among the members of the Council.

'This could be good news, surely,' Rankovic said.

Tito looked dubious. 'It would be better for us to rely on supplies from Russia. We don't want to be beholden to the British.'

'But is there any sign of an air drop from that source?' Djilas asked.

Tito shook his head. Alix could see that he was in a dilemma, torn between the possibility of getting much-needed arms and ammunition from a source he regarded as potentially hostile to his aims, and his obedience to his Russian masters.

'There have been rumours of aircraft overflying Sarajevo in the last few nights. I was hoping that this might be a Russian mission, dropping agents by parachute, but it seems not. Tempo, our agent there, has informed me that it was another British mission that was dropped, complete with a radio and some weapons. They were arrested and handed over to the Ustashe, who have sent them to Belgrade.'

'That's unfortunate, to say the least,' Djilas said dryly.

'So what do we do about this group Milutinov has picked up?' Rankovic asked.

'As you know, I have sent Mosa Pijade to Montenegro to establish a headquarters there and set up a landing ground ready to receive our Russian allies when they arrive. I shall send a courier to Milutinov and tell him to pass the group on to him. Meanwhile I shall ask the Comintern what to do with them. I suspect that their real aim is to join Mihailovic and arrange arms drops for him. Hudson chose to throw in his lot with the Chetniks rather than stay with us, so why should these men be any different?'

Next day Djilas came into the office looking solemn.

'Tito is sending me to Montenegro as a special envoy to Pijade and the supreme staff in Zabljak. He wants to set up a free territory there, like we had at Uzice. I shall be gone indefinitely, so you will have to manage *Borba* on your own.'

'Manage it?' Alix gasped. 'I… I'm not sure I'm qualified.'

'You'll be fine,' he told her. 'You've worked under me long enough to have learned the ropes and you have a talent for making clear, concise reports. And a good grasp of the importance of propaganda, which is more important.'

'Is Mitra going with you?' she asked.

'Naturally.'

'I shall miss you both,' Alix said. She meant it. Over the weeks they had worked together, she had come to know Milovan Djilas better and had realised that his apparently gloomy expression was just the outward sign of someone with a powerful intellect who took life very seriously. In contrast, there was a side to his character that came from his upbringing in the tribal atmosphere of the peasant home in Montenegro where he had grown up. Montenegrins were reputed as courageous warriors who could laugh in the face of danger and were fiercely loyal to their comrades. In the hard months they had endured together he had become almost a father figure to her, and Mitra was her closest friend.

She and Mitra made an emotional farewell as they parted the following day.

'We'll meet again,' Mitra promised. 'I think Tito wants to bring the whole First Battalion to Montenegro when we've prepared the ground.'

Over the next days Alix became aware that Tito and the other members of the Council were increasingly obsessed by the need for some sign of recognition from Moscow. It was a continuing frustration that broadcasts from the BBC consistently featured Mihailovic as the leader of the Resistance, and they also suspected that the reports were being used to pass secret messages to him. Tito sent messages to the Comintern, begging them to press their British allies to dismiss Mihailovic as commander in chief and to publicise the achievements of the partisans. Their response was to suggest that Tito had been remiss in emphasising the communist ethos of the partisans and to blame him in part for the breakdown of relations with the Chetniks.

Milutinov reluctantly agreed to send the British mission to Pijade but emphasised his suspicions of their motives. He described the English major as 'sly' and commented that they had apparently been unable to make contact by radio with their base, which he found hard to believe.

In answer to Tito's question, the Comintern ordered that he should have the British mission sent to him and get out of them what their real objective was. Nevertheless, Milutinov still delayed, until a message from Tito to Pijade threatened that they would answer with their heads if his instructions were not carried out. The three men finally arrived in Foca on 20 March. Alix saw them being escorted into the hotel but then the British officer was closeted with Tito in a private meeting and it was not until they joined the rest of the Council for dinner that she saw them again. She was itching to speak to the

Englishman, convinced that he must have been sent by the same organisation that had sent Hudson and must therefore know her mother. She wanted to ask if Hudson had sent a message informing her mother of her whereabouts, as he had promised, and if so how she had reacted. They might even, she hoped, be carrying a message for her in return.

Dinner passed, however, without giving her any opportunity. As the guests were escorted out of the dining room, Alix managed to put herself in a position to catch the Englishman's eye, but his gaze passed over her without any sign of recognition.

Back at the house where she was staying, she had, as usual, to put up with Nikola's bad temper. He could have gone to dinner with the rest of them but he refused to eat in public because he was humiliated by his inability to cut up his own food. Alix pointed out that men who had been wounded in the struggle were regarded as heroes and no one would have thought any the worse of him, but he rejected the argument.

'I wasn't "wounded in the struggle". I lost a glove and I'm paying for it. There's nothing heroic about that.'

He had, unwillingly, gone back to his duties with his battalion, who were still being drilled into the resemblance of regular soldiers by General Popovic, but he was frustrated because he was unable to fire a rifle and convinced that he was now a useless impediment to the battalion's success. Drago was sure he could learn to shoot with his left hand, supporting the rifle on what remained of his right. He still had his thumb, which would have made this much easier, but he obstinately refused to try.

When she and Drago had finally succeeded in getting Nikola to bed that night, they sat together on the balcony, looking out at the stars. She told him what had happened after dinner.

'He just looked straight through me, Drago. Surely my mother must have told him to look out for me.'

'It's possible he didn't realise who you were,' Drago pointed out. 'After all, he probably wouldn't expect to see you in uniform.'

'That's possible, I suppose,' Alix conceded.

'Also, he may have been told to speak to you privately. You may get a message asking you to meet him when he has had a chance to settle in.'

Alix consoled herself with that thought and told herself she must be patient.

Next day Tito called another meeting.

'I spoke at length to the Englishman,' he told them. 'His name is Atherton and he was a journalist in Belgrade before the war. I remember reading some of his articles and I think he has a good understanding of us as a people. He told me, however, that the British government is very ill-informed about the situation here. He says that their only source of information is what they learn from the Yugoslav government in exile and that they tell them Mihailovic is the only leader standing up to the Germans. Atherton says our existence is virtually unknown.'

'But surely Captain Hudson will have told them otherwise,' Rankovic objected.

'Hudson has not been heard from since last December. Part of Atherton's mission is to find out what has become of him. It is feared he has been killed or captured.'

Alix felt a cold hand grasp her stomach. If Hudson had not been in touch since then he could not have told her mother where she was. More importantly, he might not have had the chance to hand her letter to Steve. So Steve must still think that she was betrothed to Nikola and was working for the people he probably regarded as enemies almost as much as the Germans. No wonder he had made no attempt to contact her.

She continued to hope for an opportunity to speak to Major Atherton but it was obvious that Tito was still suspicious about the motives of the new arrivals and they were kept apart from the rest. Only he and a few of his trusted aides had meetings with them. Alix gathered that they now accepted that the partisans were the most viable force of opposition. Some weeks earlier, partisans in Montenegro had captured Mihailovic's close associate, a man named Todorovic, who was found to be carrying papers that made it clear that the government in exile was actively encouraging the Chetnik's co-operation with the Italians. Tito had shown these to Atherton to prove that Mihailovic was a traitor and asked him to pass on that information to London. It seemed, however, that Atherton had left the charger for his radio battery with Milutinov, who had promised to forward it on to him, a promise that had not been fulfilled. So he was unable to send the message.

It was an unsatisfactory situation all round, and to make things worse there seemed to be some disagreement between Atherton and Nedeljkovic, his Serbian companion. Into this already confused situation a new factor was introduced by the arrival in Foca of a stranger.

'Who is that?' Alix asked Rankovic.

'A Serbian general,' he told her. 'His name is Novakovic. He's a nasty piece of work. He tried to take over Mihailovic's Chetniks back in the summer but Mihailovic wasn't having it. Since then he's worked with the collaborator Pecanic and then tried to set up a band of his own in Montenegro. Milutinov captured him and sent him here.'

In the days that followed, the general was seen talking to Atherton on more than one occasion.

-

On the morning of 16 April, Alix woke to the sound of a commotion. Coming out on the balcony, she was in time to see the head of security and a small posse galloping out of town in an easterly direction. Word soon spread around the camp. Atherton and his radio operator and Nedeljkovic had disappeared during the night, accompanied by General Novakovic. Search parties failed to locate them and messages to other detachments produced no results. It was assumed that they had gone to join Mihailovic, confirming the theory that their objective all along had been to bolster his position and confirm British support for him.

In the following days Alix had the impression that Tito was out of sorts. He was moody and taciturn and uncharacteristically inclined to snap at anyone who disagreed with him. She understood at least part of the reason. At the end of March a message had come from Moscow to say that 'for technical reasons' it was impossible to send any representatives to him. It was a blow to his ambition to see the partisans recognised by the Allies as the principal opposition to the occupiers, and on a practical level it meant they could not expect to receive much-needed arms and ammunition. It did not help that Zdenka, his mistress, who had returned to Belgrade when they were forced to leave Uzice, had now joined him. Alix had disliked her when they were all in Belgrade for her haughty manner and bad temper and she had not mellowed in the intervening weeks.

A much more immediate problem was the growing impression that the partisans had outstayed their welcome in Foca. There were several Chetnik bands operating in eastern Bosnia, and although the local people were grateful for protection from the depredations of the Ustashe, their instinctive sympathies lay with the Chetniks. They were mainly peasants, whose loyalties were first to their village, which often meant a network of families connected by ties of blood; then to the Orthodox Church, and above that to the king. The communists had no sympathy for the peasant's attachment to his land, rejected religion, and were not royalists.

Without the hoped for support from Russia in the form of arms drops, the partisans were beginning to run out of ammunition. It was obvious that soon they would not be able to withstand the increasingly regular incursions of the Chetniks. It seemed that their idyllic stay in Foca was drawing to a close.

Chapter Thirty-Three

Cemerno, Bosnia Herzegovina, March–April 1942

'What are the British doing? Why are we not receiving any supplies? I thought we had their support, but it seems it amounts to nothing but words.'

Draza Mihailovic was pacing around the single, mud-floored room of the cottage he had requisitioned as his headquarters in the tiny village on the flanks of the mountain. He had relocated himself and his staff to this point on the borders of Montenegro to be close to Djurisic, his representative in that country.

'We Chetniks are in virtual control of large parts of Montenegro,' he continued. 'We have almost driven the communists out. But it is thanks to the Italians, our enemies, not to the British, our so-called friends.'

'Perhaps the British are puzzled by the lack of communication from Captain Hudson,' Steve suggested cautiously. 'They must wonder what has happened to him.'

'Hudson is no friend of ours,' Draza growled. 'He prefers Tito's rabble.'

'He did come back to us,' Steve pointed out. 'You refused to see him.'

Draza looked at him, his expression for once undecided. 'You think that may be the reason?'

'It is quite possible that they think in Cairo that he is dead, or perhaps that we are dead too – or captured by the Boche.'

Draza's face expressed the conflict between his reluctance to withdraw from his previous position and the logic of Steve's argument. 'Perhaps,' he said at length, 'it is time to send for him.'

'You know where he is?'

'I can find out. I heard he was somewhere in the Sandjak. I will give orders for him to be found and brought here.'

A week or so later, Mihailovic sent for Steve. 'Send a signal to London. Captain Hudson is with us and hidden in a safe place.'

Steve frowned. 'Forgive me, sir, but that is not strictly true.'

'It will be, very soon. He has been located and is being transported here. Send the signal.'

Steve had no option but to obey and hope that Draza's prediction proved correct.

It was almost another week before an Italian truck drove into the village and a shabby figure in peasant dress climbed out. Two strangers in Chetnik uniform followed him out and escorted him into Mihailovic's cottage. Steve followed. He had expected the newcomer to be Hudson, but now he decided he must be mistaken. Inside the single room, the man was facing Draza across a table. He turned at Steve's entry and for a moment Steve stared in disbelief. It was only when he heard an unmistakable English voice greet him with the words 'Hello, old chap' that he was sure he was, in fact, facing Bill Hudson. He was emaciated and filthy and his sunken eyes peered out from a tangle of overgrown hair and beard. Steve had the impression that he was having difficulty keeping on his feet.

'My God, Bill!' he exclaimed, but Mihailovic cut him short.

'So, Captain Hudson. You have returned to us. Are you ready to resume your duties?'

Steve held his breath. What possible response could be adequate to the circumstances? For a few seconds Hudson was silent. Then he said, 'On certain conditions. One, I am free to report the situation as I see fit, using my own cyphers. And two, that you provide me with the means to wash and shave and give me a change of clothes.'

Draza gave orders and Hudson was escorted out of the cottage. Steve followed. In another cottage, a large cauldron of water had been set over the fire to heat, a tin bath was produced and Draza's own personal servant bustled in with his razors and shaving soap. Steve's mind was seething with questions, but some sense of tact made him hold back until Hudson had stripped off his lousy clothes and lowered himself with a groan into the hot water. The sight of his body confirmed Steve's worst impressions. The man was a walking skeleton and his flesh was covered with red, swollen patches that Steve had learned to identify as lice bites. As Steve watched, Hudson slithered down in the bath until his head was entirely immersed and came up gasping. As the barber set to work, Steve drew closer and squatted by the bath.

'My God, Bill. What's been happening to you?'

Hudson fixed him with a level stare. 'What do you imagine happens to someone left without resources in a foreign and largely hostile country? For four months I have had to beg, borrow and steal to stay alive. If it wasn't for the generosity of peasants who have scarcely enough to live on themselves I should be dead by now. Even so, a diet almost exclusively of potatoes is not one I'd recommend.'

Steve struck himself on the brow. 'Sorry! I'm a fool. You need food. Wait, I'll—'

He was interrupted by a woman's voice calling timidly from the doorway. Steve's intention had been pre-empted. She was carrying a tray on which was a hunk of bread, a plate of fried eggs and a mug of milk. In spite of his hard-bitten response, Draza had not been unmoved by Hudson's condition and had given orders accordingly.

Steve set the tray across the rim of the bath and watched Hudson cram the food into his mouth. Twenty minutes later, clean and fed, shaved and with his hair trimmed, Hudson sat on a stool with his back propped against the wall and felt ready to ask what had been happening in Draza's camp during his absence. For the first time, Steve was able to express his worries about the Chetnik leader's objectives.

'Draza is completely obsessed by the need to conquer the partisans. Fighting the Germans is second by a long way to that. He's been encouraging Chetnik detachments in Croatia to attack them and the Montenegrin detachments have almost succeeded in clearing them out of the country. And they are doing it all with the help of the Italians.'

Hudson looked grim. 'Then the rumours I've heard are true. Is there any resistance activity going on at all?'

'None. But Draza is blaming that in part on the fact that there have been no air drops of supplies for several months.'

'What does he expect? We are not going to waste our precious resources helping him to fight fellow Yugoslavs.'

'There's another thing.' Steve spoke with some hesitation. 'Draza has this project to create an ethnically pure country within the bounds of what he calls Greater Serbia. That means getting rid of all the Croats and all the Muslims.'

'Getting rid of them?' Hudson queried.

'His idea is that all Croats should be persuaded to return to Croatia and all Muslims should be sent to Turkey, or Albania. But from what I've heard some of the Chetnik leaders of other detachments have taken it as giving them carte blanche to carry out mass executions. Some of the rumours are horrifying.'

Hudson sighed and shook his head. 'What a country! First of all you have the Ustashe trying to exterminate the Serbs, now Draza wants to do the reverse. As far as I can see the only man who is interested in creating a united Yugoslavia free from German occupation is Tito.'

'Is that what you will tell London?'

Hudson stretched and yawned. 'I'll have to make my own enquiries, of course. The first thing to do is let them know I'm back in business.'

Chapter Thirty-Four

Cairo, April–May 1942

The SOE in Cairo was in turmoil. Leo had been aware since her arrival that there had been repeated upheavals due to the conflict of interests and policies between Cairo and London, which had led to several changes of senior personnel. She had kept herself aloof from the rumour-mongering and back-biting that seemed to afflict her colleagues, but now the general atmosphere of uncertainty had permeated through to the Balkan Desk. Masterson was leaving.

'I shan't be sorry to go,' he told her. 'I'm not a young man and my health is not what it was. To be frank, I've had enough of trying to sort out the affairs of that benighted country we call Yugoslavia.'

Leo looked at him. There was no doubt that he had aged considerably in the time she had known him. 'You deserve a rest,' she said. 'But you will be missed.'

'I doubt it,' he responded. 'Klugmann at least will be glad to see the back of me. We've never seen eye to eye.'

'I shall miss you,' Leo said.

'I shall miss you, too,' he told her. 'I've enjoyed working with you. You're a link to the old days when we worked together back in Belgrade.'

'Will you look Sasha up when you get back to London and give him my love?' she requested.

'Of course. I'm looking forward to having a long chat with him. I haven't lost interest in what's going on and I want to find out what the government in exile is really aiming to achieve. If anyone can tell me it will be Sasha.'

On the morning of his last day, Masterson came into Leo's office brandishing a slip of paper.

'At last! We're back in touch with Mihailovic and he says Bill is with him.'

'Oh, thank God!' Leo exclaimed. 'Can I see?'

She read the transcript of the coded message that had been forwarded from the listening station in Malta. 'He says he's safe and hidden. Why hidden?'

'There has obviously been a serious problem. I guess there may have been a German operation against them and they have had to keep their heads down for a while. I expect we shall learn more when we hear from Bill directly.'

'Hmm.' Leo handed back the slip of paper. 'I suppose that must be the explanation but I shan't be happy until we get a message from him, in his own code. But it's good that you have a bit of positive news to take away with you.'

'It's a weight off my mind, certainly,' Masterson agreed. 'I hated the thought that we might never know what became of him. But there's still Atherton out there somewhere. God knows what has happened to him.'

Leo went to the station to see him off that evening.

'Give my love to London, what's left of it,' she said.

Masterson nodded. 'I'm prepared for a shock. I haven't been home since before the blitz.'

'I'll keep in touch,' she told him. 'I'm sure Baker Street would pass on a message.'

He smiled grimly. 'I wouldn't take that for granted. But you'll hear any news from Sasha.'

The guard blew his whistle and Masterson turned to the carriage door. 'Better get aboard.'

She reached up and kissed him on the cheek, in defiance of military protocol.

'Take care of yourself,' she told him. 'And have a good rest.'

'You look after yourself too,' he said.

He climbed into the carriage and settled in his seat. The engine gave a belch of steam and the train began to move. All along it men and women hung out of the windows, waving to loved ones or taking a last look at what they were leaving; but Masterson stayed in his seat. Leo had the impression that he had at last allowed himself to believe he was escaping, escaping from the heat, from the constant bickering among colleagues, from the responsibility. She wished him well.

She had to wait several weeks for a message from Bill himself but before that she had the pleasure of forwarding a message to him from their superiors in London. He had been promoted to major and awarded the DSO.

The message, when it finally arrived, said no more than that he was now 'on terms' with Mihailovic and would be continuing the work he had been sent to do.

Chapter Thirty-Five

The foothills of Mount Durmitor, Montenegro, May 1942

A cuckoo called from the forest fringing the valley. Alix turned her head with a smile. She had always loved that sound as the harbinger of spring, whether at home at Kuca Magnolija or at school in England. It gave her a comforting sense of continuity to hear it here. For a few moments she allowed herself to revel in her surroundings. The river they were following was in spate from the melting snow, cascading down over its rocky bed and sending up showers of spray that the sunlight painted with rainbows. On either side of the valley the limestone peaks rose into a sky of intense, unsullied blue. The mountain air was fresh but the sun was warm on her face. She was on horseback and Mitra was riding beside her. What more could she ask? But she knew that the happy mood could be shattered at any moment. They were in hostile territory and danger could strike without warning.

As the situation in Foca became increasingly untenable, Tito had decided to make a personal visit to Montenegro in the hope of finding a place there where his increasingly large army could base itself. Over the recent months more recruits had joined them and he had been able to establish a second Proletarian Brigade, in pursuance of his aim to create a mobile force no longer tied to a particular village or area. Leaving the bulk of his forces in Foca, he had come with only his personal advisers and the Escort Battalion to look at the situation on the ground.

At first sight, the prospects did not look good. Milovan Djilas had greeted them sombrely and reported that the Chetniks, with Italian support, had made themselves masters of most of the country. Today, however, they were on their way to a meeting with the leaders of other partisan detachments at the Black Lake and on the way they had been promised a picnic. Most of the Battalion had been left in Zabljak, where Djilas had set up his headquarters, and Tito was accompanied by Djilas and a small escort under Nikola's command. Alix's cheerful mood was shared by the rest of the group. Even Nikola was exchanging jokes with one of his men, but it only needed the weight of her rifle on her shoulder to remind her that this was no holiday.

As if to emphasise the point, she became aware of the distant drone of an aircraft engine. All round her, heads were raised and the conversation stopped. Seconds later the plane appeared over a shoulder of the hill ahead of them. There was no doubt about who it belonged to. They were all far too familiar with the outline of a Focke-Wulf.

A short distance ahead of them was a dense stand of pine trees. Tito stood in his stirrups and waved his arm towards them.

'In there! Quick!'

Alix put her heels to her mare and joined the others in a reckless gallop towards the shelter of the trees. She flung herself down over the horse's neck to avoid low branches as they crashed into the little copse, and even as she did so she heard the spatter of bullets hitting the ground just behind her. All around her she heard the trampling of hooves and the snap of breaking branches as the rest of the troop sought cover. In the centre of the copse the trees were taller and the canopy a little higher and it was possible to sit up. Tito had drawn rein there with Djilas beside him and the rest assembled themselves around him.

The sound of the plane's engine was fading but Tito warned, 'He'll be back,' and sure enough they heard the engine's note change as it banked and turned for another run. Once again they heard the chatter of the machine guns but the tree canopy was so thick that the pilot was unable to pinpoint their precise position. Twigs and pine needles rained down on them but aside from a few scratches they were unharmed.

Djilas looked around at them and grinned. 'Well, it strikes me this is the moment for our picnic.'

He swung down from his saddle and opened his saddlebag to produce an object that raised a murmur of surprise that swelled to a cheer. A whole ham! Something almost unheard of in these straightened times.

Tito threw back his head and laughed. 'Brilliant! Let's eat!'

The German plane was not done with them. It came back for a third attempt but once again the trees sheltered them and then they heard its engine fade away into silence as it left the valley.

'He's gone to refuel,' Tito said, 'but it will be some time before he gets back.'

More cautiously than in their headlong retreat, they found their way out of the copse and dismounted on a grassy bank. Djilas's servant produced a sack of flatbreads from his saddle bag and Djilas carved slices of ham and passed them round. Biting into an improvised sandwich, Alix thought she had never enjoyed a meal so much.

As soon as they had eaten they resumed their journey and a short while later they crossed a shoulder of the mountain and found themselves looking down on the Black Lake. It was so called because the hillside flanking it was covered with a dense pine forest and the dark trees were reflected in the mirror-like surface of the water. Alix gathered it had an almost iconic value to the Montenegrins, which was why it had been chosen as a meeting place.

On the bank opposite the forest there was a collection of small huts and tents and they rode into a camp prepared for them. Tito was introduced to half a dozen bearded and well-armed men who represented different partisan bands and he and Djilas sat down with them around a rough log table to talk. Alix, still the unofficial record keeper, sat with them. The mood was grim.

'We can't fight the Chetniks and the Italians,' one of the men said.

'Take this as an example,' another continued. 'We had surrounded one of the Chetnik strongholds in Danilograd but the Italians attacked us and broke through our ring, and that allowed the Chets to break out and massacre our men. We are in danger of being wiped out.'

'Mihailovic's man, Djurisic, has an agreement with the Italians,' the first man went on. 'They haven't the manpower to police the whole country. They stay in the main cities, like Podgorica, and they leave him and his Chetniks to police the rest of the country. He is able to recruit freely among the local peasants. Even some of our own men have deserted and joined him.'

The mood on the return ride was very different.

Tito had taken up residence in the governor's house in Zabljak. It was a beautiful place, set among orchards and beehives, but Tito found no comfort there. He sent for his old friend Mosa Pijade, whom he had dispatched to Montenegro early in the war. Pijade was not a young man and an unlikely rebel leader, it seemed to Alix. He was a Jew, an intellectual, and an impressionist painter. Tito had been in prison with him before the war and he and Tito were close friends, but if Tito hoped to find support from him he was disappointed. Pijade had decided to set up a state farm and seemed interested only in his sheep and cows and the produce of the land.

To add to everyone's discomfort, Zdenka had travelled with them and her temper had grown worse than ever. She seemed to feel that the hostility of the Germans and the Italians was directed at her, personally, and shouted at Tito for his failure to protect her. Nobody could understand what Tito saw in her, but he seemed totally infatuated with her. She detested Alix and repeatedly accused her of wishing to seduce Tito.

'We all know why you refuse to marry Count Nikola Dordevic,' she ranted. 'You think you can do better for yourself. But you watch out, you scheming little bitch. You'll get your comeuppance. Tito wants nothing to do with you. Do you hear?'

Nikola took his cue from Zdenka and became increasingly jealous.

'It's no good you hanging around Tito like a lovesick puppy,' he said one evening. 'If you have no respect for your own reputation you might at least show some for mine.'

'It's got nothing to do with your reputation,' Alix responded sharply. 'I've made it clear that you have no claim on me. And I'm not hanging around Tito in the way you imply. I respect him and I admire him and I want to be useful, that's all there is to it.'

This did nothing to pacify Nikola. He resented any time Alix spent in Tito's company and tried to find ways of keeping her at his side, constantly demanding small attentions. Tito, meanwhile, became increasingly depressed. The atmosphere in the governor's house was more and more oppressive.

One afternoon Tito called them together.

'I have made a decision. There is no place for us here. We must establish a free territory in Bosnia. I shall incorporate the detachments here into a third Proletarian Brigade. There are others in the Krajina district of Bosnia who can be brought together to form another brigade. We shall head west, away from the main cities. The Italians have withdrawn to the coast and the area is controlled by the Ustashe, who are hated by the people. We shall find a welcome there.'

'Go west?' Djilas queried. 'How? The Italians control the railways and we have no way of acquiring trucks, or petrol.'

'Then we march!' Tito declared.

Chapter Thirty-Six

Cmerno, May 1942

Steve finished decoding a message and hurried to find Mihailovic. He was glad to find Hudson with him, poring over a map.

'According to my spies, Tito and his rabble are somewhere here, in the mountains west of Sarajevo,' Draza was saying. 'We drove them out of Foca but only God knows where they are heading now. The Croatian Independence Party under Pavlic have taken over Bosnia and he won't tolerate partisan operations in his area. With any luck he'll finish Tito off without any further action from us.'

He looked up at Steve. 'What is it?'

'I've got a message from Major Ostojic.'

Hudson looked up. 'Ostojic? Where is he? I haven't heard from him since I got back.'

'He's not here,' Draza told him. 'He is in command of our forces in the Sandjak now.'

Steve saw that this gave Hudson pause for thought. Ostojic had been sent from Cairo along with him, supposedly to gather information and report back. It seemed that his real objective had always been to join the Chetniks.

'What is the message?' Draza asked.

'It is about that British mission that was rumoured to have arrived a couple of months ago.'

Hudson sat up sharply. 'What mission? I've heard nothing about this.'

'According to my informants, a British major and some others were landed from a submarine, as you were,' Draza told him. 'They fell into the hands of the partisans and that was the last we heard of them. I've no doubt the partisans killed them.'

'It seems not,' Steve told him. 'Ostojic says he has picked up a Yugoslav officer by the name of' – he paused to refer to the signal – 'Nedeljkovic, who was wandering about in his area. He says he was part of a British mission led by a Major Atherton. They were with Tito but now Atherton is "somewhere in Bosnia" and wants to see you.'

'What sort of double game is being played here?' Draza asked. 'If he was sent to me, what has he been doing with Tito? Why was I not told to expect this mission? There are rumours of other British parties active elsewhere in the country. If the British are our allies, why am I not being kept informed?'

'We have been out of touch for some months,' Steve pointed out.

Mihailovic's response was a glare. 'Send a signal to London. Say I have been informed that there is a mission in the area but I don't know who they are or what they want. Ask them to elucidate.'

'If Atherton is wandering about Bosnia, we must try to find him as soon as possible,' Hudson urged.

'All in good time,' was the curt response.

A few days later a courier brought a letter from Atherton himself, asking to be escorted to Mihailovic's headquarters, and in response messages were sent out to other Chetnik groups in an effort to locate him.

'I'm going to Ostojic's HQ to talk to this Nedeljkovic,' Hudson said. 'We need to get to the bottom of this.'

He was back in a few days but the only information he had gleaned was that Nedeljkovic and Atherton had quarrelled and the Englishman had left in the direction of Serbia.

A message arrived from London.

> *Atherton is our man. He was sent in January. Help him and take his advice.*

Cairo, May

Leo had waited impatiently to hear from Bill himself and at last a message arrived in his own cypher. As a bonus, it also brought the first news she had received of the fate of Terence Atherton. Bill's report that he was lost somehow in Serbia was worrying, but at least they knew now he was still alive.

Her hopes were dashed by a second message a few weeks later.

I have made extensive enquiries, Hudson wrote, *and this is a summary of the information I have been able to obtain. Atherton and O'Donovan, his radio operator, escaped from Tito's camp at Foca on 15 April in the company of a man called Dakic, the leader of a small Chetnik band in eastern Bosnia. They hid for seven days in a cave until Atherton quarrelled with Dakic and left for the village of Tartaravina. No one seems to have any knowledge of where they went after that.*

Leo conveyed this message to her new boss, Basil Davidson. He was another ex-journalist who had been recruited into SOE and had already had a varied and exciting career, including a spell as an Italian prisoner of war, from which he had been freed in a prisoner exchange. Leo found he had a lively mind and a great sense of humour, but she was never able to feel the same connection to him as she had to Tom Masterson. More and more she found herself missing Sasha. He wrote regularly but with the vagaries of the wartime postal service she often did not hear from him for weeks, and then three letters would arrive at once. He was becoming increasingly frustrated with the internal bickering that plagued the government in exile. He was also concerned about Peter. The young king had finished his year at Cambridge, which he had apparently enjoyed, but now he was determined to join the RAF. *I'm afraid he has visions of leading a daring raid to somehow liberate his country, maybe even of parachuting in to lead the Resistance*, Sasha wrote. *It's hard for him to accept that there is nothing he can do.*

Bill's next message sent a chill through her.

> *Yesterday the man Dakic appeared here, carrying Atherton's binoculars and wearing his boots. Of course he claims they were given to him, but I feel certain he has murdered Atherton and O'Donovan. I assume Atherton was carrying a considerable amount of currency, probably in the form of gold sovereigns, as I did when I arrived. It is true that ready money for bribes, etc., can be a great advantage, but we must rethink that policy. It is too much of a temptation in such a lawless country.*

Chapter Thirty-Seven

Konjic, Bosnia, 7 July 1942

Alix scrambled down the steep slope, clinging to the overhanging branches of the trees that clothed it to stop herself from sliding. Below her, the surface of the River Neretva gleamed in the moonlight, but it was not the river that was the focus of her attention. High above it, carried on a slender bridge, ran the railway line that connected Sarajevo to the Adriatic. That was her target for tonight.

A scuffle and a small fall of pebbles told her that Mitra was close behind her. They reached the bank of the river and crouched under the cover of some bushes to watch the bridge. There were sentries patrolling it. That much they knew, but now they needed to study their movements. How many were there, and how often did they pass across the bridge?

Alix eased a heavy rucksack from her shoulders. There was no donkey this time to carry the sticks of gelignite and the fuses and wires and other paraphernalia they needed. Instead she and Mitra carried them between them. It crossed her mind that a few months ago she would have found this hard. Recent weeks had toughened her and pared away every ounce of surplus flesh until her body was nothing but muscle and sinew.

The plan Tito had conceived in Montenegro had, by then, brought them halfway across Bosnia. Partisan detachments from all over the eastern part of the country had rallied in the foothills of Mount Zelengora, just south of Foca, in June. From there they had moved west, keeping to the mountains well away from the main centres of population. It had been hard going. To begin with, in Herzegovina, the slopes were bare, denuded of trees and without shelter from the mid-summer sun. Men had collapsed from thirst and heat stroke. Further on, the landscape changed and the mountains were covered in thick forest. There were brown bears here. Often they saw the prints of their paws on the paths they were following and sentries had to be posted every night to guard their meagre supplies. At night they heard wolves howling not far away. The peaks of the mountains rose to over 7,000 feet, where the air was thin and it was cold, even in summer. The ridge they followed was bisected by frequent gorges, entailing a precipitous descent and the crossing of wild, foaming rivers and then another long, hard climb on the far side. As always, as they marched, Drago had been there to offer a helping hand or to carry her rifle; but she was no longer the girl who had struggled to keep up as they left Uzice. She was a *partizanka*, tough and battle hardened.

There had been battles. First they had had to clear a strong Ustashe force from around Treskavica mountain. Then they had fought their way westward with frequent skirmishes with Chetnik units supported by Ustashe. Initially, Alix had found it hard to reconcile the taking of human lives with her conscience, until an incident that branded itself on her memory. Of necessity, the partisans had to live off the country they passed through. Tito made a point of paying for supplies where possible but the store of silver they had carried with such difficulty from Uzice was beginning to run out and often units were forced to rely on the hospitality of local peasants. One village belonging to some Serbian people agreed reluctantly to house a partisan detachment overnight. Next day, horrific rumours about the aftermath reached the Supreme Headquarters and Djilas was sent to establish the truth. Alix went with him and what she saw banished any scruples she had about fighting. The Ustashe had taken revenge by slaughtering every man, woman and child. Dead bodies lay in the streets, obscenely murdered. In one corner they found a heap of severed limbs. In the houses they found the bodies of women clutching their dead babies in their arms. From that day on, whenever they had to fight Ustashe forces, Alix cast aside all inhibition and fired until the barrel of her rifle was red hot.

Tonight, however, she was not required to fire a shot. The skill she had learned from Tomaz had given her a different and more vital role.

Above their heads, the shadowy outline of a figure moved across the bridge heading for the far side. A cigarette glowed briefly and hissed as the butt hit the water.

'Fifteen minutes,' Mitra whispered. 'That's how long he spends walking to the far side and back.'

'Time enough,' Alix responded. 'Let's go.'

They inched their way along the bank until they were directly under the bridge. There they unloaded their equipment and prepared the charges. Then Alix wound a rope around her waist, slung her rucksack round her neck and felt her way to the edge of the river. Mitra took a firm grip on the other end of the rope. The water was flowing fast and they could only hope that Alix would be able to keep her feet. She lowered herself down the bank and stifled a gasp as the cold water rose round her legs. In one hand she carried a stout staff, cut from a tree branch higher up the bank, and with that she probed the ground ahead of her. As she had hoped, at this point the water was not very deep, not quite up to her waist, and the riverbed was firm and not too rocky. Step by step she moved forward, until she reached the base of one of the piers supporting the bridge. She wedged her staff against it, bracing herself against the flow, and reached into the rucksack. Working with numbed fingers, she strapped the charge in place and inserted the fuse. Now came the tricky bit. She had to make her way back to the bank, unrolling the wire which would be attached to the detonator.

She was about to start the return journey when an owl hooted close by on the bank. Alix froze. This was the agreed warning. Seconds later she understood the reason. There were voices above her on the bridge. She could not hear what was being said but it was obvious the sentry had returned and he had company. She gritted her teeth. Her legs were numb from the cold water and she was beginning to shiver. Moments passed, then two cigarette butts hissed into the water a few feet away and the bridge vibrated under the movement of feet. More time passed, perhaps only seconds but it seemed endless, then the owl hooted again, twice. With great relief Alix grasped her staff in one hand and thrust the other arm through the centre of the roll of detonating wire. It was a struggle to remain upright, but eventually she reached the bank and Mitra reached out to take the roll of wire and pulled her up onto dry land.

While Alix took off her boots and emptied out the water, Mitra connected the wire to the detonator. Then they moved back up the bank until they were concealed among the undergrowth.

'All set,' Alix whispered. 'Now all we have to do is wait.'

It was critical that the explosion was not set off too early. In her imagination Alix saw her comrades moving stealthily through the forest surrounding the little town of Konjic, heading for the railway station. If her bomb was set off prematurely, the garrison stationed in Konjic would be forewarned and the men attacking the station would come under fire. Timing was vital.

Alix squeezed water out of the hems of her trousers and tried to rub some warmth back into her feet. On the bridge the sentry continued his beat. Then, a mile away to the south came the sound they had been waiting for. The crackle of gunfire. The attack on the station was underway.

'Now!' Alix said, and Mitra depressed the handle on the detonator.

There was a breathless millisecond of suspense; then they saw the flash and a blast of warm air swept over them. The sound of the explosion reached them a fraction of a second later. They both jumped to their feet, peering through the pall of smoke and dust to see their handi-work. The pier had collapsed and the bridge had fractured, leaving one end of the rail line sticking out over a void, while the other drooped down to touch the water.

'Well done!' Mitra squeezed Alix's arm. 'Let's get moving.'

They scrambled up to the small road that ran along the rim of the ravine. Here they had hidden the rest of their kit, including a pair of dry socks for Alix. As soon as she had put them on they shouldered their rifles and set off at a jog towards the noise of the battle that was still raging around the station.

By the time they reached the town, the firing had died down. The garrison had been subdued and prisoners were being herded into a warehouse by the tracks, while another detail was collecting the bodies of the dead. Around the station, groups of men led by some who had worked on the railways before they joined the partisans were destroying points and signals and rendering several locomotives immobile. This railway was important, not just to the Ustashe but to the German war effort, since it carried vital supplies of bauxite and coal from the Bosnian mines for the factories in Germany. Alix looked around for Tito and found him standing on the platform with his personal escort. Nikola was sitting on an upturned bucket nearby and close to him, to her relief, was Drago. The Escort battalion was always held in reserve to protect Tito and the members of the Supreme Headquarters but that did not mean they did not take part in the fighting. Once the dispositions of the battle became clear they were often sent in to reinforce any weak spots.

Nikola no longer insisted that he was unable to do his duty. He had finally, after much persuasion, allowed Drago to teach him to shoot using his left hand on the trigger and supporting the barrel of the rifle on the thumb and what was left of his right. Only Alix knew the extent to which he relied on Drago's help and support.

As she moved towards them, Drago saw her and hurried to meet her. 'Are you all right?'

'A bit damp, but all right otherwise,' she told him. The summer night was warm and the run from the bridge to the station had dried out her trousers.

'And the bridge?'

As he asked the question, Tito turned and saw her.

'The bridge is down, comrade,' she told him.

He gave her a quick smile. 'I never doubted it.'

Nikola looked up. 'Decided to come and join in now the fighting is over?'

She ignored him. Since he had failed to restrict her to what he regarded as suitable roles for a woman, he had changed tack and lost no opportunity to suggest that she could never be as effective a fighter as a man.

The demolition experts had finished their job. The men who had been detailed to replace the garrison in the now 'liberated' town were moving into position. Orders were given and passed down the line and men shouldered their rifles and formed up. By the time the first rays of the rising sun gilded the tops of the trees on the eastern side of the gorge, the main partisan force had melted away into the forest.

Chapter Thirty-Eight

Cairo, 1 July 1942

Davidson called all the staff of the Balkan Desk together for an emergency meeting. In place of his usual expression of wry amusement, his manner was tense.

'I don't wish to spread alarm and despondency but there's a bit of a flap on. Our men have been driven back from Mersa Matruh and Rommel's army is advancing. Unless Auchinleck can hold them at El Alamein there's nothing to stop them taking Alexandria and then moving on to Cairo. We have been given orders to burn all sensitive documents and prepare to evacuate. Go back to your desks and collect anything that might be of help to the enemy and take it all down to the courtyard to be burned.'

Leo sorted through the files on her desk with a sense of unreality. All through the summer she, like all her colleagues, had listened avidly to the reports coming out of the desert as the British Eighth Army struggled to contain General Rommel's Afrika Corps. The fall of the vital port of Tobruk, which had become a symbol of resistance, had sent a shiver of alarm through the population of the city, both military and civilian, but somehow life had continued as if the war was happening elsewhere. It had been an ongoing source of amazement to Leo that Cairo seemed to exist in a parallel universe, where rationing and blackouts were unknown and the main purpose of life was enjoyment – at least for the Europeans and the wealthy Egyptians. The officers played golf and polo during the day and drank at Shepheard's Hotel or the Continental in the evening, or took their lady friends to the open-air cinemas that had sprung up all round. At dinner there was no shortage of steaks or whisky or fine wine. It was a life of luxury beyond the dreams of many of those who had come up through the ranks.

The common soldiers too were making the most of what was on offer. The British Tommies had now been joined by contingents of New Zealanders, Australians and Indians, but it was for the Brits that the contrast between life at home and here was most marked. Many of them had come from the backstreets of industrial cities or from remote hill farms or rural backwaters. For most of them life had meant grey skies and the struggle to make ends meet. Here they found sunshine and plenty to eat and no shortage of beer and available pretty girls. It was no wonder that many of them seemed to exist in a haze of heat and alcohol.

Now it seemed that all that might be about to come to an end, not only for them but for Leo herself. The question at the back of her mind was, if Egypt fell, where next? But that was a problem for another day. Right now, she had to concentrate on sorting papers to be burned before they could fall into enemy hands.

In the courtyard there were already several fires burning and staff from various departments were busy feeding the flames. Looking up, Leo saw plumes of smoke ascending from other points in the city as the headquarters of the various military commands destroyed their files. Men and women were scurrying in and out of the building with armfuls of paper and there was an atmosphere of barely controlled panic.

When she was finally able to leave for her little flat on the houseboat, Leo found the streets even more packed than usual. Cars crammed with whole families, with their possessions strapped on the roofs, were struggling to make their way out of the city, some heading south towards Sudan, others east to the border with Palestine. Men and women on foot lugged suitcases towards the central station. Taxis were impossible to find, so she had to walk and before long found her way impeded by a long queue of army officers which wound its way round the block and out of sight.

'What are you all waiting for?' she asked a red-faced lieutenant.

'Barclays Bank,' he said. 'The military branch. All my money's there. I want it out before the Huns march in. Same for all these other chaps.'

Leo's mood of anxiety deepened. 'Well, good luck,' she said, and threaded her way past the waiting men.

The panic of that day was succeeded by several days of tense waiting. Then the news came through. Auchinleck's men had succeeded in stopping Rommel at the little railway town of El Alamein. Intelligence suggested that the German lines of supply were over extended and there would be no further advance for the time being.

Somewhat sheepishly, they all returned to their desks; but the mood of carefree enjoyment had vanished. For some weeks, both armies licked their wounds and regrouped but it was inevitable that before long the fight would begin again.

Chapter Thirty-Nine

Steve was increasingly disturbed by the deterioration in the relationship between Draza and Bill Hudson. Mihailovic had never lost his suspicion that Hudson secretly favoured the partisans and seemed unable to overcome his distrust. Hudson was growing more and more frustrated by the Chetnik commander's refusal to undertake any direct action against the German occupiers. He had never really recovered his health after the deprivations he had suffered during his 'exile' from the Chetnik camp. Steve noticed that although he had put on weight he no longer had the muscular shoulders and agile movement of the amateur boxer he had once been. His cheeks were hollow and his eyes sometimes had a haunted look, as if he was still reliving the horrors of that period.

Matters came to a head one afternoon. Steve had just transmitted a signal from Hudson to his superiors when Draza came into the radio cabin.

'What are you telling them in London?' he demanded. 'What lies are you feeding them?'

Hudson stood up. 'I am telling them the truth. That you are collaborating with the Italians and doing nothing to disrupt their operations or those of the Germans.'

'What do you expect me to do?' Draza demanded. 'I have said before, if I cannot rely on supplies and funds from those who purport to be my allies I must take what I can from those we call enemies.'

'So,' Hudson said, 'if I can arrange a substantial drop, can I assure my superiors that you will use what they send to sabotage enemy communications?'

Steve saw that Mihailovic felt he had been pushed into a corner. After a moment he said, 'I shall understand it as proof that the British Government is aware of my situation and is prepared to support me.'

Hudson heaved a sigh and turned away. 'Very well, I shall see what I can do.'

A week later Steve found himself standing with Hudson on a windswept plateau a few miles from Zabljak, watching the sky and listening for the sound of engines. Since Tito and the other members of the partisan Supreme Headquarters had abandoned the area, Mihailovic had made it his base. There were still a few bands of partisans holding out in some areas but Montenegro was now almost entirely under Chetnik control, apart from the few towns still garrisoned by the Italians. Around Steve and Hudson, a large force stood ready to receive whatever the RAF sortie had brought them, and to repel any possible enemy intervention.

Steve shivered. It might be high summer, but Zabljak was the highest town in the whole of the Balkans and at this altitude the night was chilly.

'Hark!' Hudson said, and at the same instant Steve's ears picked up the drone of a heavy aircraft. At Hudson's signal torches were put to bonfires arranged in a careful formation around the plateau, a pattern that would enable the pilot to recognise the dropping zone. The drone of the engine grew louder and Steve experienced a sudden flashback. He could feel himself crouched over the bomb-sight in a Blenheim fighter/bomber, peering down, not at the mountains of Montenegro, but at the fields of France. Nearly three years ago! Was it only that long? It felt like a lifetime ago.

He shook himself mentally. This was not the time for dreaming. The plane that overflew them was not a Blenheim. It was something much larger but Steve had been too long away from his RAF squadron to recognise it. A signal light flashed from the cockpit and was answered by Hudson and then two parachutes blossomed in the moonlight and began their descent.

'Is that all?' Steve asked.

'He may be going to make another pass,' Hudson suggested.

But the plane flew on and very soon the sound of its engines faded into silence. Gazing up at the parachutes, Steve saw that what was being dropped was in fact two men. His heartbeat quickened. Could these be two more British agents come to join Hudson? The thought of contact with men of flesh and blood rather than disem-bodied Morse bleeps was appealing.

'Are we expecting anyone?' he asked.

Hudson's tone was grim. 'Not to my knowledge.' He turned to the Chetnik officer standing beside him. 'Tell your men to bring them here.'

A small reception committee was ready when the two men hit the ground and freed themselves from their para-chutes. The 'chutes were quickly brought under control and bundled up and the men were led over to where Hudson and Steve were waiting. As they drew closer Steve saw that their uniforms were not British, but belonged to the Royal Yugoslavian air force. They were obviously expecting to be gladly received and Steve saw that Hudson was hiding his disappointment as they shook hands.

'We were expecting an arms drop,' he said. 'But you're very welcome.'

The two men introduced themselves and one said with a broad grin, 'We may not be machine guns, or whatever you were hoping for, but we have a gift that will be more useful than that.'

'May I ask what it is?' Hudson enquired.

'That is something that General Mihailovic should be the first to hear,' was the response.

'Of course,' Hudson agreed. 'I will take you to him now.'

Back at the house where Mihailovic had settled, Hudson and Steve found themselves dismissed from his presence. It was not until after the newcomers had been treated to a welcome dinner that Hudson was readmitted.

'So what did they bring?' Steve asked when he came out again.

'Money,' Hudson replied. 'Thirty million lire and a considerable sum in American dollars.'

'Wow!' Steve murmured. 'So what is Draza supposed to do with that?'

'That remains to be seen,' Hudson said. 'But it doesn't immediately provide the equipment he needs to carry out sabotage attacks. I fancy the government in exile must have persuaded whoever makes these decisions that the money would be more useful. My guess is they don't want Draza taking any action that would risk reprisals any more than he does himself.'

Steve shook his head despairingly. 'They're a devious lot, aren't they?'

Hudson raised an eyebrow. 'I thought you were an admirer.'

'Of Draza?' Steve shrugged. 'I used to be. When the Nazis drove in and the Yugoslav army fell apart like a piece of wet tissue paper in a gale, he seemed to me to be the only senior officer with any fighting spirit, and the only chance of creating some form of resistance. That's why I decided to throw in my lot with him. And to begin with I thought he was on the right lines, sending men to build up detachments in different parts of the country. I could see the logic behind waiting for an allied invasion before launching a full-scale uprising. But I didn't expect him to be so... so passive, just sitting back and letting the Boche have their own way, refusing to take the slightest risk. I think it was the massacre at Kragujevac that did it. He can't bear the thought of Serbs being killed because of his actions.'

'Well, I certainly haven't seen any sign of that fighting spirit you mentioned,' Hudson said. 'If that's what you're looking for it's the local Montenegrin commanders who have it in abundance. I think if Djurisic, for example, was in charge we'd see a very different approach.'

Next morning Steve caught Hudson's eye as they left the mess hut. He joined him and they strolled around the perimeter of the camp.

'You remember what I said about Djurisic yesterday? Well, it feels like he wants to prove me right. He nabbed me last night on my way to bed with a proposal of his own.'

'Which is?'

'He wants some of the money that was dropped. His idea is he'd use it to either buy equipment from the Italians or bribe someone into letting him have it. On that basis he's prepared to take a company into Serbia and carry out sabotage attacks, with or without Mihailovic's permission.'

'What did you say?'

Hudson shrugged. 'What could I say? Draza has the money. I can't make him part with it. And anyway, I couldn't be party to any kind of negotiations with the occupying power.'

The next message Steve decoded was a direct request from General Alexander, the commander in chief of Middle Eastern forces, that Mihailovic should sabotage the Belgrade–Nis railway line. Hudson was unsurprised.

'The main reason the Germans want to keep hold of Serbia is because it gives them a safe passage to bring troops and supplies to Thessalonika and from there across the Med to North Africa. With things hotting up in the desert that could be crucial. The Belgrade–Nis rail connection is a vital part of that.'

Nevertheless, Mihailovic refused to be pushed into action.

'Send this message in reply,' he told Steve. 'To carry out the sabotage as requested would require a sortie to drop explosives. Please do not drop anything of the sort until I tell you we are ready to receive them.'

Steve ground his teeth in frustration but there was nothing he could do but obey.

When he told Hudson, the Englishman shook his head grimly. 'You know, I can't help thinking we are backing the wrong horse here. From what I saw of Tito and his partisans they would jump at the chance to do something that would really hurt the Nazis.'

'You were pretty impressed by them, weren't you?' Steve commented.

'Yes, I was. From what I saw in Uzice and on their retreat over Mount Zlatibor I would say they are well-organised, well-disciplined and brave. If only Draza could have been persuaded to join forces with Tito we would have a really formidable force, but at their last meeting…' He stopped suddenly. 'My God! I've just remembered something! Wait here.'

He disappeared into his hut and Steve waited, puzzled, for several minutes. Eventually Hudson returned, holding a yellowed and crumpled piece of paper.

'I was supposed to give this to you when I returned to Draza after my last visit to Uzice. But then there was the German attack and the retreat and when I finally found my way back to Ravna Gora he wouldn't let me anywhere near the place.' He held out the piece of paper. 'I thought I'd lost it but it was stuffed in one of the pockets of that stinking sheepskin coat. I'm afraid it's not in very good condition but it might still be legible.'

'What is it?' Steve asked, mystified.

'It's a letter to you from that girl you once met in Paris. You saw her briefly, remember, at that meeting between Draza and Tito, and then some oaf snatched her away.'

'Alix!' Steve murmured. 'You mean Alix?'

'Alexandra Malkovic,' Hudson confirmed. 'She told me you knew each other in Paris before the war.'

'Yes.' Steve's thoughts were in such turmoil that he found it hard to speak. 'Yes, we did.' He turned the paper over in his hands and discovered it was an envelope addressed to Stefan Popovic.

Hudson said gently, 'I'll give you time to read it – if it's still readable.'

He moved away and sat down on a log that had been carved into a seat.

Steve's hands were shaking. The envelope was so delicate that he was afraid of destroying the contents as he opened it. He succeeded in extracting a single sheet of paper. The ink had faded and the paper was so stained that it was almost impossible to make out the words, but he persisted and read:

My dear Steve,

It was such a surprise to see you at the meeting at Brajici and I would have loved to talk to you properly. I was furious with Nikola, the man who dragged me away. I want you to know that I am not engaged to him, whatever he said at the time. He is the man my father wanted me to marry. Getting away from him was the reason I was in Paris. Do you remember me telling you? Since I came back he has tried to take up where we left off but I've told him that I don't want that sort of relationship.

I've been hoping that there might be another meeting, another chance for us to get together, but it seems that is not going to happen.

Do you remember how you used to walk me back to the college when we left the café in the evening? I treasure the memory of those walks. Ever since you left to join the RAF I've regretted that I didn't give you more reason to stay. I have often wondered what you were doing and prayed that you were still safe, but I never imagined that you might find your way out here. I suppose I should have guessed. After all, this is in a way your country as well as mine.

If you get this letter, please try to get in touch. I should so much like to see and talk to you again.

With my love,
Alix

Steve raised his head and looked around him. His eyesight was blurred but he was not sure if it was the strain of reading the faint writing or because there were tears in his eyes. He struggled to give his thoughts some order. Alix was not engaged. That was good news. And she remembered their time together – treasured the memory. She wanted to see him. Even better. But that letter had been written… When? A year ago. So much could have changed. She might have formed a new relationship, or perhaps the man she had resisted for so long had finally forced her into some kind of betrothal. The partisans had fought battles, he knew. She might, God forbid, be dead.

One thought clarified itself. She had asked him to get in touch, but she must think he had received the letter months ago. She must by now have decided that he did not want to renew their relationship.

Hudson was still sitting on the log. Steve dropped down beside him.

'Good news?'

'Yes. Yes, it is.'

'I'm sorry it's a bit late arriving.'

'Not your fault.'

'I should have remembered to give it to you earlier.'

'It's not surprising, after all you went through. Thank you for preserving it for me.'

'So, what now? Is there any further action?'

'I'd like to reply, but I can't see any way to do it.'

Hudson shook his head. 'Nor can I, at the moment.'

'If we contacted Cairo… But I can't see what good that would do.'

'Ah!' Hudson reacted as if he had been stung. 'That's another thing. God, my brain! I need to get a message through to Cairo.' He looked at Steve. 'Did Alix ever mention her mother to you?'

'Yes. She seems to have been a remarkable lady. I know Alix was very keen to live up to her example. Why?'

'She still is a remarkable lady. She's the woman who has been dealing with all our signals traffic between here and London.'

Steve stared at him. 'Alix's mother is... where? In Cairo?'

'Leonora, yes. She was recruited by SOE two years ago and was involved, with her husband, in the Belgrade coup. They got out when the invasion started and got back to London, but then her boss at SOE asked her to come out and join the team at the Balkans desk in Cairo. She's ideally qualified, of course. Not only fluent in Serbo-Croat but in Greek and Arabic, among other things.'

Steve was still staring. 'You've met Alix's mother?'

Hudson smiled. 'Yes. I was in Cairo for several weeks. We became good friends.'

'That's incredible!'

'Small world, as they say.' Hudson became serious. 'The point is, Leo has no idea where her daughter is. I promised Alix when I met her that I would let her know. If I compose a message, can you send it?'

'Yes, of course,' Steve said. 'But is it wise? We don't know what... what's happened to Alix since you saw her. I wonder if it would be kinder...'

'No.' Hudson was definite. 'Leo would want to know. I know she has been worrying about what might be happening to her in occupied France. It's right she should know where she is now.'

'OK,' Steve said. 'But that doesn't solve the problem of how I'm going to get in touch with Alix. Doesn't Cairo have any contact with Tito?'

'Not to the best of my knowledge. I offered to give him the necessary codes but it seems he prefers to take his orders from Russia.'

Steve grimaced. 'That doesn't sound very hopeful.'

Hudson frowned, thinking. 'Draza has spies keeping track of Tito. We might be able to persuade one of them to carry a message.'

'Yes, great idea!' Steve exclaimed. He went on more soberly. 'But they come and go at irregular intervals and I don't know if the men who come here are in direct contact with Tito's people. It's more like a network, or a grapevine.'

'It's a long shot, I know,' Hudson agreed. 'But it's the only way I can see of getting in touch. Why don't you write a letter and have it ready? Then, next time one of them comes to report to Draza I'll see if I can persuade him to take it.'

'OK,' Steve agreed. 'I've no idea if it will work, but it's worth a try.'

Hudson said, 'Don't you have some kind of back channel you could use? Who sent you out here in the first place?'

'Some Brigadier chappy in Baker Street. Code name's M. He's the head of SOE, I think. And I do have the cyphers for a direct link. I haven't used them in a while because when you brought new ones I assumed that was now the official channel of communication. And anyway, Draza forbade me from using the radio for months while we were in hiding.' He frowned. It was true that he had stopped using the direct channel he had been given to report through, and now he was wondering if he had failed in his duty. 'I don't see what he could do but suppose I ought to let him know what we've learned.'

'I agree,' Hudson said. 'He must be the one who sent Leo to Cairo. I got the impression that Leo knows him personally. You'd better contact him.'

Chapter Forty

Alix got to her feet and wiped sweat from her forehead. She was standing at the base of a tall cliff and in front of her the ground sloped away to a grassy plain, a *polje*, the kind of flat field found often in karst mountain areas. The plain was dotted with the red roofs of a large town. Livno had grown prosperous from its situation controlling access from the coast to the inland cities and it was an important centre of Ustashe power. It was the largest town the partisans had attempted to capture, and yet as she watched she could see that the advance troops were already in the outskirts.

The partisans had come down from the mountains, as was their normal practice, as dawn was breaking, following the valley created by the River Bistrica, which ran through the town. Spreading out, company by company according to plan, they had filtered through clearings in the forest until the town was surrounded. Then, on a bugle call, the attack had commenced. The Escort battalion had been held in reserve, as usual, but now the order had come to advance.

Alix shouldered her rifle and looked ahead. Tito was riding forward, Nikola close behind him. The officers were mounted now, but as a simple *partizanka* Alix did not qualify for such a luxury. Nikola had been at pains to make it clear from the moment she volunteered that she could not expect special treatment – not that she would have asked for it. There were no bridges here to blow up, so she had resumed her position in the infantry, but it seemed that today she would not need to fire her rifle.

As they reached the outskirts it became clear that the town was not completely undefended. There were concrete road blocks and wire fences which had been cut and trampled down. Here they saw the first bodies, the majority of them bearing the insignia of either the Ustashe Militia or the Croatian Home Guard, but there was no sign of any continuing resistance.

Drago had dropped back to walk beside her. 'Looks like we caught them by surprise.'

'Maybe they thought we'd never attempt anything against a place this size,' she suggested.

In the main square they found the remaining defenders herded together under guard. Tito had taken up a position in the Town Hall and was issuing orders. Alix and Drago crowded in along with any others not immediately required for duty. A hangdog gaggle of men in Ustashe uniform was marched in and lined up in front of him.

'What do you want us to do with this lot?' the officer in charge enquired.

'Ustashe?' Tito queried. 'Why ask? Take them out and shoot them.'

The men were marched away and their place was taken by a dozen men in civilian clothes. One or two of them were putting on a brave face, but the rest, Alix thought, looked completely terrified.

'So, who are these?' Tito asked.

'They are Germans, comrade,' came the reply.

'Germans?' Tito moved along the line, studying the faces. 'What are German civilians doing here? What are you, spies?'

'No!' one of the braver ones replied. 'We are engineers overseeing the working of the Tusnica coal mine. We are non-combatants. You have no jurisdiction over us.'

'That's what you think, is it?' Tito smiled. 'Look around you. My men are in control of the town. You are surrounded by guards with rifles. That gives me as much jurisdiction as I need.'

He looked back at the officers of the Supreme Headquarters who had accompanied him. 'What shall we do with these gentlemen?'

'They're German,' Rankovic said. 'That's enough, isn't it? Shoot them, along with the Ustashe they are working for.'

'We do not work for the Ustashe,' the German who had spoken before protested.

'No,' Tito agreed. 'You work for the Fatherland, don't you? Germany needs coal to drive its trains and heat its furnaces. That is why you are here.'

'All the more reason to shoot them,' Rankovic insisted.

Tito mused for a moment. Then he said, 'No. We won't shoot them – not yet anyway. There may come a time when they can be useful, either as hostages or to be exchanged for some of our men.' He turned to the officer who had brought them in. 'Take them away and keep them under guard. They are coming with us.'

With the prisoners disposed of and the dead buried, there was time for celebration. Tito presided over a grand dinner. Nikola was included, as captain of the escort, and Alix and Drago squeezed in at his coattails. There were two strangers who seemed to be guests of honour and at the end of the meal Tito stood up.

'Comrades, let me introduce you to Florian Sucic and Ivan Pelivan. They are leading members of the Croatian Peasant Party and they have decided to throw in their lot with us. I do not have to tell you that that is good news as many other Croats will follow their example.'

There was loud applause, and toasts were drunk to freedom and brotherhood and the defeat of Nazi Germany. When someone suggested that the Italians should be included in that last one Pelivan shook his head.

'The Italians will collapse soon. Their soldiers' hearts are not in this fight. And while they are here they have not behaved badly towards us. They hate the Ustashe as much as we do.'

The partisans remained camped in and around the city for several days. Tito saw to it that the civilian population was unharmed and businesses were encouraged to continue as usual. Nikola took over a house that had once belonged to a Ustashe officer and it was taken for granted that Alix and Drago would move in with him. Catering to his whims was no less irritating than it had been in Foca but at least she had the pleasure of sleeping in a proper bed again.

The quartermasters used the opportunity to stock up with supplies. Recruits continued to join up and Tito now commanded over two thousand men, all of whom needed feeding. Other officers, meanwhile, searched the town for arms and ammunition. One morning Alix received a message ordering her to present herself at a building that had been a Ustashe barracks. She found Mitra there and Tomaz, with a handful of other men and women he had been training over recent weeks in the use of explosives.

The man in charge was one of the few officers to have real military experience, having fought with the republicans in the Spanish Civil War.

'I've sent for all of you because I understand you like things that go off "*bang*". Am I right?'

There were murmurs of agreement and glances were exchanged. The unspoken question was, *What are we letting ourselves in for now?*

The officer opened a large crate. 'Know what these are?'

'Grenades,' someone said.

'Exactly. Grenades. One of the most useful weapons in attacking a defended position. Now, I am forming a special unit of *bombasi* who will specialise in the use of these weapons. I am looking for volunteers. Anyone?'

Alix looked at Mitra. They had felt they were playing a special role in blowing up bridges and this seemed to be an extension of that. Alix raised her hand.

'Count me in, sir.'

'And me,' Mitra added.

After that, all the rest volunteered as well.

'Excellent!' the officer said. 'We start training this afternoon.'

Cairo

Leo was studying a lengthy report she had just received from Bill Hudson. The main conclusions were that Mihailovic was waiting for the Italians to surrender, whereupon he would be able to seize their arms and equipment, and that he would refuse to carry out any acts of sabotage until that happened. He was waiting for victory over the Axis powers to be assured before making any move and intended at that point to establish a dictatorship ensuring Serb supremacy.

She was still assimilating the implications when one of the FANY girls, who now operated the radio signals room on the top floor, came in with a sheet of paper in her hand.

'This has just come through from Major Hudson, ma'am. It's addressed to you and marked personal, but I had to transcribe it, of course. I hope that's in order.'

'Yes, of course. I understand.'

Leo reached for the paper with a slight sense of foreboding. What could Bill have to say to her that could not be part of his normal communications? She read:

> *Leo, I have seen your daughter. She is with Tito and his partisans. I should have sent this message months ago but as you know I was out of contact for a long time and since then events have pushed it to the back of my mind. It was last December, when I visited the partisan centre in Uzice. I should have recognised her at once. She is so like you! As soon as she said her name was Alix I knew who she was. I am sorry to say that since then I have had no further contact with the partisans. They were driven out of Uzice by a German offensive and are now known to be somewhere in western Bosnia but Mihailovic forbids any communication with them. All I can tell you is that when I saw Alix she was well and working as an assistant to the editor of Borba, the partisan newspaper. From what I saw of Tito and his people they are well organised and formidable fighters, so I have every reason to believe that she is safe with them. I shall make every effort to garner any information I can and if I learn more*

*I shall, of course, let you know immediately. I hope
you can forgive me for being so tardy in sending you
this information.*

Leo sat staring at the paper, unable to take in what she
had read. Alix was not in France but in Yugoslavia? How
could that be? When had she arrived there? And why was
she with the partisans? A sudden thought stabbed her. Had
she come home, expecting to find her mother and father
waiting for her, and been at a loss, not knowing what to
do next? Was that why she had turned to Tito and his
companions?

She became aware that the FANY girl was still
watching her.

'I hope it's not bad news, ma'am.'

Was it? Or was it good? Leo was unable to think
straight.

'No, no,' she murmured, then pulling herself together
she said, 'Thank you, Jean. That will be all.'

The girl retreated and, above the confusion in her own
mind, Leo registered that she was disappointed. Of course,
such a strange message would be the hot gossip in the
FANY mess and Jean had hoped to learn more.

Leo's thoughts returned to what she had just learned.
Of course, she should have realised that when the country
was invaded her daughter would have felt it vital to return,
though how she had escaped occupied France she could
not guess. And of course, she would have wanted to
join the Resistance, if such a thing existed. Leo knew
her daughter well enough to guess that. But why the
communist partisans, rather than the royalist Chetniks? It
struck Leo that Sasha would be furious when he learned
that. Then she remembered that in one of her letters

from Paris, before the war broke out, Alix had said that many of her friends were communists. It had surprised her then, but later she had recalled that even as a young girl Alix's instincts had been egalitarian. She had disapproved of the hierarchical structure of Yugoslav society and the way the aristocrats treated the peasants. In that she had been in tune with her parents' thinking. The difference was that they had been intent on reforming society from within, with the co-operation of the new king. Now, it seemed, Alix had joined a party that would, if it prevailed, overthrow the whole structure.

Leo pushed such abstract speculations out of her mind and concentrated on the immediate position. Alix had been alive and well last December, but that was nearly a year ago and since then no one had been able to discover exactly what was going on in the country. There had been some fighting, she knew from Bill's reports, but lately his knowledge had been confined to Montenegro. What Tito and his partisans were doing was a matter of speculation. Anyway, what was it Bill had said she was doing? She referred back to the message. *Helping the editor of a newspaper.* Not in the front line, then. With any luck, if there had been any fighting, Alix would not have been involved.

She comforted herself with that thought, but knowing her daughter she could not convince herself that she would be content to remain a 'back room' girl.

Her next problem was how to communicate what she had learned to Sasha. Letters took weeks sometimes to reach him and the telephone connection was erratic, to say the least. She longed to speak to him face to face but travel, too, was almost impossible with war raging in the desert and enemy planes patrolling the Mediterranean.

It would have to be a letter, then, but how to explain the position to him without initiating an explosion of wrath was a matter that would require a good deal of thought. If only she could give him some more up-to-date information, it would be easier, but until they heard from one of the missions they had sent in, or until a new one was organised, the chances of that were remote.

It occurred to her that there was one person who should be given this new information, and who might also pass it on to Sasha. She abandoned the report she was writing and went back to her room on the houseboat. There she retrieved from her suitcase the cyphers and wavelength information she had been given by Brigadier Gubbins when he had sent her back into Belgrade two years earlier. She had not used that channel since she had arrived in Cairo, but now she sat down to encode a new message.

—

In an office in London's Baker Street, Brigadier Colin Gubbins looked up from a document he was studying as his secretary came into the room.

'Sir, Grendon Underwood has just sent on two messages addressed to you. They are both from recognised sources, but we haven't heard from either of them for some time.'

'Which sources?' Gubbins asked.

'One is from Falcon, on his original wavelength and using his personal cyphers. The other is from Fidelio, sent from Cairo but again using the cyphers you gave her two years ago.' Falcon was the code name Steve had been given and Fidelio was Leonora, a nod towards the Beethoven opera in which her namesake was the heroine. 'Curiously, they both seem to deal with the same subject.'

Gubbins reached out his hand. 'Let me see them.'

He read Leo's first.

> *I have just received information via Hudson which is causing me some concern. You will recall that we spoke when we met about my daughter Alix, whom I believed to be in Paris. Bill tells me he saw her last December in the company of the man called Tito and his partisans. It seems she is working with them. He has had no further contact and we have no channel of communication with Tito, who is now believed to be somewhere in western Bosnia. You will understand that I am anxious for further news. If you have any means of getting intelligence from that quarter and can give me any news of Alix I shall be eternally in your debt.*

Gubbins turned to the message from Steve.

> *Sir. It has come to my knowledge that a young woman by the name of Alexandra Malkovic is believed to be working for the communist leader, Tito. Hudson saw her with him last December but we have no intelligence as to her whereabouts or welfare since then. I understand her mother works on the Balkan Desk in Cairo. She has been informed, but I am sure she will be anxious for further information. If you can offer any means of contacting her I am sure her mother will be most grateful. With respect, S. Popovic (Flt Lt.)*

Gubbins studied the two missives for a few minutes. Then he picked up a telephone and dialled an internal number. When it was answered he said, 'Roger, do we have anyone on the ground in Sarajevo?'

'Sarajevo?' The voice on the other end of the line sounded puzzled. 'Not any longer, I'm afraid. We lost contact when the Croatians declared for Germany.'

'See if you can get back in touch. I've got important information for him.'

Chapter Forty-One

Alix lay on her stomach in a muddy field. There had been rain the day before and she could feel the damp beginning to seep through her trousers. It was still dark, with no hint yet of dawn behind the mountains to the east, but from time to time a break in the clouds allowed a gleam of moonlight to show her her target for this operation; the outline of a row of concrete bunkers encircling a small village. Dressed from head to foot in black, with a dark scarf wrapped round her head and her face smeared with mud, she knew she must be invisible to the defenders manning them. On her back she had a bag containing half a dozen grenades and to left and right of her, unseen in the darkness, there were the five other members of her team, all young women like herself.

It had taken a long time to get this far. First it had been necessary to take control of the towns and villages between here and Livno, to establish a free territory with lines of communication back to Foca. Jajce, Arzano, Bosanski Petrovac, Dvar… The names formed a kind of litany in her head but she could no longer recall any of the battles in detail. Kupres – now that had been a tough one! Livno itself had been captured by the Ustashe and then retaken. What really mattered now was that each one of them had given her and the rest of the *bombasi* time to hone their skills and develop their plan of operations.

Bihac had always been the ultimate target. On the borders of Bosnia and Croatia, it had important rail connections to Sarajevo and beyond and was the Ustashe's headquarters. As such it had been given elaborate defences. Outlying villages were heavily defended to prevent attackers from even approaching the town itself. Within that perimeter there were a number of strongholds, linked by wire fences, and in the city itself, their spies told them, every major building had been turned into a fortress. The Ustashe had had plenty of warning and had used the time to import concrete and iron to strengthen their defences.

Preparations for the attack had taken many days of planning. Over the last two days battalions of troops had made their way through the forest, unseen by the defenders, until the city was surrounded. Now the moment for action was almost upon them.

Alix raised her head enough to peer eastwards. There was the faintest hint of dawn in the sky. *Not long now*, she told herself.

Even as the thought formed itself in her mind, the signal she was waiting for came. The boom of a howitzer somewhere to her left, closer to the city, was followed by a crackle of gunfire. She raised her head and waved one arm, signalling forward, and began to snake her way across the intervening ground between her and the nearest bunker. Behind her, machine guns opened fire, the bullets whining over her head, and the gunners in the bunkers returned fire, the flashes allowing her to pinpoint the openings in the structure. When she was only a few feet away the machine guns ceased fire, as planned, and she knew this was her opportunity. She reached into the sack and took out two grenades. This was the most dangerous moment. The gun ports were above ground level, so to reach one she must raise herself up. She fixed her attention on the one nearest to her. There was a burst of fire and then a pause while the gunner reloaded. Alix took her chance. She ripped the pin out of the grenade with her teeth and launched it into the hole. Without a pause she pulled the pin from the second grenade, twisted to her left and threw it into the next embrasure. Then she flung herself flat, covering her head with her arms. The ground shook with the explosion and lumps of concrete showered down around her. There was a risk of being hit by a piece but there was no way of avoiding it. One of her team had been knocked out in the last attack and they had been lucky to be able to evacuate her without further damage.

Along the line of bunkers, similar explosions were going off as the rest of the team found their targets.

As soon as the debris had stopped falling, Alix got to her feet and, keeping low, ran for the dead tree that marked the rallying point. She passed through the line of machine gunners who were now running forward to join the fight for the village without fear of being mown down by the fire from the bunkers. By the time she reached the tree, two more of the team were there and within moments the others came running in. She counted them as they arrived... Four, five, six! Mitra was bringing up the rear. They were all safe.

'Right!' she said. 'On to the next target.'

Their next objective was one of the blockhouses forming the inner circle of defence. It was protected by a barbed wire encirclement and Alix dropped to the earth and pulled a pair of wire cutters from her bag. It took a few minutes to cut a hole large enough for her to crawl through, followed by two other girls. At the approach to the next blockhouse Mitra would be doing the same with the rest of the team. Once inside the wire they wriggled on their bellies towards the concrete bulk of their target. Behind them their comrades had mopped up the Resistance in the village and were advancing and the machine guns in the blockhouse opened up to repel them. With rapid gestures Alix directed the others to right and left where the flashes of gunfire indicated the gun embrasures. She pulled the pin from another grenade, scrambled to her feet and hurled it through the nearest one, then dropped down again to await the explosion. This time there was less debris. The structure was solid enough to withstand the impact, but gouts of fire issued from the gun ports and from inside she could hear the screams of the wounded. She lobbed another grenade in for good measure.

As she dropped to the ground again she heard a short burst of fire from a nearby embrasure and a cry of pain, not from inside but from close to her. She crawled across and found one of the team, a girl called Natalia, clasping her upper arm and struggling to suppress her cries. Alix rose up and threw her last two grenades into the opening then clasped Natalia in her arms.

'It's OK. I'm going to get you out of here. Where are you hit?'

'Here,' the girl choked. 'My shoulder.'

The light was growing. Soon the sun would be up and they would be exposed. Alix pulled open Natalia's tunic, trying to find the wound. It was too dark to see how bad it was but when she withdrew her hand it was sticky with blood. She unwound the scarf from her head and made it into a pad, which she pushed inside Natalia's tunic and pressed onto the area where the blood seemed to be coming from. Then she pulled the girl's own scarf free and bound her arm close to her body. That was all she could do in the way of first aid. The problem now was to get Natalia back through the wire and to the medic who would be waiting behind the lines. They dared not stand up in case there were still men alive inside the blockhouse. Against the flames they would be perfect targets.

'Natalia, can you crawl?' she asked.

In response the girl turned onto her side and tried to drag herself across the ground but after a few feet she collapsed, sobbing quietly.

'I'm going to have to drag you,' Alix whispered. 'I'll be as careful as I can but I'm afraid it will hurt. Be brave!'

She took hold of the girl's shoulders but her involuntary cry of pain told her that this was not the way. Instead she changed her position and grabbed her feet. Crouching, partly on her knees, she backed towards the gap in the wire, pulling the supine form with her. It was lucky that the ground was flat and the rain had made the mud slippery, but it still took all her strength to move her unwieldy burden. They reached the gap at last but the wire caught on her clothes and she had to straighten up to free herself. She had just succeeded when something struck her and she felt a searing pain in her left arm. Choking back a scream, she bent again to grab Natalia's ankles and with a supreme effort hauled her through the wire.

Movement nearby brought her round with a jerk but Mitra's voice reassured her.

'What's happened?'

'Natalia's been hit. We need to get her back to the medics.'

The first wave of their comrades had just reached the area, intent on pressing on towards the city. More troops were advancing behind them. In the dawn light the scene was a nightmare vision of running men, flashes of rifle fire seen through earth and smoke thrown up by shells from the defenders' guns. Alix and Mitra helped Natalia to her feet and staggered back through the lines.

'Medics!' Mitra yelled. 'We need a medic here.'

Out of the smoke and dust two figures appeared carrying a stretcher. Natalia was taken out of Alix's hands and placed on it.

Mitra said, 'Wait a minute. Alix, you're bleeding! Your sleeve is soaked.'

'No, it's just...' she started to say, and then darkness overwhelmed her.

–

When full consciousness returned, Alix was lying on a pallet in the forward dressing station and a nurse was bandaging her arm.

'What happened?' Alix asked.

'You got shot,' was the reply, 'but it's only a flesh wound. You lost quite a lot of blood, but you'll be right as rain in a day or two.'

'But the battle...' Alix started up. 'I should be there. I've got a job to do.'

'You are not going anywhere,' she was told firmly. 'And there's no need to worry. Our men have got the upper hand. Bihac will be ours in a few hours.'

Later she was transferred to the hospital tent. In keeping with Tito's principles about the care of the wounded, a well-staffed mobile hospital accompanied the partisan forces wherever they went. In addition, they had created secret hospitals, hidden in the forests well away from any roads or tracks. The approaches to these were carefully concealed and anyone arriving with casualties or leaving to return to the army made sure to obliterate any traces. Those too seriously wounded to remain with the main force were assured of expert care, out of danger from any enemies.

Alix was injected with a local anaesthetic while her wound was stitched. When it was done she was offered some more painkillers.

'No, I should be getting back on duty,' she protested.

'They can manage without you for the rest of the day,' she was told. 'Everything is under control. If I were you, I'd take the pills.'

'How is Natalia?' she asked. 'The girl who was with me.'

'We had to remove a bullet from her shoulder,' the doctor said. 'She'll be all right, but it will take a bit longer for her to recover. She's been asking for you, but she's sleeping now so leave it for a bit.'

Towards evening, Drago arrived, his face and hair grey from the dust of battle and his eyes red from the smoke.

'What's happening?' Alix asked eagerly. 'People keep telling me we're winning but I don't know whether to believe them.'

'It's true,' he told her. 'We are in control of all of the city on the west bank of the River Una, but the Ustashe are still defending the bridgehead over the river. There's some fierce fighting going on there but it's only a matter of time.'

'And you? You're not hurt?'

'A few scratches, nothing more.'

'And Nikola?' she asked.

'He's fine. The Escort battalion weren't committed until we entered the city itself. You should have seen him an hour ago, leading the troop into the centre like a conquering hero.'

She caught his eye and they both grinned. It was not hard to imagine Nikola's demeanour.

By midday next day Alix had persuaded the doctor to discharge her and, after spending a short while with Natalia, who was pale but cheerful, she went to rejoin her unit. She found they had installed themselves in a large house that must have once been occupied by someone fairly high up in the Ustashe. Whoever it was had kept a good cellar and the *bombasi* were making good use of it.

'Shouldn't we be at the front?' she asked.

'No need,' she was told. 'The Second Kraijina Brigade are mopping up in the local villages. Otherwise, it's all over.'

In the middle of the afternoon word got round that there was to be an announcement. They all made their way to the main square, which was soon packed with men and women in the uniforms of the various partisan battalions. Tito mounted the steps of the Town Hall, accompanied by General Popovic and other members of the Supreme Headquarters, and was greeted by a cheer that echoed round the buildings surrounding the square and went on for several minutes.

When the noise died down, Tito spoke. The city and the surrounding villages had all been taken, he announced. He praised all the troops for their courage and picked out one or two battalion commanders for special mention.

He ended with, 'Today I announce the establishment of the Bihac Republic, free from the Ustashe, free from the control of the Italians or any fascist power.'

This time the cheering went on even longer.

Chapter Forty-Two

Cairo, 9 November 1942

Weeks had turned into months since Leo had received Bill Hudson's message and she'd sent off her desperate plea for news to Colin Gubbins. She had written a difficult letter to Sasha, emphasising Alix's courage and patriotism in joining the Resistance and trying to play down the fact that she had allied herself to the communists. After a long wait she had finally received his response.

> *You say Alix is with this communist Tito. How could she do that? It is a betrayal of everything we have believed in and worked for for so many years. How can I tell Peter that the girl he played with as a child, who was like a big sister to him, has turned against him? But it is all of a piece with her earlier behaviour. If she had married Nikola, as I wished, she would never have been allowed to do anything so foolish. But you chose to ~~frustrate~~...*

The word had been crossed out but was still readable, and instead Sasha had chosen to write:

> *...to join with her in negating my plans and took her to Paris instead. It must have been there that*

she was indoctrinated with this communist ideo-
logy.

*You say we should be proud of her for wanting
to resist the Nazi occupation. I would agree with
you if she had joined General Mihailovic, who is
fighting for the restoration of the king and the legal
government. How can I be proud of a daughter
who allies herself with a man whose aim must be
to overthrow both king and government?*

*I am praying that you have been misinformed.
That perhaps there has been a case of mistaken
identity, or if it was truly our daughter who
Hudson met that she has now seen the error of
her ways and changed her allegiance. Otherwise I
shall find it hard to acknowledge her as my child.*

Leo wept bitterly as she read the letter. Sasha had stopped
short of blaming her for what had happened but it was
obvious that this was what he meant. She thought they
had been reconciled when she returned to Belgrade from
her self-imposed exile in order to work with him for the
overthrow of the regent and the installation of Peter as
king. Now it seemed they were back where they had
been in 1938 when she had taken Alix away to protect her
from a marriage she did not want. Now, when her anxiety
about their daughter's fate had reached almost unbearable
levels, when she most needed her husband's support, it
seemed she had lost it. The terrible thought struck her
that Alix might not survive the war. If Sasha remained
obdurate she would be alone indeed.

Her first impulse was to ask for leave and try somehow
to get back to England. She needed to see Sasha face to
face, though what good that would do without further

knowledge of Alix's fate it was hard to see. In the event, her request was turned down.

'There are new developments,' Basil Davidson announced. 'We cannot go on like this, with only the sketchiest knowledge of the situation on the ground. Hudson's reports are all very well but they only give us one side of the picture and it seems he is more or less confined to Mihailovic's camp. Atherton is dead, and we have had no contact from any of the other missions we sent in, so it has been decided to send in someone with enough authority and backing to convince Mihailovic that unless he pulls his finger out and starts some sabotage action he will lose any support we may give him.'

'So who are we sending?' Leo asked.

'Bill Bailey. You must have met him in Belgrade.'

'The manager of the Trepca mine? Yes, I met him socially before the war.'

'You probably didn't realise that he was also acting as the head of the SOE circuit out there.'

'No, I had no idea.'

'Well, he's a colonel now, with enough rank to impress Mihailovic, hopefully. He speaks the language perfectly, enough to pass as a native, so he's ideally qualified. When he arrives here I want you to brief him on what we know of the current situation.'

'Of course,' Leo agreed. She added, 'Will he be tasked with making contact with Tito and the partisans?'

'That will not be his primary objective. We don't see Tito as a serious player in this game. To the best of our knowledge, he and his partisans have been driven out of Montenegro and eastern Bosnia and are holed up somewhere in the west. They show no sign of attempting any sabotage. If there is going to be a real prospect of seriously inconveniencing the Nazis it has to be with the Chetniks. Besides, Mihailovic has the backing of the government in exile. He's our man.'

Leo returned to her desk with a sigh. The chance of someone being able to give her news of her daughter seemed to be as far away as ever.

Next morning she woke to the sound of cheering from the streets across the river. Hurrying out, she found some of the other residents of the houseboat gathered on the shore.

'What's going on?' she asked.

'The news has just come through. There has been a great victory at El Alamein. Rommel's been given a bloody nose.'

Huddled over her radio later to listen to the BBC news, Leo heard Winston Churchill proclaim, 'This is not the end. It is not even the beginning of the end, but it is, perhaps, the end of the beginning.'

Chapter Forty-Three

Bihac, November 1942

After the conquest of Bihac itself, various units of the partisans were sent out into the surrounding area to clear out Ustashe and Italian forces. In the process, 860 Ustashe fighters were arrested, a number of Italian soldiers were killed and a large quantity of arms and ammunition was captured, including a mountain gun and three antitank guns. Adding these to the towns taken on the march towards Bihac meant that the partisans now controlled an area that stretched from Karlovac in the west to Prozor in the east, an area roughly two hundred and fifty kilometres long by fifty to seventy kilometres wide.

Under Tito, the Bihac republic took on the same attributes as the now abandoned Republic of Uzice. Schools and libraries reopened; the staff of the hospital were augmented by the doctors and nurses from the travelling hospital and it was made free to use by anybody; courts were set up and captured members of Ustashe were brought to justice; and freedom of worship was established for Muslims and both Orthodox and Roman Catholic Christians. *Borba*, the newspaper, was published again and Alix found herself once more directed into the role of assistant editor. She approached this with mixed feelings.

She knew she should be glad that peace had been established in this corner of her country, but after the dangers and excitements of the previous months it was hard to settle into something so mundane.

One of the perks connected to her job was access to a radio that was able to pick up BBC broadcasts. On 10 November she was thrilled to hear that there had been Allied landings in North Africa. Casablanca had been captured, but more exciting to her mind was the fact that General Darlan, the Vichy French commander in Algiers, had changed sides and refused to oppose the landings. Algiers was now in the hands of the Resistance. She knew how great a boost to their morale this must be to the friends she had worked with in the Resistance on the mainland.

One of the most far-reaching decisions taken by Tito at this point was to establish a formal governing body for the area and for any other areas that might be liberated in future. Messages were sent out to all the provinces where partisan groups existed, asking them to send delegates to a conference to be held in Bihac. Men arrived from Croatia, Serbia and Montenegro to join those from Bosnia and Herzegovina. At a meeting held in the hall of the secondary school on 26 and 27 November it was agreed to set up the Anti-Fascist Council for the Liberation of Yugoslavia, the AVNOJ. Tito had sent to Belgrade for Lola Ribar's father, Ivan. He had been president of the Parliamentary Assembly before the war and was now elected as president of the Executive Council of the new body.

At one of the sessions of the Council, Tito made a speech thanking the loyal troops who had accompanied him on the long march from Montenegro and whose courage had enabled the partisans to take Bihac and its surrounding towns. He made a particular point of complimenting the women who had fought alongside their menfolk and who had played a significant role in their victory. As an example, he described the work of the *bombasi*, who had disabled the guns in the strong points surrounding the city and had thereby saved the lives of many of the attacking partisans. Many of them, he told the delegates, were women. At this point his eye fell on Alix, who was sitting in the front row with her notebook.

'One of those who took a leading role in the operation is sitting among us now,' Tito declared. 'Alexandra, come up here.'

Red-faced and confused, Alix did as he bade her and climbed up the steps to the stage. Tito laid his hand on her shoulder and turned her to face the audience.

'Comrades, I present to you one of the heroines of the new republic.'

One or two of the delegates stood up and began to applaud. In a moment their example was followed by all the rest and it was several minutes before the noise subsided and she was allowed to return, glowing with pride and embarrassment, to her seat.

Outside the hall the other *bombasi* were waiting for her and she was met with hugs and handshakes and vociferous congratulations.

'It was meant for all of us,' she insisted. 'I just happened to be on the spot at the time.'

'No.' It was Natalia, now discharged from hospital, who spoke up. 'You were our leader. You were the first to volunteer and you inspired the rest of us.'

Alix made her way to what, for the time being, she could call 'home'. As soon as they were settled in Bihac,

Nikola had been awarded the occupancy of a pleasant house close to the River Una, once occupied by a Ustashe officer, and he had insisted that she return to live with him. Her first instinct had been to refuse, but she thought of Drago, still serving as his batman, and knowing how demanding that could be she felt she must share the burden with him. It was obvious that Nikola had missed her and had decided to switch tactics. He had dropped his surly manner and reverted to the use of pathos, insisting that he was still in love with her and desperately in need of her care and attention.

When she arrived it was clear that the news of what had happened at the meeting had preceded her. Drago met her at the door, his eyes shining with such love and admiration that she threw her arms round him, and for a moment he held her close. Then Nikola called.

'So the heroine has decided to return to her humble suitor. I am honoured.'

Her elation vanished. 'Don't be sarcastic, Nikola. It doesn't suit you.'

'Forgive me. I didn't mean to annoy you. I am just very glad you can spare the time to be with me.'

Alix exchanged looks with Drago and he shrugged. They were both used to coping with Nikola's changes of mood.

Alix was preparing for bed when she heard a tap on her door. Her first thought was that it might be Drago, and for a fleeting second she imagined herself admitting him and allowing herself to fall into his arms. It was three years now since her affair with Raoul had come to an end, three years since she had said goodbye to Steve, and there were times when she longed to feel a man's arms around her.

It was Drago, but the look on his face banished her momentary fantasy.

'There is a man downstairs who says he must speak to you.'

'What man?'

'He wouldn't give me his name, but he says he has an important message for you.'

'Who from?'

'He wouldn't tell me that either. But he looks… harmless. Shall I tell him to come up?'

Alix hesitated. If Nikola found out that she had entertained a strange man, however 'harmless', in her bedroom there would be hell to pay. But she needed to find out what this mysterious message could be.

Reading her thoughts, Drago said, 'Nikola is fast asleep. I'll keep watch outside the door, just in case.'

'All right,' Alix said. 'Send him up.'

A small, middle-aged man with thick glasses and a receding hairline came diffidently to her door.

'Forgive me for intruding on you so late,' he said softly. 'I have been waiting for an opportunity to speak to you alone.'

'Speak to me?' she queried. 'What about?'

'You are Alexandra Malkovic?'

'Yes.'

'I have a message for you – two messages. But not messages I could convey in public. May I come in?'

For a moment Alix still hesitated.

He sensed her doubts and added, 'It may help if I tell you that one of the messages is from your mother.'

'From my mother!' Alix's heart quite literally skipped a beat. 'How? Who…? You'd better come in.'

She stood back for him to enter and Drago softly closed the door behind him. Alix gestured to the only chair.

'Who are you?'

'My name is Bogdan Kovac. I am a professor at the university of Sarajevo. I teach English literature – or I did until the faculty was closed down by the men now in charge of the government of Croatia. But that is beside the point. I have also been, for some years, employed by certain people in London to provide information which they were unable to access through the usual channels.'

'You're a spy?' Alix said incredulously.

He gave her a small smile. 'That is one way of putting it.'

Alix lowered herself to sit on the edge of her bed. 'So how do you know my mother?'

He shook his head. 'I have never had the privilege of meeting Countess Malkovic. The message has come by a somewhat circuitous route, via a contact in London. I should have brought it to you sooner but circumstances made it difficult for me to leave Sarajevo. It was only when I heard that delegates were being invited to a meeting here that I found an excuse to take leave of absence.'

'And the message…?' Alix was torn between eagerness and dread. Surely only bad news could be serious enough to warrant the attention of these mysterious people in London.

'I am asked to tell you that your mother knows where you are – or at least that you are with the partisans some- where. She is understandably anxious to know more and to be assured that you are safe and well.'

'How…?' Alix was struggling to order her thoughts. 'How does she know where I am?'

'That is not something I can explain, except that the people I work for in London have many other sources of information apart from me.'

'And will you be able to get a message back to her?'

'I shall communicate with my contact in London and say that you are, indeed, safe and well. I was in the hall today and I saw you being congratulated by Tito himself.'

'Can you also say...' She floundered for a moment. 'Can you ask them, whoever they are, to tell my mother that I am longing to see her, and my father. Do you have any news of him?'

'I'm sorry, no. But I will certainly pass on your message.'

Alix was silent for a moment, absorbing what she had heard.

'You said something about two messages?'

'Ah, yes. Thank you for jogging my memory. The second message came from a different source. A letter was passed on to me by someone in contact with General Mihailovic, the Chetnik commander.'

Alix caught a sharp intake of breath. There was only one person who could have written that letter. It had to be Steve. She had believed for months that Hudson must have handed over the letter she had written and that Steve had chosen to ignore it. But now it seemed she was mistaken.

'A letter? You have a letter for me?'

'Here.' Kovac handed her a crumpled envelope.

She opened it and read:

> *My dear Alix,*
> *I have no idea if this letter will reach you but if it does I must start by apologising for not responding to yours sooner. It is not Major*

Hudson's fault. Circumstances far beyond his control meant that he no opportunity to give it to me until today.

I can't tell you how happy it made me to know that you too have fond memories of our time together in Paris. So much has happened in between, but I have always kept the memory of those days as something very special.

It was a terrific surprise to see you that day when Tito and Mihailovic met at Brajici. I wanted very much to talk to you. I'm glad to know that that brute who grabbed you is not your husband or your fiancé. I hope that our brief encounter did not lead to any bad effects for you.

It seems that by chance we have ended up on opposite sides in this crazy fight, but I know that for both of us the real enemy is the Nazis and perhaps one day there will be an opportunity for us to work together against them.

As I said, I don't know if you will ever receive this letter, but I am praying that you are still safe and well and that we shall meet again one day.

With my love,
Steve

Professor Kovac was looking at her with a sympathetic gleam in his eye.

'Perhaps more than a casual acquaintance?'

'Yes,' she agreed. 'A little more than that.'

Kovac got to his feet. 'Well, I have delivered my messages and I shall endeavour to deliver yours in return. I mustn't keep you up any longer.'

She rose too. 'I can't tell you how grateful I am, and how much it means to me. I wish I could do something in return.' She looked round the bare room. 'I haven't even offered you a drink.'

He smiled. 'Thank you, I have been very well supplied with food and drink. Mr Tito's hospitality is extremely generous. I will wish you good night.'

He had almost reached the door when Alix said, 'Oh, just one thing more. Is there any chance you can get a message back from me to... to the man who wrote that letter?'

Kovac lifted his shoulders. 'It's unlikely, I'm afraid. I can pass it on to the man who brought me your letter, but the link is very tenuous. There's no guarantee it will reach him.'

'Can you wait while I scribble a note?'

'If you can be very quick. I have already stayed longer than I should have done.'

Alix grabbed her notebook and tore out a page. She wrote rapidly:

> *Dear Steve,*
>
> *I was so happy to get your letter. I can't write much now because the messenger is waiting, but I just want you to know that I still think of you and our time in Paris. I pray that you are still safe and that we will meet again when this dreadful war is over.*
>
> *With my love,*
> *Alix*

Chapter Forty-Four

Cairo, 8 December 1942

Leo received a call over a crackling and distorted phone line.

'Leo, it's me, Sasha. I'm coming over. I should arrive sometime late tomorrow.'

Leo gasped. 'Sasha! That's wonderful. How have you managed it?'

'I can't say much over the phone. It seems one of your friends is able to pull some very long strings. We'll talk properly when I get there.'

'Sasha—' she began, but the line had gone dead.

Leo was amazed that her husband had been given clearance to travel to Egypt. With the ongoing fighting in the North African desert civilian flights had been grounded long ago, and even for military personnel, seats on the few planes that made the journey were at a premium. She knew Sasha was taking a great risk to get to her.

She looked forward to his arrival with mixed feelings. She had longed to see him face to face ever since she got the news about Alix, but the tone of his last letter made her wonder what sort of a mood he would be in. Surely he would not come this far just to resurrect their old argument about her role in frustrating his marriage plans for their daughter. What could have prompted him, she asked herself, to attempt this hazardous journey? And who was the friend who had pulled those strings to enable him to come?

On the 9th, a brief phone call from Alexandria told her that Sasha's flight had arrived and that he would be on the next train to Cairo. As she watched the tumultuous mêlée of people pouring out of the train, Leo's heart was beating fast. Then suddenly she saw him and all her doubts evaporated in a surge of tenderness. His suit looked as if he had slept in it, which he probably had, he was unshaven and she could not be sure whether it was the dust of the desert or not, but his hair looked greyer than she remembered. She ran to meet him and threw her arms round him and he held her tightly for a long moment.

'Oh, my darling,' she whispered. 'I'm so glad to see you!'

'And me to see you, my sweet,' he responded, looking down into her face.

'But how have you managed it?' she asked. 'Who organised it for you?'

He smiled wearily. 'Can we talk when we get somewhere more comfortable, and not quite so noisy?'

'Yes, of course,' she said repentantly. 'You must be exhausted. We'll go back to the houseboat. Let's find a cab.'

They said very little in the taxi but he held her hand while she made occasional observations about conditions in the city, notably the marked increase in American uniforms on the streets. When they reached the houseboat she poured him a long glass of cold lemonade from the fridge and led him out to sit in the shade on deck. It was evening and a cool breeze was blowing down the

Nile, carrying the scent of a frangipani tree growing in the gardens.

'So,' she said when they were settled, 'tell me everything.'

He took a long drink and ran his hand through his hair. 'Well, it seems we have a heroine for a daughter.'

'What? How do you know? What do you mean?'

'A week ago I received an invitation to visit someone in the Inter Services Research Bureau in Baker Street... Ah, I see that name means something to you. I was directed up to an office where I met a man in the uniform of a brigadier in the Royal Field Artillery.'

'Don't tell me,' Leo interrupted. 'Small, neat moustache and a Scottish accent?'

'Right. He didn't introduce himself...'

'His name is Colin Gubbins. He's the man who sent me out to Belgrade to join you back in the autumn of 1940.'

'I thought he must be. He is obviously at the head of some kind of secret intelligence service. He told me that he has an informant somewhere in Bosnia whom he tasked with finding out what he could about Alix. It seems that this Tito character, whoever he may be, has taken control of a large swathe of the country centred on Bihac.'

'Bihac?'

'Yes, I'd heard rumours through... various channels. I don't know any details. Is Tito really in control? Apparently there have been several battles and he has cleared out the Italians and their Ustashe allies.'

'Battles? And has Alix been involved?'

'I'm coming to that. The informant managed to get to Bihac and sent a report back. Your friend Brigadier

Gubbins very kindly gave me a copy of part of the transcript.' He reached into his pocket and pulled out his wallet and extracted a sheet of paper.

Leo read:

> *I have made contact with the young lady you mentioned. She is in Bihac with the partisans. The man who calls himself Tito has declared the area a free republic and invited delegates from all over the country to a conference. I was present at one of the sessions, where he called the young lady up onto the platform and presented her as an example of the courageous contribution made by the women who fought alongside the men to free the city. He referred particularly to the bombasi, of which she is a member, who were responsible for putting the enemy guns out of commission before the main attack started. I spoke to her later and she asked me if it was possible to pass on a message to her parents, saying that she longs to see them again…*

Leo looked up, blinking away tears. '*Bombasi?* What does he mean?'

'It translates as "grenadiers". Gubbins thinks they were probably responsible for throwing grenades into the gun emplacements.'

'Dear God!' Leo murmured. 'And I thought she was just writing articles for the local newspaper.'

He raised his eyebrows. 'Can you see Alix sitting in an office somewhere while all this was going on? She takes after her mother too much for that.'

'I never fought,' Leo protested.

'Not in the sense of actually firing a rifle or throwing a bomb,' he agreed. 'But I am reminded of the young lad who, thirty years ago, put on Turkish uniform and came with me to reconnoitre the Turkish trenches.'

Leo laughed. 'Oh, that!'

It was true that, aged eighteen, she had reacted to the mud and filth of a forward dressing station by cutting her hair and putting on trousers, and when Sasha had mistaken her for a boy she had not disillusioned him for fear of being sent back behind the lines.

'So you don't disapprove?' she asked. 'You always hated the idea of women in the fighting line.'

'I still don't like it,' he said, 'but it has taken me two great wars to understand that they can play a valuable part.' He paused, shaking his head. 'I still cannot approve of a commander who allows women to undertake such dangerous work.'

'Why not if they can do it as well as, or better than, the men?' Leo asked. She looked at him. 'You're proud of her, aren't you?'

'How could I not be?'

'Even if you think she's fighting for the wrong side?'

'Your friend Gubbins has made me see that a bit differently,' he admitted. 'According to him, Tito's forces are doing more to disrupt enemy communications than the legitimate resistance under Draza Mihailovic. So on that account it seems Alix has picked the right people to work with.'

'That's interesting,' Leo said. 'Bill Hudson has always said in his opinion the partisans were better organised and more disciplined than the Chetniks. He thinks we are supporting the wrong people.'

'But how can we do otherwise?' Sasha asked. 'Mihailovic is fighting for the king and the legitimate government. We have to make sure he takes over at the end of the war, not Tito's communists.'

Leo sighed. 'It's a minefield, in every sense of the word. But surely what matters now is just to get rid of the Nazis and if Tito is best placed to do that we have to back him.'

'On the basis that my enemy's enemy is my friend?' Sasha said.

'That's about it, I think,' Leo agreed. She sighed, her thoughts returning to her daughter. 'But Alix… They are calling her a heroine. Heroines take risks… Heroines get themselves killed…' She bit off the last word on a sob.

Sasha took her hand. 'She's a fighter, we know that, and pray God she'll be a survivor too. We'll see her again when this bloody war is over. We must just hang on to that thought.'

Leo moved closer and he put his arms round her. 'I suppose that's all we can do… Just hang on. I'm so glad you're here, and you understand. I couldn't bear the thought that you were angry with her… With me.'

He nuzzled his face in her hair. 'I was angry, I admit. But I was being unreasonable. We all have to do what seems best to us in difficult circumstances. Alix has made her choice and I can only applaud her courage.'

Sasha intended to stay on for Christmas, and preparations for the festive season helped to take Leo's mind off her worries about Alix. Meanwhile, her work preparing Colonel Bailey for his expedition continued.

Shortly before Bailey was due to leave for Yugoslavia, one of the FANY radio operators brought Leo a message for him from SOE's central office in London. She handed it to the colonel at their next meeting.

Special request. Please inform Flt Lt. Stefan Popovic, currently serving as radio operator to

General Mihailovic, that the young lady hopes
they will meet again after the war.

Bailey looked at Leo. 'It's some kind of code, yes?'

Leo lifted her shoulders. 'I really couldn't say. If it is, I don't know what it means.'

'Oh well, I'll pass it on as requested,' he said.

'Best thing you can do,' she agreed.

Bihac

Tito sent for Alix. His eyes were glowing.

'Here is something important for you to put in your paper.'

'Yes, comrade? What is it?'

'Great news. Our brave Russian comrades have fought off the German attack on Stalingrad. They have surrounded the German army. It cannot be more than a few days before Field Marshall Paulus is forced to surrender.'

'That is good news indeed,' Alix agreed. 'Perhaps Hitler will need to withdraw more of his forces from here to replace those he is losing.'

'We can hope so,' Tito responded. 'Certainly it must mean his attention will be elsewhere.'

Christmas was approaching; according to the Roman Catholic calendar at least. And as all sects had been granted freedom of worship, the Catholic inhabitants of Bihac were preparing to celebrate it. For the Orthodox Christians the festival would not arrive until 7 January. Alix had grown up with this contradiction, so it seemed quite natural to her. As a girl at school in England her friends had been envious of her having two Christmases every year, though she always made it clear that she only got one set of Christmas presents. As she watched the preparations being made, she found herself remembering English Christmases at Bramhall, her mother's estate in Cheshire. Alix remembered the high-ceilinged room hung with swags of holly and paper chains, with a huge Christmas tree in the centre, and games of hide and seek with the children of Jonty, the farm manager.

She remembered other less joyful Christmases. Her first one in Paris at the beginning of the war, cold and lonely and missing her family. The second one had been brighter, pooling her resources with her friend Marie Louise to buy small luxuries on the black market, to be distributed to the children of those working at the Musée de L'Homme, the birthplace of the Resistance. That brought Marie Louise to her mind for the first time in many months. Had she and her parents escaped the Nazis after the network was betrayed? Were they still safely holed up in their gîte in the Auvergne? Would she ever hear from them again?

The thoughts made her nostalgic for a past she was afraid might never come again. She opened the pack where she carried her few personal possessions. Inside her passport she had a worn black and white photograph of her parents, taken outside Kuca Magnolija. Behind that was another picture, a slightly blurred image of a young man in RAF uniform. Steve! She remembered receiving it, back in her college room in Paris. How long ago that seemed! But Steve remembered her. He had sent her a message. He had her letter and he hoped to see her again. One day, she told herself. One day, when all this is over, we shall all be together again.

Epilogue

Berlin, December 1943

In the Reich Chancellery, Adolf Hitler was haranguing his generals.

'The situation is serious. The coward Paulus has surrendered and let the Russians take thousands of our men prisoner. In Africa, that turncoat Darlan has handed Algeria to the British and Americans. Tobruk and Benghazi are in their hands. We must anticipate an Allied invasion somewhere in southern Europe. One possible landing site is on the south coast of France. To guard against that eventuality we have already taken over the whole country from the ineffectual Vichy regime. But in my estimation the most likely place for an invasion is in the Balkans, probably on the coast of Dalmatia. It is vital that we retain control over Yugoslavia for its important mineral products and also for access to the Danube and the barges bringing coal from Romania.

'There are two rebel forces in the country, the Chetniks and the partisans. If the British and Americans land on the Adriatic coast it is inevitable that they will rise in support and the results of that could be irretrievable. Therefore it is imperative that we crush them before any Allied landing can take place.'

'With respect, mein Führer,' one of the bolder generals said, 'the Chetniks are the mortal enemies of the partisans. The Italians have already had some success arming them to fight Tito's men. Would we not be well advised to encourage that co-operation?'

'No!' Hitler was adamant. 'The Chetniks are pro-British. The Italians were wrong to arm them. Both groups must be wiped out. But we will deal with Tito first. Your orders are to plan an operation to capture or kill him and destroy his organisation. We shall call it Operation Weiss.'

On Christmas Day 1942, Colonel William Bailey along with his radio operator dropped by parachute into the mountains of Montenegro and were welcomed into the Chetnik camp.

A Letter from Holly

Many thanks for choosing to read *A Call to Service*. This is the second book in a three-book series following the adventures of Alix and Steve and Leo and Sasha through World War II, comprising together a sequel to my earlier Frontline Nurses trilogy.

Like all my historical novels, this one is based on extensive research and all the major events described in it really happened. While the main characters are fictional many of the subsidiary ones were real people. Josip Broz (Tito) is, of course, familiar as the man who ruled Yugoslavia from the end of the war until his death in 1980. His rival, Draza Mihailovic is perhaps less well known. He was an officer in the Royal Yugoslav Army and an ardent royalist and the main purpose of his campaign was to ensure the return of King Peter when the war was over. Unfortunately he was distracted by his determination to destroy the communists and became overly dependent on the assistance of the Italian occupation forces. He was arrested at the end of the war, tried as a collaborator and executed in 1946.

Many of the characters in the book who are portrayed as working with Tito or Mihailovic are also historical and have left first-hand accounts of the events they lived through. Milovan Djilas was a writer and political thinker who was one of Tito's closest allies. Ivo Lola Ribar and

Alexander Rankovic were also his trusted companions. The names of many of Mihailovic's friends are also taken from the historical records.

The leaders of the Yugoslav Government in Exile were also, of course, real people, as was the ill-fated King Peter.

The British members of SOE who assisted in the coup that put the young King Peter on the throne (see *A Call to Courage*) were also real people who left their own written records. The story of their escape from Belgrade in this book is taken from Alexander Glen's account in his book *Target Danube*.

The personnel of the Balkan Desk in Cairo are likewise very largely taken from the historical record, with the exception, of course, of Leo. Duane 'Bill' Hudson was the first Brit to be parachuted into Yugoslavia and his adventures are described in a book which I have found an invaluable source, *The Embattled Mountain* by F. W. D. Deakin. Deakin himself was dropped into the mountains of Montenegro in April 1943. (More of him in Book 3.)

Obviously I have had to deploy a writer's imagination to portray these characters but I hope I have given as truthful an account as possible and done them justice for their courage and determination.

If you've enjoyed reading *A Call to Service* please mention it to your friends and family, as a word-of-mouth recommendation can really help make a book successful. And do please leave a review – it can be as long or as short as you like. The number of reviews has a direct bearing on the extent to which Amazon recommends a book to other readers. I'd be very grateful.

I love hearing from readers, so feel free to get in touch, via my website: hilary@hilarygreen.co.uk. I am also on Facebook at Hilary Green Author.

I should like to thank my editors at Hera, Dan O'Brien and Keshini Naidoo for their invaluable help in knocking this book into shape.